THE SHORT LIVED YOUNG

SGT. HAWK BOOK NINE

PATRICK CLAY

ROUGH
EDGES
PRESS

Rough Edges Press
An Imprint of Wolfpack Publishing
1707 E. Diana Street
Tampa, FL 33610

roughedgespress.com

Paperback ISBN 978-1-68549-519-0
eBook ISBN 978-1-68549-731-6
LCCN 2024944738

To my grandchildren: Raylee, Paige, Nicholas, Michael, Eli, Adalee, Zoe, and Gianna. May they have long and happy lives without any wars.

THE SHORT LIVED YOUNG

"We are the short-lived young, who know what the old ones know, who know time does not heal all wounds, and that there is not always a tomorrow. We have learned it is not our past that is dying, it is our future."

1

MISTAKES FROM THE EDGE

EVERYONE MAKES MISTAKES, AND MISTAKES ARE LONELY things. We can usually find someone to blame for our poor choices and yet stand alone with the responsibility. What of the mistakes made for the right reasons? Do we have only ourselves to blame for those? Sergeant James Hawk had grown accustomed to being alone and living with mistakes. So much so, he little noticed himself committing one of his greatest errors in judgment.

"Bringing third squad out of the pocket at this point in the attack results in losing more men. You have to weigh loss against return, and there is no return," said the captain. "It's simply a tactical decision." The officer's face flushed red, with both the blazing heat and the anger coursing through his system. He had heard enough of the argument in favor of removing the unit from its predicament. "They never should have been there in the first place. That's a factor to consider, but that's not why we're doing this. They're serving a purpose now, by keeping the line in place. If they hold, they'll be all right when we move forward. That's the last word from the colonel, and I fully support it."

"Yes, sir," said Lieutenant Kirk. He walked back toward the sound of the artillery pounding the ridge above them. His platoon gathered around him as he entered the draw, where they had been tensely waiting.

"What did he say?" Sergeant Reaves, the platoon sergeant asked.

"He said we can't get them out right now," said the lieutenant.

"Write them off?" Reaves asked. "That's not how we do things, sir. Leave a whole squad to the Japs, *and* let the ridge fall?"

"It's more than a squad, Lieutenant," said another man standing beside Reaves. "They sent the weapons platoon to carry ammo up there. They're stuck in the pocket, too. The Japs have tanks, pushing them right off the edge of the cliff. Our men have to be relieved."

"We are not 'writing them off.' The captain gave us our answer. He said, 'not right now,'" the lieutenant insisted. "The captain assured me they would be all right. I tried. Our orders now are to move on toward the assault on the left flank. That's the end of the discussion about the ridge. If we weaken the Japs on the left and attract enough of the enemy forces our way, third squad may be able to fight their own way out of the pocket. When everybody does their job right, things will work out. We will be doing our job right, starting now."

The men stared mutely at the answer; stunned, and not pleased. The noncommissioned officers returned to their squads.

One of them, Sergeant James Hawk, rejoined first squad. He looked up at the ridge, flashing black and red with pulsating explosions, a vision of hell emblazoned across mortal earth's blue sky. A Japanese plane circled over the boiling smoke, an impatient buzzard darting in and out of the foggy blackness with a rattling machine gun. Hawk knew his men were not going to like the news he had to report to them, and he quickly considered his options.

"What did they say?" asked Hawk's corporal, Joe Canlon.

"The captain said to write 'em off. We're moving around 'em," said Hawk.

"*What*?" said Joe. "He said that? That ain't right. They can't do that."

"They did it." Hawk took out a block of chewing tobacco. "He says they're okay for now. Maybe later."

"My cousin is up there," said a young man named Welch. "I can't do it, Sergeant. There's no way I can do something like that. They must be crazy. We have to do something about third squad *now*. Not later."

"What are you gonna do? Go up there by yourself?" Hawk asked. He spat while still looking up at the ridge, and avoiding the eyes of everyone.

"If I have to, I will," Welch answered, adjusting the rifle on his shoulder. "One more man—is one more than they have." It was a bold stand for a comparatively inexperienced young man to take. Welch had two close friends, Rayburn and Epley. Hawk was certain they would go with Welch if Hawk permitted it. Welch spoke for three men, and not just himself.

The sergeant finally looked around the ring of accusing eyes fixed upon him. He chewed calmly. "They said the Japs are pushing them off the escarpment with tanks and a plane. It looks like they're gonna take the pocket from us. It's a bad bet, boys. Sometimes you gotta face the music."

"I don't give a shit what they've got," Welch persisted. "I'm not leaving here."

"We let it go? Just like that? Walk off?" asked Joe. The order violated everything Joe felt he had been trained for. Hawk took off his helmet. He had already conveyed to them what both the captain and the lieutenant had ordered. That should have been the end of the matter. It was a rare circumstance for a Marine to even consider going against a command. Family ties can be strong. The ties in a combat unit can be just as strong. All these factors had just arrived at a major showdown.

"I guess...I could go on up there," Sergeant Hawk drawled slowly. He knew this meant throwing away his stripes, if not his life. But then, he did that sort of thing. He couldn't ask anyone else to do it. "I don't mind giving it a shot. I might be able to lead 'em out. It could be...they don't know what a bind they're in. Nobody has to go with me if they don't want to. Welch, you can go with me, it's up to you. It *don't* look good, and it *is* against orders. They might just blame me, but they might go after all of you if you try to come along. We'll probably end up dead or in the brig."

Hawk looked around with a pained expression. "Like Welch said, I figure they'll need any help they can get up there. They won't make it without us and probably won't make it with us. If I was them up there, I'd be hopin' for somebody to show up. Y'all kick it around for a minute. Then we gotta shove off before the lieutenant wonders where we are and comes after us. The line ain't standing still over there."

Joe stood next to Hawk as the men gathered in small groups to discuss the matter. "You think this is a good idea?" Joe asked. "I ain't never done nothing like this before."

"Shit, no. A *good* idea? It's about the second worst idea I can come up with. Leavin' 'em up there is an even worse idea." Hawk spat. "I don't like none of it. But maybe I can do something, if I can get up there. Are you comin'?"

"Yeah. If you're going. We got to. I figure we can help somehow. I just don't want this on my conscience. This is the kind of shit that sticks with you the rest of your life. I'm serious. Sometimes an extra hand pays off big. You don't just leave guys in something like that. The captain is gonna get his ass in trouble for doing this. This ain't right. You don't do this kind of shit."

"Tell you what, Joe. I wouldn't count on any of that. If I was you, I'd give this some real thought. That conscience of yours ain't telling you that you gotta kill yourself or get court-martialed."

"Oh, yeah? What's your conscience sayin'?" Joe asked.

Hawk shrugged. "I ain't got none. I don't care about shit like that."

Several minutes later, each man had made his decision. Four would go with Welch, Canlon, and Hawk. The rest would join up with the lieutenant on the left flank, as ordered. Epley and Rayburn were not among those choosing to follow Hawk and Welch. In spite of their friendship with Welch, it looked like a losing proposition to them, all the way around. They could not persuade Welch to forget it. Changing the stubborn young man's mind was the last hope, for there had been a remote chance Hawk would drop the matter, if Welch did.

Hawk gathered the six volunteers around him.

"There's two ways up there," he said. "We can climb the front of the slope and come up behind the Japs. If we do, they'll fire down on us the whole way when they see us coming. We can't link up with third squad without bustin' through Jap lines. And we're gonna have to go through our own artillery, because we can't ask them to stop, without the captain and the lieutenant steppin' in." Hawk spat.

"The only other way is to climb the back of the escarpment," Hawk continued, "and come up behind our own men. We have better cover that way and a better chance of getting up there. We can link up with third squad right away. The only thing is, I don't know if we can climb it. It's straight up, without any ropes or anything. It'll take a while. If the Japs wipe out third squad while we're going up, they'll be looking over the cliff and down our throats. We'll be trapped." The men looked at one another. Finally, Joe spoke.

"So, what do *you* say? Go behind the Japs, or behind our guys? I don't like the artillery thing. And the plane is covering the slope. I say stay away from all that shit and climb the cliff in the back. The plane can't see us there. We get in behind third squad, link up, then we all bust out together."

"Yeah," Hawk agreed. "I'm thinking we climb up the back way and hope for the best. If we can't do it, we can't do it. We'll just come down and go the other way. Gotta start somewhere. Maybe the captain will come around and help out the longer this drags on."

"Sounds good," said Joe. "Trial and error."

"Trial and error?" Hawk asked. They looked at one another. Joe did not elaborate on the statement. Hawk had a wry smile. "Anyhow, let's go."

The cliff side angled sharply up, as expected.

However, it also provided numerous handholds, allowing for a fairly rapid and unchallenged ascent. As the self-appointed rescuers neared the top of the cliff, the sound of gunfire became louder. Enemy tanks directed both their cannon and machine guns at the defenders. A fighter plane swooped and dove, occasionally firing a burst at the earth below whenever finding a target of opportunity within third squad. It banked and turned its attention elsewhere on the broad front before inevitably returning to harass the beleaguered squad. Hawk stopped below the crest, short of climbing onto the ridge itself.

"We gotta be careful," he shouted as they crouched beneath the overhanging rock. "Third squad don't know we're here. Stay down. I'll see if I can tip them off that we're behind them."

The other six men waited under the sheltering cliff top, cringing under the rising crescendo of noise above them. Everyone had their second thoughts about going through with the rescue, but no one voiced any misgivings. Never having had a second thought in his life and having had only a few first thoughts, for that matter, James Hawk scrambled over the top. It was impossible to tell whether he had drawn any additional fire, as the roaring of the explosions had already reached a deafening, nerve-splitting maximum level. Several minutes later, the sergeant returned, with fountains of spewing leaden dust following him along the rim of the ridge, until he could jump down and huddle beside his companions, holding down his helmet with one hand.

"Okay. I done told 'em we're here," Hawk said. He had to spit the words out between bullets striking the stone above. "But, listen up. It's a son of a bitch out there. It's about twenty yards to the first line of holes, and any decent cover. The Japs know we're here now. It won't be easy getting across that open stretch again. They're watching it."

"Did you run, or crawl?" Joe asked.

"I did everything but swim. I mean, there ain't *no* cover at all, till you get to them holes. The son of a bitches ain't worried about runnin' out of ammo, that's for goddam sure. They're pouring it on us."

"How many tanks did you see?" Welch asked.

"One was burning over there off to the left. I think they knocked him out. He ain't moving, anyway. I really only saw one other tank, unless there's more back down the slope, out of sight. There's Jap infantry behind that one, though. I don't know how much. It can't be a whole lot, behind one tank."

"That's kind of good," said Joe. "Except for the cover thing. Are you saying there ain't *no* cover?"

"Well—shit, the ground ain't level, so you can try to stay low in some little defilade. But the fact is, there ain't no rocks to get behind. And the tank ain't no tin can armored car, it's a real tank." The men looked at one another, as another train of machine gun fire dashed along the brim of the cliff. The latest outburst suggested the enemy tank had located them.

"You still in, kid?" Hawk asked Welch.

"I'm ready," said Welch, his eyelids clenched tightly together. "Do we go out there one at a time?"

"I figure, all at once. We spread out," said Hawk. "If we go one at a time, they just get in a lot of practice shots for the men going last."

"*You* made it," said Joe. "We can do it."

"When you go over that top, buddy, there ain't no guarantees. Aw'ight, then. Everybody's in but the devil. Let's deal the cards." Hawk rolled over the brim of the cliff with fluid agility, recklessly tempting fate yet again. A hail of bullets landed all around him as he charged forward toward third squad's line of defensive entrenchments. The other six men jumped up after him and plunged over the top in one unified motion. The slashing deluge of humming white streaks hit three of them immediately: their bodies twisting, dropping and hanging over the edge of the cliff before being able to take a single step. Two helmets fell spinning, back down the escarpment. The hellfire that had been a magnet for James Hawk proved to be a leaden snare net for them.

Upon seeing the massacre, and seized with discouraging terror, Welch and Joe Canlon forced themselves to sprint after Hawk. The last man alive, Keegan, then ran ahead of them all with blinding speed, diving headlong into a third squad trench. The other three soon joined him there.

Reaching the fighting holes had been the life-and-death goal of the four newcomers, but upon arriving in the shallow protection afforded there, they gained an entirely new perspective upon the battle for the ridge top. They had entered third squad's world of only temporary survival. The tank loomed mere feet away, large and loud, raking the defensive holes with merciless machine gun fire. Its cannon aimed low and blasted at them periodically, but it could not be trained low enough for a direct or damaging hit.

Nevertheless, the massive explosions from the advancing cannon, splattered waves of rock over them, taking a toll on their already shattered and barely functioning nerves. Behind the tank, a dozen supporting Japanese riflemen bobbed and darted about, firing shots at the Americans. The intense fusillade left the Marines scarcely a chance to return fire.

This new situation was much different from the relative safety they had enjoyed under the rim of the escarpment. The pressing noise and fire paralyzed flesh and blood. Hawk looked over and saw Welch, motionless, with his face buried in dirt churned and plowed by endless lanes of machine gun fire.

"Hey! You hit?" Hawk screamed at him.

Welch looked up and shook his head. "No! No! He's dead! It was all for nothing! Mark is dead!" Two dead Marines lay still in firing positions on the other side of Welch. Hawk assumed Welch's cousin was among them. Lifting his tear-streaked face up, the boy grabbed a grenade. He pulled the pin and stood, arching the lit bomb toward the infantrymen behind the tank. His gracefully outstretched form created the perfect target. The armored vehicle's 7.7 mm machine gun cut into Welch's torso, holding his shuddering body hanging in midair as it pounded it. Welch finally dropped outside the hole where the metal teeth released him. Hawk ducked as the endless flood of machine gun slugs hit inside the back and flanking walls of the hole. The dry and rocky soil spouted funnels of swirling smoke where each bullet struck. Welch's grenade exploded—somewhere unseen—and with no discernible effect on the deadly madness swirling all around.

Hawk knew he had to get out of the shallow trench. He was too close to the tank's machine gun. The bullets landed inside the depression as easily as they struck the outside. He felt a heavy weight land behind him and turned to see Joe had dove into the hole with him.

"Keegan's dead. All them third squad guys are dead. This was a mistake. All of that shooting out there is for us, Hawk," Joe told him. "We're all that's left. I think the goddam tank is going over us."

"They were alive a minute ago," Hawk managed to say.

Joe screamed back at him to confirm his original message. "*They ain't now!*"

Hawk at last understood the reason for the intensity of the massive volume of fire. As Joe had guessed, the steel-shod source of the volley moved toward him. He heard the rattling of the bogey wheels, sprockets, and return rollers edging closer. The shallow hole would not prevent the whirring tank treads from crushing the two of them into its rocky floor and grinding their remains.

"Shit. We gotta take off!" Hawk shouted.

"Where? Back over the cliff? We can't make it that far," said Joe. Hawk straightened the pin on a grenade and pulled it, holding the safety lever down with his hand.

"They're too close to get a good shot at us—they're planning on running over us. I'll put this in their tread, maybe it'll stop the goddamn thing."

"There's more of them behind the tank!" Joe shouted. "You'll run right into them!"

"Damn sure might." Hawk pushed his helmet down and rolled over the top of the hole. He was startled to find the Type 97 Chi-Ha tank directly before him; he had practically rolled against the front of it. The forward-moving monster towered over him. He did not have to run more than a step or two and found himself so close that the view of the following enemy soldiers lay blocked by the huge armored vehicle. He planted the grenade atop the inner workings of the sprockets and dove back for the hole. The grenade exploded behind him just as he hit the ground. The abbreviated fender enclosed a good deal of the blast and blocked the shrapnel from hitting both Hawk and Joe. The tank jolted perhaps a foot toward the side opposite that where the grenade had been placed. The narrow tread on the stricken side parted, coming unspooled and trailing out in a straight line behind the tank as the vehicle tried to continue moving. The gunners inside had stopped firing.

"It...slowed it down," Hawk choked.

"But, it didn't stop! We got to jump off the cliff. It's still coming," Joe answered.

"The drop is too high. You can't jump, you'll kill yourself," said Hawk.

"It's that or get flattened. You better jump!" Joe pulled a leg under himself.

"Hang on, hang on, it's damn near stopped, I tell you." Hawk unslung the Thompson. "It's right there. Let's climb over the top of the goddam son of a bitch."

Joe lifted his eyes out of the hole. The crippled tank crept and jerked steadily in his direction, making odd noises and barely moving now. Climbing up the front of the tank did not sound inviting, but it suddenly looked slightly better than being chased over the cliff. "There's Japs behind it!" Joe screamed.

"We climb up this side and stop on the top of it. We use the damn thing for cover," said Hawk. Joe did not know what else to do. His brain shut down, leaving Hawk's indomitable will to supplant his own. He jammed the rifle butt on the floor of the hole to aid himself in standing.

"Let's do it," said Joe. They stood, right when the tank began bulldozing over the hole. The roaring mountain of rivets and camouflage-painted metal pushed into their faces with uncompromising might. The makers of the tank had affixed a ring shackle towing loop along the bottom of the front of it. The loop served as a good foothold, and a caged head lamp directly above the foothold served as a handhold for the two Americans to mount the jostling, sloped front surface of the vehicle. They clawed their way up the tank, which still inched forward in a lurching manner, closing all the while, as well, with the dizzying edge of the escarpment.

Joe managed to wedge between the driver's front view hatch and a machine gun, making himself invisible to the crew inside. Hawk, less cautious, climbed quickly to reach the turret above and pulled himself up on a bar, which encircled the closed hatch like a railing. He looked over the top of the hatch down at the crouching enemy, following behind and using the solid tank body for their cover. The brims of their caps pointed downward, covering their eyes so that none had seen him, or even considered looking up. A dozen or more of them inched forward, intent on following their source of cover and making sure the Americans were sufficiently crushed by their iron protector.

Hawk quickly pulled back the breechblock of the Thompson. He thrust the submachine gun over the top of the tank and held back the trigger, dragging the flashing muzzle across the faces of three of the startled infantrymen. A moment later, another lightning bolt zig-zagged from the mouth of the Thompson and into the crowd of men, crippling two more. Momentarily shocked, the rest of the Japanese dropped back, to put a greater distance between them and the tank, and between them and the submachine gun. Hawk felt the tank dip into and pass completely over the hole, near where Welch lay torn and dead.

Both the tank crew inside the vehicle and the Americans clinging to the outside of it, rolled inexorably together toward the high and deadly drop from the mountain. Joe attached himself as best he could to the front of the tank, a little below where Hawk perched on top of it. Hawk faced the Japanese infantry, and Joe faced the cliff. The infantry continued to fire at them from behind, but the two Americans cringed, safely hidden, from the bullets on the front side of the moving barrier. Hawk and Canlon had the tiger by the nose, rather than the tail, which did not look like the more advantageous position.

The tank jerked unsurely forward, toward the drop, on its one functioning tread, and aided by a few splintered wheels on its damaged side. Once at the edge, it could only plunge over the cliff, deliberately pinning its two attackers under fifteen tons of steel. The driver's front hatch flapped open. The driver evidently intended to study the situation, though the two Americans could not know whether he studied it in order to halt his forward progress or in order to commit suicide, taking everyone over the cliff with him. Hawk, positioned above the trapdoor of the view hatch, brought a boot down on it, slamming it shut in the face of the driver, leaving him to maneuver and make his decisions blindly.

"Grenade the bastard!" Hawk screamed at Joe, who clung next to the now-closed viewport. The driver struggled to lift the hatch open from beneath the pressing boot. From his higher position by the turret, and looking over his shoulder, Hawk's eyes filled with a panoramic view of earth meeting sky, as the breast of the tank slowly crossed the edge of the escarpment. His eyes took in the treetops waving far below, beckoning him to dive into them. The front hatch lay right at Joe's elbow, and he pulled at it as Hawk removed his boot. Joe fumbled the pin out of a grenade and dunked it inside. The resulting blast flapped the hatch open twice, and then tore it loose, flinging it like a knife edged discus over the cliff. Dancing flames shot from the sides of the stricken monster. The tank stopped, with a little less than half of its body hanging over the edge. It was too heavy to tip over, however; and planted itself solidly there, leaning out in midair.

Though the forward movement of the tank had stopped, the overall contest with the enemy had not been resolved. In addition to the remaining infantry behind the tank, a fighter plane still hovered overhead, looking for an opportunity to strafe the embattled men below. Hawk and Canlon heard it barrel toward them, its machine cannons blazing. Leaden ingots, the size of coffee cans, ripped into the rear of the smoking tank, causing its metal hide to vibrate under the jagged penetrations on all sides.

After it had passed, Hawk looked over the top of the turret, to fire down again at the enemy still trailing them. The Japanese had taken cover now, and he was unable to tag any of them. They returned their own volley and he had to duck beneath the criss-crossing firebolts, ringing as they slid along the curved, burning metal surface of the tank.

Joe lay plastered like a bug on a windshield against the front of the tank, facing forward with both hands clawing into the face of it, trying to keep himself from sliding off into the blurry, colorful oblivion yawning below. His legs splayed, he formed a large X on the iron grill. Inches away, the fuel burning flames leaped closer to his face. Convection from beneath him scorched his skin.

"Come up here and help!" Hawk called down to Joe.

"The bastards are gonna charge us. There's a whole platoon of the goddam son of a bitches."

"I...I can't move. We're hanging over the cliff. I'm sliding." Joe could not have helped anyway, he had lost his rifle. It had fallen and been crushed beneath the treads.

Bullets rang on the other side of the turret. Hawk could not look over it, but he held the Thompson on top of it, without raising his head, and fired down at the enemy, unable to see them. He would have to fire blindly, unless he stood up completely, and guaranteed his being riddled. The blind shots fell far from accurately. He could hear the plane returning. He huddled down to await the coming storm. There was no possibility of his being able to deal with a hurtling missile as fast and powerful as the low-flying fighter plane. Again, the rattling anvil chorus of the machine cannon played across the opposite side of the tank as the plane flew over. The propellers roiled the vibrating air like giant egg beaters.

"Help me! I'm falling!" Joe called. He had done all he could, and the end had come. Hawk slid down a foot or two, and grabbed Joe's outstretched arm, steering the corporal's hand toward the barrel of the tank's machine gun, where his clawing fingers could latch onto something for support. Joe clawed madly at the hot barrel, and the machine gun slid forward until the gunport stopped it from pulling all the way through. It sounded quiet on the other side of the tank now, other than for the distant airplane motor and propellers.

Hawk saw this would be his only opportunity to fire at the supporting infantry below, as their plane banked for another run. Throwing caution aside, and with a backward glance at the inevitable fall awaiting him, he rose to plant an elbow up on the closed turret hatch and aimed down at the soldiers below.

To his surprise, they lay strewn over the tread ruts, torn asunder, flaming, smoking, and in horribly dead positions behind the tank. The plane receded into the distance. Hawk climbed higher on the tank for a better look and pushed back his helmet, reflexively flinching in adrenaline fits, still ready to duck for cover if necessary.

"Hey, Joe!" He called to his companion, desperately clinging to the torrid outcroppings of metal below. "That was *our* goddamn plane."

* * *

KARL WEITZ KNEW he had waited too long. Things had been going well at the jewelry store, and for the most part, the local home front had been rather quiet. In fact, he hadn't even thought much about leaving Germany. People had mentioned it, as they had for years, but he put it to the back of his mind. He knew for certain he could not travel to Denmark or France, and he had not heard of anyone getting into Switzerland in quite a while. He didn't know where he would be allowed to go, should he want to leave. Germany had seemed fine, or fine enough. This afternoon, as luck would have it, everything changed. He would have to show a little more initiative in finding a destination. This afternoon, he had a new mindset: he needed to leave Germany.

The mailman had already told Karl about two of Karl's friends in the neighborhood being picked up last week. He had been alarmed, but such things happened periodically, and people had grown to expect it; it was like auto-pedestrian accidents: things happened, and then were forgotten. Was an occasional unfortunate event worth uprooting your family and losing everything you owned? The odds were still low that it would happen to him. All of his fellow workers at the shop, and all of his customers were friendly.

This afternoon, however, the policeman on the block told him two more neighbors had been arrested, only a few houses down. The entire families had been removed. A truck came and took away all their belongings. It was like they had never existed. This was perfectly legal, chilling, and not subject to any form of objection. Would the mailman and the policeman be talking to him this time next week? Would his customers?

2

GOD SAVE MANILA

UPON REJOINING THE PLATOON, HAWK AND CANLON expected the worst. Not only had they disobeyed orders, five men had been lost in the bargain. To make matters worse, the entire embattled third squad had been lost, just as the captain had predicted, in spite of the valiant efforts of all involved. Hawk and Canlon had committed the unpardonable sin of surviving. The heart of the insubordination, Welch, was gone and beyond any rebuke. He was entitled to burial with full military honors. In addition to all of this, the psychological well-being of the two survivors had taken a rather severe beating, something that no one bothered to waste any solicitude on.

Lieutenant Kirk found Hawk and Canlon immediately, and they assumed they would be standing before the captain within minutes. But it did not even go quite that well.

"Colonel Clark wants to see both of you at battalion headquarters, on the double," said Lieutenant Kirk. "He didn't say why, but I'm sure you know. I haven't heard from the captain. He saw what you did."

"Aye, sir," said Hawk. He stood there, covered in Welch's blood and other grime, and still breathing heavily. He could see with remarkable clarity now, previously undetected, that his job had been to control Welch, not go along with him.

"Do you mean the Quonset hut on the beach, sir?" Joe asked, in an innocent and conversational tone. His lips trembled as he spoke, though not from any fear of Kirk, or a meeting with the colonel. He had enough genuine fear still coursing through his veins.

"Is that battalion headquarters?" Kirk snapped.

"Uh...yessir."

"All I can say is, I can't believe you did such a thing," said the lieutenant. "Don't expect any support from me. You know how I am going to testify. Carry on."

"No, sir," said Hawk. The statement meant little to him. He had never had an opportunity to expect help or support from anyone in his life. The warning was not accepted as easily by Joe.

They had a lot of time for thought and conversation as they traveled on foot through the battleground, and down to the lower elevations along the beach.

"Do you think we'll go to a brig, or to like a real prison in the States?" Joe asked.

"Hell, if I know. Probably, neither one. Probably just back on the line," said Hawk, from his unique perspective as a lifelong member of the lowest rung of society. He figured they would rather throw him into the Japanese meat grinder than warehouse him in some secure prison where he had to be taken care of. *Nobody* —wanted that.

"I'll take the line," said Joe. "I don't want to get

kicked out of the Corps just yet and lose my pay and everything. My mother counts on that money for the rent. She's not gonna like this. How do you explain this to your mother?"

"Ah, shit. You won't get kicked outta nothing. We took the ridge for them, didn't we? Nobody else could've done it. They didn't lose nothing more than they would have lost anyway. You ought to get a medal out of it, if you ask me. Don't worry. Your mother will still get that ten thousand bucks life insurance—after you get blown to pieces on the line. And your medal."

"Yeah, right. My metal shackles." While Joe had yet to reach the bottom rung of society, he knew how things worked down there.

When they arrived at the headquarters, Hawk was ordered brusquely before the colonel, and Joe ordered to stay outside.

"It's the old split-'em-up trick," Hawk told Joe before entering Clark's office. "They want us to rat each other out."

"What do I say?" Joe asked, detaining him with a hand.

Hawk muttered a few obscenities. "Say anything you want. Just tell 'em what happened. It ain't no secret. They can go to hell."

They took Hawk away, and Joe felt even worse than before. Without the other's defiant and baseless bluster, the future looked dark.

As ordered, Sergeant Hawk stood calmly before the desk of Colonel Clark. On it lay a map of the Philippines. Unlike Joe, Hawk comfortably wore the battlefield filth clinging to him; it made him feel as if still in his element, instead of here. He looked out the window, watching sea birds playing in a nearby palm tree. The colonel rose and paced back and forth behind his desk. He could think better that way.

The portion of their conversation devoted to introductory small talk ended abruptly. They knew one another. Clark said nothing about the incident on the ridge, nor had he raised his voice or sounded in any way accusatory.

"We have a developing situation on our hands here, which may need a delicate touch," advised the colonel, with his features assuming a serious expression.

"I guess that leaves me out, sir." Hawk tried to lighten the mood with a bit of self-deprecation.

"You would think so. I have to agree with that. But the general likes you, for some reason. No, Hawk, once again, they've roped us into something we have absolutely nothing to do with. The Corps has no connection to this upcoming campaign, whatsoever. Supposedly, that's why they want us in on this limited aspect of it."

Hawk looked silently attentive, in spite of having little of interest to occupy him so far, other than the gangly birds outside. He reserved his interest for when it came time to invest in some life-and-death commitment. He was sure such a proposition would be coming his way soon. Otherwise, he would have already heard about the disaster on the ridge.

"It has to do with Manila and its invasion by the Army. MacArthur is putting on quite a push in the Philippines for the newspapers, you know. While we and the Navy close in on Japan, he's doing God knows what down there. There's no reason for any of it, if you ask me. And I'm not alone in this. But that's neither here nor there. Not my call. It's done," said Clark.

Hawk smiled to himself. All he cared about at the moment was getting beyond any discussion concerning the ridge. The cares for tomorrow were sufficient unto themselves. He was certain now that Joe sat outside stewing over nothing. The mental image was kind of amusing.

Clark paced silently. Hawk wasn't sure if he was supposed to wait or speak. He remembered the colonel said something about the Philippines. The comment must have been some philosophical introductory observation, as the Philippines had no relevance to either of them.

"I heard they landed there, sir," Hawk offered. He had not received much news in the sorts of places where he had been of late, but everyone everywhere had heard about MacArthur, and his "I have returned" speech. Hawk knew Clark would disapprove of anything MacArthur did. It was a safe subject, an offer of something to bond over.

"Exactly. That he has. The Supreme Commander. The word is Leyte Gulf was the biggest naval battle in history. Can you imagine that? At least, it crippled the Jap navy, for the real battle to come in the home islands. *Japan* is *our* battle. Now, MacArthur is on a tangent, after the capital of the Philippines, his old homestead. Manila could turn into the biggest land battle in history, in my estimation, and for nothing."

Hawk remained silent, having insufficient information to give an intelligent response. Weren't all battles for nothing? He had been fighting for years over islands abandoned by time and mankind. As an afterthought, someone usually explained the necessity for the fighting was to establish an airfield. No one ever explained why with thirty thousand islands in the Pacific Ocean, only a half dozen were worthy of airfields, and those coincidentally teemed with entrenched Japanese.

"I'll give you a little rundown on the order of appearance, as of today." Clark shook his hand in the air. "Don't worry about remembering any of this." He pointed down at the map. This subject of the Philippines was obviously not mere small talk. "They have the Sixth Army landing up in the north of Luzon and driving south toward Manila. The First Cavalry Division is landing midway up the western shore of Luzon at San Fabian, and moving east toward the capital. The Eighth Army and the Eleventh Airborne Division are coming at Manila from the south through Tagaytay, along with the Filipino guerrillas."

Hawk realized he was being told all this for a reason, and that it meant something to him. The subject of the ridge suddenly became preferable. At least it was over.

"Sounds like they have the city sewed up," said Sergeant Hawk. He didn't look at the map. Talk of armies and divisions exceeded the power of his imagination. His expertise involved matters more of the closeup and personal nature: the ridge, for example. He did have a degree of interest in the discussion, however, as a military creature involved in a global war. He would not be hearing news of such a grand nature back in the company.

"Yes. We have a lot of power aimed at them, but it's not quite that simple. The Japanese Army, under the command of General Yamashita, has about two hundred fifty thousand men in and around the city. This is not going to be an easy undertaking. When we lost Manila in 1942, MacArthur withdrew, leaving an open city for the Japanese. He did it in order to preserve the old historical quarters, and the civilian population, of course. We hoped Yamashita was going to—politely —do the same thing for us. And damned, if it didn't look like that was going to be the enemy plan, from the intelligence we received. But now we're getting mixed signals. Army's G-2 isn't sure what the Japs are doing."

"That's what war's all about, ain't it, sir?" Hawk asked. "Gettin' the other guy to turn around, so you can shoot him in the back."

"To a point, yes. But our command doesn't want to destroy an ancient cultural center like Manila and thousands of civilians if they don't have to. You've seen what it takes to get a thousand Japs off this little, uninhabited island. You can imagine what would happen in a fight with two hundred fifty thousand of them over a large urban center like that."

"Yessir. I can. I'd probably forget the open city idea. I don't see that happening. Sir. They don't give up nothing."

"I'll level with you. It's a terrible situation. There is some hope an all-out battle can be avoided. That's why I asked you here. Here's where you come in. They've contacted us because they don't want any scuttlebutt circulating among those different Army units I mentioned. You will go into Manila with a detachment composed strictly of Marines. The flow of intelligence from the city has suddenly stopped, and we need to find out a few things and get back in the loop. *You* have to find out what's going on in there for us. Is Yamashita leaving us an open city? Or not? Feel up to the task?"

"Uh...into Manila? A Japanese city, sir?" Hawk asked.

"Yes, yes. I know it sounds bad. It's not as bad as it sounds."

Hawk's features remained set. In his experience,

things always ended up being a lot worse than they sounded.

"We think Yamashita is evacuating. We're...*almost* sure. The Japanese troops are draining out of most of the districts of the city, and they appear to be congregating to the north of the urban center. We were convinced that was Yamashita's intent a few weeks ago. He was moving into the mountains in northern Luzon for a last stand. At least, that was the most recent word we had received from our intelligence operatives in the city before things fell silent. The Army is willing to let the Jap general withdraw, if in fact, he *is* leaving. If he is *not* leaving, the Army wants to proceed rapidly with the securing of Manila, and as I've said, they are poised on all sides to go in. When they go in, they're going in with everything they've got: no holds barred. There will be enormous casualties on both sides and among the civilian populace."

"I would guess inside information about that general would have to come from the locals, sir. Unless you can get it by intercepting Jap radio messages. I mean, you need people who know the country and the languages and all that," said Hawk. He was having difficulty envisioning himself serving any military purpose by sitting on a street corner in enemy-occupied Manila. "And besides, nobody can get inside the head of some Jap general."

"Absolutely, right. Oddly enough, we were able to do just that, for a while. We had been getting regular, accurate intelligence reports for the last two years before they simply...stopped. We had our own prophet, that had seldom been wrong. There may have even been a little pillow talk going on, from what I hear. I don't know all the sordid details. For now, we are hoping there may be one last delivery of information out there, that they were unable to get out of the Philippines, or maybe even out of Manila itself. It would be the key to all of this, to possibly saving the city. It would change everything if we knew more about the enemy's planning. We think you might be able to dig up the missing intelligence drop for us before catastrophe strikes."

"The Philippines is a big place, sir. And that's a big city. It sounds a little over my head. To be honest, this ain't exactly a job for a sergeant and a few men. If you wanted something blown up, or somebody shot, that's one thing, but intelligence gathering in Japanese—in a place like that—is beyond me. I been there, and..."

"I know you've been there. That's one reason we brought you here. Now, pay attention, Hawk. You haven't been to Manila. This is a different type of operation from what you're used to. This isn't beaches and jungles. The operative we were getting our key information from ran a type of cabaret, on the southern outskirts of the city, in an area called the Qebu District. It is one of only two or three of the districts in the city now officially open and undefended. It hasn't been *declared* open, mind you. It has just been left, de facto, open.

"This nightclub was an elaborate affair, built on a sandbar in the middle of a canal there, to avoid some sort of legalities, I've been told, back in the days of the American occupation. A regular palace. The reputation of the dive has never been the best. But it's perched high on this island with a very good view of the city. It was a hangout for celebrities and the well-to-do in the American days. Movie stars, baseball players, millionaires, they all went there. After the fall of Bataan, the high-ranking Japanese military stooges replaced them and began to party there. The current owner of the bar was supplying us with all sorts of reliable first-hand intelligence, until just a few weeks ago. Drunks talk, I'm sure you know. The club was shuttered by the Japs. It is out of business, and so are we.

"We suspect the Japanese military police were onto us and arrested the owner. That's just speculation; there could have been an illness or a death, some sort of accident, or a business dispute. Who knows? But it's suspicious that the cutoff happened when it did, right when we needed the information the most."

"You might want to contact the owner of the bar, sir. He must have had a ring of spies working with him. Some of them are probably still hanging around the area," said Hawk.

"It's a she. Yes, that would be nice. We can't locate her. We're afraid she's been locked up in the Fort Santiago prison for interrogation by the secret police, and there won't be any getting her out of that place without MacArthur flattening the city. If—she's even still alive, which is very unlikely. The *Kempetai* don't have the forethought of the Gestapo: their idea of interrogation is execution; after, a suitable amount of torture, that is. That would be the one and only reason she isn't dead yet, they aren't through torturing her.

"The woman's name was Mademoiselle Eugenie Rossier, and she ran this place, the Club Arashigaoka. And you're right, we suspect she had a staff, a large staff, at the club, and that some of them are still out there. Most, if not all of them were probably spies, and loyal to her. We received a weekly mailbag full of documents from her. Some were handwritten accounts of what she had learned, either from the general staff or personally from the Japanese. Many of the documents were original, stolen Japanese reports, or photos and sketches. Local Filipino resistance fighters picked up the drop, and then transferred it to us. It's certain, at least one delivery was sent out the day Rossier was arrested, as that is the day we were due for a pick up. It may be hidden in that abandoned building, or it could be in the possession of one of her cronies." Clark took a photograph from his desk and handed it to the sergeant. "This is the Club we're talking about."

Hawk looked at the picture. It was not what he had expected. He had imagined a beer joint surrounded by narrow gutters. The black-and-white photo contained an image of something resembling an Italian villa leaning out from the Amalfi coast over the Mediterranean Sea.

"Is that a hotel?" Hawk asked.

"That is the Club Arashigaoka. Quite a beach house, eh?"

"Is that Manila Bay? It looks like it's sitting on the ocean."

"No, it's just a barge canal, running down to the harbor. It's a wide one, and it surrounds the building. You can see there, the mansion is up on a sort of a hill, a man-made island. Notice the bulkhead they've built there along the water. The windows have a good view of the city, the harbor, everything. And yet, it's fairly well isolated, in an otherwise poor outskirt of the city—which is good for us."

The colonel reached back to his desk for a sheet of paper. "This is the general floor plan. It's nothing official, just something an American drew from memory. It's the way the inside looked before the occupation. It could be different now." Clark took the photo back as he handed Hawk the floor plan. "Did you see that sign down there in the water, at the bottom of the picture?" The colonel pointed at the photo. "I was trying to make that out with the magnifying glass. I was wondering what the sign said."

Hawk shook his head. "It's probably not in English." He glanced at the sketch of the floor plan. "If this is an island, how do you get onto it?" Hawk asked.

"There's a footbridge on the back side there. You can't see it in the photo. The bridge is on the narrow side of the canal. The ships pass on the wider side, in front of the building. That picture was taken from a boat, no doubt, as it approached the Club."

"I don't know if there's any point to checking out a place like that, sir. That's a long shot, on top of the long shot of getting in there. I think I would be monitoring the Jap radio messages, myself."

"Yes, well—that's *not* what you're going to be doing. I'm sure others are doing that, and have been doing that all along. *You* are taking a patrol into the Qebu District, securing this dance hall, and searching it. You can't tear out walls and rip up floors, because we don't want the Japs to know we've been there, or that we're looking for anything. We don't want them looking for any of those documents at their leisure after we leave. There are probably names and all sorts of things in there, that are best kept secret. If this lady hid something on the run, she didn't have time to cement up any walls or dig any pits or anything of that nature. She only had time to put the satchel in a good hiding place, and *you've* got to find it." Clark pointed at Hawk.

"It might be like a needle in a haystack, sir. Walking into Manila with twenty-five divisions of Japs around us —looking for something like that? A mailbag? Some of her people probably got it. Somebody might have burned it or thrown it in the river. More than likely, the Japs already have it. I reckon when they picked her up, they weren't real gentle with the furniture. They're an untidy bunch."

"Sure, sure. There are alternative scenarios, that's for certain. You can stand there and nitpick all day. No time for that. Now, once you're in Arashigaoka, we suspect you will find her employees. Some of them probably didn't have anywhere else to live. Those people will know the details of her arrest, the events of the day, her contacts, and her ordinary routine. You'll have to play some of this by ear." The colonel paused. "By the way, you won't be '*walking* into Manila,' as you say. You aren't going to march up Main Street. The Japanese have withdrawn from the area south of the city, congregating in the north, and left this particular district open. We are going to get you in there with the help of the resistance, very quietly. Understand, however, Command doesn't want the object of your mission leaking to the resistance, or even to the Army. If the Japanese get word of this, we'll never find what we're after, and if she's alive, Mademoiselle Rossier will be killed, for certain." Clark sat on the desk.

"I guess I don't have to tell you the next part, Sergeant," said the colonel. "You're savvy enough to know these things. We've been through this before. But —not everyone is on board with this mission we're sending you on."

"Like, General MacArthur?"

"Let's not get specific. A lot of people. Our object is to save the city and save thousands of lives. If we have to go in there with planes, tanks and artillery, thousands of people will die and the old city will be destroyed. Not to mention what all the Japs will do. They'll no doubt execute civilians, prisoners, themselves, and burn the place down, leaving us the scorched earth. The city is old, from colonial days, and highly flammable. We can avoid all of that if we know what's going on with Yamashita. There is no need to destroy an open city or attack people who did not intend to resist. If you ask me, they aren't going to give us the courtesy of telling us whether it is open or not, the way we did for them, because they don't care what happens. Right now, we think it's open. But air recon has uncovered some inconsistent information, preparatory indications of a possible defense being arranged." Clark looked up. "Time has run out. You're our last hope, before the total destruction of one of the world's classiest old cities. We have only a few days. Maybe hours. As I said, not everyone is on board. Things are happening. What I need to know right now is, are *you* on board? I'm not sensing any enthusiasm here, for a project that is going to need it."

Hawk had been put on the spot before. He made it a point to avoid being put there for long. "I ain't one to argue. If that's what y'all want. It wouldn't be my idea of how to go about it, like I say."

"Very agreeable of you, Sergeant. It is voluntary, of course. Do you want to advance any other arguments, or expand on any of your recalcitrance?"

"No, sir. I don't mind taking a crack at it if it's me you've settled on, and this is what you want. How many are going in with me, sir?"

"I want you to have enough of a force so you can defend yourself from nosey constabularies, and so forth. Enemy units may stray over in that direction in the chaos developing, even though it's supposed to be an open district. You obviously won't be able to slug it out with organized armies, under any circumstances. If you can get in and get out, maybe it won't take long. No more than a few days at the most. That's the plan, anyway. We'll be in radio contact so we can act immediately upon receiving any information you pick up, without waiting for you to get out of there. You'll have... something approximating a platoon, I would say."

Hawk didn't like the sound of not waiting for him to get out. Usually, the colonel was not as direct about referencing Hawk's indefinite ability to exit bad spots.

"Aye, aye, sir. I wouldn't want too many going in there with me, anyway. I imagine the Japs are moving all their POW camps to Japan after this."

"Now, now." Clark laughed. "There's no room for any negativity in this type of undertaking. Negativity doesn't inspire success. I need *enthusiasm*, it's an important part of an important mission."Hawk smiled, baring his teeth like a hunted animal. Hunted animals have no use for enthusiasm. They just do what hunted animals do.

"Undertaking. Yessir." Hawk saluted.

"And tell that Canlon outside that he's volunteering, too," said Clark, without looking up. "I know he's your buddy. Partner in crime, is more like it. Tell him he's going to Manila—and if he doesn't want to go, he's headed somewhere else not as nice."

"He is?" Upon hearing this, Hawk knew his own participation in this venture was probably not as voluntary as it had been presented.

"Yes. I heard about the debacle on the ridge. Frankly, I personally, wasn't the least bit surprised. Your captain thought a lot of you until you pulled that stunt. Those young fellows aren't used to dealing with people like you. You know, Sergeant, your captain was really hurt by that. In fact, it hurt me to see the way he took it. And look at you. Coming in here like looking that." Clark shook his head disdainfully at the sergeant's blood-streaked face.

"I didn't mean to hurt anybody, sir."

* * *

KARL WEITZ HAD to face the grim truth. The nation he had fought for in the First World War and that had meant everything to him, now hated him. The fact that there was no logic to it little mattered. He had to make a move. The formerly idle consideration of evacuating had turned into his first priority. He started inquiring about the ways others had managed to leave the country. The process sounded much more difficult now. It would have been easier a year ago. He wasn't worried for himself so much, as for his family, his wife, Marta, and the four small children. He had heard harrowing stories of escapes. How would all of them be able to carry out a clandestine operation, hiding in trucks, and sneaking onto boats, in order to escape the country? It sounded virtually impossible. Marta was very particular. She would not do anything undignified. Rumor had it war was going to break out at any minute. Such a declaration would make things a hundred times more complicated than now.

It all seemed hopeless, until in the course of asking around, Karl's friend, Jacob, told him of an interesting possibility. He would have to convince Marta of it, however. It sounded extreme, but he would have to make her understand that extremes were what the situation required. As expected, he met resistance.

"My aunt went to Denmark," offered Marta. "It is very nice there. She can understand them."

"It is *very* nice there, Marta, but we cannot get into Denmark," said Karl.

"She got there. A man took them in a produce truck to the commuter train, and it just slipped over the border, like it always does."

"I know. I know, dear. And *when* was that? Such trips are illegal now, and dangerous. Did you know that?" Karl asked. "They shoot people for doing those things."

"I suppose I did. People do things now. Karl, we are Jews. The government itself is illegal. Everything is dangerous."

"Indeed. But, you see, Denmark is not exactly a safe haven for us. Germany could easily walk into Denmark, and do the same things there they are doing here. You have to listen to my idea, to what I have discovered," said Karl.

She sat quietly, waiting, a pitying expression on her face. Karl could be so simple. His ideas were always outlandish.

"I talked to Jacob. He is well informed on emigration and such matters," said Karl. "In light of...the current political situation."

"I don't like Jacob. He cheats on his wife," said Marta. Karl started sweating. He knew this would be difficult. Perhaps dealing with Marta was the main reason he had been putting things off.

"Yes. Be that as it may, Jacob tells me the president of the Philippines has invited Jewish émigrés to come there." Karl smiled broadly, as he paused for a reaction.

"Are you talking about *the Philippines* in the Pacific Ocean, Karl? Do you know how far that is? Didn't it take Magellan two years to get there?"

"Marta, you are going to have to listen and stop saying things like that. This is very serious. You well know Magellan lived four hundred years ago and went on a sailing ship. The Philippines are an American commonwealth. It will be the same as going to America. It may even be one of their states by the time we get there. You can travel from there to America with very few complications, once you become an established resident. Here is the best part: it is *all* perfectly legal. The government will allow us a visa and passport to get there. It is almost too good to be true. We won't have to worry about being arrested or hiding with the chickens under a tarpaulin on a ship, or any of that."

"Did it ever occur to you there might be a reason for that, Karl? No one cares if we go there. They *want* us to go die in some outpost like that. You are not an explorer, or...Jungle Jim, you're a jeweler. You can't be a jeweler in the Philippines. You can't fish and trap, or whatever they do there. We will be destitute, stranded on an awful island. Thousands of miles from my family? No, thank you." She folded her arms. "Besides, they are not part of America. They did some nonsense. They are a separate country now." Marta often knew a little bit more about the world than she let on.

"The alternative is death," said Karl, with a grim expression. "They are not merely relocating people, they are putting them in work camps. This is a gift from God, and you had better accept it."

"Karl, there are a hundred countries in the world, and half of them are civilized. Why can't you pick one of those?"

"Because these civilized countries are all hauling off Jews, and quite likely killing them, because they never come back from these camps. The Philippines *is* civilized. It is more civilized than any country here. It is at peace. It has urban centers. The people are very religious, moral people. And, it is inviting us. The United States government is allowing it, which they don't, in most places. *Germany*, is allowing it, which is nothing short of a miracle. You have to think of the children. Four families have been taken from our neighborhood. They know who we are, Marta, and they know where we are. We are on some list, right now. We need to get on a safe list, instead. A perfectly legal, safe list."

"I don't like it one bit. Do whatever you want. You're going to do it anyway." Marta began to cry. "I will just have to wear a grass skirt and live in a hut. And—speak gibberish."

Karl frowned as he looked down at her. Nevertheless, he didn't hesitate to pick up the phone and call Jacob. Three of the children came into the room, shouting and laughing. One was no more than a toddler. The fourth, the baby, slept peacefully in the other room, in a Germany she would never know or remember.

3

NIGHTCLUBBING

A TORPEDO PATROL BOAT LANDED HAWK'S PLATOON OF volunteers on a deserted beach near Balayan, on a bay south of Manila. He had been given three squads, two of them composed of riflemen. The third squad consisted of a light machine gun crew, and a bazooka team. They climbed down from the boat and into the lapping, shallow water under the cover of darkness. Within an hour, according to plan, they were met by a member of the Filipino resistance, who led them to a group of carts parked on the side of the dirt highway leaving the beach. Inside the carts lay scattered loads of beans, mangoes, and papaya. The carabao drawn wagons, with solid wooden wheels out of the Middle Ages, were to transport the Americans through Tagaytay to the southern outskirts of Manila.

The darkness hung oppressively over them. Visibility extended in only a rudimentary fashion in the lightless hinterland. From here, it looked as if they had been dropped into a pre-electric age, or some lost planet. Considering the Japanese controlled the nation, however, the utter isolation was more welcome than alienating. The countryside had been in enemy hands for three years, and remained in those hands, in spite of the sanguine plans of the nearby American Eighth Army.

"What is that damn thing?" Joe Canlon asked, as he ran a hand along the back of the carabao.

"Looks like a longhorn," said Hawk, disinterestedly directing the men over the unfinished wooden sides and into the carts. "Probably some kind of water buffalo, or ox thing. Don't stir that big bastard up; it looks loud." The creature pawed the dirt, to show its approval of Joe's attention.

"I like to know who I'm riding with, you know?" said Joe, slapping the beast affectionately. "Right, Bessie?"

"Yeah, well, he don't look like he's gonna go running off too fast with you, if that's what you're worried about," Hawk continued waving his arm toward the others.

"That *is* what I'm worried about. I wouldn't mind something that could move a little faster than this guy. Ain't these people on the government tab? They can't afford a goddam truck or something?"

"Too noisy. It ain't far. Shut up and get the hell in the son of a bitch." With everyone hidden in a cart, Hawk climbed into the last one with Joe, and with the man named Sandoval, his connection to the resistance, and guide. Sandoval called to the cart driver, who in turn shouted at the carabao, launching the whole line of carts into lurching motion. The men leaned against the rough sides of the cart, surrounded by the fresh smelling fruit.

"You go in and out of Manila a lot?" Hawk asked his

guide. Splinters jabbed at his back and he shifted uncomfortably with the listing wagon.

"Yes," said Sandoval. "I will take you to a road which will lead to Club Arashigaoka. It is not far into the city. There will not be any Japs in the area. Or...not many. You will always have to look out for the *makapili*, wherever you go."

"What is that?" Joe asked, thinking immediately of some swarming insects.

"The traitors. People who work for the Japs. You will never know who they are, or what they are doing. The Japs, you will know. You will never know a *makapili*," said Sandoval. The cart creaked steadily, and always jerked in a curious sideways motion, as if it were trying to fold and collapse.

"Did you know anything about the people at this Arashigaoka place? The spy ring, and how they got any messages out?" Hawk asked. As the man on the ground, he did not take Clark's admonition as to silence about the mission very seriously. He wanted to know details, and he knew everyone else in this area knew a lot more of them than he did—or Clark, for that matter.

"I knew many of the workers. They did not talk about what they did in the club to me. Talk is dangerous here. It is better sometimes not to know all. They did many things. I knew Mademoiselle Rossier. She bought many supplies from my family. She was very young and beautiful, and very private. The Americans did not like her when they were in charge, the Japanese did not like her when they took over. She did very much for the people. The people liked her. I knew this. She is a saint in heaven now."

"You mean, like dead?" Joe asked. He adjusted his

helmet, which had been jostled over his eyes by the cart's violent jerking.

"They said she was locked up in some fort. I thought they had her in a big Jap prison. Alive," Hawk said.

"No one comes out of Fort Santiago. She is in heaven. She was very brave. I did not carry the messages for her. What I do is risk enough for me. Her messages were delivered to Commander Astorqui, in the mountains. She had to have many messengers, because they often disappeared. The job lasted only a short time. The Japs could see you going into the mountains. They could follow you with airplanes. They knew what you were doing."

"I imagine that's why she's gone, too," said Hawk. "Too many people knew what was going on."

"Yes. She trusted too many people. The things she did, they must be done carefully. Most of what she did was in public. I was surprised she was not killed before. She was very brave. Very *too* much brave, you know?" Sandoval looked meaningfully at Hawk.

"Yeah. I know what you're sayin'. Like us?" Hawk asked, catching the inference. "Kinda stupid?"

Sandoval smiled. He nodded his head. "Yes. It is true. This thing you do is not a good idea. The Americans think the Japanese are leaving Manila. I do not think the Japanese leave anything. They will even return to Qebu, and to Arashigaoka, someday. I worry for you. But you are soldiers. Mademoiselle was not. Still, I do not want to see you dead."

Hawk smiled. "That's mighty kind of you. Don't worry about us. We ain't the undercover type of folks. We don't mind a little daylight. You wouldn't by any chance know the names, or the whereabouts, of any of the fellas that carried all them messages up into the mountains for this lady, would you?"

"Yes. I know many names. I know all of their whereabouts. They are all very dead, except for one. He, too, could be in Santiago by now, which is the same as being dead."

"So, ain't nobody alive would know anything about a missing delivery from this woman? Something she might've sent out before she was captured?" Hawk asked.

"Many people have asked me this. I can only tell them one thing. You must ask Commander Astorqui. He would know who the last messenger from her was to be, or if the messenger ever arrived. Most people believe the messenger did not arrive. That is what I was told, and Commander Astorqui has said this to others. Not to me. But no one knows for certain who the messenger was. I think he was not one of her regular messengers. I think maybe he was someone from the Club, trying to escape. He may be alive. He may be hiding and got rid of these last...dangerous messages. He...may be a *she*."

Hawk looked at Joe. "Hmmph. That sounds like a lot of maybes. Loose ends."

"That ain't our loose end," said Joe. "They can ask the commander guy what he knows over the radio. I would guess they've already done that."

"I guess." Hawk bit off a plug of tobacco. "Nobody said anything about that fella. I'll have to check with Clark. Maybe we can radio the guy, if Clark hasn't already done it. I asked him to do that kind of stuff, and didn't get much of an answer." He turned back to Sandoval. "Have you been inside the nightclub place? Is anybody still hanging around in there?"

"When the Japs took Mademoiselle, everyone ran. I

think, lately, some came back. Some lived there. Everyone is talking about this open city agreement. Open city, open city. The Japs will leave us the open city, they say. I say, the Japs don't leave you anything. They don't agree to anything. They will leave *no* city."

"I have to go along with you on that one," said Hawk. "You gotta understand, though, a lot of Americans ain't got no common sense. They think everybody likes old buildings, and civilians, and shit like that. The people at the top ain't been wrasslin' with these son of a bitches like we have. They think the bastards are gonna do like the Germans did in Rome or something, you know, saving old statues and shit like that. All real civilized. We gotta play their game here."

"Your game is very unwise. The Japanese Army, in only this one city of Manila, is about the size of the Army in Japan. There is one soldier for every two people in the city. You could end very dead doing this thing you are doing. Even if you were in your army right now, with thousands of men with you, you could be very dead. Many will die here soon. If they catch you here, they chop off your head. They save their bullets for the invasion. This is no joke. They all carry swords to chop off your head. Many die every day. And many of those have not caused any trouble for them, and have only tried to get along with them."

"Shit," said Joe Canlon. "This story is taking a bad turn." Hawk spat at a crack between the slats of the bed of the cart.

The carts rolled to a stop a few hours before dawn. The persistent and steady jolt of the sideways motion of the old wagons left everyone with the sensation of moving, long after they had stopped. Sandoval directed the Americans to get out of the crude transports and follow him into the brush at the side of the road. Before everyone had gathered, the carts began moving again, down the road toward the center of Manila.

As promised, Hawk would not be going through the center of the city. The men formed a single file and proceeded into a helmet high thicket of cogon grass, with a narrow path winding through it. Sandoval took the lead, and Hawk walked beside him, his Thompson slung on his back.

The men talked in low voices, although smoking had been ruled out. The enemy were not supposed to be in the area, but it was their country, and anything was possible. While there might not be a significant military presence, small units of police were always known to scout about, harassing the populace for no particular reason; and the police carried radios. In addition to the patrols, there could always be a wandering soldier on leave, or a passing informant.

The cogon grass gave way to a stand of bamboo after a while, and Hawk grew more comfortable. The map, as well as his briefing, had indicated he would have to cross an open area before reaching the outskirts of the city. The terrain had instead offered a sufficient degree of concealment to permit his men to travel rapidly. When the bamboo ended, a scraggly forest of secondary growth sprouted, affording even more concealment. The wooded area provided a good deal of evidence of its having served as an informal dumping ground for the city.

"We are near," said Sandoval, walking beside Hawk, "and I am about to leave you. I will not go into the city. You must enter Arashigaoka to hide, to get out of the eye of the people, and the police. There will be patrols on the other side of the canal, and they will use glasses to look up into the Club. You must be careful. Patrol boats may also stop there. The *makapili* will be everywhere. They will know you are there. Pray they do not become interested in you. You must act and think like everyone is *makapili*. Do not speak with vendors. Do not walk around in your uniforms."

"We have to. They'll shoot us for spies without uniforms," said Joe.

"They will shoot you whatever you wear, or if you are naked. They don't care. I would take off the uniforms and burn them. Forget all this spying and regular army thing. Those rules are not for here. The Japs do not follow such rules. Trust me, I have been doing this a while. You can play army when your army gets here. Until then, you better play it smart."

"I imagine we're finished if they spot us, no matter what," said Hawk. "Might as well go out looking good." He leaned over toward Joe. "You should have brought your dress blues."

Sandoval noted Hawk took his words of warning lightly. "I tell you these things," said Sandoval. "You can joke. You do not have to listen. You have a radio, I have a radio. You need anything, you need to get out, you tell me. If the Army is chasing you, you tell me. I will tell you how to get out. We may not come in to help you fight. You may not have much chance in a fight. Many, many Japs are stationed here. We fight only in the hills, not here. If you fight here, it will not be for long, unless your army comes very soon to help you. The Japanese Army is not like us. They not only have more men, they have artillery, mortars, machine guns, trucks, boats. They are very bad. We will help you run, but we cannot help you fight here in the city, against so big an Army. Do not fight them. Hide."

"The thing is, we're going in that place to try and stop the fighting. We're hoping none of that happens," said Hawk.

"People hope for many things in a war," said Sandoval. "The other things are what happen."

"More truth than poetry to that, my friend," Hawk said.

Sandoval saw the burning blue eyes and the set mouth of Sergeant Hawk in the night. He sensed this man was not sent here strictly as a peacekeeper. One did not have to know much about Sergeant Hawk to feel the presence of some deadly grudge, waiting to be avenged. He did not have the demeanor of one prone to run or hide. Sandoval guessed that Hawk was quite possibly not the right man to place within the Manila city limits at this time in its history.

The forest ended, and below them spread an extensive grouping of shanties, made of tin, bamboo, cardboard and any other available material. Weak lighting from coconut oil lamps shined in some doors and windows. The raggedly shaped roofs stood as dark silhouettes against the approaching dawn.

"That is Manila," said Sandoval.

"*That's* Manila?" Joe asked. It did not look like much.

"It is the edge of the Qebu District. Very poor people. Not always good people. Only two or three streets away is the Club Arashigaoka. It is very tall. You look there, over the trees, you can see the top of its roof against the moon. It is in the river."

"Oh, yeah," said Hawk. "Damn. I never thought we'd get this far. How do we get through this little...town... thing here?"

"You will walk through. You do not talk to anyone. *Anyone* you talk to will be talking to the Japs. You look at no one, you talk to no one. No one will come out to look at you. Everyone is afraid of soldiers. Any soldiers. They cannot understand you, so, do not talk to them. Very dangerous. You will come to the canal, and there will be boats there. We put boats there for you. People have probably already stolen the boats, but we put many. So many, that some will still be there."

"Boats? I was told there was this little footbridge," Hawk stated.

"Bridge, no more."

"Bridge—no more?"

"The *Kempetai* chopped bridge down. It was just a foot walk. Not big. It is okay. It is not far. That is not your biggest problem." Sandoval sweated profusely.

Everything their guide had told them indicated that the man did not think the mission of the Americans was going to end well. And, it also sounded like he knew what he was talking about. "When you get over there, the building may be locked. I cannot tell you. There may be people living in there, maybe the workers of Mademoiselle, maybe others. It is a nice place to get in out of the night and the rain. Much nicer than here." He gestured toward the shacks. "It is the dry season now. People may be scared to go in there, because of the Jap signs. But maybe not. People do crazy things."

"You been a big help, buddy." Hawk slapped his shoulder. He could tell Sandoval was getting nervous. "We got the radio, if we need anything. You better get on back to your buddies. You never know what might happen, with all this old shit here." Hawk gestured at the grimly lit shacks.

Sandoval smiled. He felt good to be released. "This is very, very true. You will be careful, and good luck to you. You must not rely so much on your guns and bullets. There are many more Japs than bullets. You must rely on hiding and running. It is your only chance." He shook hands with Hawk and Joe, turned, and ducked back into the stunted forest.

Hawk advised silence as the men filed through the widest of the crowded streets in the small neighborhood on the edge of the city. Only one or two residents remained awake, and they stared curiously. The dogs barked a more vocal greeting at the visitors, setting up a disturbing racket that ultimately awakened more of the human residents. Hawk hurried the men along, before the children of the barrio could come out and demand gifts. They would not be as bashful as the adult residents.

The winding column descended a slope, the base of which bordered the barge canal. There before them, directly across the water, loomed the castle-like Arashigaoka, on its own lofty island. The château rose perhaps three stories high, looking much larger because of the earthen elevation beneath it. The moon was setting behind a salient tower on the impressive multi-angled roof.

Hawk took a breath as he surveyed his objective. The canal smelled of petroleum, sewage and death, and yet the hovering water vapor in the air was somehow pleasant; it was another part of the new day, with the portent of unimagined adventures. He had no idea as to how any of this would play out, and he enjoyed that aspect of it. This humble perversity was probably how he ended up in these chancy and less than desirable situations in the first place.

A half dozen battered and ancient rowboats lay turned upside down on the bank above the water. The men set to righting them, and sliding them into the canal. Beneath the boats, on the recently dehydrated grass, lay scattered, handmade paddles.

"We better get across quick," Joe whispered, "before these old bastards sink." Hawk tested the bottom of one of them with his boot, and his foot promptly plunged right through it, with a mushy, wet slurp.

"Well, that's one less," he said, pushing the wreckage into the water. "Hurry up, it's getting daylight. We need to get inside the damn building. Let's shove off." They could see the shattered little pilings where the foot bridge once stood. It appeared to have been an unworthy, narrow and flimsy means of access to the grand palace beyond the waterway.

The cumbersome flotilla sailed haphazardly across the canal, which had little or no cross current. The sound of the paddles, struggling to move the heavy, water-logged old boats, echoed sharply over the still surface. Exhibiting little skill at navigating the aimless craft, the men managed to wobble across the pungent channel. They soon beached upon the narrow shell and gravel shore of the other side, under the gloomy predawn shadow of the Club. Beyond the gravel, for another dozen feet, rose the jagged bulkhead, a jumble of broken concrete and rock, stacked there tightly to keep the island from eroding into the water. Crude steps mounted this seawall, leading up to an iron bar fence surrounding the hall.

Hawk ran up the slick steps, and gathered the men around him, as he crouched at the top of the stairs. He cast a cursory glance up at the dozens of glistening windows peering down on him. In a quickly passing five or ten minutes, as the sun rose, his patrol would be sitting ducks here, for anyone with evil intent and watching them, either from the windows within Arashigaoka, or from the other side of the canal.

The far side of the waterway lay much more distant than that which they had just crossed; but over on that foreign side, the forbidden city of Manila bustled, a major contrast with the sleepy barrio behind them. Electric street lights were already being turned off. An occasional headlamp of a passing vehicle could be seen moving, back within the maze of streets and buildings. The men could hear the faint drone of motors. Clearly defined shapes of Model A Fords were visible. They could feel the pounding heart, and throbbing power, of a massive awakening city leaning toward them: a Japanese city.

"We'll circle the building," Hawk told his men. "Stay low by this fence, about ten yards apart. Me and Baker are going in the front door to check it out. When we get it open and give the signal, all of you come in one at a time up through the front door. Got it?"

They nodded approval.

The men began, running in a crouch, staying close to the fence and stopping at the indicated intervals. The sound of shuffling boots seemed loud in the surrounding quietness. One man carried the machine gun, his bulky form always the easiest to identify.

Hawk stopped Joe Canlon by grabbing his sleeve. "You and Blackwell take the back door. If you can climb the fence back there, do it, and go up to the door. But stay outside."

"That fence is high. With them pointy things on top."

"If you can't get over it, just cover the door. Don't go in the place. I'll let you in after we go through it. You're going behind there just in case some Jap comes flying out the back. Or—goes flying in."

"Okay, I got it," said Joe, looking around. "Wait, Blackwell already took off."

"Then get him. If you can't find him, get somebody else. Get going," Hawk said.

Joe scrambled away, with weapons rattling from the straps criss-crossing his body. Hawk ran to the head of the line of crouching men and proceeded with Baker toward the iron gate below the large front doors of the building. A chain with a padlock held the gates shut. A high, persistent wind whipped across the water and into his face.

Hawk took another long look around, his gaze finally landing on the padlock. Baker carried an M1, the butt of which was heavier, and more substantial for bashing things than his own firearm. The thin, old shackle did not look capable of putting up much of a fight.

"Bust it open," Hawk ordered Baker.

Baker brought the sharp edge of the butt of the rifle down on the lock. The contraption fell dustily into two pieces, and onto the grass. The chain drooped partially open and Hawk pushed the gate farther, causing the rest of the links to drag across the iron with a sharp metallic sound.

"You ain't worried about being too quiet, are you?" Baker asked.

Hawk shook his head. Sneak thieves burglarized buildings all over the world as easily as this. Rats even made homes in them. Sergeant Hawk was a little of both, and a lot more of something worse.

"Get up there and see if them doors is locked." Hawk

nodded toward the roofed portico at the top of the steps, watching the canal behind them all the while.

Manila stared curiously back at him from across the gray, dappled water.

"Pull that goddamn board off the door."

Baker ran up the walk, up the steps and pulled at the door. He ripped off the white signboard nailed across the double doors and dropped it. It had Japanese letters stenciled on it, and below those, hand painted Latin script read: "Tachiirikinshi," and in smaller letters "Umiwas." Baker understand none of it. He kicked at one of the doors. Condensation from the canal hung in beads all over the old wood. He turned and looked down at Hawk.

"It's locked. Or nailed shut. It's a heavy assed thing." Baker's voice cut clear and crisp through the damp morning air. "We could shoot it open, if it's just locked."

"No! Shit! No, wait up there," Hawk called.

After another look at the city, he ran up the steps and stood beside Baker. A mortise lock sat emplaced in one of the doors, with a cylinder requiring a key. Hawk stared at it.

"Got the key?" Baker asked.

"Right," Hawk answered. "Kick it again."

Baker kicked the door. "I'm gonna bust my goddamn foot," said Baker.

He looked at the concrete porch they stood upon. A large pot filled with dirt lay next to a column. The plant it had hosted had long since departed the land of the living. "I can throw that son of a bitch through it," said Baker, pointing at the heavy pot.

"Hang on, we ain't supposed to go tearing shit up," said Hawk with a thoughtful look. He bent down and peered along the area where the double doors met.

"We could get shot out here," Baker reminded him.

"Give me your bayonet."

Baker slid out the long blade and handed it to him. Hawk stuck the blade between the doors and ran it down a little. He felt it hit something.

"It's one them kind with the push bar that opens it," said Hawk. "You push the bar down, and push the door forward to open it."

"Yeah. If you're on the inside," said Baker.

"It's a piece of shit, it doesn't know where you are," said Hawk, angling the blade inside the door downward and lifting the handle of the bayonet high on the outside.

"That's about right. Kick it up, hard."

Baker kicked the handle of the bayonet from below. The blade inside pushed the bar down and tripped the latch. The door popped opened, perhaps an inch.

"It worked!" said Baker. "I gotta remember that."

"It won't do you no good. It'll never work again in a hundred years," Hawk replied in a low, cautious voice, motioning him to get to the side of the door. If anyone lurked inside, they had been well forewarned of visitors. Hawk unslung his Thompson, stood to one side, and holding the stock with one hand, pushed the door slowly open with the other. It squeaked gently. "Anybody home?" he whispered to the darkness.

Baker went to one knee and peered inside. "Dark," he said. "The thing might have a light switch. This is the big city. I seen a light pole out there."

"We're already lit up like Christmas in this goddamn doorway," said Hawk, crouching and moving over the threshold. "Stay back."

From force of habit, he checked the floor for a trip wire. He pivoted inside, crouching close to the floor with his back to the wall and pointing the submachine gun toward the dark emptiness in front of him. It smelled like dust, and spilled alcohol. He raised his arm over his head, and behind himself, his hand searching wildly for the place where a light switch should be. His hand found the round, bakelite container jutting from the wall and twisted the switch in it. A couple of clicks back and forth did not produce any light.

"No electricity," he told Baker. His voice echoed.

The dawn light began to shine through upper windows high above the floor, but all he could see here below was its silver threads on black walls. A constant sea breeze, blowing in from the bay and down the canal, battered the prominent old manor, swirling around its tower and producing a mournful, music inside, like a low and distant train. It was not a comforting sound, impressing one more as hellish and depressing.

He pivoted back outside and leaned against the wall. "I don't like it," said Hawk. "We can wait a couple minutes, for a little more daylight to sink in. No sense making it too easy for some Jap son of a bitch."

Baker craned his neck, looking inside. "It's big. Must be like a dance hall or something. I don't see nothing on the floor. I doubt anybody would be hanging around an empty joint like that. Kinda...stinks. Hear that wind?"

"I hear it. It'll keep," said Hawk, biting off a plug of tobacco. "Just stay outta the door. We'll go inside in a minute. Sun's comin' up."

"You wanta give 'em time to set up their machine gun?"

"Yeah." Hawk spat. "No sense being chickenshit about it."

"We ought to throw a grenade in there," said Baker, shifting about anxiously.

"What the *hell*? Hold your horses. We're sittin' in the middle of twenty-five divisions of Japs, and you're gonna start throwing hand grenades in an empty house? I told you, we can't tear shit up. Can you wait one goddamn shittin' minute?"

"I guess it'll be okay if they throw a grenade at us, though, right?"

Hawk shook his head. "No. That *ain't* gonna be okay. I thought there would be more light in there by now. Just give it a second. Listen to that damn wind. It'll be hard to hear in there. Do you wanna get shot in the ass?" Although it remained dark inside, it grew brighter outside. Hawk fumbled with his pocket, and handed Baker a sheet of folded paper. "Here. This is a map of the inside. Keep yourself busy."

Baker sat on the other side of the open door, studying the map.

"This is interesting," said Baker, shaking the paper at Hawk.

"Shit, yeah." Hawk did not recall anything interesting about the floor plan, but at least it occupied Baker. He spat, all the while listening for any sort of human movement from within. It was not unreasonable to suppose that as they waited, someone inside also waited for them. Perhaps, the inarguable logic of it created an uncomfortable conviction in Hawk. Quite probably, if anyone hid in there, they were not Japanese at all. Japanese soldiers had other things to do besides sit around a vacant building waiting for visitors.

The Americans could not just bound inside, randomly shooting. Former staff members might be living there, as might any homeless local looking for a dry place to stay. Hawk looked at his men, gathered wide-eyed and wary down near the fence. He snorted a short laugh as he thought of Joe Canlon, waiting expectantly somewhere in the rear of the edifice. None of the mounting tension was going to rush Hawk into anything.

His eye noticed a sign jutting just above the metallic gray surface of the barge canal, about thirty feet from the bank. It was the same sign Clark had seen in the photograph back in his office, and had been unable to read. Hawk felt strange to be this close to the real thing now, and to be able to clearly see what it said: "No submarines beyond this point."

"Hmmph," Hawk grunted. He never would have guessed that, or that it would be in English. It looked old. It was probably a leftover relic from the US Navy. Baker had no idea what Hawk was staring at.

Finally, Hawk stood. "I'm going in there. It sounds quiet enough."

"That's what we're here for," said Baker, who had been ready to go in ten minutes before. Hawk motioned downward with his palm, indicating the other should lower his enthusiasm a notch.

Hawk stepped inside. The interior no longer lay shrouded in utter darkness. The faint dawn light filtered through upper windows and through the cracks around curtains over the lower windows. The ceiling vaulted to forty feet or more in height, with the second and third floors taking up only half the space of the first floor, creating a mezzanine. Hawk could see all the way to the top of the structure from the first floor, as well as the balconies on the lofted second and third floors. He saw no sign of life in any of the vast interior. Keeping his weapon trained on the inside of the Club, he backed toward the large front window and slid a heavy curtain open, letting in a flood of light. Dust particles sailed in the swirling shafts of the incoming rays of the sun. Suddenly, the large and mysterious structure did not look as intimidating. The barrel of the Thompson moved across the interior, keeping in time with the sweeping motion of Hawk's eyes.

To the far left side of the cabaret nestled the bar, glasses still on the countertop. Hundreds of colorful bottles stood stacked on shelves around the bar, and a long mirror took up the wall behind it. Hawk immediately recognized his own reflection without registering any alarm. In front of the bar, a wide hardwood dance floor extended across the building. Near the front window, at the head of this floor of inlaid wooden slats, stood a raised platform, only a foot or so tall, for the band or orchestra. Chairs and music stands lay scattered over it in no arranged pattern, some overturned or lying on top of one another.

An open space ran from the front door to the rear wall, where a door to a kitchen or some other work area could be seen. Beside the door and to the right was an elevated stage, much higher than the orchestra's stand. Facing the stage sat rows of round tables, each with its own ornate, antique lamp.

Partitioned booths lined the far right part of the building, having settees on either side of the rectangular tables placed inside them, and some of the inner portions of the booths were hidden by beaded curtains. Behind the tables and to the left of the booths stood gaming counters, for card dealers, and a roulette wheel with a cage for a croupier. Other than the dance floor, the concrete had been covered in most places by a heavy carpet. Low walls, or partitions separated the various areas, likely as a means of muffling noise. Paintings, both large and small, hung at various heights and intervals along every wall. A stairway led to the second floor, where the sergeant saw several closed doors; but the third floor lay obscured by its height, with only its mezzanine railing clearly visible from the ground. Any third-floor doors were hidden. Hawk eyed this highest floor suspiciously. It would be an excellent place for an enemy to launch an ambush on the people below; not that the closed doors on the second floor inspired any greater peace of mind.

Besides these upper recesses, which held the most obvious places of concealment, he studied the closed kitchen door on his own floor, and the area hidden behind the bar. The curtain behind the stage gently swayed with a life of its own, probably from the ever-present breeze now coming through the open front door —but perhaps, for other reasons. Hawk walked slowly toward the bar first and looked behind it. From there, he walked across the dance floor to the kitchen door and opened it. The spacious galley contained a massive stove and appeared vacant from his quick surveillance. He then climbed onto the stage and moved the rear curtain aside with his gun barrel. The area behind the covering hovered, cool, stale, dark, and empty. He was safer here, under the overhang of the upper floors. No one hiding above could attack him here.

He climbed down from the stage and searched each booth, parting the beaded drapery where necessary. Each was raised about a foot above the floor. All appeared well to him, on the first floor, at any rate. As he surveyed the main room one last time, before heading for the stairs, a huge painting, far up the wall beneath the second-floor overhang, caught his eye.

A beautiful young woman in a black evening dress peered down at him with a heavenly, serene expression.

Her luminous, oval white face and piercing eyes reminded him of portraits of angels. Thick dark hair, arranged in an elaborate style, framed the face, accentuating its alabaster glow. He stared at it for a moment, ignorant and unattuned to beauty of any sort as he was, his full attention arrested by this vision floating in the half-light. As unique as the portrait was, another picture equally as arresting hung on the other side of the kitchen door. Much smaller, the same supernatural face appeared to be on the image of a different woman, facing at a slightly different angle. This picture more deliberately depicted an angel, as the woman with the mystic gaze wore a suit of armor and held a sword.

Hawk walked closer to the hypnotic eyes in the larger painting. They drilled into him, as he approached. He touched the painting, perhaps to see if it was real, instead of some sort of floating spirit. The image had an eerie, three-dimensional cast to it, which drew him in, as if a person may have been imprisoned there, telling him something he wanted to hear.

"See any trip wires?" Baker's no-nonsense voice shot across the room from the front door, exploding Hawk's fascinated trance, and his daydreaming soul backed out of the portrait at the speed of thought.

"Uh...no. Check upstairs. It looks pretty clean down here. Be careful with all them shut doors. Some son of a bitch might be layin' for us." He looked back at the paintings as Baker cautiously trudged up the stairs. If the woman in the black dress was a real person, why would she have another painting made of herself as an angel? Was this supposed to be the Virgin Mary, or a real woman? He had never seen the Virgin Mary portrayed in such contemporary attire. The light struck both of the faces so dramatically that he was not sure if it was part of the art, or an effect of the morning sunrise. He walked to the front door and motioned for the men outside to enter the Club.

After the patrol came inside, Hawk picked up the signboard Baker had torn off and jammed it into only one door, using the heel of his hand for a hammer so that it did not block both doors as before but still appeared to be in its place. He closed the door behind him.

He assembled the men around the large dance floor. The immensity of the interior of the club became more apparent with all of them gathered here, dwarfing their combined human presence. The height and breadth of the expanse created an atmosphere similar to one of an airplane hangar. A gigantic chandelier swung over the middle of the floor, hanging far down and in front of the balconies of the other two floors. Though the men looked small, few, and out of place here, Hawk was undaunted. He did not see men, or faces, or eyes, or anything else, other than weapons. He knew how much firepower his patrol could produce, and on how short of a notice. Though someone may still lurk in the building, anything capable of overpowering the rough invaders was no longer in here, and would have to come from the outside. Or, so the thinking went at this early stage.

4

THERE ON THE DESK

"WE'RE LOOKING FOR A MESSENGER BAG," HAWK announced to the men. "Something like a canvas sack with a carrying strap, like you might put a satchel charge in. It could be a foot or two square, and kind of a yellow or brown color. What we really need is the papers that should be inside this thing. Then again, they could be just layin' around here loose somewhere. The people that used to run this honky tonk, left in a hurry. The papers are probably in some kind of a hiding place, but don't go ripping out the walls or nothing. If a board is already loose, that's okay, check behind it. Stuff is gonna be old and tore up here, just don't wreck anything else, or make it worse. Don't be afraid to look at a place somebody else done checked. I want every inch of these rooms to be eyeballed before we go. Kick the floorboards around. Look for anything loose." He paused to drop his rucksack on the floor and shoved it with his boot.

"Be looking for anything that might be a clue to where stuff like that is. Like torn papers, or a part of the canvas bag. We want to go over and over this bar, until they tell us it's okay to leave." He waved a hand around the building. "Find a place to throw your shit along the walls. That's where you might be sacking out for a while. Keep it to the ground floor. I want two men on each of the four sides keeping a lookout for any surprises. We'll do that now." He nodded at Joe Canlon, the corporal. Hawk shrugged. "We'll get some chow first and get busy."

The men looked curiously about their surroundings and milled around, dropping their packs along the walls. Joe approached Hawk.

"We just look around until they tell us to leave? That don't sound to me like you plan on finding anything," said Joe.

"I'm damn sure gonna be trying. We didn't come all this way for nothing. Somebody thought this was a good idea for some reason."

"Yeah. About that looking out for surprises part. Did they think we might have company showing up here?"

"No, they didn't. But then, they weren't sittin' in this dump with just a ditch between them and a million Japs. We gotta keep a sharp eye out. Probably can't do much to stop 'em, but I want to kill as many as I can before they get me."

"The whole thing is spooky. Like this...hotel place." Joe suddenly spotted the large painting. As vast as the room soared, the picture managed to dominate it from every corner. "Did you see that?" Joe asked. "Look at that babe. What a knockout!" He walked closer. "That's one of them paintings like in museums. I bet that's Cleopatra or something. I wonder what it's doing in a low rent place like this."

"I don't know." Hawk looked over his shoulder at it. "I noticed that. It was supposed to be a high rent place."

"I'm serious. I bet that's some original Galileo or something. That thing is probably worth some money. I knew a guy in New York who bought old shit like that cheap, and then sold it for big bucks to dumbasses with money. I could do something with that thing, if I wasn't stuck here. I might take that with me."

"Right. Nobody would notice you carrying that around. I doubt it's some famous thing. It would be in New York or somewhere," said Hawk. "Some son of a bitch would've stole it by now."

Joe said: "New York, my ass. That ought to be in Paris, with all that other old crap." Joe shook his head. "The women sure looked a lot better back in them old Roman days. Before they started burning up their hair with them irons, and cutting it short. Nothing worse than burnt hair, all welded together, you know. They sure looked better."

Hawk looked up the stairway. *What had happened to Baker?*

"Yeah, that one sure does," said the sergeant, walking toward the stairs. Without thinking, he unslung the Thompson.

"What's the matter?" Joe asked.

"Uh...nothing. Just gonna look around up here a minute."

"Okay. This place is too big. There could be things going on in one end of it and you wouldn't even know about it at the other," said Joe. "It's like a haunted house."

"More like a haunted beer joint," Hawk answered, proceeding slowly upward. It had been very quiet up here. "All the hiding places can set you on edge."

Joe waved his hand and turned back toward the booths, where he had dropped his pack. "Them million Japs out there can do that all by their self."

As Hawk reached the top of the stairs to the second floor, Baker backed out of an open door. He held his rifle pointed toward the inside of the room.

"Where you been?" Hawk asked. Baker kept his eyes fixed on the room.

"Looking around. I found something."

"Yeah? What?"

"Have a look." Baker gestured with the rifle barrel. Hawk stepped beside him and looked inside. It was much darker in the windowless room. At least a dozen perspiring faces huddled together there, looking back at him.

"*Damn.*" Hawk quickly surmised they must be the former employees of the Club. Most were women, but a few were men, and the men looked the most frightened.

"Are them Japs, or what?" Baker asked.

"No," said Hawk, although he had not seen every face clearly. "They're Filipino. Anybody here speak English?" he asked.

"Yes," said an attractive young woman, stepping forward. "I am Ana Mangubat and I speak English. We all speak a little. You are with the American Army? The city is free?"

"No, ma'am," said Hawk. "I'm Sergeant James Hawk, United States Marine Corps. I'm afraid we're a little out front of the Army. Did you folks work here or something?"

"Yes," she said. "We worked for Mademoiselle Eugenie Rossier, until the Japanese closed the Club. We have waited here. There have been no soldiers around here for many days. The Japanese have left Manila?"

"No, ma'am. They sure ain't. We've been sent here on a little fact-finding mission. Some of it has to do with Miss Rossier. Maybe you could tell us a few things and help us out."

"I will be happy to tell you anything I know. I wish your friend would not point the gun at us," she said. "We are not soldiers. Accidents can happen."

"Oh. Sorry," Hawk said. But he didn't tell Baker to lower the weapon. "Maybe y'all could all come on out of there, out in the daylight, and we can go downstairs and talk all this over. Y'all can come out real slow, so nobody slips and falls. Or bumps their head, or nothin'." She told her companions something in Tagalog, and the group filed cautiously out onto the balcony. Several shapely women, two boys, and a few pretty beat up looking older men gathered on the mezzanine.

"Take 'em downstairs," Hawk told Baker. "Have you checked all these rooms?"

"All but that back one. I got sidetracked by this bunch," said Baker.

"Okay. I'll check it." Hawk walked to the railing and looked at the men below. "Blackwell," he called down. "Get the battalion on the radio. Let the colonel know how things are going here. Tell 'em we're here, and found some people." Blackwell waved up at him, and went toward the radio, which lay with the rest of the gear along the front wall. It was the size of a backpack, with the heavier, lower half consisting of the battery.

Hawk walked to the last door and stopped in front of it. He had a strange feeling the room behind it was not empty. He didn't hear anything. He took the knob in hand. Then he released it, stepped back, and unslung his Thompson. The whole hall was a little secretive, a little threatening, and this closed door just might be the dark corner hiding the reason for it all. It was possible the Filipino caretakers had made a few unintroduced friends recently. Hawk knew the group must have had some sort of relationship with the Japanese, having been here for the duration of the enemy occupation.

He reached out, snapping the knob to one side with a movement like the striking of a snake, and dropped to one knee. The door swung open. The greater light from the walkway outside lit the center of the dark room, but not the corners. Hawk pushed the door open a little wider. He still didn't like it. He *knew* something was in there. Did he smell breath? Had he heard something?

He took a grenade from his belt and without pulling the pin, tossed it high and heavily into the lighted center of the room. The metal bomb casing hit with a loud crack on the wooden floor. The grenade produced no response. He stepped in. A cozy little place met him, with a bed, a chair and a washstand. A floor lamp stood in the corner, plugged into the wall. His reflection pointed a Thompson submachine gun at him from the top of a dresser against the opposite wall.

"Lotta goddam mirrors in this son of a bitch," he muttered. He looked around quickly. He saw nothing. The little space could not conceal anyone. And, yet...

He looked up at the ceiling. Pressed tin covered it. Beadboard covered the walls. A little room like this might have a few secrets: places to hide something. The whole building would need a thorough going over. He picked up the grenade. The bed was made, but the covers weren't exactly Marine Corps tight across the top of it. Someone may have slept there, lying on top of it, without moving the covers. It was something a male would do. A man, like a soldier? He left the room without closing the door. When he walked in front of the line of doors on his way to the stairway, he opened each one and left them open.

As he came down the stairs, he passed Baker. "Did you check the third floor?"

"No. You want me to?"

"Why, hell yes. What do you think? Any of our friends there got any knives or anything?"

"Not that I could tell. There's the ladies, and all."

"Yeah, well, find out. Something ain't quite right here."

"All these rooms get on my nerves," said Baker. "This house has a lot of doors. Every time you go to a new one you got the last one at your back."

"I was just thinking that. We need to search all this pretty close," said Hawk. "And we gotta do it in the daylight. It's probably a bastard to spend the night in something like this, when you can't see shit. All these doors, and curtains...and mirrors." In his experience, he had seen Japanese soldiers pop up from behind rocks and trees, but things were a lot closer, and darker, in here. He didn't want any jack-in-the-box surprises with this kind of intimacy.

While he proceeded down the steps, he could see out the panes of the large front window, where he had pushed the curtain back. Crane-like birds took off and landed along the abbreviated, trash strewn shore outside. As if rolling past on a large movie screen, a looming object appeared on the other side of the glass. A barge piled high with what looked like soil glided by, pushed stubbornly by a dirty old tugboat. The two watercraft were so close, they appeared to be floating on the island itself, as Hawk could not see the water beneath them.

"Shit! Close that curtain!" He called down to Blackwell. Fortunately, he had seen only profiles of the crew on the boat, for none of them had been inclined to peer inside the shuttered establishment during the moment it took for them to pass by. Then again, would the Filipino boatmen be interested in any strange sights they happened across during their ordinary workday? Working men generally reserved their energies for their work.

His own men were the exceptions to the rule, for the moment. They gathered around, and engaged in conversation with the newly discovered Filipino girls, making the floor of the Club resemble the way it looked in its heyday. This did not meet with the approval of their sergeant, who lapsed into some of his more routine obscenities to disband the frivolities. As they scattered, the girls included, Hawk approached Ana Mangubat and steered her toward a booth. He took note of her tight, sequined dress for the first time, and assumed it was her working garb. Large, round earrings swung with the movement of her head.

"Get them goddam bastards looking around for stuff," Hawk ordered Joe. "We're surrounded by a city full of Japs, and they're standing around scratching their ass. We need to get outta here as quick as we can." He sat down. Joe rolled his eyes and walked off, saying nothing. "Have a seat there, Miss..."

"Mangubat."

"That's right. Tell you what. Y'all are probably gonna have to get out of here pretty quick."

"I am sorry we have caused trouble."

"It ain't only the trouble. We're all kind of sitting on a bull's eye. If the Japs find out about us, they can drop a couple of artillery shells in here, and that's all she wrote. That could happen in two minutes, or two days. Y'all would be better off with them people in the shacks down to the south, or even somewhere out in the grass in Tagaytay, than you would be sitting here." Hawk shook his head to indicate the urgency. "They could surround us and capture us, and you wouldn't come out too good, if you're with us. I don't know how familiar you are with Japs and all."

"I am very familiar. I had hoped your army was coming." Her voice was high, soft, and heavily accented. He leaned forward to understand her. She had no difficulty understanding his deep, Mississippi delta accent. "And coming soon," she added.

"Yeah, that's the thing. We're here, trying to stop all that from happening. If our Army comes in here shooting, it's gonna be the same thing as the other side, as far as artillery going off. Artillery is artillery. You don't want to be sitting around in a place like this in an American artillery barrage. Ours would be even worse than the Japs. They sent us in here because..." he caught himself, and said, "we don't have a lot of common sense."

"I do not understand much. What *are* you doing here?"

"That's what I need to talk to you about. It's not good for you to know, but I have to ask you some questions anyway. You're the only ones around I can ask any of this stuff. This lady that ran this place, you knew her pretty well, right?"

"I knew Mademoiselle Eugenie very well. She was very smart and very beautiful. Most of all, she was very kind."

"Not enough of them folks around, is it? Was she like...really old or something?" Hawk fidgeted with his block of chewing tobacco and then decided against it. He pulled out a part of a cigar instead.

"Old? No. She was very young. She was younger than you. In her early twenties." Ana turned to look over her shoulder. "That is her picture. She looked just like that. Sometimes when I walk into this room, I think it is her looking down at me."

Hawk looked up at the fascinating painting. "That's her?" he asked with surprise. So much for Cleopatra.

"Yes. Is she not beautiful?"

"Damn sure is. Who's that other picture there? That looks a lot like the same lady."

"It is. It is her, as Joan of Arc. She often said she thought of herself more as Saint Germaine. The man who painted it did it as a joke, you understand—on the Japanese. They did not know of her support for the poor people of Manila or of her helping the resistance and the Americans. She was very powerful and always helped those in need. The Japanese did not know—until the end. They thought her only a bar owner. She was a warrior, as brave as Joan of Arc. That is what the picture means."

"Hunh." Hawk stared at the painting. He shook his head. He did not know a great deal about Joan of Arc, but the armor and the sword filled in the missing details. "She must have had a lot of guts."

"Yes. More than her beauty. More than her kindness even, she had courage. Too much courage. Courage is good only to get you killed by the evil ones, who have none."

"Ain't that the *gotdam* truth?" Hawk agreed. "What happened, at the end, and all?" he asked, lighting his cigar with the matches lying there. He slid the translucent, marigold depression glass ashtray toward himself. "I ain't got no cigarettes. I can get you one, if you want."

"No, thank you. At the end, a week ago and three

days now, I believe it was...we were preparing for the show. The Club opened at six that night, it was a Friday. Mademoiselle Eugenie only sang every other week or so, but she was going to sing that night. An important Japanese general was coming with some visiting friends from Japan. She was going to sing a French song. I do not know these songs, you probably do. Many are on the American and European radio. They are very beautiful."

"Yeah," said Hawk, who didn't know many songs, French or otherwise. Nor did he have any interest in knowing any. Jack Benny messing around with his violin on the radio was about the extent of his musical knowledge. He had listened to Tokyo Rose for entertainment at times.

"She was standing there, on the stage, the band played but she had not begun her song, when the *Kempetai* pushed the door open very hard." She made a pushing motion. "They did not have to do this, it was open, you see? They wanted to scare us. But they pushed it very hard, and twenty or more of them came in saying loud words, and pulled her from the stage. She did not say anything. She did not scream." Ana shrugged. "And that is how this ended." She gestured at the room around them. "There was no show that night. They nailed the door shut. The general and his friends did not come. We planned to be happy. It was very sad."

"Ain't that some...something?" Hawk pushed aside the Victorian table lamp with its gaudy lace shade, that he might better see Ana, who had pulled to one side, and was looking down. Perhaps she was sniffling. His mind ran more toward the possibility of her pulling out a pistol, as she avoided his gaze.

"They took her to Fort Santiago, where things are

done to people. You know about that, I am sure. And she died. And they threw her body in a ditch with all the others killed there every day. It was said she would not tell them anything. She did not say a word to them. This I can believe. If you knew her, you would understand."

"Damn," Hawk squinted through the swirling smoke. "I guess you knew she had been sending out information to the Americans?"

"Yes. We knew. Everyone knew. The wrong people finally knew."

"Sounds like it. Did you know how she went about doing all that? I mean, like, the general routine of the spying and all? The way you described it, she wouldn't have had time to send out any last messages, would she? The end was unexpected."

"She did not have time to even drop the microphone," said Ana. "It was in her hand, with the cord dragging, when they carried her out that door."

"Hunh. How about right before all that happened? Or maybe even the night before?"

"I don't know. It is possible, because she was up late that night, writing something. It took her a long time. I have been in her room, and I saw no writings left there. I have asked myself about that many times. Where are those writings? What was so important to her? I did not see the police go upstairs. They did not want anything, or anybody, but her. The *Kempetai* took her out, and left on a patrol boat. The station is that way on the canal: right down there, not very far. You should know that you are very close to it here. I walked outside to watch. We stood there, not believing it. Soon, we cried. We did not even think how lucky we were to be alive. We only thought of her, and how sad we were."

Hawk nodded. "That's kind of interesting to me. On account of, we're looking for those papers you're talking about. Our S-2 thinks she may have known whether the Jap in charge of Manila is planning on leaving an open city." Hawk threw caution to the wind now, telling her everything, in the hopes of finding out something.

"Mademoiselle would know this. She would know everything the Japanese do. They tell her everything. We all tell her everything. She sat there, looking like that." Ana pointed at the painting. "And we would tell her everything in our heart. She never asked. People just wanted to talk to her. To look at her eyes. This is hard for anyone to believe who did not know her. This is how she kept this Club open for three years, under the Japanese occupation. Some in the resistance, not many, but some did not trust her because she was not Filipino. They believed she would betray them someday, and that she was really in sympathy with the Japanese. Others thought she was just a woman running a bar, and had no loyalties to anyone. Those who knew her, knew the truth. Someone knew the truth and betrayed her anyway."

"It *is* odd; how she was able to do all that, I mean. I can see why people would wonder. Didn't the Japs round up all the Americans and Europeans and take them to some camp, when MacArthur left? She just slips their net and opens up a gin joint? That's kind of... odd. First off, if I could get away, I would be on a slow boat to China, not hanging around here with some juiced up Japs."

"Many told her to do this. Yes, that very thing. It was not easy to do. She took over the Club when the Americans were here. It was Club Starlight then. She took the Club from an American—I don't think they liked her even then. The whole country here changed with the war. In the beginning, when *they* came, the Japanese did not arrest her because she was exempt as a German citizen. In fact, the Americans had been preparing to deport her, before war was declared. She was from Alsace, on her papers. It is part of France since the First War, but many Germans live there because it is on the border and changes hands. The authorities here all had been told that Hitler had transferred the province back to Germany when he took over France. She was exempt as a German for many months and kept the Club. Like Joan of Arc, she was from a place where the French and the Germans meet.

"She liked to sing, not so much in front of people, but she wanted to be on the radio. Then the authorities found out, Hitler did *not* transfer Alsace back to Germany. That meant she was really a French citizen, not German, and *not* exempt from arrest. This was a very frightening time. We were closed for...I think more than a week. The magistrate then ruled Vichy France is an ally of Germany and Japan, and that she was exempt again. Some say a Japanese general talked to the magistrate to make this happen, because of the great influence of Mademoiselle, but I have heard since that this is really the law for everyone. I know other Vichy French, and most have no problems with the authorities. For a long time, they did not.

"The Japanese fear everyone now. All Europeans. Everything was fine then, until now. People that look as if they may be Western can have trouble. For a day or so, after the police raid, I thought, these things happen all the time, she will come back. Like before. Because of her influence? But this time, it did not happen. And now she will never come back." Ana looked down as her voice dropped.

"I been told she sent messages to this Commander Astorqui, with the resistance, up in the mountains. You know about that?"

"Yes. I knew this. I could be killed for telling you this."

"Sweetheart, you can get killed for sitting there blowing bubbles. Did you know how she got the information to the mountains?"

"She had many messengers. She even took them herself at times. All of the messengers were captured, or shot, one by one."

"She lost a lot of messages, I guess? But they never figured her out, while all that losin' and shootin' was going on?"

"The messengers were all killed on the way *back* to Manila after the messages had been delivered. Mademoiselle had only one messenger left, one who she could rely upon. He was very sly. He delivered the message, but then, he would not come back. He would stay in the mountains until everyone had forgotten about him. They never caught him. He still lives."

"That might be a fella worth talking to. Do you know him?"

"I know him. He is called Ulupong, the snake. He charged a lot of money for the deliveries. He did not do it for the Philippines, he did it for the money—American money. He would not take Japanese money. You would probably never find him, because he is—a *snake*."

"You didn't know where he lived, or where he hung around?"

"I stayed away from him. He looked like a snake. He did anything for money. There are criminals here, with gangs, that do not care about the war. He works mostly with them. But he will work for anybody with money. The boys over there may know where he is. Mademoiselle would send them to get him when she needed him. But I did not see him the night before the raid, because I would certainly have remembered. He always leered at me with his big teeth. *Kamusta, Ana,* he would say. I would not look at him. He knew my father. He would always tell me that, that my father would like it if he were my boyfriend. But my father said stay away from him."

"Sounds like the Mademoiselle should have taken some advice from your father," said Hawk. "I would guess the snake sold her out for a few bucks."

"None of that would surprise me. I did not think of that. He was just another person around here. Not all were nice. There were so many with the war. It makes me very sad to think of him doing this. I would like to kill him."

"Hey, don't pay no attention to me. I was just taking a wild guess, there. A lot of people around here could have turned her in, but he's the only one I know about, so far. If he was getting paid well, he might have wanted to keep her alive. I ain't tryin' to put the Black Hand on nobody."

"No, I think you are right the first time. He would not think that far ahead. If he wanted money that night, he would do anything to get it. He would worry about tomorrow when he needed more money."

"I probably have to try to find Mr. Snake. I'm short on time. I ain't sure exactly what all I'll do yet." Hawk set the cigar down. "Tell me something. I noticed your get-up there. What all went on in this place? You got all these rooms and beds. How did y'all get the Japs to do so much talking? In my dealings with 'em, they ain't been real sociable. It must have been loud in here with the band, dancing and singing, and a roulette wheel. Folks boozing it up. Seems like with all that hoo-rawing going on, it'd be hard to pass around too many secrets."

"This dress is for a musical number. Nothing unclean went on here. We had fun. We drank with them. They drank liquor, a lot of sake, we drank tea. They got silly, we listened. If someone wanted to leave with someone, that was their business, not the business of Club Arashigaoka. It did not happen very much. But...people are people. This was a happy place. We worked with cleaning it, cooking, and rehearsing, but when the door opened at six, it was fun. It was not like work. The war, of course, made it something else. More of a...contest."

"Yeah. Sounds real lively: a lot of dancing and drinking Japs. Can't beat that for fun. Was Miss Rossier in on all this? Was she a live wire, too?"

"Mademoiselle was not a happy person. She was a serious person. She spent much time counting money, and ordering supplies. She did not cry, but she did not have fun. I believe she thought of killing herself. She wore black, like when someone dies, you know? Maybe she was not well. Everyone wanted to hear her sing. She did sing, but not very often. It was always a special occasion. And always a sad song."

"What was her name again?"

"Mademoiselle Eugenie?"

"*You-jah-nee?*" he asked.

She nodded, with a smile, and did not correct his pronunciation.

"So, was there a Mr. Eugenie in on all this fun Jap stuff? How did he jive with the bastards?"

"No. She was never married. She had no companions. Men desired her, but I think they were afraid of her. She was very powerful. Men do not like that. You could tell she was powerful. She did not laugh much, she was serious. She carried a gun. Some people who talk a lot said she had used it. I never believed this. I was more afraid she carried it to use on herself. Men chase a woman to bother her, but not if they think they will be shot. Most of the men left here when the Japanese came. Only the very old and very young stayed."

"Did she have the gun the night the police picked her up?"

"I do not know. It did her no good, if she did. She could not kill them all."

"I don't know, either," he said. "She sounds like a tough customer. Somebody might have got nicked in the deal."

"No," Ana disagreed suddenly. "She was not a rough person. There was no killing or anything dirty here. The priest, Father Deharo, came here every week. He blessed the building, to protect us from the devil, and the Japanese. He heard the confession of Mademoiselle and stayed many hours."

"He was probably putting the bite on her," said Hawk.

"The *bite*? This means?"

"You know, looking for a handout. Trying to get a cut of the take here."

"You mean, money? Yes. He helped many people with the war. Many people are suffering. Mademoiselle had a lot of money, and she wanted to help them, too. She gave him money. This is not wrong. He was a holy man." Ana sounded indignant at the American's cynical and crude implication. She had no understanding of

Hawk's innate crudeness. It would have been impossible for him to communicate without being crude. "And she paid us very well. More than she should. She was a good person."

"I bet she was, at that," said Hawk, not knowing exactly what to think of Mademoiselle Eugenie. Everyone agreed she was a saint, or perhaps an angel, and yet she ran a gin joint for enemy combatants, (not a dirty one), ran a *very* deadly spy ring, carried a gun, told Japanese generals what to do, knew what they were thinking, passed out cash like Al Capone, and—nobody messed with her. Then she ran off and got herself killed, leaving Hawk holding the bag, or not holding it—and she still could get him killed after the partying was over. It was an involved portrait. Hawk looked up at the real portrait. It looked back at him, and not with a great deal of approval on its soft brow.

"Who did that painting? Is he a famous guy? Like, from Italy or something?"

"No, but he was a genius. He was from here. It took him weeks. He is dead. The Japanese killed him. I am glad there is something left of her, of both of them. I am afraid something will happen to it, but where else could I put it? It is large."

"Yeah. It ought to be somewhere...else." He looked around. "How about a bouncer? Got anybody like that? When things got rowdy? Can't have a joint for old drunks without rowdiness. Anybody with a gun? Somebody to lay out folks having too much fun?"

"Our doorman was Pablo. He was very large, but did not have a gun. It is dangerous to have a gun here when you are not Japanese. He left over a month ago. It frightened him here. We did not have much trouble, because the clients were mostly Japanese officers. No one would cause trouble with so many Japanese officers around. You would get much more problems, than just being thrown out, if you made trouble for them. They *are* the trouble."

"Yeah. I imagine those...gents...run a tight ship."

"I am so tired. We were so afraid of you. But I am glad I talked with you. Now, I am not as afraid. You are nice."

"Oh, shit, yeah. Everybody'll tell you that. Well... maybe nobody here. But you can go on about your business. No need to be afraid. If you don't mind, keep them ladies away from the men. Like I say, you might have to get out of here pretty soon. It's risky being around us. I have to talk to the colonel about everything, to see what's next. We would like to find those papers the lady was working on, if they ain't been torn to pieces or something."

"I will think about it. I can show you her rooms, on the third floor."

"Okay. Yeah. Let's do that right now."

They stood and climbed the stairs. Joe Canlon leaned there, eating a bag of peanuts he had found somewhere.

"We're going upstairs. Come on," said Hawk.

Joe folded up the bag. "Okay. Afraid she'll jump you?"

"Yeah. Did you get the lookouts posted on them sides?" Hawk replied, continuing up the stairs.

"Yes, Mister Sergeant. Don't worry, I'll take care of her for you."

"Yeah. Okay. Try shuttin' up." They reached the third floor, and Ana opened the only door there and entered the room. "This was her office. We came to talk to her here, sometimes," she said.

"Nice place," said Hawk. The room contained a large desk, a filing cabinet and two chairs for visitors. A banker's lamp dominated the desk, and there were other odds and ends. He opened a filing cabinet. It was bursting with folders and papers. "Shit! Look at all this shit!" Joe walked over to look at it.

"What? Just a bunch of papers?"

"Shit, yeah—*papers*. Do you know why we're here? Papers."

"Congratulations," said Joe. "End of the treasure hunt. Box 'em up. Let's get the hell out."

"More like the start of it. I'm gonna have go through all this shit, and see what it is." He pulled out the desk chair and fell into it. "We can't carry off this whole son of a bitch."

"Sure, you can. Take 'em outta the cabinet and divide 'em up."

"Those are mostly records," said Ana. "Marie was the bookkeeper. She can tell you which ones are important. I don't think any of that is what you are looking for." Hawk rifled through the desk drawers, finding little of interest. "A lot of this old shit ain't in English," he mumbled.

He stood and noticed a cabinet, fashioned into the wall. It had a lock on it, but nothing more secure than a little wafer tumbler desk lock. The latch was unfastened and he opened the door. Inside, the empty storage area contained one shelf. "Odd."

"What? A cabinet?" Joe asked. "Maybe it's where she kept her toothbrush. Gotta keep the choppers polished in the entertainment business."

"Yeah, but it's empty. With a lock on it. You ever see anything in this cabinet?" Hawk asked Ana.

"I saw that there were things in it, but I never looked

in there. I think it always had...little booklets in it. Pamphlets? Maybe about the church."

"Church, huh? A fancy looking thing cut into the wall with a lock on it, sitting there empty. It's kind of funny," Hawk looked at Joe.

"Not too funny," said Joe, with a blank expression. "My grandma had a lot of empty cabinets, because she didn't have any shit to put in them." Hawk looked at a door on the other side of the room.

"Where does that go?" he asked.

"Into her bedroom," said Ana, walking toward the door and opening it.

They entered the room. It contained a large canopied bed. Windows extended across three of the four walls, and the place looked bright and clean. Hawk stepped to the window. He could see the shanty town the patrol had passed through when arriving in Manila. He saw the grimy canal on the other two sides. Conspicuously, there was no view of the city from here, which lay to the north.

Hawk walked to the blank wall blocking the view of the city and tapped it. "You can't see Manila from here. That's kind of stupid. What's this wall here for?"

"I don't know," said Ana. "There is an attic over there, I believe. But you *can* see Manila. Come with me." She brushed aside a curtain, exposing a little door, of the type that usually concealed a fold-out ironing board. When she opened the door, a narrow stairway extended behind it. She had to almost turn sideways to climb up it.

Hawk bent down to look up the spiraling steps. "Joe, I hope your fat ass don't get stuck in this thing." They had to lower their heads a bit to climb it. At the top, they found themselves in the open air of a cupola, with a domed roof over their heads and a railing around the sides. One could see across Manila, all the way to the bay. The wind was high and the view impressive.

"Whoa! Look at that! I wouldn't mind living in a place like this," said Joe, walking to every side to check the view. "After the war and all, when there ain't no Japs."

"I imagine, if there ain't no Japs, there ain't gonna be no place here, either," said Hawk, surveying the Pearl of the Orient, stretching out forever before him. "Stay back from that rail. Somebody could see you up here." In the middle of the floor was a small round table and one comfortable chair. The tower appeared to be Mademoiselle Rossier's private retreat.

"Where did you see her do her writing, on that last night? Was she here, or sitting at the desk down there?" Hawk asked.

"Yes. When I saw her, she was at the desk. It is dark up here at night. The wind blows out a lamp."

"Baby, I wouldn't mind living in a place like this," said Joe. "You know what this reminds me of? The Statue of Liberty. You look down from the top of it, and you're on this little island, surrounded by water. You know you been someplace when you go there." Joe looked down at the water lapping the shore right below him, thinking of home for a happy moment, and better days.

"Okay. We better go back down, and get this stupid ass off here," said Hawk, "before somebody spots him." The winding descent proved even tighter than climbing up the narrow stairwell. "A man could get hisself hung up in something like this," Hawk commented, as his shoulders jammed and dragged across the close walls. The smell of paint was strong in the cramped quarters.

"Yeah, you know, they don't let you climb up in the arm of the Statue of Liberty anymore, but you can still go up into her hat," said Joe, struggling to twist and turn. "My mother was one of the last people to go up in the torch thing. Did you know that?"

"How in the goddamn hell would I know that?"

Hawk looked quickly around the bedroom for papers: in the chest of drawers, and under the bed. There were none. They returned to the outer office. The first thing to catch his eye, upon entering the room, was a little brass figurine on the desk: a Statue of Liberty, souvenir of New York. He picked it up, turned it around, and held it out toward Joe. Joe raised his eyebrows

"Hey! I was just talking about that! My mother had one of those."

"Did you see this damn thing sitting there, when we came in?" Hawk asked.

"No, I didn't see it," he answered.

"Me, either." Hawk set it down. "That's kinda peculiar," he said, turning to Ana. "There, on the desk." He looked around the little room.

"It is how the dead talk to us," Ana said.

5

DEAR JOHN AND JODY

By the time her family boarded the ship, Marta Weitz grew more accustomed to the idea of the family's move to the Philippines. Maybe not happy with the idea, but accustomed. Karl had been right, the passage turned out to be first class. They did not have to hide aboard a freighter, as many refugees had done before them. Several well-to-do voyagers traveled with them aboard the passenger ship. Marta could not tell if any were fleeing the country, and she certainly did not want to ask: first of all, because it was embarrassing, and only second because it could cause problems. An air of normality accompanied the whole trip, without any panic. They were able to leave Germany at a fairly leisurely pace and did not lose the majority of their belongings in the bargain. The ship made stops at Bombay, Ceylon, Penang, and Hong Kong, before arriving in Manila. The journey, and the little side trips, had been rather pleasant. The children got to see elephants.

The travelers were met by a welcoming committee

in Manila, organized by President Quezon himself. Many local dignitaries attended, wearing the traditional light *barong tagalog* shirts made of pineapple fiber, rather than formal suits. In spite of the hospitality, the Weitz family noticed not many Jews resided here. Few had taken up the President on his offer.

They were given a comfortable apartment downtown, and Karl was introduced to a local jeweler. Karl stayed there a little over two weeks, but the position was not to his liking. It was not what he had been used to doing in Germany. The job here in Manila involved more of the duties of a salesman, rather than those of an artisan, as he had been. He was also not a very well compensated salesman, receiving no salary, and working on commission. While wealthy buyers of jewelry lived here, it was not like in Germany. The customers did not come to his door to peruse his wares. He often had to beat the bushes to find them. You had to know people here. Karl did not know anyone, or yet speak the language well. People could speak anything from Tagalog to Cebuano, and from English to Spanish. The President was encouraging the use of Tagalog as the basis of a national Filipino language at the time, and Karl had developed a loyalty to the President—but loyalty did not make it any easier for him to learn things.

Karl had some savings, and he had been able to get them out of the bank, so he did not fret. It was not expensive to live here. After another week or two of asking about, he found a job as a bookkeeper for a merchant near the harbor. It did not pay a lot, and he was not a bookkeeper at heart, but it was a steady income. He had been in business and he knew how to do it, although it was not his calling, and he did not really care for it. But he could not complain to Marta, because she was still in her darker phase of appraising the move. This would fade with time, but upon their first arrival, he had to keep his criticisms of the Philippines to a minimum.

The whole family set to learning Tagalog, and made friends easily. People accepted them. They had no Jewish friends in the beginning, but they located a community group, and hoped to rectify that circumstance. It would be good to reconnect with others who had been through experiences similar to their own.

Karl and Marta began attending the Jewish group meetings and Karl had hopes of finding a better position through his associations there. He and Marta discovered other immigrants had far more harrowing stories of escape from the fatherland than did they. The Philippines had been the last choice for most of these refugees, rather than the first, as it had been for Karl. It seemed Germany was not the only dangerous place for a Jewish person trying to relocate. Even the American authorities had not been overly welcoming here, but they were at least polite and far from hostile. This was not true in every country.

Karl started looking into what it would take to emigrate to the United States. He discovered the American authorities were beset by a certain lack of enthusiasm. Perhaps it was just indifference. There were no official denials or rejections to his queries, but there were a lot of waiting lists—long waiting lists. And there were a lot of assurances that he eventually would be contacted, and to leave well enough alone. If you irritated someone, you could find yourself at the bottom of a list. Later, Karl would wish he had followed this advice. Getting one's name added to a list, even at the bottom, is not always advantageous. Governments are fleeting, but lists can be permanent.

* * *

THE WELL-STOCKED filing cabinet of Mademoiselle Rossier had to be dealt with. Hawk conceded the cabinet appeared to be the primary focus of his mission. He sat down with Marie, the bespectacled bookkeeper, Ana, and a private among his men, named Van Houten. Van Houten was a bright young man, having attended college for a year or two until enlisting when the war broke out. The sergeant assigned the three of them the task of going through the papers in the filing cabinet, and the few papers he had seen in the desk, as well as some from other stray places. Ana assured him several times that they would find nothing, until he grew tired of hearing it. He disliked everything about this aspect of his assignment.

"Then don't do it," he told Ana, as he sat in a booth downstairs. "Let them do it. We gotta go through everything, like it or not." Ana's face flushed. "I am sorry," she said. "I will help."

When they left, Joe came and sat across from Hawk. "Kinda rough on the girl, weren't you?" Joe asked. "You don't like her or something?"

"Why?" Hawk asked without interest.

"I think she's crying over there."

"Ah, she can go to hell. I'm getting tired of people telling me stupid shit," Hawk said. "We gotta get this done and get out of this son of a bitch before a mortar comes through the roof. Japs are crawling around like ants out there, and here you are blubbering about how somebody got their feelings hurt."

"I said *she* was blubbering. Did you talk to the colonel?"

"Yeah."

"That's what this is about? What'd he say?"

"Ah, he's full of shit."

Joe understood he would have to be satisfied with the brief explanation. He looked around the room. Most of the men browsed other floors, searching or pretending to search, and a few checked the outside area. Dusk fell, signaling the unwelcome and swift passage of time. In particular, two of the men were looking around the bandstand but were obviously more fully engaged in a conversation with one another.

"See them two guys," Joe said suddenly, nodding toward the bandstand. Hawk looked up slowly. "Yeah. That's...uh...Rayburn, and Epley is the one on the floor, crawling around," Hawk said. Though most of the men had been newly assigned to him, Hawk knew them all by name. These two were not so new. "They were in the squad when we took Welch up on the ridge. Welch's *buddies*."

"Yeah. I know. The buddies who *didn't* go up on the ridge," Joe said quietly. "They're from this same place in Illinois, these two little towns, and they went to the same high school. The two had been trying for a year and a half to get in the same outfit together. The Corps never would help 'em out. They finally got together, when that ridge thing happened and then the Corps split 'em up again. They volunteered for this rotten mission, just to get back together."

"Hmmph. That wasn't such a good idea," said Hawk. "This looks like a damn good way to get killed."

"And people do it. Look, that's why I'm here, because you're here, ain't it? I didn't want to do any of this."

"Yeah, but we been together all along. That's different. And Baker and Blackwell are here with us. There's a little more to why you're here, anyway. It ain't all for hugs and kisses. *You* had a little help from the colonel. He appealed to your patriotism, and told you you'd be bustin' rocks, if you didn't come along. Epley and Rayburn came outta nowhere, for no reason, to do this."

"Maybe the two felt bad about backing out of the ridge—on account of what happened to Welch. If you went on the ridge, or you didn't go on the ridge—we all end up in this shit. You don't have to try to be hero in the Corps. They'll take care of that department for you."

Rayburn and Epley had stopped looking around and stood facing one another, speaking in gradually rising voices. Rayburn waved his arm angrily, and the clipped sound of obscenities echoed across the dance floor.

"Looks like one old buddy done stepped on the other old buddy's sore toes," said Hawk, winking at Joe.

"Yeah." Joe laughed stupidly. "Hey!" Joe shouted at them. "Knock that shit off and get busy!" The two men ceased arguing and looked over at Joe, and at the silent shadow of the sergeant behind him. The dark presence of Hawk had a way of dispelling bad feelings, as much as it dispelled the eerie light filtering inside. Rayburn and Epley drifted apart, one returning to the search along the front wall, and the other behind the bar.

"The two of them went through all that trouble of volunteering to get together, and now they're stuck with somebody they hate," said Hawk.

"Yeah, looks like it," said Joe, with a more serious expression. "It's like gettin' married."

When night came, the patrol bedded down in the dark hall, without the benefit of lights. Hawk did not want any form of illumination shining through the windows, which were easily seen for miles from the elevated island. Enough moon and star light came through the big windows to allow the men to move around comfortably. The first day had passed quietly enough, but without realizing any particular accomplishments. Hawk knew the Sixth and Eighth Armies moved in on the city, tightening their grip, and that all hell could break loose any minute. The first day had passed, but were days supposed to pass?

The sergeant briefly reported to Clark on his inability to turn up anything, and was told to keep looking. Later, he lay on the floor and studied the copper plated ceiling as he prepared to sleep. Maybe the fidgety U. S. Army would move unopposed into this vacated area, as the Club with its island was purportedly located in an open district, and all would be well. The patrol would be surrounded by thousands of American soldiers, and could pursue their search of Club Arashigaoka in relative safety. If the city received a preparatory bombardment, however, one sufficient to vaporize everything Japanese, all would not be well. Artillery shells were notoriously bad at distinguishing one nationality from another.

All hope was not lost. Manila could yet turn into an open city, or failing that, Qebu could remain an open district.

The next morning, Hawk sat near the front window, squinting as he held the curtain back and watched a barge pass by. The tugboat's airhorn blasted a mournful warning, after it had passed. There was a sharp turn in the canal, just after passing beyond the Club. The light grew brighter inside the dark, humid building. The old smells of alcohol and stale perfume saturating its walls grew stronger in the morning warmth.

The men ate C rations, shuffled about, and prepared for the day. Hawk looked over at them. He noticed several bottles of liquor missing from the shelves behind the bar. The lines of bottles had been pulled closer together to hide the spaces once occupied by the missing selections. He had made a mental note of the size of the inventory when he first entered the club. He yawned. *The bastards.*

Amid the ordinary, groggy morning sounds, one noise rose above the rest. Hawk immediately recognized the same two angry voices from the night before. Rayburn and Epley had resumed their prior, interrupted disagreement. This time, it was much louder, and the two of them appeared to be facing off. The other men stood or sat in amused interest as to what would happen next. Hawk rose to his feet with a groan.

Can you believe this shit? He thought. *Every Jap God ever created out there, and they're in here cutting up like kids?*

Epley stood a couple of inches shorter than Rayburn and had a slightly smaller build. He was the aggressor, however, in terms of the screaming. The verbal argument stopped when Rayburn threw a straight right at Epley's head in response to some particularly provocative insult. Although the punch connected rather well, it did not soothe Epley's ardor. He launched himself upon Rayburn, coming inside and under the taller man's reach, and pummeling him mercilessly to the floor. This brought a few expressions of admiration from the crowd, until the angry Rayburn rose to his feet, unbeaten by any of it. They traded blows toe to toe for a minute or so, until Epley decided he was getting the worst of it, and dove into his opponent, tackling him to the ground, where they both set to rolling about and clawing. At this point, a resigned Sergeant Hawk crossed the floor.

Hawk reached down and grabbed the back of Rayburn's utility jacket, pulled him free of Epley's grasp, and slid him like a hockey puck across the dance floor. After the raging Epley rose to his feet and came at Hawk, a quick punch to his nose from the sergeant left him sitting back on the floor.

"Awright, knock that shit off. What the hell do you think this is? Girl's night out? You're in the goddam US Marine Corps. When we fight, we kill people. We don't do shit like this. Do you know where we are?"

Assuming the matter resolved, Hawk turned with the intention of returning to his own quiet ruminations in a booth. Rayburn, however, who had not had the force of the sergeant's fist applied to his nose, was not quite satisfied. He ran and dove at the seated and dazed Epley. A dozen hands reached out and restrained him. Hawk stopped and looked over his shoulder at the continuing uproar.

"He's all right," Joe said to Hawk, from the middle of the heavily breathing group holding Rayburn. "The guy didn't hear you." Hawk continued on his way back toward a booth.

Several minutes later, Joe Canlon joined Hawk, smiling broadly.

"Pretty good, huh?" Joe asked as he sat down.

"Yeah, that was great. Your two *buddies*? What the hell is that all about? Is this gonna go on forever? I ain't having all that. We got too much shit going on here. Everybody acts like it's a sure thing the Army is gonna show up and pull us out of this vise."

"Here's what happened, it's kinda good. Epley had this girl back home, see? She's been writing him, crazy about him, blah, blah. So, it turns out she's been writing Rayburn, too, says she's crazy about him, and sick of Epley. She can't wait till Rayburn gets back. Pretty funny stuff, huh?" Joe took out a cigarette. "High school kids, you know. Don't know the score yet. Important shit."

"Yeah. That's a laugh a minute. That's gotta stop."

"Well." Joe blew smoke in the air. "I don't think it will. They hate each other's guts now. And we're stuck with 'em. Just another pain in the ass. When I was in camp, they would let guys fight it out with gloves when shit like that happened."

"Right, and they let guys play with footballs and Tinker Toys, too. This ain't no camp. Have any of these simple son of a bitches figured out who's outside the windows there?"

"Yeah," Joe answered, disappointed at not being able to arrange a fight. "It's bad. I kinda hated to see it."

Hawk shook his head. "Which one got the girl? Never mind. Tell the one who lost the girl to come over here, I want to talk to his ignorant ass. He must be the one stirrin' this up."

"That's Epley, the one you hit."

"Even better. He's gonna be willing to listen. It looked like the other one might need a little more convincing." Joe brought Epley over and sat him down in the booth, across from Hawk. Joe slid in next to Epley, with a ridiculous grin on his face.

"Hey, useless? Ain't you got something to do?" Hawk asked Joe.

"Oh. Yeah," said Joe, getting up and leaving, looking to one side and another, with a bit of an indignant swagger in his walk.

"Listen, kid. I know you had a little falling out over there, but you understand, don't you, that you could get your brains shot out in this place, right? And real quick. We're in a tough spot here. You got any family?"

"Yes, Sergeant. Sorry. That was dumb. It won't happen again."

"The thing is, we're all depending on you two to act right. This is serious bidness. I could tell you I'm gonna do this or I'm gonna do that—don't none of that matter, if you're dead. I ain't talkin' about some captain gettin' his skirt blown up over his head and erasing your name from the party invites. I'm talkin'—dead." They stared at one another. Sergeant Hawk knew all about dead. "So, what's the matter here, he stole your girl?"

"Yes. The rat's been sneaking around behind my back the whole time. He's a liar, he's a thief..."

Hawk held up a hand. "Listen. He ain't the rat. This here girl ain't some prize pig, with no brain. She knows exactly what she's doing. She started this shit. She's the rat. He's doing you a favor taking her off your hands. You know, people end up marryin' rats like that, and causing all kinds of shit? He might just do that himself. You ought to feel sorry for the stupid ass, not go startin' fights with him. Just because we're stuck out here without no women around ain't no reason to go nuts over something ten thousand miles away. We got Japs right outside there that can settle all your problems."

Yes, Sergeant." Epley was unbowed. He looked straight into Hawk's eyes, and did not seem to be buying it. Blood streamed out of his nostril. "I apologize. To you."

"Mighty big of you. You're mad right now. At him—at me—who knows? But you know who you ought to be mad at. She's over there probably running around with half a dozen other dumbasses. You gonna fight every 4F guy in Illinois? You need Rayburn and he needs you, and we all need both of you. Y'all were big buddies before all this came out. You need to get over this shit and go back to being buddies. You gotta get over stuff fast here, just like you gotta eat fast, shit fast, shoot fast, and go to sleep fast. Awright?"

"Yes, Sergeant."

"Now, you're the one in control of this. You're the one that can get over it, and get it done. He ain't got no reason to be mad at you. He thinks he's the big winner. Let him think that. He might get killed tomorrow. And so might you. Her stupid ass ain't gettin' killed. She's gettin' a big laugh outa all this, see? Some jerk, that ain't worth a second thought, laughing at two US Marines. We don't allow that. Now use your head and settle this, or I'll settle it for you—because as of now, it's over."

"Yes, Sergeant. Sorry. It was dumb."

Hawk sighed. "Okay, kid. Take off." Hawk had no idea whether any of what he said registered with Epley. He was dealing with emotions, not reason. With a kid like that, sometimes a woman had to kick them in the teeth a dozen times before any light bulbs went on. He motioned Rayburn over. Rayburn did not have an expression indicating he was any more pleased than Epley.

"Sit down there, shithead. So, you want to fight me, right?"

"No, Sergeant. I was a little out of line. He hit me, and I was mad. At...everything."

"Yeah. I noticed that. It's over some girl, right?"

"Yes, Sergeant. I can't help it if he met her first. I mean, so what is that? Like, she's a cow or something?"

"A really nice girl, eh?"

"Yes, Sergeant. She's beautiful. She's the most wonderful girl in the world."

"Ain't that some shit? Them are sure hard to find. You got a real...prize...on your hands there. Hey, listen, kid, you got the prize, right? You ain't got no reason to be mad at Epley, right? He says he's willing to forget all this. It was just kind of sudden, you know, and surprised him. He had been getting some different messages from the home front. It takes some adjusting. Two Marines don't fight over stupid shit like that. Do you think y'all can be buddies again?"

"Yes, Sergeant. I have nothing against him. He just started calling me...things. He's...a bastard."

"Okay, Rayburn. He ain't a bastard. I sure hope you two can take up where you left off and be friends. I'd hate to have to break your neck before the Japs get a chance to. But—I will. Take off. And, congratulations. You're the lucky one." Rayburn smiled, nodded and left. Joe Canlon returned.

"What'd they say?" Joe asked.

"Nothing. We'll have to wait and see. I think it's done, but who knows? Couple of jackasses." Hawk shook his head. "I tell you what, though. If there's a next time, there ain't gonna be no talking. What am I? The chaplain? I ain't having that crap going on."

"Did you tell 'em that? Maybe I oughta tell 'em that."

"Do what you want, I don't give a shit. Go get me one of them bottles over there, before they drink 'em all up. The son of a bitches."

"Is that a good idea?"

"Shit, no, it ain't no good idea. What's with the good idea business? Do I look like Alexander Graham Bell?"

The routine of searching for, and finding nothing in the way of documents, had been well established by midday, when Hawk was contacted by Clark. Clark was not as satisfied with the routine failure as Hawk.

"Okay, okay, Sergeant. Then who did that bar woman say the contact was, on the night of the raid? The go-between? Is he there with you now? Is he in there with the rest of those crumbs? Over," Clark demanded. The patrol's radio sat on the table in the last booth, the one Hawk usually occupied.

"It was a local, called Ulupong," Hawk replied. "It's like a nickname, I think." Blackwell, the radioman, sat next to the sergeant with a cherubic smile on this face, elbow bent and chin in hand, watching Hawk sweat. He could hear the excited voice coming over the headset, as Hawk was not holding it tightly to his ear.

"Hang on, hang on, spell that goddam shit!" the colonel screamed.

Hawk spelled Ulupong. "He ain't really with the resistance, he's just some kind of a crook that hung around the bar. They scraped the bottom of the barrel, since everybody was getting picked up and killed by the Japs. Over."

"Okay. Listen to me, Sergeant. The guerrilla leader, Astorqui, never received anything from that Club. No documents, no messages. *Nothing*," said the colonel. "Everything disappeared somewhere between that damn bar of yours and the hills. Or maybe between the bar and this messenger. Keep looking, but get that... Ulupong...character, too. Don't just talk to him. *Get* him. Bring him with you. He may have sold those papers. I don't want some asshole playing both sides of the fence floating around out there. This is a very sensitive period of time right now. I would say shoot him, but he probably knows things that'll help us down the road. You might have to...get rid of him...later, but for now, let's just say you're bringing him into battalion for questioning. Don't alienate him, or act like he's a prisoner, just tell him he's doing his patriotic duty, if you can. But remember, he *is* a prisoner. I want that man. Over."

"Yes, sir. The thing is...I think the fella's out there running loose in the city somewhere. I imagine he's doing his business, chiseling people. He's moved on since his Club Arashigaoka days, and ain't worried about the war or nothing like that. It might not be so easy to get at him wherever he is. Over."

"*Easy*? What are you talking about—*easy*? You're in the city now, aren't you? Nothing's happened, has it? Find that son of a bitch, today. Those sorry jokers lying around there know exactly where he is, you can bet on it. Get him. And find those papers. If you get him, you'll probably get the documents, too. You know that bastard knows something. He either had those papers, or he was picking them up that night. Offer him money, make up any amount. Look, I can't be explaining all of this to you every five minutes. You're the man on the ground. You should be able to figure things out—and take the initiative. Over."

Hawk looked at the ceiling. The daily chats with the colonel always tended to be a bit stressful, but Clark was outdoing himself today. The colonel was very creative when it came to dreaming up impossible things for somebody else to do. Hawk's eyes met those of Blackwell. The radioman, at least, was enjoying the conversation. Blackwell quickly looked away, rubbing the back of his head.

"Aye, aye, sir. I'll get on it. Over." Hawk hung the headset back on the radio. "Get that son of a bitch away from me," Hawk said, shoving the radio at Blackwell, who picked it up and left. This was Joe Canlon's signal to come over and find out what was happening.

"Did he say we can get out of here?" Joe asked, his face bright with hope.

"Yeah. He sure did. He said get your ass out there in the city and find that messenger."

"What the *hell*? Wander around Manila, knocking on doors? Is he trying to get us captured?"

"You'd have to ask him that. I gotta talk to this Ana again. Maybe they know how to get the shithead to come to us. The problem is, he might be afraid of us. He may be working with the Japs, too. If Ana tips him off we're looking for him, he may dig in like a dung beetle, and we'll never find his ass. The colonel doesn't care about all that, he just wants us to get the sneaky pile of shit."

"Yeah," said Joe. "I hate to say it, but the colonel may be right. Maybe we got to pick this guy up. Surprise him and clip his wings. He could rat us out, if we don't."

"Yeah. Funny how things always work out where the colonel's right, and we're the ones gettin' shot."

Hawk discussed the matter with Ana and was informed that he would not be able to find Ulupong in the city without someone to guide him. The situation became further complicated by her reluctance to send one of the young boys with the Marines, on such a perilous endeavor. She suggested instead the taking one of the older men. Hawk wasn't fond of the alternative idea, as the two "volunteers" she offered both had all indications of being alcoholic medical cases.

Joe Canlon, intrigued by the sight of Hawk and Ana huddled together, joined the end of the discussion. He liked to know things, especially if his life span was involved; and in this patrol he had the ability to freely insert himself into matters, as long as Hawk was the only authority over him.

"This place where he is, how far are we talking about?" Hawk asked Ana. "Because those old guys don't look like they can hobble across the room. Where exactly is this Ulupong character?"

"I have been told that it is maybe a kilometer or two into the city. He stays in the place of business of a family member. We could send for him, but I don't think he will come," said Ana. "He will surely know Mademoiselle has been killed, and the Club is closed. Ulupong would not come here, for fear of a trap. More so, he would not come because there is no one here now who could pay him anything. He no longer has a reason to come. As you have said, he may have helped the *Kempetai* arrest Mademoiselle. We don't know. He may be avoiding all of us. We could not mention that it is you looking for him. You will have to surprise him, if there is any hope of getting him."

"How old are them kids over there? There might be some running and hiding involved. You know...climbing, crawling. They could handle it a lot better than them old winos," said Hawk.

"Thirteen and fourteen. They are children. They could go alone, easily, as they have done many times. But to go with you would be risking their lives. I would rather go myself than send them. Though, I would rather not go at all."

Hawk ran his hand through his sandy hair. There was nothing like a few vague, half explained objections when trying to get something done. He suspected the colonel would not have this much trouble. "How about a map? Can you draw me a map of where to find him?"

"I can try. You understand that Ulupong may not be

there. He is not a reliable person. He may be anywhere," she said. "You may have to go somewhere else. He could be in the mountains with Astorqui. Anything could happen, and you would be lost out there in the city."

"We could take a kid, and if something happens, just tell him to fade into the background," Joe suggested. "He'd look like anybody else out there." Ana looked down and said nothing.

"Sounded good to me, but I don't think she liked that idea," said Hawk.

Ana looked up and shook her head. "No."

"Awright," Hawk said at last. "Draw the map. And we'll probably take one of the crazy old coots. If he drops dead, he drops dead."

"We'll end up having to carry him around like a garbage bag," said Joe. Hawk waited until Ana was looking away, and shook his head slightly, communicating they would *not* be carrying the oldster around.

Ana looked back at them, suspecting some sort of understanding had passed between them.

"I was just...thinking out loud," said Joe.

"Yeah. Don't do that. You make the lady nervous. It's bad enough when you talk out loud, without any of them other noises." Hawk stood. "Okay, let's get something put together here before the colonel gets back to us. Don't want to be listening to any more of his shit." Ana slid out of the booth and left them.

"If you ask me, the colonel is pushing it too far," said Joe. "Letting everybody in the whole city know we're here ain't smart. Especially some old low life guy on the take. Clark's gonna screw up everything with trying to pick this sack of shit up."

"Nah. Colonels don't screw up. That'll be your fault. Get wise, stupid."

* * *

A BENEFIT of being in the Philippines, for the Weitz family, was that it was at once a peaceful location, and a location under American control. War in Europe began soon after they left Germany, confirming that Karl had made a timely decision to leave when he did. England and France declared war on Germany, though Karl and Marta had never understood the details as to the reason.

Not only had the war failed to reach the far Pacific, no one would dare consider expanding it to here, due to the American protection. Luzon boasted an enormous American military presence. Karl would be able to wait for a conclusion to the war in Europe, and then return home, or God willing, transfer his family to the United States permanently.

Two years passed and the Weitz family began to become a part of the Manila community. Karl went to games at the Rizal Baseball Stadium with some of his coworkers, and Marta even joined them sometimes. Babe Ruth and Lou Gehrig had played there in the 1930s, but celebrities were few and far between in the war years. Besides learning the language of the local residents, Karl and Marta made many friends among them. They learned some English, and even a little Spanish. Contacts with the Jewish community were not as strong, because there were not as many of them.

Some of the German refugees acted suspicious, even with one another, and proved difficult to get to know. The response to the President's invitation to Jews had been lukewarm, and perhaps the United States had not been as supportive as it could have been. The community consisted of sufficient numbers, however, to join together to buy property for a synagogue, and Karl stayed connected to the group through this program. He had never been a particularly religious man, but he was having a change of heart in that regard. Adversity had a way of working its magic.

All was going well, when the unexpected happened. In hindsight, everyone said they knew it was coming all along, and that it was inevitable. Of course, that was nonsense, as is any claim to foreknowledge of future events—with apologies to meteorologists everywhere. The Philippines *did not* remain peaceful, and someone *did* challenge American control there, and very successfully.

The Japanese surprise attack on Pearl Harbor was quickly followed by a surprise attack on the Philippines and Southeast Asia. If these blows were not a surprise, the American reaction was one of the greatest acting performances by a military force in world history. The Japanese invaded the Philippines, bottling up the American Army around Manila Bay, and eventually accepting its surrender five months later. Needless to say, the sudden development turned society upside down. The Jewish community, in particular, expected the worst. Allied with Germany, the Japanese were expected to adopt a similar hostility toward the Jews. Their fiery method of entry into the country did not suggest a mood of peace and goodwill.

6

THE SEWER RATS

HAWK HAD HOPED THE LAIR OF THE SLIPPERY ULUPONG would be in some easily accessed area, preferably to the south, where shaggy tree-covered rights-of-way and untended fields of grass abounded. Unfortunately, the enigmatic go-between was a city dweller, known to abide more toward the center of Manila, where he kept close to the easy money operations. When the sergeant examined Ana's roughly drawn map, he became of the opinion that the abduction of Ulupong was unlikely.

As local residents, the fleet of subsidiary messengers serving Mademoiselle Rossier had been able to travel in broad daylight, and able to do so generally unchallenged. They could cover the mile or two to the designated residence of the primary messenger, Ulupong, without any problems, unless there were some sort of curfew issues. For much of the time, there had even been telephone service. Hawk could not pick up the phone, nor go walking around, however, unless he undertook to wear some sort of disguise. The colonel had not sanctioned the conducting any operations of that nature. The colonel would probably frown on such behavior, keeping in line with the terms of the Geneva Convention.

When the cautious Joe suggested traveling out of uniform, Hawk responded: "That ain't according to Hoyle." The discussion ended there without any exploration of his rationale on the matter.

Ana introduced the sergeant to Ferd, who would serve as the agreed-upon guide of the expedition. Ferd appeared to be approximately two hundred years old, with thick white hair slicked back and sported only a few teeth. His eyes were a hard to look at red, and his thin body appeared as tough as a well pickled vegetable, with jaundice. His wages at the club had been paid in liquid installments, and it showed.

Ferd spoke English rather well, and assured Hawk that according to his plan, the Americans would not be exposed to the unwelcome eyes of the murderous city garrison during their journey. The Marines could wear all of their uniformed finery and bring along any weaponry they chose. The guide knew passages through the sewer system that would get them extremely close to their destination. If they also traveled in the dead of night, there should not be any major difficulties.

Hawk did not consider this especially good news. It removed any reservations he had about a trip he did not care to take. Ferd made the journey sound entirely reasonable to him. They would have had to travel at night anyway, in order to get off the island, and cross the wider portion of the busy barge canal.

Hawk left Joe Canlon behind, and in charge of the platoon. This also left Joe in charge of finding the missing documents and dealing with the colonel, if the worst happened to the Ulupong expedition. Lance Corporal Baker would accompany Sergeant Hawk in an effort to locate Ulupong, as would four other men, along with the indomitable Ferd. The four chosen: Lawson, Moreno, Lacoursierre, and Hobby, were young and experienced in warfare, though not in this particular clandestine aspect of it.

But they grew in experience with each passing minute. Merely being in the enemy-occupied city endowed them with a certain rodent-like caution. Everyone, Hawk included, found themselves looking jerkily over their shoulders, and everywhere else, just as did the careful tree sparrows, trying to find their breakfast scattered on Manila's cruel sidewalks.

Moreno and Lawson received an approximately five-minute lesson on the operation of the bazooka from the team originally assigned it. Hawk wanted to take the weapon, but he didn't want a team limited only to its use tagging along. Moreno would carry the light burden, along with the not-so-light BAR. The rockets for the launcher could become heavy over time, and he restricted the load to two of these rounds, which were left for Lawson to carry. They might come in handy, though two shots would not be enough for a prolonged engagement. It was rather a moot point, as firing American rockets in the middle of a Japanese city could only be the prelude to imminent death. The loss of an encounter had never meant as much to Hawk, however, as did killing the enemy. He wanted the bazooka along.

He also wanted Baker rather than Joe. Joe was fully capable, but he was also the nervous type, and this was not going to be a smooth job. Baker was handy to have around when things were not looking well. He had a certain, "let's tear shit up" attitude, that Hawk could identify with. Joe was not as attuned to the attitude.

They waited for nightfall and crossed the main branch of the canal in the same rotting skiffs that brought them to the island. The passage was not a sure thing. This side of the channel had more of a current and had been dredged to greater depths to allow for the passage of ships. They struggled to get across in the unwieldy boats. One of the disintegrating old watercraft decided in midstream that this would be an excellent time to retire from sea duty and sank precipitously to the bottom. The men in the rapidly sinking skiff had to double up with those in the other two boats, forcing the gunwales on those down to a nerve-rattling inch above the water level.

The unsteady armada landed near a large culvert, jutting high up on the side of the far bank. Slimy, thick liquid oozed out of it, to plop rhythmically onto the ground. Ferd informed them that this opening indicated the inauspicious entryway to their subterranean route beneath the city. An overpowering smell burst forth from the metal tube.

"That sewer gas can kill you," Baker observed with scientific detachment, as the men stared at the opening with universal revulsion.

"And that's while we're standing out here. What do you say about that, Mister Ferd? Are you sure people can go inside this thing and live?" Hawk asked. He looked up at the clear sky, full of heavenly, pure stars burning above him. He could feel God looking down from eternity, and perhaps laughing, as his men backed away from the sick, gaping hole.

"Yes, you will get used to it," Ferd said, dismissing all concerns with a wave of the hand.

"Yeah. Okay. How long will it take to get through this bastard?" Hawk stood, legs cocked on the slope of the bank for balance, looking skeptically into the big, uninviting pipe.

"Less than one hour. No more," said Ferd. "Very easy. Very safe. Then it gets much bigger, and better. This is just the entrance. This part is very short. Do not be alarmed."

"Our flashlights won't last an hour into it and an hour back," said Hawk. "We should have brought something else."

"When we get to the main sewer, there will be electric lights," said Ferd. "This is only a drain. If you do not like it, you do not have to go in here. This is the safest place, but there are many ways in. We can go farther into the city, to another place with more light, which will be cleaner. But you will have to open an iron cover in the street there. I warn you, if you do that, someone could see you. It looks bad to be doing something like that."

Hawk considered it. Strolling around Manila did not sound any better to him now than it did when first presented with the idea in Colonel Clark's office. He knew from experience that unorthodox methods often paid off well. "Nah, this is fine. Looks good. Shit. Lead the way."

"Some kind of boat is coming," said Hobby, pointing at a light upstream, which grew quicky larger. Hawk judged its speed as uncharacteristic of a working tugboat. The small craft zipped right along.

"Aw'ight, everybody get in the pipe, hurry it up," Hawk ordered. "There ain't no better place to hide around here."

"Leave our rowboats laying there?" Baker asked.

"Yeah, git in," Hawk repeated more urgently. Everyone had planned a more delicate entry into the foul opening so as not to saturate their hands and clothing with the emissions from the culvert any more than necessary. That plan would be the first of many to be left behind. Hawk was the last to put a boot up, and latch onto the sharply bent sides of the pipe, propelling himself inward.

He turned around in the dark, narrow space, to watch the speeding boat pass. The others breathed heavily in the dampness behind him. The light from the launch threw a weak silver beam ahead of it, gliding across the corrugated surface of the canal. The patrol boat sported a searchlight, but the searchlight remained turned off, and the quick craft used only its running lights. A shadowy rising sun decal on the bow indicated it was a police cruiser.

Hawk turned on his angle headed flashlight. It provided little illumination against the opaque darkness all around them. He turned it off and unscrewed the bottom of the light to check if the batteries were tightly in place. A burning liquid touched his hand. The batteries were leaking. He cursed and replaced the bottom.

"Government issue," said Baker.

The men were packed into a tight world of varying shades of a rust-brown color. They could see down what appeared to be something akin to the gullet of a decomposing dragon. A six-inch wide stream of semi-liquid matter occupied the bottom center of the cylindrical enclosure. Ferd had traveled here before, which was the only encouraging thing about the dismal setting. Accepting his veracity, they knew the task could be done, and they could get through it unseen. It did not smell a great deal worse than it had from the outside, another questionable selling point.

"Lead the way, captain," Hawk said to Ferd. As the others followed the guide, Hawk and Baker stayed back to watch the rear. "The old gent looks kinda shaky already," Hawk told Baker.

"I got a little something to fortify him, if his transmission starts to grind," said Baker, with his lopsided grin. He pulled a flat half-pint bottle of whisky out of his shirt. Hawk nodded. "Good idea. We might all need that. This is getting a shade western."

They could not fully stand in the cramped pipe, having to duck their heads as they proceeded deeper into it. Hawk felt twinges of claustrophobia as he bumped along the rivetted, rusty walls. They all gasped, rather than actually breathing, which helped to slow the progress of the living, squirming odor entering and saturating the inner cells of their bodies. Hawk opened his shirt as the sweat poured off him and soaked his clothing.

Finally, a light shone at the end of the pipe. It opened out into a ten-feet high bricked chamber. On the concrete floor of the chamber ran a little rectangular channel, still filled with the same black liquid meandering through the pipe. A small naked bulb glimmered near the top of the cavern. The weird, larger space presented them with the appearance of an inner earth, fairyland hideout—which was by comparison, a welcome sight.

"It is the dry season," said Ferd. "In the rainy season, this whole sewer fills with water," he pointed at the ceiling far above them. "Some people still try to walk in here then. Not me."

"It's better than the pipe," said Baker, looking

around the strange environs, expecting rats, rather than trolls or elves. "I was getting a crick in my neck. Them bricks in the wall look old. Does it go across the whole city?"

"No, only the rich people in the downtown businesses, and the government, have use of the main sewer. The Spanish built it, long ago," said Ferd. Hawk, as impressed as Baker with the underground structure, had expected it to go on endlessly. Arches periodically supported it. Sometimes the lights flickered, but they never went out. They could hear water rushing quickly somewhere; obviously the sound did not come from the stagnant, slow moving and oily gel in the winding channel at their feet. There had to be real pipes carrying water—somewhere.

"I don't suppose Japs ever mosey around down in this thing?" Hawk asked, trying to look into the darkness ahead. The passageway curved this way and that, dropping and rising, never allowing a level and straight view for very long. Ferd's eyes widened at the mention of the Japanese.

"I have never seen them down here," said the guide. "But there are many things I have not seen."

"I know what you mean." Hawk bit off some chewing tobacco. It tasted remarkably like sewage. Water dripped from the cracked and broken bricks overhead. He hoped it issued from condensation, rather than some threatening leak, or total collapse. All of the walls looked slick and wet. Some of the bricks jutted out of place from the others, like misplaced teeth, grinning at them. The shifting earth had likely pushed them around over the decades.

"Do not worry. The Japanese can walk on the street. They do not need to come in here. Would you come in here if you could stay up there? We will get out of the sewer soon and into the fresh water supply. It will smell much better and be even nicer," Ferd told them.

"Nicer than this?" Hawk asked.

"You're darn tootin'," Baker mockingly answered in a low, echoing voice. Within minutes, they came to some steps with a rusty iron ladder extending up.

"We could go on in this part," said Ferd, gesturing ahead, "but up above, up there, will be much better." He smiled with pride at the grandeur of the underground maze and his knowledge of it. He climbed the ladder. Hawk looked at Baker and shrugged. They followed their guide.

The passage at the top of the ladder looked similar to the one below but did not have the same odor. Ferd led them through an iron door with heavy, felt edges, and the passage contained a floor channel identical to the one in the sewer, except it carried fresh water. Ferd took a handful of the silver liquid and drank it.

"It is very cold," he said, holding out his hand with the water dripping through his fingers. No one else appeared thirsty.

"Ain't this some shit? How much farther?" Hawk asked, growing impatient.

"Not as far as we have come," Ferd assured him.

After a few minutes, the freshwater tunnel opened out into a large reservoir. The huge lighted room looked like the interior of an ancient Greek temple, with neatly spaced columns. Hawk marveled at the underground spectacle, being an essentially rural creature, unused to such urban ingenuity. In the distance, he heard the muffled sound of some sort of machinery.

"All this shit," he whispered. "Way under the

ground." Ferd nodded his head proudly, showing his toothless grin.

Upon crossing the floor, which had only inches of water on it in places, they came to a low wall. On the other side of the wall, what appeared to be a huge fan, lay on its side, whirling around, pushing water into the channel running across the floor. Beyond the fan stood another low wall, so that it sat recessed into a deep tank between them.

"This is the pump," said Ferd. "You know, pump? Like a valve? Water wheel? I may not know the English word."

Hawk looked at him blankly. "Yeah, I get the drift," he said. "I can see the goddam thing. Is it much farther? We been down here a while." Ferd pointed behind them and up toward the ceiling. A water pipe ran from floor to ceiling into what looked like yet another tunnel running parallel above them.

"Up there is for utility workers. Sometimes I hear them. They will stay up there. Down here could fill with water, so they stay up there. The water does not go up there. You know, workers? Maintenance?"

"Yeah. Got it." Hawk walked over to the pipe and looked up. "How the hell do they get down here? They slide down that pipe?"

"I don't know. I think they have stairs. They could not climb up the pipe," said Ferd. "We are safe here." Hawk studied the pipe. As long as only workers dwelled up there, and not Japanese, the skeptical American willingly accepted Ferd's opinion as to the inaccessibility of the reservoir to the upper chambers.

They tight-roped along the low brick wall surrounding the spinning blades of the pump, hovering atop the surface of its tank. Each blade, half submerged, extended to about a twelve to fifteen feet length. The blades pushed the agitated water in what appeared to be a bottomless pit, and the well was not something anyone cared to fall into. On the other side, Hawk noticed the same type of slender water pipe he had examined before, rising upward, and once again, he went over to look up at it and to make sure no one was looking back down at him.

"Workers," Ferd reminded him, pointing up.

"Right."

They reentered a tunnel, this one without lights and with a lower ceiling. The clammy pathway wound around for several minutes, with the men using flashlights, before Ferd informed them they had arrived at the end of their subterrestrial journey. He pointed to a ladder leading up to a manhole cover.

"We are under a street corner, inside the water maintenance building," said the elderly man. "Usually, it is empty, but sometimes it is not. I will go up and see if workers are in there. They know me and will not say anything. If I don't come back, you wait here for me, and when they go, I will come back for you. They would be afraid of you. They will not stay long. They only look at gauges and turn valves and then leave."

"Yeah, good deal. Tell me something. How far is the place from here, where this Ulupong is at?" Hawk asked. "I'm tryin' to get a notion on the time we got ahead of us here."

"He stays in a shop on the other side of the street. It will be one block away. It is not far, but you will have to walk down the street up there. If you stay in the shadows by the businesses, you should be able to get to it without being seen," said Ferd. "It is very quiet here in the city at night. There are only closed businesses now."

"Okay," said Hawk, closing his eyes and nodding, as if he believed everything he was being told—which, he *never* did. He knew the above-ground exposure would be the riskiest part of the evening. "I might have to go up by myself, if it looks bad. We don't want to put on too big a show here. I can probably get this asshole by myself and bring him back."

Ferd shrugged. None of that aspect of the venture mattered to him. If anything indicated failure, he planned on just walking off, like any good citizen of Manila on a midnight errand.

"Go on. Check it out for us," said Hawk, urging Ferd upward with a motion of his hand.

Ferd climbed the ladder and with great effort pushed the lid off the manhole. He went up two more rungs, and looked around. Without climbing out, he looked down and said: "I see no one in the building. You may come up."

Hawk ordered everyone out of the underground passage. They assembled in the tin shed sitting over the manhole, where several large pipes arched out of the ground, each having various valves and gauges attached to them. An approximately twenty-five-watt light bulb illuminated the entire thirty-foot-long shack, so that its interior shown rather dim and hazy. A gentle hissing noise came from some, or all, of the pipe conduits. The windowless metal structure had a single door.

"Leave the top off the damn thing," Hawk said, gesturing at the manhole cover. "You're gonna take me to this place where the guy stays," he told Ferd. "Baker, come with us. Let me have a look outside first, to make sure there ain't no shindigs going on out there." He crouched low and opened the unlocked door. Only a spring held it shut. Darkness reigned outside, without any streetlights.

"It looks pretty damn good from here," said the sergeant, glancing back over his shoulder. "Lead the way, chief." Ferd stepped in front of him and left the building. They crept onto a wooden sidewalk, only three to four feet wide. Two-story shops lined the street, all made of tin alloy, or some sort of sheet metal. The dark, bent structures leaned against one another for support, without any sign of human habitation. The area looked like a rundown industrial district, rather than a residential area. The heavy metal debris thrown about in the few vacant spots, appeared related to welding, repair, or machine shops. The tin double doors on the businesses were festooned with chains and padlocks. The three of them reached the end of the block without incident. All visible evidence indicated the type of neighborhood the Japanese would not be very interested in patrolling.

Ferd stopped and pointed at a dirty storefront. "Ulupong lived in a room above this shop the last time I was here. He is probably there by this time of night and asleep. He falls asleep drunk and would be hard to wake up." Hawk looked at the tall, padlocked doors. They resembled gates more than doors, consisting of sheets of tin, crudely nailed onto wooden two by four frames.

"How do we get in? We'd need a bolt cutter to get past them chains, without making a lot of noise," said the sergeant. He tugged at a door and noticed a little play in it. He thought he might be able to squeeze in between the double gate frames.

"We do not go in. I call to Ulupong, and he comes down," said Ferd. "He may not do that for you. If you hide, I may be able to get him out. Do not let him see you."

As they were speaking, they did not notice a head stick out of the second-floor window and just as quickly withdraw back into the black interior.

"Okay, take your shot," said Hawk, pushing Baker back into the shadows. He then heard rustling inside the building and suspected they had been spotted. He unslung the Thompson.

"Ulupong! It is Ferd, from Arashigaoka!" Ferd called in a loud whisper as he looked up. "Are you there? Ulupong!"

The belch of a gasoline engine firing up could be heard in the numbed quiet of the night. It was followed by a tinny mechanical sound, like the small engine of a lawn mower or generator. Seconds later, a figure on a motorized bicycle came around the back of the building, headed for the street in front of them. The contraption moved rapidly and did not show any intention of slowing down. The rider leaned inward, turning the corner in front of them. Without consulting anyone, or even thinking, Hawk ran out into the street and gave the back fender of the bicycle a powerful side kick.

The bicycle spun around, and its rider pitched headlong over the handlebars into the street. He landed roughly, and the bike spun another half turn, colliding with his head, which had been lying in the stone roadway. The high-pitched little motor continued to whine madly, like a wound-up child's toy.

"Kill that engine," Hawk told Baker, and grabbed the collar of the man lying in the street. He dragged him up onto the sidewalk. He propped the unconscious captive against the double doors of the building. "Out like a light," he said. "Is this the guy?" Hawk asked Ferd.

"Yes," said Ferd. "I do not know why he did that," said the old man. "I am sorry. He is used to running."

"It ain't your fault. It's just what chiselers do," said Hawk. "Guilty conscience." He slapped the man's face. "Probably won't be able to get no sense out of him anyway. Goddamn crooks are so fulla shit."

"He may be in one of them coma things," said Baker.

"Shit," said Hawk. "Just what we need: a chiseler in a coma. The stupid bastard. We gotta get off the goddamn street." The sergeant pulled at the double doors, spreading them to a limited degree. "Can you get in there?" he asked Ferd.

"Yes." Ferd squeezed inside the building. But Ferd probably weighed under a hundred pounds. The two Marines stuffed Ulupong through the opening, almost ripping his shirt off, along with a few of his more loosely attached body parts; and then they followed, with considerable difficulty. The inside was much darker than the street, and contained pieces of boats, being the site of some sort of marine repair shop.

"Are we gonna sit around waiting on him to wake up?" Baker asked. "Shit, he might just die here. If he ain't already dead."

"Let's find a water hydrant. Maybe we can wake the son of a bitch up. I hate to leave him after all this, but I don't want to carry his dead ass around, either." Hawk shook the unconscious man, likely not improving the pending medical situation. "Wake up, you shit eatin' little horse's...I tell you what, if he don't wake up, I'm gonna kill his ass right here. I don't like nothin' about this. What was he runnin' for?"

Upon hearing the angry, and final sounding pronouncement, the eyes of the formerly unconscious captive opened wide. "Who are you?" Ulupong asked. "Why do you chase me? I do not even know you."

"Pleased to make your acquaintance, shit-for-brains. We're with the United States government. I'm President Roosevelt, and this is my son, Elliott. We need to talk to you. We need to know some things about Club Arashigaoka and Mademoiselle Rossier, see?"

"I know nothing. She is dead. The Club is closed. I had nothing to do with the place. I have never seen it. Leave me alone. I have done nothing. Why are you here? You do not know me. I do not know you."

"Slow down, asshole. Maybe I wasn't clear. We need to find out some things, *now.* Without no bullshit from you. If you don't talk sense, you might as well be dead to us, get it? *Dead*?"

Ulupong got it. He struggled mightily to get up and was shoved down.

"Look, stupid." Hawk took a deep breath. "Just listen to me. We're your friends, see? Your buddies? Americano? We need your help. They want to talk to you at battalion headquarters. They really like you. You're like a hero to them—one of them...Freedom Fighters. Like on the posters." Hawk backed away, to give his newfound friend some friendly space.

"Oh, good. Then I can go? Tell me when to meet them. Who shall I ask for? It will be such a pleasure. So nice to know all of you. Now, I must go." The formerly incapacitated captive jumped to his feet with great alacrity.

"Whoa. Just a minute, Kemosabe." Hawk grabbed his arm. "We have to take you with us, and look after you. There might be some traffic problems around here pretty soon, and we could get separated."

"I had better not go with you," said Ulupong. "I think you are going to get in trouble very more soon than you think. Bad trouble. I do not like trouble. I am too much blamed for things I do not do. You do not need me for anything. I am very poor."

"No—now—simmer down, you're gettin' on my nerves. I don't like all that high-strung shit. Don't you like us? You remember Ana? She said she really liked you, and told us where to find you. She wants to see you bad. She likes that greasy shit you stick in your hair there."

"Ana? Ana, said that?"

"Shit, yeah."

Baker had been looking out the crack between the double doors. "Something's going on out there," he announced. "And it ain't so good. It looks like bicycles with battery headlights on them. I don't think it's no midnight bike riding club, either."

"Maybe *Kempetai*," said Ferd. "Very bad. They will kill us. They chop off things first. Very, very bad." Ferd licked his lips. He was breathing fast. The military police had a galvanizing reputation. This shadowy junkyard was not the best place to be galvanized.

"Shit," said Hawk. "Let me see the goddam..." He squinted outside and saw the straight beams of the headlamps of a half dozen bicycles lancing jerkily about in as many directions, while uniformed men climbed off them. They spoke in low voices. "They're looking around for something. They probably heard that kazoo's motor, when our buddy tried to take off."

"Are there windows in here?" Baker asked Ferd.

"Yes, but the glass is too dirty to see out. They are hard to find in the dark."

"Do they know where we are?" Baker asked Hawk.

"Don't look like it. Not exactly. Not yet," Hawk answered, watching carefully. "Crap. One of their flashlights just hit our guy's bent up bicycle there." Hawk rubbed beneath his lower lip. "They'll be rattling doors any minute. Is there a back way out of this joint?"

"Yes," said Ferd. "But it will be locked, too. I don't know if we can get through the rear doors. I think it was just an accident the door chains were loose in the front. Someone put them on too quickly. They don't open and close the back doors as much."

"How did you get out of here, Houdini?" Hawk shoved Ulupong. The man pointed at the second floor. "I jumped out the window."

Baker looked desperately around the old shop. The hull of a plywood launch, twice his height, leaned against the wall next to him. "What do we do? Hide? Run? Fight?" he asked. He pictured himself crouching behind the flimsy boat frame.

Hawk pulled his face from the door, his expression tense with indecision. "Run, I guess. It's quite a pack of 'em. Let's try to go out the back." Upon winding through the motor launch paraphernalia and arriving at the rear, they heard voices outside in the back alley. "Shit. They already got this door covered. They done zeroed in on this place somehow."

"Now what? Hide?" Baker asked.

"Maybe we can bust into the place next door," said Hawk.

But that proved impossible, as they could not get through the heavy piles of equipment to even find a party wall. Hawk led them back toward the front, passing the stairs leading to the rooms on the second floor.

"We ain't gonna be able to hide for long in here, when they come bustin' in," said Hawk. Now they heard voices near the front doors. The Japanese were gathering on the sidewalk.

"That leaves one thing," Baker said with resignation. "Fight."

"Yeah," said Hawk. "That's about the size of it. We gotta knock 'em out and get back to the sewer, or the show's over."

"It sounds like a *lot* of them," said Baker. "I don't know if we can do it."

"Yeah, well," Hawk growled, "that's what you get when you go sneakin' around in downtown Japan." He leaned against the front wall to listen to the searchers outside and shook his head. "They're *right* there, shootin' the shit, on the other side of the wall," he whispered. "We might as well start it."

The other three looked on in horror as he stepped back, and pointed the Thompson at the front wall. The muzzle aimed at about waist level. He blasted a half dozen rounds through the thin metal, as if operating a rivet gun. The flickering flash lit their faces and the wall. The incredible noise, flapping through and about the metal enclosure, left their ears numbed. Screams erupted from outside. Large jagged holes ripped through the wall. Despite the ringing in their heads, they heard loud banging coming from the back doors. The Japanese in the rear alley feverishly threw themselves, or something, against the barrier in an effort to break it open.

"Up the stairs," Hawk shouted. Baker and Ferd ran rapidly. Ulupong acted confused. A rough push from Hawk helped him to focus.

They reached the upper landing as the chain fell

from the front doors and the gates swung heavily outward. The angry battering continued in the back. Three men with rifles and flashlights rushed through the front doors, making excellent targets. Both Baker and Hawk opened fire immediately. The hands and arms of the invaders lashed violently about, dropping their weapons. They fell over one another and across the entranceway. Outside, another man had seen where the fire came from and ducked outside the doorway. Moments later, he fired up at the two trespassers hiding in the darkness atop the stairs.

The banging, along with raging shrieks, increased on the other side of the rear doors. Hawk fired at the lone man in the front doorway, aiming his shots through the wall the man used for cover. A groan indicated the bullets had punched smoking holes through more than the metal, connecting with flesh and bone.

"We gotta get outta here," said Hawk. "We thinned 'em out up front. Let's go that way before they break in the back." Ferd shook in terror. Ulupong's narrowed eyes looked for opportunities.

"I have a gun under my bed. I can help you," said Ulupong. "Let me go get it."

"Skip that. Let's go," said Hawk. Throwing caution aside, their boots thundered down the steps. Reaching the door, Hawk pulled a grenade off his belt and looked quickly outside.

"Hey, I don't see nobody. Let's make a run for the sewer," he said. The back doors caved halfway into the interior with a nerve shattering crash, deciding the matter for everyone. Even Ulupong did not want to remain standing there, relying on the kindness of the frothing *Kempetai* officers.

Running out into the street, they picked their way

through the bicycles lying strewn about, headlamps still burning. Within seconds they pulled open the spring door of the maintenance shack on the corner, where the other four men waited.

"What happened?" Moreno gasped as Hawk entered the shed with his captive in tow. "The Japs saw you?"

"Yeah. We got this shitbag, though. Get down the ladder, quick. They might not know where we are," said Hawk. The Americans jumped into the opening one at a time, with Ulupong in the middle, all climbing rapidly down the clanging steps. Hawk took up the last position, struggling at the top of the ladder to close the manhole.

Ferd shouted up at him. "Push the lever on it!" He told Hawk. "Then they will need a water key to open it." Hawk struck and shoved the ancient machinery with the heel of his hand, to lock it shut. He jumped from the ladder to the floor.

"Get movin'. I don't know if they're after us or not," said the sergeant. Ferd led them down the dark tunnel and back toward the lights of the high-ceilinged reservoir. There they threw themselves down against the walls to catch their breath.

"We lost them. They don't know where we went," said Baker.

"Even if they did, the locked iron cover will slow their ass down," said Hawk. "Where is the water key they need to open it with?" Hawk asked Ferd, who was breathing heavily, to a degree much more dangerous than that of the younger men.

"Hanging on the wall," Ferd answered.

"*What? Shit!*"

"But they have to see it there first," Ferd added. "It will take a long time."

Unfortunately, the time was not so long; it was already over. A drunken transient sleeping on the sidewalk pointed out the maintenance shack to the pursuers, where their prey had hidden; and the frantic secret policemen easily noticed the T-shaped key hanging there, as it was the only thing on the bare walls of the tin shed. The sound of the heavy cover being slid off echoed throughout the subterranean chambers, followed by angry voices, and Hawk knew immediately what had happened. There were no intervening tunnels for the Japanese to become lost in. The path to the Americans was a singular one.

"They found it! They're coming!" said Baker. "We can use these columns for cover, if we hold them here." More reserved, questioning Japanese voices now filtered down the passageway.

"That sounds like a whole army," said Hawk. "This place ain't no good. It's too wide open. Let's get down to the pump room. It had all kinds of twists and turns. There was a little wall there we can get behind. We can at least put the pump and the big tank of water between us and them."

Bumbling to their feet, the foot race was on. The advantage of a head start soon evaporated. The eight of them made it to the pumproom, jumped the first wall of the tank, tight-roped along the side wall of it, inches from the rotating blades of the pump, and crouched behind the opposite wall. Hawk pointed his weapon over the wall, waiting for the enemy to enter the chamber. Upon surveying the scene, he only now saw the *Kempetai* would have the wall on the other side of the pump for cover, just as did he. The two sides of the room were mirror images of one another.

It was too late to reconsider the set up. Perhaps they

could stop the Japanese before they got under cover. Hawk was ready for a fight, ready to settle this contest here and now, without any more running, regretting, or thinking. Luckily for his companions, he was much better at fighting than planning.

7

THE BATTLE BENEATH THE EARTH

"Do we shoot out the lights?" Moreno asked. He carried the Browning Automatic Rifle, which would be able to make short work of the bulbs. Hawk looked up. What would this bizarre place be like in utter darkness? Who would have the advantage?

"Not yet," said the sergeant. "I want to see how many of the son of a bitches we can kill first."

Hawk trusted his men and their weapons. They were all combat-tested veterans. The oncoming enemy likely consisted of untested garrison troops, or even actual policemen, unaccustomed to the roaring, blinding horror about to unfold. The Japanese pursuers had been the terror of shopkeepers and little old ladies, but they were about to run into something out of their ordinary fare. Along with Hawk's Thompson, and Moreno's BAR, Lawson carried an M3 grease gun, so that half the Marines had automatic weapons. The other three carried semiautomatic M1s, which were still far superior to the bolt action standard issue rifles of most of the enemy.

The Americans also had the bazooka, but use of it was burdened with a nagging concern that even one rocket blast might bring down the city's entire sewer system. The bazooka round had to hit a hard target to detonate, and the only hard targets in here were keeping the planet earth from collapsing on the Americans for the moment. Firing the rocket launcher had not been ruled out, though relegated to reserve status for the time being; to be brought out only in case of a Samson versus the Philistines final act.

Hawk noticed Ulupong looking nervously behind them. The messenger had no stake in this deadly clash. A mortal confrontation of this nature was not to his liking. "Shithead," Hawk jabbed him. "You stay put." The sergeant looked over at Hobby. "Keep an eye on this guy. Blast his leg if he runs."

Ulupong's dislikes grew exponentially.

Hawk glanced again at the lights. It was entirely possible the lights would not survive the encounter anyway, with lead flying and ricocheting in every direction in the close quarters. The bulbs had moderate protection, aligned as they were along a brick ledge close to the overhead, and recessed inside metal cages. As Hawk awaited an appearance by the first of the attackers, he understood anything could happen here. Either side, desirous of victory, could be wiped out in short order with some unexpected advantage found by their opponents. They were too far apart at the outset to grenade one another, but the shrinking and expanding of the distances could soon alter the circumstances, including the possibility of putting the combatants too close to one another. At some critical, game changing moment, things might quickly degenerate from point blank range to hand-to-hand combat.

"How did they get here so fast?" Baker muttered quietly as the excited voices grew closer.

"Ask 'em that, when we all get to hell," Hawk answered. "Okay, boys." He raised his voice. "All we gotta do is change their attitude. Then we can get outta here. They ain't gonna follow us too far, with us shootin' at 'em. We're just gonna show 'em a little of what we got. Stay loose. It's gonna be awright." Quiet followed, as if the Americans were not the only ones listening to the order.

Not suspecting an ambush or having ever been exposed to organized resistance, a half dozen of the fastest of the enemy ran headlong into the vast chamber, under the mistaken notion that they had the upper hand. The Americans opened with a blast of room-encompassing fire, bowling their targets over instantly. The dozen or so who followed close behind the stricken men promptly dropped to the floor and crawled to the pump wall ahead for cover. They were unable to return fire as they wiggled forward, and the Marines continued to empty their magazines in an effort to augment the opening advantage. Yet another dozen Japanese stragglers followed, advancing in a crouch and firing, as they too sought cover behind the wall surrounding the pump. By now, the first dozen were already returning fire from cover, and had slowed the American volley to a trickle. Hawk's plan to prevent the attackers from reaching the wall and using it for cover had been instantly thwarted. But Sergeant Hawk was no stranger to thwarted plans.

The Arisaka rifle rounds chipped at the ancient bricks in the wall around the pump, some of the old blocks shattering like glass, with red powder blowing over the Americans' helmets and down into their faces.

In reply, the powerful thirty and forty-five caliber rounds of the Marines pulverized the bricks the Japanese hid behind. Rivulets of shining fresh liquid spilled from the tank where the retaining wall sank below the water level. It would not be long before the two sides reduced the walls to rock dust and would face one another in a wide-open duel. The inch of water randomly scattered on the uneven flooring rose to two inches in places.

Though not as well armed, the Japanese had the invaders outnumbered four to one. All of their force had arrived. Rifles aimed at the Americans from every angle, and the Marines found it difficult to rise and fire at their tormentors.

"There's too many of them," Baker shouted over the noise. "We can't get away from here." Hawk crawled toward him and slouched down, his back against the wall. Any reservations about blasting their way free with explosives evaporated. It would take everything they had to get out of this catastrophe. Unfortunately, the barrel of the bazooka, jutting up over the shoulder of Moreno had been penetrated by at least two Arisaka rounds.

"It probably still works," said Baker.

"Check. You gonna be the one firin' it?" Hawk asked. "We'll give you all the room you need."

"Maybe not," Baker conceded, forgetting the bazooka for the moment.

"We have to get close enough to hit them with a grenade," Hawk said, "and make sure they don't do it to us."

"We better come up with something fast, there's a lot of them," said Baker. Hawk had relied too heavily on the American's superior firepower. He only managed to keep the enemy at bay. The situation deteriorated rapidly.

"I see something we could try," said Baker, jumping up to take an aimless shot and quickly dropping back down. "You know how those pump blades go around? If you could hang onto one, it would spin you over to their side, and you could lob a pineapple in on them."

"Those blades are underwater, in a fifty-foot-deep tank," said Hawk, resting the Thompson on top of the wall and squeezing off a couple of rounds. The idea sounded too far-fetched to him.

"The blades are only a few inches under water. You could hang on to one. It rotates over there toward them, and...bam," said Baker. "They won't see you coming, down in the tank. Never know what hit 'em."

"Yeah, but you gotta get *in* the tank. How the hell are you gonna get over the wall and into the tank without getting shot to pieces?"

"I can do it. Just give me a little cover," said Baker. "They won't be expecting it." Hawk faced the area behind them. Around the little corner, where the passage turned, he could see the water pipe going up into the maintenance area above.

"Wait, just a minute. We can't give you *that* much cover. We're already pouring it on them," Hawk answered. He easily envisioned Baker being struck by dozens of shots the moment he rose from behind the wall, just as the men following Hawk over the top of the ridge had been.

"I got another idea. See the water pipe back there? It's like a fireman's pole. It goes upstairs, and there's a pipe just like it on the other side, in their rear. I can distract them from the back, if I can get up there and go over them to the other side and behind them."

"That's a hell of a long way up. You're gonna climb that little skinny pipe?"

"Like a monkey," Hawk assured him. "They cain't see what I'm doing back there around that corner."

"But when you get on the other side, you can't see them too good, either. The pipe is around a corner over there, just like it is here. How are you gonna shoot at them from way up there? That's no good. We lose the Tommy gun for that?"

"I can probably get a grenade close enough to scare the shit out of them, then you can jump in the tank and onto the fan blade, like you said," Hawk offered.

"Ye-aah," Baker drawled skeptically. "That's a lot of grenades. You think this old brick pile will cave in on us?"

Two enemy soldiers jumped over the wall and ran at the Marine position. Because the Americans stayed under cover, they did not see them charge around the whirring pump until they had nearly made contact. Moreno's BAR quickly dispatched them as they reached the defender's wall, but the charge foreshadowed the enemy's future strategy. A larger charge, or multiple charges, would be difficult to stop. At least, the first effort had eliminated the boldest of the enemy attackers.

"*Shit!* I don't know if you can do any of the climbing, but we better do something," said Baker, spitting out a mouthful of brick dust.

As he said this, the Japanese opened up on the overhead lightbulbs. Within seconds, the battle had been plunged into semi-darkness. Three feet of dim circular light filtered down from the openings for the maintenance rooms in the ceiling. Flashing muzzles lit the walls, but the area between the two groups remained in smoldering, deep shadows.

"Killing the light didn't help us any," said Hawk, surveying the disorienting darkness. "It made it easier for them to pull a run at us. I think we better make our move. We can't get out of this without some grenades whittling down the odds."

"Man, they're too hard to see now," said Baker. They heard a pop and a hiss from their own side of the conflict. Hobby shot a flare, which rammed into the ceiling with a blunt crack, and sizzled back down to the floor upon impact, where it continued to blaze, lighting about half the room with a sputtering, silver glow.

With Hobby thus engaged, Ulupong drew a knife from his own waistband, stood, and spun toward the back of the distracted Marine. Catching this stealthy action out of the corner of his eye, Baker threw a leg under the unsuspecting assassin, tripping him. Baker kicked the knife out of Ulupong's hand. Hobby turned around, and assessing the situation, started punching the captured messenger with his fist, and with the part of the flare gun jutting out of it.

"Did you see Hobby and that bastard?" Baker asked Hawk.

"Yeah," said the sergeant, still looking instead toward the Japanese. The flare made it even more difficult to see anything, causing a blinding chrome glare on one edge of the fight. "Look. When I hit 'em in the ass with a grenade, you jump on the fan blade and give 'em another one. Mine might not do much, but yours will. You'll be right underneath 'em," said Hawk. Baker nodded and raised a hand.

Hawk slid over to Ulupong. "Lay your hand on the ground," he ordered. He held the butt of the Thompson up, clearly preparing to bring it down and break the other's hand.

"No, no!" Said Ulupong, pulling his hand away.

"Okay, stupid. I warned you once. I ain't tying you up, because I ain't gonna have to. Understand? I'm gonna fix your running gear for good, if you so much as move."

"I was afraid. It is so loud. I am better now," said the messenger. "Much better."

"Shut up. Lay on your face there. Push your nose into the ground. Shoot him if he gets up," Hawk advised Hobby.

"I'm gonna shoot him if he does a lot less than that," Hobby answered, ducking beneath a furious cluster of slugs striking just above his head.

Hawk crawled away from the wall, around the corner and out of the line of fire, to the base of the water pipe. He slung the Thompson and looked up at the circle of soft light above him. He hoped he had correctly surmised this location as safely out of the sight of the enemy, behind the corner of the twisting walls of the chamber. He would be well lit, all the way up.

He stood, jumped, and pulled himself up with his arms, locking his boots around the pipe. He pushed up with his legs and again pulled with his arms. It was done so quickly; it looked as if the hand of God had drawn him up. He gained the opening above and lifted himself into the lighted upper chamber. There he found the metal slats of a catwalk leading toward the water pipe on the other side of the pump room, located behind the Japanese. Running across the clattering steel to the far opening, he peered down at the floor below, hoping to see the backs of his foes.

But as expected, the enemy was out of his line of

sight. The strobe of gunfire lit the walls, and the flare still spat somewhere in a corner. Hawk sighed. It was difficult to tell precisely how far away the embattled enemy soldiers lay. If the distance from the pump wall to the water pipe measured the same as that on the American side, the position of the foe likely lay beyond the range of a grenade. Hawk had climbed into the maintenance area to get the attention of the enemy, rather than to attack them. He was to serve primarily as a distraction, enabling Baker to deliver the fatal strike. He could still accomplish that much, even without being able to see his opponents.

Regardless of Hawk's modest objectives, a thrown and rolling grenade anywhere in the region at the rear of the *Kempetai* was certain to produce some benefit. The unexpected noise alone would render their eardrums useless. As he straightened the pin on the grenade with his knife, he harbored a good deal of vengeful optimism.

Baker, lying behind the wall on the other side of the pump from the Japanese, had ceased firing in order to devote his full attention to Hawk's awaited diversion. The sergeant's grenade would give him a brief moment to dive into the pump tank without being shot. He held his own grenade tightly in his hand. He would have no opportunity to study the moving fan blade before jumping onto it. The simplest of these matters become very complicated when unrehearsed, and life hung in the balance. He began to doubt the plan as he waited interminably for Hawk to act and watched the whirring pump blade. Its speed increased in his imagination. What had seemed simple, now seemed impossible. Could he grab the thing? Would it rip his hand off?

Hawk tossed his spewing grenade blindly down into

the concealing, flickering darkness below. It crashed onto the wet concrete floor and spun like a smoking top. The brick walls magnified the sound of its subsequent blast, causing Hawk to more seriously consider the possibility that all of old Manila might collapse on top of them. The tensely waiting Baker leaped over the wall he had been using for cover, pausing only an instant before he dove into the tank, down onto a huge, darkened, and rotating fan blade, hugging it with his arms and legs. In seconds, he swirled all the way around to the other side of the tank. Ill prepared for a throw, he tried to adjust his grip on the slick metal of the fan as he rode half under the water through another rotation.

Baker held his right hand awkwardly over the safety lever of the grenade, while using his right wrist to press and grip the fan blade. After a second rotation, he became unsure of his orientation. Where were the Japanese, and where were the Marines? Gravity pushed at him and slung him toward the top of the blade at every rotation. After a third spin, he recognized the sides of the conflict by the sound of the American automatic weapons, and was able to pinpoint his target in that manner. He lobbed the bomb into the Japanese position. Continuing to whirl beneath the water, he heard the grenade detonate above him. Only then did it occur to him, he had no exit plan. He hugged the fan blade securely, using both hands, lest he be suctioned into the bottomless well, or slung into the wall of the tank and chopped to pieces.

As the ringing aftereffects of the sound of the second explosion receded, Hawk could see little but the additional smoky dust floating in the glow of the dying flare below him. Ultimately, the ghostly figure of a wounded soldier staggered through the swirling, reddish cloud. This was all Hawk needed. He had no intention of using his vantage point strictly for observation. His raging anger led him to leap onto the slender water pipe, Thompson in hand, and slide down, firing into the retreating and confused *Kempetai*. When his boots hit the floor, his magazine empty, he plunged into the confused, wounded and stumbling men, in full retreat from their position along the pump wall. He swung the empty gun like a club, bashing them senseless. After half a minute, none remained on their feet. Several rolled groaning on the floor. He replaced the spent clip, and stood over each one, dispatching them with as few shots as possible. In this way, the entire encounter abruptly ended.

Hawk walked over to the pump. Hobby shouted at Baker, telling him to give him his hand, in order to pull the half submerged man out of the tank. Baker was nonresponsive to the command. Hawk saw the wire running to the fan motor and fired a burst into it. The wire parted, sparked and flamed, and the pump blades slowly stopped turning. The dizzy Baker tried unsuccessfully to rise. Several hands pulled him out before he could sink to the bottom. They propped him against the wall. He threw up.

Hawk slung the Thompson. The victory had been complete, but he did not want to sit around in these alien surroundings rejoicing, or in any way waiting for Baker to recover his senses.

"Go down there and shut that manhole," Hawk told Moreno. "Lock it and leave the key on our side of it this time. We're gonna head out. You can catch up." Hawk bent over and grabbed Baker's arm. He slung him across his shoulders as the moaning man again threw up, this time on Hawk. Fortunately, there was not a great deal inside Baker's stomach. A whisky bottle fell out of his shirt, shattering across the floor.

"Let's get back to the sewer! We have to cross the canal before daylight," said Hawk. "Ain't no telling what all kind of shit we done stirred up here."

It took more than a total of two hours to both navigate the sewer, and cross back over the canal to the island. In the early morning hours, the city reflected a minimum of activity. There was confusion in the *Kempetai* headquarters as to where the infiltrators had emerged from, or where their own missing officers had disappeared. This allowed for an uneventful return to the Club by the Americans and their newfound companion. The patrol saw little commercial traffic crossing the canal during the early hour.

As Hawk shoved Ulupong through the door of the Club, he became painfully aware that someone untrustworthy now knew the whereabouts of their hideout.

Without resting, Hawk questioned Ulupong for half an hour about his connections to the Club. The messenger continued to insist he had not participated in any dispatch runs for Mademoiselle on her last day, nor had he been scheduled to do so. He knew nothing of any last-minute communications. He finally admitted to traveling between Mademoiselle and Astorqui on occasions in the past, but none of those trips had been conducted recently. This conflicted with what Ana had told Hawk and left suspect the rest of everything Ulupong claimed.

"I have told you all. I tried to help you all I could. I should probably go. I think more bad things are going to happen to you here. You should probably go, too," said Ulupong. Though his words and speech generally projected a fearful, weasel-like impression, Ulupong himself did not. His menacing presence, wiry, athletic and scheming, with a scarred, mean face, suggested something more akin to demon possession.

"We're leaving here any minute," said Hawk. "Don't you be worrying none about that. But we need you to stay with us. What's your hurry? I mean, I'm really gettin' my feelings hurt. Nobody wants to kill you, but you got to start cooperating with us. If you make a break for it, we gotta figure it's because you're in with the Japs, and trying to rat us out," said Hawk. "Now, do you want something broken, so you can settle down in one place and take care of it for a while? You're too damn healthy. You move around too much, you make me edgy." Hawk moved his hands back and forth, imitating Ulupong's unsettled demeanor.

"No, no. It is very nice here. I will wait with you until you leave. Everyone is very nice to me. I should apologize, you are a very nice man. I will not hurry you."

"Okay, yeah. Go get yourself a jug over there and settle down somewhere. No—just sit over here by the goddam mirror so I can keep an eye on your ugly ass. We got a couple more things to do before we go." Hawk next interviewed Joe Canlon.

"Did you hear from the colonel?" Hawk asked.

"No. You talked to him last. Did you have some kind of trouble out there?"

"A little. Nothing ever goes smooth. Everybody made it. Did Epley and Rayburn give you any more shit?"

"No, they're getting along again, it looks like. They've been talking together even more than before. I guess the fight's over. I don't know what the hell they got to talk about so much. We haven't found any satchels or anything. Don't you think we should leave this little corner of paradise?" Joe asked.

"Yeah, I guess we played out our string. The Ulupong guy don't know nothing, or won't say, and we can't find that other stuff. It's a dead end. I just gotta clear it with Clark. He's probably come up with ten other things for us to do by now. If he keeps it up, the Eighth Army is gonna be knocking on our door."

"The Eighth Army would look pretty damn good to me right now," said Joe. "I'm more worried about the Jap Eighth Army knocking on my door."

"That's gettin' to be more likely," said Hawk. "When I was down in the sewer, I figured the whole pack of them was going to be after us. I guess we got away with it. But either way, the American artillery ain't gonna be much better. We need a new address—*fast*. This fancy little building, propped up here like this, is a forward observer's dream target. It'd be fun to turn this thing into confetti."

As the afternoon wore on, besides growing more exhausted, the sleepless Hawk grew concerned about not hearing from Clark. To a certain extent, he did not particularly want to hear from him, but without the word to evacuate, they could never get out of here. Nothing good could come from the incident in the sewer, it was time for a swift departure.

The physical aftereffects of the skirmish did not go away after the last shot was fired. Hawk was still conscious of something like a rolling ocean wave, pounding in the back of his neck, as if his nerves were telling him the conflict was ongoing. He jumped at sounds he shouldn't have and turned too quickly at the sight of the slightest movement. Prompted largely by this steady physical discomfort, and the desire to be free of it, he had Blackwell initiate contact with Clark and eyed the bottles behind the bar.

"You mean, you brought that bastard back? Over," Clark asked about Ulupong.

"Yes, sir. Got him right here," Hawk answered. He looked around. He didn't see the son of a bitch.

"I told you there was nothing to it. Did you ask him anything? What does he say? Did he speak English? Over."

"Yessir, he speaks English. As good as anybody else around here. He says he doesn't know anything about the lady sending out anything that night or any night close to it," said Hawk. "They didn't find any papers while we were gone. It may be time to pull us out of here, sir. We caused quite a ruckus in the city. Over."

"It can't be helped. That's our mission. I understand your fear. But you have to understand, Sergeant, you are in a unique place there. I'm not quite ready to give it up, just because somebody gets a little antsy. We're working on something new you may be able to help us with from there. It's important. The Japs are making some... unusual...moves. I'm not ready to give up on those papers yet, either. I'm going to have to get back with you as to any timeline for a withdrawal. Over and out."

Hawk looked at the dead radio. "Over and out?" Blackwell was smiling. "Was that funny, Blackwell?"

"No, Sergeant."

"You heard all that, didn't you? He said to stay here, didn't he?" Hawk asked.

"That was my impression. But I couldn't hear it as well as you."

It would be dark soon. Hawk paced the room, checking with the lookouts, and he climbed up to the tower to look over the city, in time for a beautiful sunset. There was nothing left to do, or accomplish. His nerves still fought the memory of the unsettling and claustrophobic encounter beneath the city. Explosions had loosened needed connections in his brain. His unchecked thoughts rolled over and over. As evening approached, he knew he had better concentrate on getting some sleep. It would do no good to stay up another twenty-four hours. Especially, if a quick retreat became necessary in the morning. He did not look forward to escaping the Club, and returning south. By now, the Japanese would have set up some sort of defensive line to meet the Eighth Army down there, and he would have to pass through it.

It all depended on Yamashita, and whether he was leaving the city or defending it. It occurred to Hawk that he would like to know that himself now. Suddenly, the goals of his abstract mission had practical implications for him, personally. The fate of Manila had become his own; a place he had known little to nothing about not so very long ago.

Things became quiet as dark fell, with a greater calm than the night before. Having no deadly or impossible errands to run tonight, Hawk settled down to sleep on the floor, between the booths and the roulette table, against a low partition wall. Hobby, who had slept during most of the daylight hours, was one of the men on watch. He was posted at the front window, and Ulupong had been ordered to sleep near him. Hobby had no warm feelings for their guest, due to the latter's efforts at stabbing him in the back; which, Ulupong denied. He insisted it was all a misunderstanding. Hawk wanted someone awake to be watching the shifty messenger at all times, lest he slip his tether.

* * *

As the night wore on and the rather nervous Ulupong awakened, he and Hobby played a couple of hands of cards. In spite of this, they did not exactly bond. Ulupong had a small bladder, and Hobby did not care for his tendency to want to roam around.

Most of the men slept near the front of the hall, either on the dance floor or under the tables. Joe Canlon slept on the band stand, beneath a front window. The exceptions were Epley and Rayburn, who had selected a rather recessed location on the far side of the bar, near the kitchen wall, and far from the front. All of these mundane arrangements would prove significant the next morning.

Not long after dawn broke, and the first light of day entered the vast dark hall, Rayburn was discovered to have been savagely stabbed to death in the night. The mission had never run smoothly, of course, but it had at least had an element of adventure to it, which was the thing often leading men with too much adventure in their souls to participate in such things. The murder of Rayburn in his sleep was an inglorious and grim reminder of how the adventure could end. No one had volunteered for that sort of ignominy. To make matters worse, the identity of the perpetrator remained unknown—meaning he was probably still inside the unfriendly confines of Arashigaoka, and looking for another victim.

Hawk surveyed the scene. A long knife, or bayonet, had passed entirely through Rayburn's neck while his head was turned to the side. He had been stabbed again in the torso, and though no one there was an expert in anatomy, the conclusion was that it pierced the heart. The knife was not present.

"Kneeled on his head, and stuck it through his neck," said Hawk.

"How do you know?" Blackwell asked.

"Well...I've...heard about that stuff," said Hawk distractedly. Joe, standing next to them, knew exactly how Hawk knew of such things. Hawk knew a lot of other things, too, and Joe knew a lot about Hawk.

"Should we bury him here, or take him with us?" Joe asked. "Is GR coming here—into this place?"

"I'll have to think about it," said Hawk. He looked away from the disturbing sight of young Rayburn, and around the room for Epley. He had the same first impression that most of the observers there had: *looks like Epley wins the hand of Miss Illinois.* It wasn't cut and dried by any means, and no one demanded a hanging, but it certainly didn't look good for Epley. Epley himself soon joined them at the crime scene. He had been the man to discover the body.

"Y'all were bedded down over here in this corner together and you didn't hear *nothing*?" Hawk asked his wide-eyed charge.

"No, Sergeant. The thing was, he kept talking and moving around, and I was tired, so I moved away, over by the bar, maybe around 0200," said Epley. "He was kind of by himself over here. I...feel like it's my fault, kind of."

"I know what you mean," said Hawk, and it was no idle comment. "When you got all tired, and moved, did you see anybody on watch?"

"I believe it was Hobby by the window, but I didn't really look close. It may have been Lawson by then," said Epley. "It was about that time."

"But they were awake? The guard?" Hawk asked.

"Oh, yeah. I think he and the Filipino guy were playing cards or something. They were like bent over, looking at something," said Epley.

"And you seen Rayburn was alive, when you got all tuckered out at 0200?"

"Yes, Sergeant. He turns over a lot, and talks in his sleep. You never know if he's awake or asleep. It's aggravating. But he was definitely alive and well."

"Alive and well," repeated Hawk. He left the group and found Hobby, sleeping peacefully under the bar. Joe followed, wanting to hear the exchange. "Hobby, get outta there," Hawk shouted. Hobby crawled out groggily.

"Rayburn got killed last night. Did you see anybody moving around?" Hawk asked.

"Killed? No! Uh...yeah. I saw a few people get up and move once or twice," said Hobby.

"I mean, they didn't go over that way or anything. It's real dark over there."

"You didn't see Epley move?"

"Oh, yeah. I saw him come away from there, carrying his blanket and his rifle, like he was going to sleep somewhere else. I saw that."

"And you didn't hear any noises, like somebody getting knifed or something?" Hawk asked.

"No, I never heard anything like that," said Hobby. "You would have known, if I did, that's for sure."

"How about our buddy, there? The gay blade? Did you keep an eye on him all night?"

"Yes. I was with him the whole time. We even played cards for a while, just to kill time. I could still see out the window. I don't see how it could have been him. Not that I wouldn't put anything past him," said Hobby. "He went to sleep when Lawson came on watch. I guess Lawson would know what he did after that."

"Hunh," Hawk grunted. Hobby didn't see how it could have been Ulupong, *but* he wouldn't put anything past him. There might have been something missing in his logic, and in the story. Did Ulupong slip off, unseen, and Hobby was covering it up? They asked Lawson about Ulupong. He never saw him get up, nor did he see Epley get up, for that matter. If either of the two of them did it, they did it before 0200 and before Lawson's watch. Upon questioning, Ulupong insisted he had been asleep all night, had never played cards, and had never seen anything.

"I did not know this man," said Ulupong. "This young soldier. I had no reason to kill him, or know who, or even where he was. I am new here. The only person I would know to kill is you, Sergeant. I know you." Ulupong did not realize how that sounded, but Hawk had to acknowledge the honesty of the statement. Of course, everything else the man had said was a lie. Hawk had to admit that Hobby was right. You couldn't put anything past the guy. Ulupong did, however, have two men on guard vouching for his innocence to a certain degree, whereas Private Epley did not have anyone providing him an alibi.

Hawk went back to his booth with Canlon and Baker.

"I don't trust the snake guy as far as I can throw him," said Baker. "He tried to stick Hobby in the back that time."

"He says he didn't," said Hawk. "A lot was going on."

"Well, shit! What do you think he's gonna say?" Baker asked. "I seen it. I trust Epley. But that other guy? Unh uh."

"The thing is, Epley had a reason. Not a real good one, that's for sure. But they did get in a fight. This Ulupong bird had no reason. Why would he pick Rayburn out of the pack to kill?" Hawk asked. "A guy he didn't know? But incidentally, Epley knew, and didn't like a whole lot."

"Because Rayburn was off by himself, in the dark," said Joe. "Once Epley got up and moved, Rayburn was an easy mark. I'm with Baker. I trust Epley. Not that other cross-eyed guy."

"Yeah, okay, but why? Does this character think he's gonna kill all of us? Why didn't he make a run for it after he did it, if he was runnin' loose enough to do that? And Hobby was watching him do all this? It don't make sense. Now, Epley moving around in the dark, at about the time it happened, *does* make sense. It really don't look too good for the kid," said Hawk.

Baker could not conceive of one Marine stabbing another in the night. His suspicions remained with Ulupong. Joe agreed. Joe added: "The snake guy don't need a reason. That's what snakes do. Hobby's a kid. He probably fell asleep and missed it all. He sleeps a lot."

"Maybe," said Hawk. "After all, it don't have to be either one of them. It could have been anybody, for all we know."

"Yeah," said Joe, "I can see where it might not be the old snake, but I don't think that makes it Epley." Baker nodded. "Because, look," said Joe, "so Epley kills Rayburn. Will that make the dame back in Illinois fall madly in love with Epley, now? I mean, that's no reason."

"No, but gettin' punched in the balls and the face a half dozen times might be a better reason," said Hawk. "There was some bad blood there for a while."

Joe shrugged. He still didn't believe it. High school kids from Illinois didn't do things like that. Joe had a New Yorker's high opinion of middle American, cornfed youth. The kid had joined the Marine Corps, for God's sake! That had to be a good kid.

"I don't know what to think now," said Baker. "It could be somebody else. It doesn't have to be them. If, you could find somebody else with a better reason. I don't know what it would be. I mean, Rayburn? It ain't like he went around pissing people off. But you could tell every word out of that Ulupong's mouth was a lie."

"Yeah. That's his deal, though. He's a goddam liar. His mind don't work right. He can't tell the truth about anything. It don't mean he did it," said Hawk, who had some familiarity with reprobates of every sort. He had not forgotten Ulupong's little episode with Hobby and the knife, however. The Club's prior messenger was no saint, nor was he limited to minor, sneak thief antics.

"That was funny, how he said he would have killed *you*," said Joe. "The dumb guy. Probably a lot of guys would say that, but not to your face." Joe laughed.

Hawk lit a cigar. "Yeah. That's real funny, awright. I don't think Rayburn liked me too much, either."

"Maybe you did it," said Joe.

Hawk blew smoke into the air, without looking at Joe or acknowledging his comment. "Now, I gotta tell Clark about this. It would damn sure help if we knew who did it," said Hawk.

He looked from the men in the booth, toward a table across the room, near the stage. Several of the former employees of the Club sat there, drinking something. The door to the kitchen stood open, and several more moved about within it. He noticed Ana occasionally looking over at him.

"That damn Ana is giving me the eyeball for some reason. I wonder if any of them got anything to do with this."

"It's probably just your good looks," said Baker.

"Yeah. No question about that," said Hawk, shifting on the settee. "I don't like it. I guess I gotta go see what they know. She knows a lot about this place. Maybe, too much." He glanced up and saw the heavenly portrait of Mademoiselle Rossier looking down at him.

"Ana?" Joe laughed. "You think she did it? She's two feet tall."

"Yeah, with a three-foot-long knife," said Baker, quite willing to throw her into the mix.

"Nah," said Joe. "This is crazy talk. It'll all come out. You'll see. This kind of shit always does. Now, I used to read the papers in New York. I know about this stuff. It's always the first guy you think it is. It's gonna be old snake, and he'll slip up and confess. The pressure gets to 'em."

Hawk growled as he stood. "That ain't gonna happen. I don't care how many papers you read in New York. That guy ain't admittin' nothing." He walked over to the table by the stage. As he approached it, Ana stood and turned toward the kitchen. Hawk detained her, touching her arm from behind. Joe and Baker watched this unfold.

Joe laughed. "She was trying to give him the slip. Did you see that? This is funny shit."

"Yeah," said Baker. "She shouldn't have done that. Now, he's gonna say it was her that done it."

"Shit," said Joe. "Wouldn't you make a run for it if you saw that coming after you?" Joe shook his head. "He scared the shit out of her. Hawk must be pretty desperate, if he plans on putting the collar on *her*. That's like them cops, when city hall puts the pressure on them. They settle on anybody. Clark will be worse than city hall."

"She had zero reason to kill Rayburn," said Baker. "If, she could even do it. I guess he thinks she got somebody else to do it."

"I don't know. That bunch has been playing footsie with the Japs for two years. I bet they'd like to get back to letting the good times roll. We're in their way here," said Joe. "We give the place a bad smell. They would all sure like to get us out of here."

"Yeah," said Baker. "I bet they'd like to *kill* us." They both laughed.

Realizing that the tone may have gotten a little too light, Joe quickly said: "That *is* a shame about Rayburn, though."

"Oh. Shit, yeah," Baker agreed.

8

SHADOW ON THE STAIRS

IN THE CHAOTIC UPHEAVAL THAT WAS THE JAPANESE invasion of the Philippines, a ray of hope appeared for the Jewish community. The Japanese victors exhibited no innately anti-Semitic tendencies. The Jewish community remained below their radar. They arrested Americans and most Europeans as enemies of the Empire, including women and children, but Germans and Italians were exempt from detention, due to their alliance with Japan. Other fringe exceptions existed, such as the Vichy French and the Spanish. The Japanese authorities initially, under their fluid categorizations, considered the Weitz family to be German. Their passports indicated Germany as their country of origin. There was no interest expressed in bloodlines or ethnic backgrounds. No subcategory, such as "German *but* Jewish," existed. Karl was not arrested, and after a brief interview by the newly invested authorities, owing to his non-Asian ethnicity, he was released to continue on with his life. By all indications, the lion had lain down with the lamb. The uneasy coexistence would last for a good while, allowing complacency to once again set into place.

* * *

AFTER A FEW INQUIRIES directed at the former employees about their observations of the previous night, Hawk returned to Joe and Baker. He fell into his usual booth.

"What did Ana say? Did she crack? Did you slap a confession out of her?" Joe asked. "The old rubber hose and third degree?"

"Nah," said Hawk. "That was a waste of time. They all think a hoodoo did it. They've been hearing things at night, moving around in the place. They've found stuff moved around. They hear voices, all that shit. I don't know if they're shittin' me, or what. They might really be ignorant. Have you seen any rats?"

"Not the animal kind. With thirty guys here, somebody is always moving around in the place. That's a dumb thing to say," Baker commented.

"They said it started before we got here," said Hawk. "They hear sounds, like knocking and popping. It's probably the old foundation settling. This island is just an old dirt pile, it shifts around. The whole rotten bastard could cave in on us."

"That probably ain't the worst thing that could happen here," said Joe. "I don't like rats. We had them babies in New York. They get huge. They'll fight ya."

"Yeah, I bet them son of a bitches could swim the canal, if they figured they could find a goddamn peanut in here," said Hawk. "They ain't so good with bayonets, though."

Clark had not checked in with his emissaries at the

Club by late afternoon. Ordinarily, this would have led to a cursing fit on Hawk's part, followed by his taking the initiative and contacting the colonel. Today, however, the sergeant had no inclination to establish any communications. He knew that Clark would sense that something was wrong on the Manila end of things by the evening. Hawk still had a little time to try to figure out the murder, or come up with some sort of a theory about it. All of the ideas eventually hit a dead end. His suspects and motives all appeared a little weak, until right before dark, when Epley said he wanted to speak to the sergeant in private.

Hawk took the request for privacy to mean the man did not want to sit in a booth and wait for the ever-hovering Corporal Canlon to slide in with them. The presence of Joe within earshot was tantamount to speaking into a bullhorn to the whole room. Hawk took Epley up to Mademoiselle Rossier's office and shut the door.

"There you go, junior," said Hawk, pointing at a chair. "What's on your mind?"

Epley did not look too happy. Hawk sat behind the desk and waited patiently for the other to start the conversation. He knew it had something to do with the murder, and fully expected Epley would confess, based upon his facial expression. He was a little surprised, since like most of the others, he strongly suspected, or perhaps hoped, that Ulupong was the culprit. He assumed Epley and Rayburn had another fight that night, and it had gotten out of hand. Still, the savagery of the murder somehow did not fit Epley, whereas, Ulupong had a history of being quick with a knife.

"I have to talk to you about Rayburn," said Epley.

"Shoot."

"The thing is—you know those letters that we've been looking for? The Jap stuff, in the canvas bag?"

"I do. You can believe that." Hawk's rough accent made it sound as if he were spitting the words out at twice the speed of normal conversation.

"Well, Rayburn found the bag," Epley declared, trailing off with a mumbled, "and all that kind of stuff."

Hawk sat stunned. He wasn't sure what he had been expecting, but this wasn't it. "He *what*?"

"Yeah, I don't know if it has anything to do with him getting killed, but it might. I figured you ought to know," said Epley.

Hawk frowned, trying to process what this could mean. "I appreciate that. You figured right. We've been sitting here waiting for that bag to turn up. This is a bad place to be passing the time, kid. We could have all taken up knitting by now. Where is it? I need that goddamn bag. The colonel is waiting on it. It might be the difference between the city being blown to shit, or totally bypassed. And, by the way, between all of us gettin' killed in here, or not." Hawk's lips tightened. "What in the *hell*, Epley?" Hawk violently slung his hand in the air, in Epley's general direction, as might an agitated gorilla, or some other excitable primate. The thrust made an audible whipping sound.

"I told Rayburn all that, Sergeant," said Epley. "All of it."

"Rayburn's dead. I'm talkin' to *you*."

"It kept getting more complicated. I...well, I don't know where the bag is anymore. But I want you to know what happened, and it might take a while to explain it. I didn't want to be in on any of this. Rayburn just dumped it all on me."

Hawk sighed. His anger worsened, but he controlled

himself. He wanted to hear this outrageous story before he exploded in some unstoppable rage. "I'm all ears. Put on some speed," he urged quietly, projecting the façade of a mature, wise confessor. Whereas, he was actually still the same poorly disguised James Hawk, with a lit fuse.

"He said he found it in the wall. I didn't ask him where. He had it, and it didn't matter to me at the time where it came from. I thought. So, I told him to give it to you. You know, so we could leave here, like you said."

"Mm hmm. Right." Hawk nodded patiently. "Good. Good plan."

"It was just a canvas bag, like you told us, about this big. We knew it was...*it*." He gestured, indicating the size. The dimensions looked bigger than Hawk had pictured. "We opened it up and looked inside. I don't know why. I thought he would give it to you without opening it. But he didn't, and I got curious, once he dug into it. We shouldn't have done that. He shouldn't have. I was just...there."

"Okay. Right. Good. Where did all this happen?"

"Over in that corner there. Where he was killed. Like I say, I don't know where the stuff came from. Anyway, inside were all these letters, and some papers written in Japanese, I guess. Chinese, or something. I saw maps. I didn't look at everything, because we didn't really care about any of that."

"Yeah? What exactly did you *care* about?"

"That's the thing. There was a *lot* of money in there. A lot of it was that Japanese occupation money, the Mickey Mouse pesos, but a lot of it was real American money, too. And, I guess, British or Australian stuff, you know, with the King on it. We just counted the American part. And there was a lot of jewelry and some gold coins, too. It was a big bunch of...stuff. There were photos of Jap positions, I guess. The thing is, it wasn't just military information like everybody thought. There were the jewels. Like women wear, you know?"

"Shit." Hawk hung his head.

"I'm sorry, Sergeant. I told you it's a long story."

"No, no. Go ahead. Don't let me stop you," said Hawk, rearing back and taking out a cigar. "We don't need no short stories. How much money did you count?"

"The American money was around a hundred thousand. We counted fast and didn't really get to the end, but that looked about right. So, you know, that was done and I said, all right, now we have to give it to Sergeant Hawk."

"That was real polite of you. Even mentioned my rank and all."

"Maybe, I didn't say it exactly like that." Epley smiled slightly. "But Rayburn tells me, no. He says that you don't know about the money, and all the diamond rings and necklaces and stuff, and that he is just going to give you the...you know, papers and maps, the military things, and Jap stuff. That's all you needed. Or, the colonel."

"Mighty big of him. That there would have been nice."

"Yes. But I said I couldn't let him go with that. So, he got all mad. You know how we had been fighting, and all? We never got back on the best of terms, I guess. It didn't look good to me. I didn't want to spark all that off again with him. So, Rayburn calms down, and offers me half the money, if I go along with the idea. Finally, I say, okay. I said okay, just to get him to give you the bag. Because, like he said, you would never know the difference about the money. And, it was the bag that was our mission, not the money, and the other stuff in it. I was also thinking in the back of my mind that you would probably get the money out of him eventually. How could he carry all that around?"

"I could've used anything, kid. Instead of what I'm gettin'."

"Yes. Well, that plan didn't last long. The next day, Rayburn had a new idea. He says..."

"Uh...hold on a second. The next *day*? How long did all this shit go on?"

"Well, you know how you went off that night? So, it was like the day before that. Well, maybe not the day before because you went off at night, so maybe it was the same day..."

"Okay, never mind. Shit. Forget that. Get on with the story."

"Rayburn had a new idea. I guess he got to thinking about it and got scared. He tells me that we can't give you the bag at all, because maybe you *do know* about the money. You and the colonel, that is. Not just you. I mean, we didn't know what all you knew, or didn't know. If we gave you part of it, the papers, you might know we had the rest of it, the money. He figured we were about to leave here, and everybody seemed pretty happy knowing we hadn't found anything, so why not just let it all go at that? To tell you the truth, I didn't know what to think of that idea, or what to do. That was just stealing. He *was* a thief, you know? I said I'd have to think about it. So...I did. I had this idea of just leaving it all laying on the floor, all dumped out. But then, he got killed. And... that was about it."

"Wait. Wait, we got to the ending kind of quick,

there. I missed what you decided after all that damn thinking about it you were doing," said Hawk.

"What could I do? I made him believe I was going along with him. Otherwise, I would never see the bag again, and nobody else would, either. What could I do, turn him in?"

"Oh, *shit*, no, that would be crazy! Okay. I get it. You made him *think* you were going along, but, of course, you weren't really going to."

"Right."

"Did you kill him?"

"No. No, I don't know anything about that. That's another reason I thought I should tell you. I couldn't kill him, because then I would never know where the bag was. I was the only other one that knew he found it, or that there even *was* a bag. I thought. Now, I'm pretty sure somebody else here knew, and didn't like us having it. Somebody killed him for it."

Hawk sighed. "Okay. Never mind. So, where's the goddam bag now? We gotta get out here."

"Like I say, I don't know. He didn't tell me. He said he found it in the wall. He must have put it back there. I never saw it again. It was gone right after he showed it to me. It wasn't with him when he died."

"You looked?"

"Well...yes."

"Son of a..." Hawk settled back in the chair, staring at Epley. "You know, this is a good way to end up in prison. In fact, this is a good way to get your ass shot by a firing squad." Hawk felt oddly like Colonel Clark, when he was castigating Hawk about the incident on the ridge. Maybe Clark hadn't enjoyed it all that much, either. *Nah. He loved it.*

"Except that I was *trying* to do the right thing," Epley

quickly explained. "He just got killed right in the middle of it all. Who expected something like that? It would have worked out, if I could have gotten the bag. At least, now you know there is a bag. You never would have known even that much."

"Yeah. You're right about that. Colonel Clark is probably gonna really appreciate that. He'll love this whole story. And as far as Rayburn expecting to get killed, *everybody* better be *expecting* to get killed here. You can't go around acting like a goose in a new world every day of your life, kid."

* * *

KARL CAME HOME from his job at the harbor at the usual time. Marta noticed his looking pale and acting a little quiet. She didn't mention it until after dinner. She had been afraid to bring it up. She dreaded any physical calamities befalling him now, in the middle of this political situation, and the latest rendering of their new nation. Perhaps it was his heart. His father had a history of heart trouble. The war news was always stressful. The Japanese broadcast glowing daily reports of how they were winning the war, but she and Karl had heard other versions of the conflict's progress. They met more and more people from different places, and the people received mail, not all of which could be censored.

"Something is bothering you, Karl. What is it?" she asked.

"Oh, business is bad. Very bad. I think the Americans must have the shipping lanes closed, and they aren't telling us. Mr. Katz said he may have to let me go. He thinks he might have to close the business."

"That's terrible," she said. "But, at least you can go

back to the jewelry shop. That doesn't depend on shipping. A lot of the inventory just circulates here in the country."

"I wasn't very good at that," said Karl. "I don't like sales. I did polishing and settings...and, then there was this." He tossed a pamphlet onto the table. It had a cartoon of a Jewish face with bushy eyebrows, an oversized nose, and leering eyes. The title on the cover, in German and Japanese, read: "What YOU need to know about the Jews."

"Oh, my," she said.

"Yes. This is the first time I have seen anything like that in this country. This is an official publication, coming from the government. This is what they did in Germany. The Germans are sending the Japanese these things, and probably telling them to distribute them, and to...act. The authorities didn't care anything about us. Until now."

She thumbed through it. The pages written in German made Marta homesick. "Well, it is only a booklet. It doesn't mean anything. People pass these things around like joke books, you know? Everyone likes to laugh at people that are different from themselves. Think of all those comedy radio programs. They do all those silly accents. I wouldn't take it very seriously." She laughed. "Actually, this looks like your father." She put one hand over her mouth and the other on his knee. Karl saw neither the resemblance nor the humor.

"Yes, it is very amusing," said Karl, taking the booklet from her, paging toward the end, and reading aloud a particularly violent passage about wiping vermin from the face of the earth. "That has always been one of my favorite little jokes," said Karl. "They are talking about our children, Marta. They are inhuman. They say we are insects."

"Where did you get this?" She set it down and did not want to touch it. She looked more serious now.

"From Mr. Katz. He said it was in our mail. There were enough of them to give me my own personal copy. They must be everywhere."

"You remember, Karl, I didn't want to come here. This was your idea. Here, we have two nations hating us, instead of one."

"I remember."

* * *

"Yessir, we had a guard posted. Four of them. No one could have gotten inside the building. It had to be someone from inside. Over."

"Obviously, it was one of those damned Filipinos," said Colonel Clark. "Probably that criminal you went out and dragged into the place. I would use a little aggressive questioning on him, and he'll spill his guts. I don't know what his game is. You need to show some initiative here, Hawk. You know things don't always fall into your lap, like you're Rockefeller or something. That go-between killed that boy for a reason. He was up to no good the second you brought him in there. Over."

"Yessir. It could have been him, we aren't sure. There's a couple others I been talking to." Hawk paused as he thought how to best present the information about the finding, and losing, of the documents. "There was a little more to it, sir. The man that was killed…had found the documents we've been looking for. He had found them, and then hid them again somewhere, when he died. Over."

There was a startling eruption of static before Clark's next transmission could come through. At least, the hope was that the eruption had been only static.

"I don't think I got that right, Hawk. Something's wrong with the transmission here on this end. Repeat that last message. Over." Hawk repeated the message. A full minute of silence followed.

"I'm trying to follow this. You *found* the documents and lost them? What in the hell is going on out there? And, you had a casualty, related to all this?" Over.

"We never actually found the documents, sir. The man that was killed found them and hid them, for his own reasons. There was a little money in with the papers, and we think he was planning on stealing it. Over."

"I've heard everything now. You're surrounded in a city, and that's all some damn fool has on his mind? There might be a ring of them, Hawk. One of the other thieves may have killed him. One of your men probably has those documents right now. Listen, you need to knuckle down. You know the satchel is there somewhere. It's right under your nose. Crack that ring, and get them to talk. Find out if any of them are from Chicago. This all sounds like Chicago business to me. Look for a fellow a little older than the rest. Some gangster," Clark stammered, as he formed his theory. "The attack on Manila might be minutes from H-Hour right now. You've got to get off the dime, Hawk. Do you read me? I can send in some more educated men to help you. Do you think that would help? I knew I should have sent an officer with you. It's going to be hard now, with the Japs setting up defenses between you and the Eighth Army. You are sealed in tight as a jug. Maybe some officer with paratroopers could get in, but it would give away your position. I'm counting on you to do something. You've got to rise above your personal limitations on this one. Do you read me? Over." The colonel sounded as if he might be losing his cool detachment and rambling on in confusion.

"Yessir. No sense risking any more lives. We'll take care of it. Like you say, I might have to get a little more aggressive with some of these...people. Over."

"Damn right. That's the spirit. I'm going to look into the backgrounds of the members of that patrol. I know (*crackle*)...Chicago...(*crackle*). Meanwhile, I'm expecting some answers from you. I'll check back later today, to see how it was all resolved. Oh, and don't kill anybody that has any political connections. It's a tricky situation with those goddam Filipinos. Over and out."

Colonel Clark set the phone attachment down and looked at Major Bearn. "Mmph. That was a mistake, sending Hawk in there," said Clark. "Have you ever heard of a more fouled-up situation than that?"

"You wanted a daredevil. That's what you got. No one else would have gone into something like that. When he went in there, it was a losing proposition. It was a well-fortified Japanese city. Now, it's a well-fortified Japanese city, surrounded by three American Army groups. Saving the city is hopeless," said Bearn.

"Yes, yes." Clark waved his hand dismissively. "It's hopeless for *him*. We're not talking about *him*, we're talking about Manila—and *me*. I should have found a daredevil with some common sense."

"That's hard to do. I wouldn't sell him short. He always comes through, somehow," said Bearn. "It should be easier now, now that he knows the documents are really in there somewhere."

"I don't know Bearn. Did you hear what he said? A

man found the documents and planned to steal them. And then he was killed? Does that sound like the United States Marine Corps to you? I mean, what is Hawk doing while these shenanigans are going on? Asleep at the wheel, that's what. I'm betting there's alcohol involved."

"I believe I heard he was in downtown Manila at the time it happened, capturing that messenger, Colonel." The major had a little more confidence in Hawk than did the colonel.

"Exactly. Exactly what I'm talking about," huffed Clark.

"That kind of business. You've got to keep your eye on the ball. Not go traipsing around..."

Hawk went from the radio to the bar and opened a bottle. Joe followed him the entire way. He then had to follow Hawk all the way back to the end booth, where they sat down.

"What did the colonel say? Are we leaving?" Joe asked.

"No. He didn't like none of it. He wants me to beat a confession out of Epley and Ulupong, I guess."

"That's not a bad idea. You start with Ulupong, and you let Epley watch, and maybe he'll crack before you start in on him," said Joe. "Just beat the livin' shit out of that son of a bitch."

"Good thinkin'," said Hawk, tipping the bottle up. "You oughta be a goddamn colonel." He shook his head. "That bag of papers is hidden here somewhere. I might never figure out who killed Rayburn, since that's a thing that happened in the past. But we should be able to find them papers. They're sitting in here right now, somewhere, just like we are. Nobody could them get out of here. Rayburn found the bag, and he did it pretty fast.

Epley figures he stuck it back in the same place. All this for a few bucks. We *got* to find it."

"Maybe he buried it," said Joe. "The ground is all rocky outside. It can't be deep."

"No, Epley says it was in the wall. That's all he knows, because Rayburn told him. Some hole in the wall."

"Okay. That sounds like a loose board. Rayburn didn't use no crowbar on it, everybody would know about it. And, somebody can't be taking things out and slipping them back into this place, unless it's like a loose board. And, if *he* found it, it's probably sticking out a little or something. I think we can find it," said Joe.

"Hope you're right. You need to get all hands a little more interested. Ulupong's front teeth depend on it."

Joe left to organize a few intensive search parties. He had renewed confidence the task could be accomplished in short order. Personally, he wanted to take a gander at all of those reported jewels. He was motivated by curiosity more than ever.

Hawk was not as optimistic. He was good at doing things; doing things that others could not, or would not do. He was not good at waiting, or as it turned out, finding things with a time limit on finding them. He considered that perhaps the colonel was right, and that there was more of a connection between the death of Rayburn and the documents than he had considered. After all, the man that recently found them, was the man that was recently dead. The colonel's theory became a little strained beyond that, however. No middle-aged Chicago gangsters lurked here, only respectable young men—with the lone exclusion of James Hawk. Hawk tipped the bottle up, poured all that was left in it down his throat, and banged it on the table.

He slid a new bottle toward him, quickly cutting its seal with a hard thumbnail.

While his thoughts remained dimly organized, Hawk reflected upon how he came to be here. How Welch had sacrificed his young life for a relative, who had been beyond help. The cousins had joined the Marine Corps for the right reasons and died because of someone else's wrong decisions. The other four Marines who had gone to the ridge with them were just as dead, with even less justification. They had been more loyal to Welch than his two friends, Rayburn and Epley, had been. And the wheel kept turning—now, the none-too-virtuous Rayburn was dead. Loyalty—ideals —right and wrong: were just cards in the game of chance fate dealt the unsuspecting young patriots. Fortune was sandbagging them all, taking advantage of their impatience, ruining their hopes with their lack of forethought. Hawk swallowed the insight bitterly, however, as he was doing no better at the game, in spite of his lack of naivete or virtue.

It grew dark outside. Gray twilight filtered into the enormous hall, leaving the upper reaches of the club shrouded in undulating shadows. The snow globes of dust particles no longer visibly circulated in the waning shafts of sunglow. A last ray of light fell across the painting of Mademoiselle Rossier. It lit her beautiful face, causing her to look like an angel peering down on Hawk from her celestial abode. In contrast, the unlit, martial picture of Joan of Arc hung back shyly in the deeper shadows, a few inches out of what was left of the light, as if waiting for him in ambush.

Outside, test sirens began to blare over the city. Searchlights were turned onto the sky, and the glare flashed nervously across the wide walls and tall ceiling of the interior of the hall. The Japanese expected a bombing that might, or might not, begin tonight. Fear saturated the air, riding in with the anxious lights, and upon the wail of the sirens.

Hawk could smell the sultry canal outside as if someone had left a door open. Perhaps they had, in the course of the latest round of seeking the dispatches. It felt damp and clammy inside, in the dark, with that strange, unclean watery odor. He closed his eyes and lowered his head, in a momentary doze. A faraway hum of boat horns droned in his ears, adding a soothing and encouraging lull to his drowsiness.

He heard a sharp rap, one of those noises the building occasionally made: the sounds that Ana had attributed to spirits. He opened his eyes at the sound and raised his head slightly. A searchlight beam crossed the front window, piercing both it and the curtain, then playing across the stairway. A figure glided down the steps, its shadowed face turned toward him. *A ghost*, Hawk thought, with some amusement, for that's exactly what it looked like. It paused at a level across from the top of the large portrait. The apparition stood in darkness, barely showing against the darker stairway, as if it were deciding whether or not to simply disappear: whether to enter this unwelcoming world or return from whence it came.

Hawk raised his head, with a little more interest. The phantom did not have the shape of a man. A mist surrounded it, with a hint of flowing garments. Who, or what, in the hell was the vision? Hawk's iron heart held no fear of it, but he waited with attentive curiosity.

Another rhythmic searchlight beam waved across the descending figure. This time the shape settled into more definite features. He no longer had to wonder at the strange sight, for he well recognized the other worldly face of Mademoiselle Eugenie Rossier.

* * *

KARL AND MARTA WEITZ stood at the window of their upstairs, downtown apartment when the Japanese marched the captured American Army down the street from Bataan. People lined the street to watch the frightening spectacle, many had been ordered to be there. The captors were none too gentle with the stumbling and emaciated prisoners.

"They look terrible. There are so many. Why would they surrender, if there were so many?" asked Marta. A guard began beating an American who had fallen, and Marta turned her back to the window. The nervous young guards were vastly outnumbered by their prisoners. Karl rubbed his face thoughtfully. He found the scene disturbing. He knew such things had happened in Germany, but he had not actually seen them happening from his own window. As he thought about it, he had never seen them happening at all. This was rather unforgettable.

"I suppose they ran out of food and ammunition," said Karl.

"You ran out of food and ammunition in the First War. Germany did not surrender," said Marta.

"Well...we did, in a way. We just didn't know we had, until the peace treaty," said Karl. "You get to a point where there is nothing more you can do. But you may be right. I have not seen prisoners treated like this before. It appears they should have fought to the death, rather than submit to this treatment. The Americans are a little naïve when it comes to warfare, I'm afraid. They may have difficulty with an enemy like the Japanese." He closed the curtain and began to pace. They could still hear the high-pitched screams of misery and the guttural grunts of anger outside. "This does not look promising to me, Marta."

"What do you mean? *Should* that look promising?"

"I am afraid the Japanese will turn on us. They are very unpredictable, and very violent. We know they will never let us go to the United States now. All of those papers we filed are out the window. If the Japanese inspect them, it may make us suspect. They may think we are American sympathizers. I must check around and see if there is anywhere else for which an exit is permitted," said Karl. "Perhaps even here in the Philippines, on a lesser island, in the country. Where...these things are not happening and we would not draw attention. No one bothers country people."

"Karl, everything is fine. Why would we draw attention? Don't go looking for problems where there are none. That is a captured army down there. We are not in the American Army. Our papers are in order. I don't want to move again. To some...island."

"I will have to think about it," he said. "You should be thinking about it."

"The Meirs were allowed to go to Japan," Marta said brightly, keeping a positive outlook.

"Yes," said Karl. "Of course. Many of those Americans lying down there in the street will be allowed to go to Japan very soon, as well."

9

THE PROPHECY

MADEMOISELLE ROSSIER WORE A BLACK DRESS, SIMILAR to the one in the painting, except it extended all the way to her throat. The real person standing before Hawk looked more austere, more Victorian, and more ghostly, than saintly, as in her likeness. The bright whiteness of her face was offset by the dark color of the dress, and by her thickly arranged hair. Though she possessed a mysterious aura of having suffered, she did not look anything like someone fresh from the torture chambers of Fort Santiago prison. She slowly walked to Hawk's table, her feet hidden beneath the sweeping dress.

"I am Eugenie Rossier. This is my place of business," she said in a calm, accented voice.

Hawk's fierce expression did not betray his surprise, nor any other emotion. He organized his alcohol-impaired thoughts. "They told me you were dead," he finally replied, coming out of his trance, after a few lost seconds.

"Yes. But I had to come back. Unfinished matters,

you must understand?" she answered with a faint, enigmatic smile.

"Yeah...uh...would you like to sit down?" he said.

He knew he should be firing a number of questions at her, but he couldn't think of any of them. The person was more stunning than the painting. She sat across from him, her eyes boring through him. The eyes steadily took him in, and the rest of the world swirled in an insignificant blur around them. He knew he should have stopped his drinking at one bottle. He was not at his best. The supernatural eyes held him transfixed.

"I recognize you from your picture," Hawk mumbled, unable to think of anything else to say.

"Yes." She glanced over her shoulder at the portrait. "It is a good likeness. Perhaps it suffers the abuse for me. Like in the novel, about the painting that does the aging for the man?"

"Yeah. Is that the one about the old man at Christmas?" said Hawk.

"I think...not. I refer to Oscar Wilde. It is very dangerous for you to be in Manila. Why did you come here? Why do you stay? Perhaps you want to see Fort Santiago?" she asked. "You must be very brave, or very foolish."

She had the slightest hint of a French accent, or perhaps it could be German. It was so slight, it was hard for one unfamiliar with such things to determine the exact origin. He found it difficult to think in the living presence of this celebrated personage. He was sure some superior creature had appeared to him for an important reason.

"Then...I guess you can tell by looking, which one I am," he said. "I'm Sergeant James Hawk, United States Marine Corps. It's been so long ago, and so much has happened, I'm not sure I can tell you why we're here anymore."

"That sounds much like the story of my own life. Why don't you try? The evening is young." She turned and raised a hand.

One of the young boys, a former employee of hers, standing near the bar, grabbed a glass and came at a run across the room with it. He smiled broadly at her. She did not look at him.

"Do you mind if I join you?" she asked, opening the bottle of whisky at Hawk's elbow.

"No. Go right ahead. Help yourself." He exhaled. "I... we...came here at first...to find if you left any final dispatches for us. We had been getting regular information drops, and then they stopped, at a kind of important time."

"Yes. I'm afraid I was indisposed. You might say it was my fault. I take responsibility. This was the reason worth risking the lives of all of these young men? I don't recall anyone being quite that interested in my 'dispatches,' before my detention. I seldom received replies." She poured a full glass from the amber bottle, and set it in front of herself, without drinking it. Her hands moved smoothly; it was clearly a task she was accustomed to. He glanced at the beautiful hands, moving through the dim light as if they were somewhere else, and he only watched a reflection.

"Things are different now," said Hawk. "You might be a little more important than you thought. They want to know if Yamashita is going to leave Manila an open city, or will he fight for it. They didn't want to blow it up, if they don't have to. We're holding up on the artillery and the bombing, hoping he will leave. It looked like he was, but then he started dragging his feet. They were hoping you had left some sort of inside information about all of that. The why, and the wherefore? You seemed to know things."

"Yes, I did have information. I left rather unexpectedly, you may have heard, and was unable to send it. I see you have found my messenger's bag, however. It is removed from its place. You have discovered what you needed to know? Perhaps, having done so, you would return my property to me before you leave? That, which was in the valise?"

"No...uh...that's the problem. We *didn't* find it. One of my men found the bag and put it back, and got himself killed before he could tell us where it is."

"Strange conduct for a disciplined soldier—and unfortunate. All of these good young men here. And, yet, you have one like that. One? You know that in the end, all of you will be killed, yes?"

Hawk frowned. "The possibility did cross my mind."

"No. It is for certain. You did not put the purse back in its place, because it is no longer there. I have looked. Where is it? It is mine. Is this the way loyalty to your country is repaid?"

Hawk shifted under the rather aggressive accusation. "We don't know where it is. We've been looking. The man that was killed told somebody it was hid in the wall, and that he put it back. We can't find it. Maybe you remember what some of those papers said. Maybe you can tell us a little of what Yamashita was planning."

"I can tell you everything. I know all of his plans. I wrote the majority of those letters. Most of the other documents were in support of what I had written. As I said, none of that will do you any good. You cannot get out of here alive. It is much too late for that. You should never have been sent here."

"Yes, ma'am," Hawk recovered himself. Her arguing lifted him out of his wondering reverie. Being threatened with death brought the old James Hawk swimming back to the surface of his foggy consciousness. "You let *me* worry about that. We have a radio, we don't *have* to get out to finish the mission. We can relay to battalion anything you tell us."

"I see. This information, it seems, means more to you than your life, or the lives of the others?"

"You might say that," said Hawk, in a low voice. His was not a pleasant voice, under any circumstances. Tonight, it was especially curt, snapping out responses like the Bourbon Street gangsters he had known. "Depending on how you look at it. When the elephant gets loose in the street, and scares everybody off, they send in the elephant handlers. That's us. Elephants are our job. If things go right, maybe the Japs will just leave, and nobody gets killed."

"You are a young man, but not that young. Tell me, Sergeant, do things *ever* go right?" She picked up her drink, let it sway near to the brim, and set it down. A searchlight lit its nervous surface.

"No, ma'am. Do you mind telling me where you left the papers in the first place? In a wall, maybe? It might give us a starting point on settling all this. A lot of people are waiting on me to come up with some answers."

"So, you believe. I believe their minds are made up. I do not mind helping you. Not at all. The courier's bag was left in the cabinet, in my office. But now that I am here in the flesh, you no longer need those papers." She smiled without showing her teeth. "Or paintings?"

A chill ran through him while her eyes held him motionless. The emotion made him begin to resist her arrogance. Whatever forces heaven or hell directed at him with this emissary, he was still James Hawk.

"We done looked there," he said, evenly.

"If you pull the cabinet out of the wall, you will find a space behind it. Yes, someone has looked there. That is quite clear. It is empty."

Hawk noticed a developing headache. All of this conversation forced a too rapid and unwelcome sobriety onto him. The complexity of the pressing problems returned to him. He began to grow less in awe of the returned Mademoiselle, and more aggravated with her. His natural stubbornness fought the vague power she exerted over him.

"I'll have a look at that," he said. "If you don't mind me asking, how did you get in here? If, it's so impossible to get in and out?" He was truly baffled. How did she get past the guards, not to mention the thirty other men?

"I was dropped off here. The Japanese have completed my interrogation. It was very unpleasant. It seems my loyalty to the Imperial government was placed in question by someone. They will be watching me. They will be watching this place. They are probably watching *you* right now. Did you think, perhaps, this château is invisible?" She smiled again and shook her head. His eyes followed the movement of the elaborate array of her hair. The great attention required for the creation of such a coiffure was not compatible with one recently tortured and released from a concentration camp. "Then again, perhaps it is. Perhaps you and I... are...both invisible."

"I don't particularly like the sound of any of that," Hawk answered, touching his chin. He had assumed his presence was unknown, as long as no one was shooting at him. The alternative now occurred to him. He noticed men gathering around, at a distance, looking curiously at the two of them; especially, at her. "Maybe we could go up to your office and finish this conversation? I'd like to see this trick cabinet of yours."

"Of course," she said and stood. She made a slight theatrical bow to the onlookers, as she turned toward them.

"Don't forget your drink," Hawk said, gesturing toward the full glass.

"Oh. I cannot drink it. I just like to look at it," she said, walking smoothly toward the stairway. He reached back, grabbed it, and downed it with a gulp, without missing a step.

Joe called to Hawk as the latter followed her. "Hey, ain't that..."

"Yeah. She's alive. How the hell did she get in here? Watch the doors. Get some men outside. Watch the water. There's something funny about this. If she got in, anybody can."

* * *

MACARTHUR INVADED THE PHILIPPINES, landing at Leyte Island. Karl's anxiety grew. Now, his family found itself in the big, ugly middle of the war. The Japanese had not been bad hosts, leaving him less than convinced that the invasion was a welcome development. It would have been better if the war had continued to have been fought elsewhere, with the Philippines surrendering to the Americans at its conclusion. Many had expected that to happen. It sounded logical, perhaps too logical for some. Regardless of all that, there was still a chance that glorious Manila itself would still be spared. It made sense for the Japanese to withdraw, as the Americans had done before them, abandoning the metropolis undamaged, in the hands of the superior force.

As he sat reading a newspaper from several days ago at the kitchen table, a sharp knock collided with Karl's door. Startled, he rose an inch out of his chair. People seldom knocked on his door, and never at this early hour. Marta and the children still slept. He walked slowly to the door, thinking many uncomfortable thoughts.

"Who is it?" he called, placing a hand on the knob.

"The police! Open this door!" a Japanese-accented voice demanded.

Karl hesitated. What else could he do? This was totally unexpected. Was this how it was to end? "Yes, yes," he answered, unlocking the door.

Three unfriendly looking *Kempetai* officers stood in the hallway. One pushed him aside and walked into the room. "Get me your papers," he demanded. "Make no suspicious moves."

"Yes, yes. Of course." Karl nodded and opened a drawer in a bureau, there in the parlor where they stood. "I have them right here." He handed a black zippered pouch to the man without opening it. The officer impatiently unzipped it, and ripped the papers out.

"What is your name?"

"It is there, on the papers."

"I am able to read. I did not ask you what was on the papers, I asked you your name?" The stale sophistry worked extremely well this time: Karl was petrified by it.

"I—am Karl Weitz."

"There are six of you? You are German?" the officer asked, quickly rifling through the documents.

"Yes, that is correct," Karl nodded. He wondered if

he had been singled out, or if everyone was going through this disturbing process. Or, more frightening, if only *certain* people were going through it.

"The city is expected to be under attack soon. It will be dangerous for Europeans to travel. No one will know who you are, because you physically resemble the enemy. Do you understand me? Danger?"

"Yes, yes, thank you for the warning. You are very kind."

"Enemies of the Empire are being executed immediately. You should be very careful. We do not want to accidentally shoot you, thinking you are American. The city may be lost to us. There are many traitors. If the Americans take over, they will capture you and shoot you. They will not ask questions. They are mad dogs. Follow all of our instructions for your own good. What does this letter—here—mean?" the officer asked, pointing and tapping several times on a "J" on the German passport. Karl's throat froze. Should he lie? Did the officer already know? Did it matter? It had never mattered before.

"In Germany...that is a designation for religion... they put that on there, for everyone," said Karl. "Everyone has a religion, but there are many kinds."

"A religion?" the officer asked. "Interesting." He did not look upset. "Why do they do that? You are all Christian, of course? Is this—Jesus?" He tapped the "J" vigorously again.

Karl could have just said yes. He held his breath and finally spoke.

"No, the 'J' means Jewish," said Karl. "We arrived quite legally. You can see the papers are all signed and in order."

"You do not know what I see. *Jewish*?" The officer

frowned and said the word slowly, as if he had heard something uncertain about that. "Is that right? What is all of this?" He shuffled the cumbersome stack of documents. "You have many papers. This Jewish is not a race? There is no country for this Jewish?"

"There is no country. Those were applications to visit America. Before the war, of course. The dates will show that." Karl began to tremble.

"You have relatives in America?"

"No, no. It was for business purposes," said Karl. "This was an American country then, you see. All of the companies were American," Karl stuttered.

"Ah, I see," said the officer. "Mind that you do what I say. Do not go out. I am taking your name and noting this *Jewish* marking. Do you know any others of this Jewish... religion?" He began talking to the other two officers in Japanese, turning his back to Karl. Karl decided he should not lie at this point. It looked as if things were going... fairly...well. The man acted somewhat reasonable. The officer was probably overworked and a little tense.

"Yes, we have a temple here."

"Ah, I see. Very good. Very good for you. There is *something* about this...this *Jewish*. I cannot keep up with all of these things. It bears inquiry. We are unsure about that. There are many different people here in this city. In our country, it is not like this."

"I am sure all is in order," said Karl. "We have never had trouble."

"Unh. We have talked to your block manager. You have not been helping with the sandbag details for two weeks," said the official. "This is not patriotic. Do you want trouble?"

"I...yes. I hurt my back. I did not realize how strenuous it was going to be. I was trying to alter my duties to another area, something of a more sedentary nature," Karl explained. "I have not received approval yet. I was unsure..."

"The Empire does not care about your back. You are free to go for now but do not go out. Not even for sandbags. Nurse your Jewish back. You are in danger. We may not be able to protect you. Our resources are taxed. Good day."

"Good day, sir." Karl breathed a sigh of relief as he shut the door with a trembling, soft click. He stuffed the dumped papers back into the zippered pouch. They slipped in much easier than they had come out. Suddenly, a cold shaft of adrenaline shot up his spine. The officer had taken his passport.

* * *

THE DOOR to Mademoiselle Rossier's office stood open when Hawk arrived on the third floor. She had lit an oil lamp on the desk and stood beside the cabinet in the wall. The light shined up her back, and her arm, from below. Her face, and the wall, were barely visible. Shadows dominated the room. She opened the cabinet. She folded down the shelf inside, and using it like a handle, pulled the shell insert of the recessed cabinet from its niche. Behind the opening lurked a larger opening, that also looked empty. Hawk peered into the dark interior. He reached in and felt the four wooden walls, as well as a top and bottom.

"So, this is where it was? A canvas bag?"

"Yes," she said. "I believe the bag was fashioned from the hide of a water buffalo. It would not have been easy to find. That is, for anyone who did not know it was in there."

"No," Hawk agreed. "It wouldn't. I don't see how Rayburn could have found that."

"Perhaps he did not," she said.

"What do you mean?"

"Did the dead man tell you this is where he found the dispatch bag?" she asked. "I would suspect someone who knew about this place, removed the documents. There may be others involved."

"No. He didn't exactly tell me nothing. It was his friend that did the talking. The man that was killed showed it to this friend of his. They took an...interest... in it."

"I see. Perhaps this friend did not tell you everything he knows, yes?" She replaced the cabinet, turned, and sat behind her desk. "I hope you will interrogate me much better than you have interrogated the uninformed friend."

He nodded and sat in the chair before the desk. Her dark eyes, her dark presence, the huge mahogany desk: it all made him feel as if he sat before a judge.

And judging, was exactly what she was doing. His intelligent blue eyes, narrow nose and well-formed face did not fit the rough voice, or the crass, slouching, uninterested attitude of the clearly threatening man before her. Had the soul of a demon possessed some masculine angel, in order to come here and thwart her plans? Who was the prey here, and who was the predator? She smiled slightly at the contest.

"For example, did the friend mention there were valuables in the bag?" she asked at last.

"In a way," Hawk answered.

"More details might produce more answers," she said.

"Yeah. I'll have to run through his story again, I guess. But...while I have you here, maybe we can get into Yamashita's plans, and all of that? That's sort of important right now."

"But of course. We must. How old are you?"

Hawk cleared his throat. "I ain't real sure. But...uh... was he planning on leaving the city open?"

"You are a farm person. Like the Maid of Orleans, yes?"

"Well, not exactly. I'm not a city person, if that's what you're getting at. My...uh...agricultural ties...tend mostly toward the cotton trade. You get a little more sunshine and fresh air out there, than on a regular farm." His deep bronze color contrasted with her whiteness. She looked as if she had never stepped out of Arashigaoka— in the daylight hours.

"I see. You are a simple man, an honest man. I know a lot about men. Why do they send a man like you, into something very dirty, like this?"

"I don't imagine they could get nobody else to do it, truth be told. That's usually how I get most things. I might not be as clean cut as you think. I deal with a little bit of dirty business now and then. And, pretty quick."

"Like...Ulupong...business?"

"Yeah. Like that. You know about that?"

"I know about him. I know you went into Manila and brought him back. One man against thousands. You are fearless. Such a thing seems impossible to me." The lamp flickered, for no apparent reason.

"Damn near impossible, at that," he said, bowing his head, and looking up quickly.

"Are you of this world?" she asked.

He set his jaw. What did that mean? Foreigners sometimes said odd things that meant something else in their own language. So, he did not dwell on its strangeness. "Near as I can tell," he finally answered.

"You know, I need a man who can do the impossible."

"Is that a fact? It turns out, my dance card is a little full right now. Anyhow...I gotta have some answers. The colonel is checking in with me pretty soon, and he'll be surprised to hear you came back to this place. He'll be wanting a lot of answers."

"To be sure, he will. Don't we all? Perhaps I can help you with this loss of your man. I am not so simple as you, and I am accustomed to the devious—and the ruthless. You may overlook many things, I fear. You are not so devious. You think you are above the devious, trusting to your strength. You think you can overpower it, yes?" She smiled. The smile faded and she shook her head. "You cannot."

"What are you gettin' at? Like...us losing the papers? Yeah, I guess it's pretty obvious Rayburn didn't put the papers back in the same place, like he said he did."

"No, that is incorrect. It is only obvious, that they are no longer there."

Hawk blinked. Maybe she and Clark were right. Maybe the details of all this were a little beyond him. But the point of it all was not beyond him, and he was more interested in the big picture. He was going to pin her down, and no amount of double talk was going to throw him off the trail. "Okay. About the General, General Yamashita?"

"Yes. He is withdrawing his entire contingent, two hundred fifty thousand men to Baguio in northern

Luzon. They are traveling in three groups: one of one hundred fifty thousand, one of eighty thousand, and one of twenty thousand. The names of these armies, the numbers they go by, I do not remember those details. They were in the papers. It does not matter. Your intelligence will know those things. Baguio is a beautiful place. Is it better to destroy it, than Manila?"

"I don't know nothing about it. That ain't my department." He shook his head. "If that's true, Manila should already be empty, shouldn't it? That's what they needed to know, I think. If all that's so, why are troops still here? There's all kind of Japs roaming around, doing all kind of sh...things."

"Yes. It should be empty. If, God had made a perfect world. Why did he not? Wouldn't it have been just as easy for him?"

"I can't tell you that, either. I guess he was busy, and slipped up. Maybe he did the best he could. People don't like it when you do the best you can. I don't pass judgment, since he's let me off the hook a few times." His expression changed from the whimsical to the serious. "It sounds like you think some of the Japs are *not* leaving?" he persisted.

"Oh, I know that they are not. They are cutting down the beautiful old trees on Main Street to use for fortifications right now. You see, Admiral Iwabuchi is in charge of the Naval forces here. He refused to follow the orders of General Yamashita, who is over the Army. The has some political influence in Japan and is able to do this. He had only twelve thousand marines, but by his boldness, he is drawing some support from random Army units as well. He is vowing a fight to the death. He is bitter about some loss he suffered early in the war. Honor, perhaps? As a man, this may make sense to you?

Honor is more important to a young man than life itself, am I right? How much more, or less, to a mature man, I cannot imagine."

"What you're saying...don't sound like what our side was planning on. The...open city...thing. This here admiral is in the way. All of this...stuff...was in your papers?"

"Yes. Had your officers received this information, Manila would already be in flames. They do not care that twelve thousand is not as much as two hundred fifty thousand. Many will die. The Japanese have already started the executions. They know they will be defeated, but they are leaving no one alive who was not loyal to them."

"It sounds a little like maybe you didn't want us to have the information written in the papers."

She shrugged. "Obviously, they would find out the truth eventually. One cannot hide reality. I would have sent the reports, if I could have. I did not write them for my own entertainment. I had hoped that the admiral would come to his senses, or that there would be a mutiny within his mutiny. I had hoped that the Americans would realize how small his unit is, and spare the majority of the city; that they would bypass it, and go after General Yamashita. I had hoped for many, many things, you see? For Manila. But the world crumbles around our hopes."

"That's...complicated. All that...hoping. It would have helped to have the papers, I think," said Hawk, unsure as to what Clark, or anyone, would make of her explanation. The facts, the size of these armies, the identities of those leaving and those staying, might make a difference to American planners.

"I think not. Can a paper plead a case? Is a paper

more ingenuous than I? I would like to explain it all. But they would not listen to me, just as the Japanese did not listen to me. Perhaps your colonel will listen to you, if you plead this case. Make him see that the admiral is not the threat, and to go instead to Baguio. If they do not go to Baguio now, they will never drive Yamashita out of the mountains. There is...nothing...to gain in Manila."

"The colonel—listen to me? I don't think so, Mademoiselle. This is high level stuff. Ain't nobody even gonna listen to a colonel, and they sure as *hell* ain't gonna listen to me. I don't see them letting this admiral just sit here in Manila, gumming up the works. This is up to the Supreme Commander. You've heard of him?"

"I have heard of him, and he has heard of me. If I could speak with him, I feel it would do some good. Though, he is not here, and he knows he will not die in the collapse of Manila. But—you and I, here we are, where we will die. We have no voice. We are the past. Our breath is like that air floating above the canal outside."

"Maybe not. If the Japs are left with a skeleton crew like you say, the Army might be able to swoop in and knock them out pretty fast."

"You do not know your own people. They do not... *swoop*...in." She mocked the word. "They bomb, they bombard, they burn, for weeks, before they come in. To save a thousand of their own soldiers, they will kill two hundred thousand civilians. We will all be dead before we see our first American soldier."

"Well...I'll talk to the colonel. I'll try to tell him about it. We'll keep looking for your dispatches. Don't give up yet."

"No. I will not give up on you. I admire your courage. Your...simplicity? Many brave people are prisoners at the *Kempetai* field office, not so far from here. In the *Buntai*. They will all die there without a fight. At least, you may be able to fight the police before you die."

"Oh, yes, ma'am. You can count on that."

* * *

KARL MET Bernard Koch just after dark. They stood beneath the streetlamp near the door of the jeweler's shop, Karl's place of employment. Koch set his heavy suitcase down on the sidewalk as they spoke to one another.

"I tell you, something has happened. It is just like Germany," said Bernard. "People are disappearing. It is so maddening. Just when the Americans are about to return, it is all happening again. I am afraid we will have to get out of here."

"*Get out of here*? Manila? The country? And go where?" Karl asked. "How? We are in the middle of the war now, in the country of the Japanese. Soldiers will be fighting everywhere. We cannot *get out of here*. We are at their mercy. They have never done anything like that to us in this country...like they did in Germany. It is hard to believe. There must be some explanation," said Karl.

"There is an explanation all right," Bernard answered. "They have come to your door, haven't they? Open your eyes. Are you going to stick your head in the sand again? In Japan, they have deported Jews to China all along. They are not your friends, Karl." He kneeled next to his suitcase. "But you are not to worry, I will take care of the getting out of here. I am working on an exit. I called you here for a reason. You will have a part in this. You must help the community, and it will help you. We have to get our assets out of here first. We are converting the liquid assets into stamps and jewelry. You must convert the jewelry into settings resembling costume jewelry. It must be unassuming, in case it is seized. Can you do this?" He stood, holding a heavy bank bag he had taken out of the suitcase.

"I suppose," said Karl. "It may take time. Depending on how much stock there is." Koch handed him the bag. Karl's face fell as the weight pulled his hands down. "This will take time, Bernard."

"Do it, and quickly. We may not have time."

"You cannot get this much jewelry out of the country. It looks suspicious. They will hold it on general principle, no matter what it looks like," said Karl. "I cannot turn jewels into feathers."

"We have contact with a German woman. She interacts with the Japanese and they do not suspect her. She is a double agent of the Americans. She can get the property out through underworld channels of her own, and we can recover it later in the United States," said Bernard. "She is trustworthy."

Karl hefted the bag with a doubtful expression. "You trust this woman? To do something like that?"

"Absolutely. That is not a problem. There are paper tags on each piece to identify them, you must transfer them to the new pieces carefully. The cheaper, the trashier looking you can make them, the better." Koch looked over his shoulder. "Someone is coming. I must go. Take that inside. For God's sake, they are always watching me."

10

A MATTER OF TRUST

Eugenie Rossier pointed at Hawk, as if casting a magic spell over him. He imagined he felt its power.

"You will tell your colonel these things about the withdrawal, about the Japanese having already departed, and he will tell you that you can leave, because your mission is accomplished. Do you think?" Eugenie asked.

"That's the plan," Hawk answered. "We want to get out of here as soon as we can. I'm not sure if this information is going to make things better or worse. If this admiral character, the one planning the mutiny, wants a fight, they're probably going to give it to him. You don't have to worry about it, though. We'll get you out of here." Hawk settled back in his chair, ignoring the creeping uneasiness of nicotine deprivation, and the sounds of old explosions echoing in his head.

"I am not worried. I will not leave here." She stood and walked to the bedroom door. "I *am* Manila, you see?" She opened the door. "Without it, I have nothing. I am nothing. I am so tired."

Hawk watched her retreat into the darkness of the room. The black clothing, her black hair, made her vanish into the shadows. Her words, and their tone, reminded him of when Ana had said the same thing: "I am so tired." Ana had been imitating Mademoiselle Rossier, repeating words she had heard Eugenie say, perhaps often. He realized Ana had missed the meaning. Eugenie was not referring to a physical tiredness. Like Manila, she had wearied of the task of trying to save herself.

As he sat there, it occurred to him that he had no reason to be in here alone. He stood and walked to the bedroom door. She stood at the window, looking down at the twinkling lamps of the shanty town toward the south. They blinked randomly, as distant lights will do, now here, now there. He could see only her compact shape, lit like the edges of an eclipse, and the white face, glowing against the night outside the window, and then reflected again in the glass, as if she were outside looking at herself.

He had known her less than hour, though it did not feel like it. It seemed as if he had known her since he first saw the portrait downstairs, as if he had been thinking of her all along. It also felt as if she had known him, like she had been evaluating him, and judging him, for a long time, before she came to him. In spite of her fatalism, she had some reason for an interest in him. And he knew that she had sized him up as a hard case. For, after all, that's what everyone did, and that's what he was. But even the hardest stones are of some use. He knew too well, that was his only value to anyone: to be even more vicious than the evil ones he fought. For while others always had some gain in mind, maybe even altruistic goals, Hawk was only vicious.

"Where did the years go?" she asked, slightly above a whisper, and without turning around. "I was a child in a place they have taken away. The people there don't even know what language to speak anymore. You, I think, were never a child. But we end together here in this fragile haven, after—all this time. How could this happen? What is time?"

"That's a long story."

"It is night again," she said. "Spirits prefer the night. It is softer and easier to pass through." She looked half toward him. "Without the light. Without reasons." His wide shoulders slouched against the doorway as he watched her, trying to understand her. As she had said, he was a simple man, and she was not simple. His head turned toward her, like that of a perplexed dog. "They say spirits return to tell us things. To tell us of matters they left undone. But I don't think the spirits know any more than we do. I think they return to find out things. What do you think?" She looked at him.

Unfortunately, Hawk did *not* think a great deal, about anything. Even so, he found himself trapped in Manila, in a situation that required a great deal of thinking. When it came to doing things, however, he was much quicker on the uptake. He walked over to her and stood beside her. It is possible, he never realized that he had been led into the room. He nevertheless cast a wary glance at the shadows in the corners, for no man on earth, regardless of strength or cunning, had any hopes of kneeling on James Hawk's head and inserting a knife in his neck.

"Why are you here?" he asked. "You could have gone anywhere."

She smiled softly. "We do understand one another, I believe. We may be alike, more than you know. I am not a gentle person. I am a lonely person. I find suddenly that I came back...*for you.* Your country has a good deal of faith in you. Now, I feel I have faith in you. The violent take the kingdom of heaven by force. St. Matthew warned us of you. You read the Bible?"

"Not lately."

He put his arms around her and pulled her to him. It felt as if he were pulling life itself against his body. She was made of an energy different from the world around her. She wilted, as if the gesture had in fact pulled the strength of that energy out of her. But—it was still there, waiting, like the infernal gale blowing outside. It waited to engulf him. He forgot all of the questions he should be asking. Her head tilted back and he kissed her. Her darkness, her force, was all around him and overpowering. The wind cried beneath the third-story eaves, and through the open deck of the tower above, the wail of souls crying for what they have lost, and can never have again.

* * *

THE WEITZ FAMILY had put the war out of their minds for the evening. The Americans were advancing, and perhaps things would all work out. Karl had complied timely with the request of Bernard Koch, but he had also heard little else of Koch's grand scheme to get the Weitz family, and the rest of the community, safely out of Manila. He began to wonder if perhaps Bernie might not be planning an escape limited only to himself, and the bag of jewelry. Such underhanded-ness had occurred in the past, and Karl did not know Bernie all that well. Everyone suspected everyone; trust levels fell to low ebb. The worst part was, Karl would probably be blamed by the community for the potential theft.

But, tonight was the last night of Hanukkah and the candles of the menorah had been lit. Marta and the children broke into unquenchable smiles as it came time to exchange gifts. Before they could, however, a light knock came at the door. Karl showed no alarm, because it was so soft. It could not be the *Kempetai*. It was likely another holiday celebrant, paying a visit. Had his song been too loud and upset the neighbors? He took the few steps to the door. A small, poorly dressed little boy stood outside. His little eyebrows raised as the smell of fried food flooded over him from inside the apartment. He reached up and handed Karl a piece of paper. Karl thanked him, and with a laugh, put a coin in his waiting hand. He raised a finger, turned to the table by the door, and handed the boy another coin, a chocolate one wrapped in golden foil. "Gelt," he said, closing the door with another parting smile.

"What is it?" Marta asked.

"Probably a note from some well-wisher." Karl laughed again, as he opened the folded paper. His smile quickly faded after reading it. "Get the luggage. We are leaving," he suddenly announced. They had been prepared for weeks, and their suitcases lay ready, stacked against the bedroom wall.

"Now?" Marta asked, waving toward the table with the food and the gifts.

"The police are on their way here *now*. We have ten or fifteen minutes, depending on how long it took the boy to get here," Karl answered.

"But this isn't Germany. They could be coming for a dozen different reasons," said Marta. "They don't even know who we are."

"They are coming for one reason. We must leave immediately. They have block managers who know everything about us."

"Where? Where are we going? We have nowhere to go. Just...leave everything?"

"Yes. We are going to Bernie's house, if we can make it. He says he can take us to the harbor. The American fleet is not far offshore. We can likely make it to Australia."

Marta looked at the ceiling. "The harbor? A ship? Not another ship, Karl. There is an invasion going on. There is a Japanese fleet in the harbor as well, you know. They are sinking ships, each other's ships, all ships. Think of the children."

"There is no time to dither about all of that. Get the bags."

* * *

THE RADIO CRACKLED. "That is impossible, Hawk. It can't be Rossier. That woman is dead. It's been reported, confirmed and reaffirmed. She is dead, dead. I don't know who you have there, but it's not Eugenie Rossier. You've been fooled again. How could she get through your perimeter? That *should* have been impossible, too. Did you investigate that? Over."

"She said the *Kempetai* dropped her off, sir. She had nowhere else to go. The thing is, she knows what those documents said. That's kind of the important thing for now. She says Yamashita is withdrawing with most of the troops, to leave the city open, and this other man, a Navy admiral is the one trying to set up some kind of defensive positions downtown. He doesn't have the approval of the Japanese high command. He's just doing it on his own. And he doesn't have a very strong force. It will pretty much be an open city. Over."

"That makes *no* sense to me. That's not the way the military operates, and especially not the Japanese military. They don't have *rogues*. And you still don't have the papers to back any of this cock and bull story up? Over."

"Not yet. The papers have to be here. I imagine her handwriting is the same as that on all of the other papers you have from her, sir. You will be able to tell if it's her. I have her right here, she can write new papers for you. I don't think any woman off the street would know this kind of stuff, or even how to make up something like that. It's her, for sure, sir. Over." Hawk looked at the painting. That was the real reason he knew that it was Eugenie Rossier. No one else on earth looked like that. But, he left that unsaid.

"No, Sergeant, a woman off the street wouldn't know those things. But a woman coming straight from the Japanese intelligence office *would* know those things, and a lot more. Like, how to dupe a backwoods sergeant. Listen to me. You're on a sandbar, with your sentries all around you. No one saw a Japanese secret police boat putter up to your doorstep and drop this woman off? Does that make *any* sense to you? She gets released from the *Kempetai* prison *after* they find out she's been supplying us with information? Does *that* make sense? Has that ever happened? Use your head, boy. She's lying to you. What the hell is wrong with you? Is she some *femme fatale* or something? She shows up and you lose a man. Wake up. Over."

Hawk had no answers for the onslaught of questions. He hadn't really expected such a hostile argument. How would he know if any of what the colonel suspected had ever happened? He thought it best not to address the question of a *femme fatale* or think about it much. If ever there was one...he looked up at Blackwell staring at him. Blackwell shrugged. Hawk opened his palms at the radioman, and said: "What do I tell him?"

"He's not going to believe anything you say," said Blackwell. "Everything you say, he finds a way to disagree with. Just go along with him. He's...a...*colonel!*"

Hawk pressed the transmitter. Though no passive follower, he had enough of the Marine Corps disciplining to know that the colonel could be right, and he could be wrong. The ridge, and a dozen other incidents like it, had proven that. Even Blackwell was smart enough to simply agree with the man. Nevertheless, Hawk took one more shot at it. "If you look into it, sir, I think the facts will check out. I would suggest trying to hold off the attack and work on locating and going after the Jap admiral with a smaller force. I think things are working out the way you wanted, without a major attack. You can still save the city. Over."

A long pause followed. Did Clark like that? Hawk and Blackwell looked at one another. At last, the static returned.

"Don't let that woman out of your sight," the radio squawked. "Don't let her talk to anybody. Not for one minute. I'll get back to you. Over and out."

Hawk looked at Blackwell. "I like how he does that," said Hawk.

"Does what?"

"The man doesn't tell you what the hell he's doing or what we're doing. He spends twenty minutes not listening, telling you how stupid you are, and crazy, and a liar, and then—over and out."

"I guess we're supposed to wait," said Blackwell. "That was my impression."

"Yeah, but for what? We've been waiting since we got here. Whatever it is we're waiting for, can't be good."

"I don't know," said Blackwell, "but I bet we're going to know it when we see it."

"No, shit."

* * *

"Yeah, he's gone. Cleared out," said Joe Canlon. "I guess he swam the canal. He must have swam it, since there ain't no boats missing. Hobby says the old snake went into the galley for two minutes to get a piece of bread. He went to check on him, and nobody was in there." Joe shook his head. "There ain't no windows or no way out of there. He's pretty slick."

Hawk asked Hobby about the missing Ulupong and received the same story. The kitchen had a rear entrance, likely as a safety measure in case of fires, or to dump trash in the canal. The rear entrance had been boarded up from the outside, and the boards had not been disturbed in weeks. The door opened outward. The missing messenger could not have passed through it, without a good deal of noisy assistance.

The sergeant assembled everyone on the ground floor. No one had seen Ulupong leave. Nothing of note had gone missing. Nothing, that is, that anyone knew anything about. He could well have left with the most important thing there: the dispatch case and documents, for supposedly, no one knew of their whereabouts. Quickly tiring of blank stares in response to his questions, Hawk dismissed everyone.

"I guess that proves he killed Rayburn," said Baker.

"How the hell does it prove that?" Hawk answered.

"He took the papers from Rayburn, and beat it back

to the Japs," said Baker. "Shit, I coulda told you that. I *did* tell you that. The bastard tried to kill Hobby, didn't he?"

"What do the Japs want with the papers? They already know everything in them. It's all about them," said Hawk.

"I don't know, but he sure as shit took them. They want them, just to keep us from having them," Baker answered. "Nobody knows what that goofy ass was up to. I bet he can make a buck out of it, though. He knows who to sell them to and where." Hawk heard a door shut on the third floor. The muffled sound stood out, even in all of the chaos. He looked up.

"Yeah," said Hawk. "Nobody knows what he was up to. But I bet some people got a little better idea than other people." He climbed the stairs to the third floor and knocked on the door to the office of Mademoiselle Rossier, opening it at the same time. She quietly told him to enter, after he was inside. She sat behind her great desk.

They looked at one another for several seconds without speaking. "He did not take the dispatch case," she finally said.

"How do you know that?" Hawk asked.

"He told me," she said. "He did not kill your man."

"And—that's because he told you that, too?"

"Yes. He would not have done it. He had no reason to do it. To do so would create a good deal of attention for him, and he does not like attention."

"Some people say there was pretty good reasons. I've been thinking—since I had my little conversation with the colonel—I don't know for sure when *you* got here. You could have been here when Rayburn was killed, for all I know."

"Yes. I was here," she admitted, without batting an eye. He stood there with an expressionless face, taken aback, first of all that she had been there, and second, that she boldly told him as much. "You have never asked me that. Do you think now that it is I who killed him?"

Hawk sat down. "I just might. Did you?"

"I had every reason to. He stole my property, which I have still not recovered. The only problem with that kind of impulsiveness would be, of course, I don't know where the property is. It would have been very unwise of me to kill the only person who did know."

"Why do you care? None of that stuff means anything to you."

"*Bien au contraire.* Something does. All of us have things that mean something to us. Don't we? I think— you do."

"You know," he said, "right after it happened, Ana acted kind of nervous. I wouldn't be surprised if she would kill somebody for you. She thinks quite a bit of you."

"Yes, she would do anything for me. But kill? No, she is not like you. You must try to understand, though it will not be easy for you. Some people are not killers. It is...revolting to decent people. It would make anyone nervous or sick. You have forgotten human nature. Your familiarity with evil has made you complacent. Good men are swept away as if by the tide, but what happens to the men like you?"

"Nobody keeps track."

"How well you know your own, and what you are."

"So, I'm a killer?"

"Yes. You are. Do you deny it?"

"I might."

"You cannot. Will *you* kill for me?"

"What are you getting at? You know what's going on around here, don't you? What did you come back here for? What's the game you're playin'? The *Kempetai* didn't just drop you off here, like you said. How did you get in here? I need some answers."

"Your words have become harsh. They were not so harsh last night when we...spoke. For such a violent man, they were very gentle. We are on the last sharp edge of existence here together, and about to leave it forever. Don't we mean something to each other? Soon we will be nothing. They romanticize about fugitive lovers in the theater, chased by the police, with a hundred guns aimed at them, as they share their last emotions. We are fugitives chased by *hundreds of thousands* of guns, sharing our last breath." She looked down, shielding her magnetic eyes, which only served to emphasize her words all the more. "I—*need*—that dispatch case, my love. And, you? You need me."

"What do you mean?"

"You are in love with me. You don't want to be, you struggle with it, but you are. Painfully so. The more you struggle, the more deeply you feel it. I am sorry. I did not mean for it. It is hopeless for you. I assumed you had no soul. They say you can get over it, but I do not know. I am not a man. Do you deny you love me?"

"I...might." Hawk didn't want something like that added into the equation. He had business to tend to. He shook his head, as if shaking off an evil spell, and quickly added, "I ain't gettin' into none of that. I need to know how you got in here."

"You did not deny it. Yes, you need to find out many things. But if I do not tell you, you will still love me. It does not matter. That is how love is. It is sad in a way, the same as leaving life. You give up yourself. I can tell that you do not understand it, and it confuses you greatly. It will be better when you accept it. I have had to accept a great deal."

"You just said I was a killer. You know me, and what I am. You ain't the first one to figure me out. That's why they picked me for this. You ain't messing with a poetry professor, ladybug. I mean...this love stuff. You're pretty sure of yourself, Mademoiselle. Don't be."

"Yes, I am. Are you as certain of my love for you? Or is that why the tone is so harsh? I think you are—still uncertain. You do not trust me. Must I tell you again? How many times? Who is there to be jealous of? There is only you here." She looked at him, showing no emotion in her face.

"How did you get Ulupong out of here? And, why?"

"This matter is a barrier between us. This bothers you. There must be nothing between us, because of the things that we must do here, together." She stood. "Because of what we mean to one another." She walked around the desk and leaned against him, touching his shoulder with a hand. "I must show you something. Come with me." He stood. She smiled up at him. He saw the portrait downstairs in his mind, it enveloped him. She possessed some irresistible power, something inhuman, perhaps something unwholesome. When she got close, he put his heavy arms around her, the arms of the hunter; but, now preying on the bait, or the trap?

"I detest the uncertain. Don't you? Come with me," she repeated and slipped from him, as all of his unfortunate victims would have liked to have done, and glided toward the door.

He followed her down the stairs and upon reaching the bottom floor, followed her as she entered the kitchen. Her chef stood busily at work on something in the wood-fired oven. Eugenie shook her head quickly, her dark hair straying a bit. The cook quickly left the room, shutting the door behind him. She opened the door to the pantry.

"This is how I entered the building," she said.

Hawk looked inside, seeing only shelves with various canned goods, bags, and bottles. He immediately guessed what was to come, however, because of the demonstration with the cabinet upstairs. The shelves attached to the back of the little room disguised the front of a large door, taking up most of the pantry's rear wall. She pulled it open, revealing the dark interior behind it. He looked inside, seeing steps leading down into a tunnel, shored up with cross beams.

"You see, it was nothing nefarious or supernatural. Just a passage," she said.

"This old castle is full of surprises," he said. He didn't know what nefarious meant, but he suspected this latest revelation might fit the bill.

"Yes. It is very old. There are so many secrets, I am afraid not even I know them all. I would like to know who built it, and why they did what they did. I suspect lovers were involved. Would you like to see where this ends?"

"I'll take your word for it. Where does it end?"

"I think you must see the end. It is important, for us and for the future. My word must always be true for you. I do not care for harsh words between us. There is no time for that. Come with me," she said.

"How far does the damn thing go?"

"No more than twenty, thirty minutes. It is slower in the dark."

"Twenty or thirty *minutes*?" He looked down the

steps. "I can't take off that damn long without telling somebody."

"You are afraid of me. You are afraid I will throw you down in this dark tunnel? And perhaps, beat you about the head and eyes?"

"Something like that. It's just how we do things. I'm responsible for thirty men. None of us can go loping off by himself without telling somebody. Things change. If I'm going into some hole in the ground for thirty minutes, a lot could happen here, or in there."

"To you? Or to the things hiding in the hole in the ground?" she asked with a smile.

"Either way. Mostly, to the thirty guys. I done lost one, like a dope. I'll be right back, I gotta tell somebody," he said.

She held him.

"You cannot. If you tell anyone, it may be someone who killed your man, and you will never find who did it. This exit is not something for an enemy to know about."

He shifted his lower jaw to one side. "Okay. What if I only tell somebody that I'm sure didn't kill Rayburn, and is not an enemy?"

"You have someone you trust that much? You, who do not trust *me*?"

"Yeah. I got somebody. I'll tell him not to let on to anybody about the tunnel, unless I don't come back. He's real ignorant, but he can do that much. It's like tellin' a hog."

"Very well. I will go to the end of the passage and wait for you there. I am not as afraid of tunnels. You will need a lamp. Let no one see you enter."

He thought this an unusual proposition. Anyone with any common sense would have probably refused the terms. She could be going ahead of him to lay a trap, for some reason. Judging by her expression, he had already sufficiently offended her by saying he needed to leave word as to his whereabouts. Without thinking about it very much, or at least enough, he said: "Okay."

Maybe it was foolish. But he would play her game.

He shut the pantry door with its false back shelf and left the kitchen. He looked around the main room on the ground floor, until he located Joe Canlon. He walked over to him.

"Listen, jackass. I gotta do something," he said. "You're gonna be in charge for maybe an hour."

"Oh, yeah? Does this something have anything to do with a certain French babe?" Joe asked.

"Yeah, it does. Here's the thing. You can't tell anybody about this. There's a tunnel out in the galley. I think she let that Ulupong bastard go out through this rat hole. I'm gonna check it out. Remember, this thing is secret. Whoever killed Rayburn may know about it, but they may not. If they find out about it, we may never catch them. Get it?"

"Sort of. Yeah, I hear what you're saying. But if Mr. Snake did the killing, and he's already gone..."

"Aw'ight. Go put a pencil to it. I ain't going through all that shit with you. All you gotta know is, if I don't come back, that's where I went. Otherwise, keep it under your goddam hat. Got it?"

"Yeah. But you're going in some tunnel, where the snake is probably hiding?" Joe shook his head. "Is that smart?"

Hawk bared his teeth with his usual, joyless smile. "For who? Me? Or him?" They laughed.

* * *

PEOPLE CROWDED the sidewalks of Manila between the homes of the Weitz and Koch families. A cloud of fear shuddered in the air above the writhing humanity. Karl had no idea where all of the travelers were going. The Americans had not attacked. For now, the residents of the city feared only the Japanese, and how they would react to the invasion. The civilians had not yet been subjected to the American bombardment, and still thought of them only as their saviors.

Karl saw the crowds as a positive development, useful to cover his flight toward the home of Bernard Koch. If anyone followed him, they would have a difficult time staying within sight in all of the flowing humanity, livestock, and wheeled vehicles. Getting to the harbor would be another matter. The military and police presence would be heavy there. But, in this vicinity at least, no one would be guarding Bernie's house. Everyone had more important things to do.

Karl pulled Marta's hand, and she pulled on the hand of the youngest daughter, Liselotte. Like a train, the young children clung one to the other, winding through the shouting populace. They stayed on the sidewalks at first, but soon the crowd pressed them into the streets, and they couldn't tell one paved surface from the other. Some of the shops they passed had Christmas decorations, and carols blared. To the children, it seemed like being part of some grand choreographed musical production. But it wasn't.

Karl glanced behind them once and noticed an Imperial policeman weaving in and out of the rest of the public. The angry-faced officer did not appear to be following Karl's family by design, however, and more importantly, he did not wear the white armband with the red insignia of the *Kempetai* on it. There were policemen, and then there were policemen. Also, of some concern to Karl were the random, ordinary soldiers scattered among the crowds. But the young men, some looking like mere adolescents, passed without a second glance at the panting family. The Europeans did not stand out significantly in all this bustle, but Karl nonetheless felt as if a spotlight shone upon their panicky flight.

"There is the house!" Karl announced to his dearest ones at last. "We are safe now. We can go inside and rest before Bernie takes us on to the harbor. Thank God, it is over!"

"This is so horrible," Marta called above the noise of the jostling, unwashed multitude. She looked behind herself to make sure all of the children remained in tow. "I am afraid we are going to be swallowed up by all this madness!"

"No, no, the worst is behind us," Karl assured her again. The raging river of townsfolk pushed him tightly against Bernard Koch's door and tried to carry him past it. He pounded urgently on the long-sought portal to safety, clinging to the doorjamb with his fingernails. No one answered until he had pounded three times. Then it opened slowly. He could see no one inside the dark interior, but he knew the house well and pulled the others inside, into the relative calm awaiting them there.

The lights snapped on. A *Kempetai* officer faced the Weitz family, and three soldiers behind the officer pointed rifles at them.

"Oh!" Karl gasped involuntarily, both startled and horrified.

"Good afternoon," said the emotionless officer without even indulging in a smile of enjoyment at the alarm of his prey. "Karl Weitz, I believe?"

"Uh, yes, yes, I am," Karl answered. "This is my wife, and these are my children. We are visiting Bernard Koch. I must have selected the wrong door. My apologies, sir."

"No need to apologize. You have correctly found the Koch residence. We have been seeking *you*, in fact. This is a fortunate coincidence, is it not? You are looking for him, and we are looking for you? Are you traveling? Or were you planning to overnight here?" the officer asked, pointing at the luggage.

"Yes, yes, it is our holiday. We were going to spend the night, you see. To...celebrate...of course." Karl tried to laugh nervously, but nothing came out of his cold, choked throat.

"Of course, I see. Your Christmas is still a week away. Perhaps, you did not refer to Christmas. This holiday, is this a *Jewish* holiday, by any chance?"

"Why, yes. Yes, it is. We celebrated it in Germany, our homeland. We are *German*, by origin. And we brought the custom with us." Karl forced a smile through the anxiety paralyzing his facial muscles. "From...*Germany*," he emphasized.

"That touches me deeply. There are questions about this, however. We are given to understand that Germany did not approve of such things. Your sudden flight from your own residence here in Manila makes us even more curious. I'm sure you must understand our concerns. There is a great deal of traitorous activity in the city just now." The officer's voice sounded robotic, more cold than angry.

"Yes, yes. I'm sure it all looks strange to those unfamiliar with our customs. I would be willing...and glad... to answer any questions. Most certainly. Of course."

"Of course, you will. You will accompany us, please,

to the *Buntai*, in order for the magistrate to hear your answers. He is very curious for your welfare. Lest you become the victim of treachery."

"Well...we are so rushed. The holiday, you understand? Thank you so much. Perhaps another time," Karl said. "I can jot down the address, if I could get a scheduled appointment, perhaps. Or if you had a form, I could fill..."

"I think not," said the officer, pointing at the door. "Your appointment is scheduled for now. I have filled out the form for you, quite some time ago. In fact, you may be our last assignment, I fear."

* * *

"I'LL BE BACK before an hour is up," Hawk informed Joe. He picked up his Thompson from the booth by the front window, slung it over his shoulder, swaggered casually into the empty kitchen, and shut the door. Joe, the cook, Ana, and Epley all saw this, along with several others, to whom it had little or no significance. Joe looked steadily at them, and one by one, they turned away.

Hawk lit an oil lamp in the kitchen, opened the dusty pantry door, shut it, and then opened the door to the damp tunnel. He entered it, and shut the disguised shelves behind him. Where the pantry had smelled of flour and spices, the passage smelled of wet earth. The subterranean shaft consisted of but a single path and no place for concealment. The only way for someone to ambush him would be to lie in wait around a sharp curve and there were very few of those. Booby traps could be hidden here, but they would be hard to cover in the sameness of the surroundings. His footsteps made the only sound in the black vacuum.

After a few minutes, the earthen walls and wooden beams ended, being replaced by a reinforced concrete culvert, seven to eight feet in diameter, being high enough for him to walk upright. He looked up at seepage where joints in the pipe had been connected.

A slight oversight came to his mind as he recalled Eugenie failing to mention where this long path led. She had done so quite deliberately. While it would be virtually impossible for one to conceal oneself in here, anything could be at the other end. The pipe constituted a waterproof means of passing under the canal. Anyone aware of the American's presence could by some method flood the passage and kill him without a fight. That same someone could be the one adamantly insisting that he walk down this route alone. Was she subjecting him to some test of his trust? Or was it something a little more...*nefarious*?

The uneasy surroundings brought on a serious evaluation of his relationship with Eugenie, as one boot followed another. What did he really know about her? Almost nothing. The few things that he did know were not reassuring. She, allegedly, came from someplace in Europe that no longer existed. In considering all of the complications, Colonel Clark came to mind. What would Clark think of this little lovers' escapade beneath the canal? That thought only served to calm Hawk. Of course, no one in their right mind would recommend his following her into a deadly underground passage, much less the colonel. And no one else would have followed her.

What was unusual about any of that? That was James Hawk. Maybe she did know him better than he knew himself. She knew that he would follow her anywhere. What she didn't realize, however, was that he would do many other dangerous things without a second thought as well. It was not a trembling, love-struck boy tracing her footsteps. It was a very mean bastard who knew just exactly what he was doing. One step at a time, he approached closer and closer to the end, wherever and whatever that might be. If anyone had bad intentions directed at him, they had better have planned them well.

One other minor, nagging detail did serve to give him pause, however. He recalled that she came in here without a lamp; into an utterly, completely, lightless, pitch-black tunnel.

A subdued circle of soft light glowed ahead. The pipe sloped upward. He saw her standing in the far opening. It occurred to him that someone, or any number of individuals, could be standing behind her, out of sight. That was how his mind operated. And yet, he did not unsling the Thompson, but only slouched confidently forward.

"Did you crawl on your hands and knees?" she called to him. "I have been here forever." Her authoritative complaint echoed in the tunnel.

"I took the scenic route. Didn't know there a rush." His reverberating answer sounded strange and apart from him. The words bounced back to his ears, trapped under yards of gripping earth and water. It gave the impression that he had left this world and entered some plane in the afterlife. If he had, she was imprisoned in the same Hades as well, and that was a consolation. As he met her, she turned and faced the outside. The sky had grown densely overcast, but daylight remained. He walked outside to look around—and—just to be outside.

"You must not be too bold. Someone could see you," she said. He looked up and saw the steep bank of the barge waterway above him. It consisted mostly of dirt and weeds, with a liberal scattering of rocks and broken concrete. He looked over his shoulder, and there shimmered the familiar, gray surface of the canal. It smelled as strongly here as elsewhere. Upstream and far away, on the other side of the water, Club Arashigaoka crowned its own high hill, glinting in the descending sunlight.

"Damn, we came a long way," he said.

"Yes. Up this bank, on the other side of a dike is the Qebu *Buntai* field office of the *Kempetai*," she said. "You may be able to hear the shots. They execute people every day behind the station, at about this time, and at dawn. I wondered sometimes how anyone could still be alive in Manila. Do they want to rule over a city of the dead?"

"No, they want us to. I don't think they plan on being in Manila much longer," he said. "You were in jail *here*? I thought you were in that Fort Santiago prison?"

"I was there for a while. Then I was brought here. The prisons and the stations are overcrowded with prisoners. They cannot shoot them all fast enough. In the prisons, they prefer to sever heads with their swords. It saves ammunition. They are not always very efficient at it. They are more civilized here, using the bullets."

He looked back at the tunnel entrance. Two small, concealing trees had been tied back on either side of it. "I uncovered the opening so that you could see the light. These trees hide it from view," she said.

"We got the Jap secret police right at our back door,"

he told her. "They could come right down this hole to the Club. That never worried you?"

"No," she said. "I cannot worry about everything. It is us, going to *their* back door, is it not? *We* point the gun at *them*. You see, over here?" She walked toward the edge of the water, and he followed with growing caution. "Over there is where barges dock sometimes, this is where they wait to enter the harbor, when it is busy. There are none now. But you can see the pilings, where they would be moored."

He looked at the metal-capped timbers jutting from the edge of the water. Little waves made a lapping, popping sound on the gravel beach. He sensed that she showed him all of this for a reason. But she didn't say anything else about it, and he didn't ask.

"You brought your machine gun. You are afraid? Of me, no doubt?"

"Not too much. I don't go nowhere without it. As a matter of fact, if I had known I would be two foot away from a Jap prison camp, I might have brought a hell of a lot more."

"Yes, you are right. It is a deadly location. We should return, but it was necessary for you to see all of this. It is hard to understand without seeing it, with your own eyes, is it not? Some things you cannot only tell someone about. People tend to believe what they want to believe and hear only the things they want to hear."

"Yeah. I guess, it's a good idea to know about the place. You're right, I might not have got a grasp of it."

"And, so, you should also see the *Buntai*? Yes?"

"Way up there? What for? This is about enough sightseeing for one day," he said. "I got a pretty good memory for what a pack of Japs looks like." He was not curious enough about the appearance of the outer trappings of a *Kempetai* field office to crawl up the steep bank in broad daylight. "They can go their way, and I'll go mine."

"Yes, but, of course. We should go." She untied the bent trees growing there, and they snapped back across the tunnel entrance. Sharp rifle reports cracked above them. Hawk flinched reflexively, and in an instant, the submachine gun leaped to his hands. She stood there, unperturbed. "I am used to the sound," she said. "The evening executions. Come." She held a tree back with her hand and gestured for him to enter the culvert. The trees fell back into place. Once inside, they were silhouetted against the grill of the leaves and the light outside: two beautiful young people, in a charred world that was anything but beautiful.

"You always have that attached to your hand?" She touched the ribbed barrel of the gun.

"Pretty much."

"It makes you fearless?"

"It don't hurt."

She slid close to him and put her arms around him. He still held the submachine gun in one hand. "We are so close to death here, are we not?" she asked, her breath short, her half-closed eyes darting back and forth across his face.

"I'd estimate...close enough," he answered.

"In both time and place now, instead of just time," she said. "You can feel it with such clarity. It makes my heart race. My head must think that I can avoid it. Is this what being alive means? Deluding yourself for a short time? Thinking like an animal, feeling like an animal, that you can live forever?" She asked. She kissed him and leaned against him. "Tell me, show me, what that is like."

"Yeah...as a matter of fact. If it's all the same to you, I'd just as soon be alive somewhere else." He glanced up at the sound of the gunfire. "I been on the business end of them bastards too many times to let all that slide."

She smiled and pushed herself away. "I forgot. You still cling to life. It is only a habit. Soon you will be mine, and I will be all that you want to hold." She lay pressing, demanding fingers on the submachine gun. His hand instinctively gripped it tighter as another shot sounded above, and he gestured down the tunnel with the barrel.

11

THE EIGHT HUNDRED POUND SHELL

LIEUTENANT HAYASHI INDICATED KARL SHOULD SIT AT the long table parallel to the extreme left wall of the hearing room. The young officer had been assigned the task of defending Karl. A similar table for the prosecution faced them across the room. To their left, in the center of the facility, stood the raised bench of the three magistrates. For the moment, three empty chairs sat behind the bench, one ominously higher than the others. A modestly sized plaque behind the bench read "Bureau of the Constabulary," written in *romaji*, and above the plaque, a giant rising sun flag took up most of the wall.

Hayashi arranged the Weitz children and Marta in chairs behind Karl. Beside Karl sat a little bent over interpreter, provided as a courtesy of the Empire, in case the accused should have difficulty with the more complex aspects of the hearing.

"Everyone, look like this," Lieutenant Hayashi told Marta and the children. "See my face?" He looked at the ceiling and drooped his shoulders, making a sad face.

Then he smiled. He pinched Liselotte's cheek and then turned to Karl. "She is so sweet. Pay attention to me. The head magistrate is a captain, but as head of the court, he is referred to as 'Commander.' *You*, however, do not call him anything but 'Honorable Sir.' If he addresses you, which he probably will not. Understand?" Hayashi straightened his papers.

"Yes. You will do most of the talking? I must trust to your knowledge of these matters," Karl whispered, leaning forward, and sweating. His voice hung barely audible between them, most of it trapped in his breathless chest. He didn't know how much trust to place in his Japanese defender. "I know nothing of these proceedings."

"Correct. Most definitely not. That is my expertise. I have your defense well planned. I warn you, though. Things have not been going well for me lately. I had a case very similar to yours this morning," said Hayashi in a business-as-usual tone. "He was a Russian. I thought I had a good case, but you know, the status of Russians is so difficult. They won't commit to the war. I did what I could. The commander did not listen, he said 'nah, nah, nah,' Hayashi, 'nah, nah, nah,' mocking me. I hate that. It is all this subversive activity, the penalties are much harsher now for irregularities. Russia, you know? Are they in or are they out?"

"I...I don't know. What happened to him? To this Russian?" Karl asked nervously, not entirely following the conversation.

"Oh, he was shot. Between you and me, I think the Russians are in, but they are not telling us about it. But do not worry. You are Germans. Germans are the best. Very best. It is entirely different. I think we can give them a grand fight. Watch how skilled I am. I know what they are up to. They are going to say you are *not* Germans. If you are Germans, there will be no problem. And—*you are!*" He smiled, and held out a hand as if he had just performed a magic trick.

"We have done nothing wrong," said Karl. "We have complied with all the laws and the wishes of the authorities—of every nation. Always."

Hayashi put his hand on Karl's shoulder. "You must have read my opening statement?" He gave him a friendly pat. "I will do my best for you. No one could do better. I like you. We must be careful of their moods. Moods are very important here. *They can be ugly.*" Hayashi whispered the last sentence.

Karl had no time to answer or to reflect on this. The three magistrates entered. Everyone stood, and the three of them sat ceremoniously. The people in the room bowed respectfully, and then all sat. Only a half dozen people sat beyond the railing in the space reserved for spectators, all of them Japanese.

Commander Nakaya began rapidly reading charges in Japanese and Karl could not follow all of the legalistic phrases. He recognized the mention of his own name several times. The interpreter sat even more bent over, with his eyes closed. Karl had no knowledge of what language the little old man spoke, other than presumably Japanese. He hoped the man spoke a language Karl was familiar with. Apparently, the charges themselves had been deemed unworthy of translation.

"The Imperial Army has commissioned me, Commander Nakaya, as Justice Minister in this affair of Weitz, to set sentencing under the authority of the *Naikin Han*. You understand this?" The commander concluded with an angry look at Karl.

Hayashi stood quickly. "Honorable, accused Wietz understands perfectly, Commander, and humbly submits himself to the authority of the tribunal."

"Very well. Proceed. The Empire shall state the matter of...what is it...*Weitz*?" The commander snapped his head toward the other table, where Karl deduced the prosecutor sat. A nasty-looking, slender, man of medium height in a *Kempetai* uniform stood, leaving several other dour-faced individuals seated and stone-faced next to him. They glared as if they hated Karl. Hayashi bowed and sat.

"Karl Weitz, the man seated there, illegally entered the Philippines under the authority of the American forces, hostile to the Empire of Japan. He has aided the enemy throughout the war and plotted against the emperor. The prosecution urges the death penalty, honorable Commander." The prosecutor returned to his seat. Karl thought the chilling remarks too perfunctory, and totally inaccurate.

"This is true? Speak, Lieutenant Hayashi!" the commander shouted louder than before. Karl was intimidated by the angry emotion his accusers were injecting into the rather simple, and baseless, charges against him.

"This is *not* true," Hayashi replied bravely. Karl was relieved to hear this, and to have an advocate. Karl could not have voiced it as forcefully himself. "This person is a German national. He entered the country legally. It is true the Americans were in control of the puppet government at the time. He had nothing to do with that. All of his papers were in order. The German nation approved his departure. Under the terms of the Imperial Liaison Conference of 1942, all citizens of

Germany, Italy, France, Austria...*and Russia*...are under the protection of the emperor as his trusted allies."

The commander waved his hand impatiently. "We have litigated the *Russian* issue. Do not start that again with me, Hayashi, or you will be subject to a sentencing of your own."

Hayashi bowed twice. "My humble apologies. It is only my prepared speech in such cases. I had memorized and repeated it many times. I meant no disrespect. I will have to rewrite it...after the events of this morning. I will remove Russia. In any event, Commander, the accused is *German*, and Germany is his majesty's staunchest ally. There is no question of that. I invite anyone here to dispute this." He smiled at the prosecutor, who did not smile back.

"Sit down. In spite of his insolence, I believe the advocate is correct." The commander spoke to the other two magistrates and turned to the prosecutor. "Is that the conclusion of the matter?" He looked over the bench and down at his female assistant. "Are we done here?" he asked her in a low voice.

The prosecutor rose. "No, honorable Commander, this is far from settled. A well-known exception applies in such matters. A *refugee* is not considered a citizen of the allied nations and is an exemption to the rule. The Jewish populations are well established as refugees throughout the world."

The commander raised his hand. "Hayashi, you said nothing about the accused being Jewish. Are you being clever with us again today? We had a refugee case yesterday. You know very well what the law is on refugees." The commander motioned impatiently for Hayashi to stand, and he promptly did so.

"The law is very clear, my commander. The accused

is *not* a refugee. A refugee flees his nation illegally without the color of law. This man has papers approved by both Germany and the admitting nation of the Philippines. He is a legal resident. In addition, the admission was even approved by the colonial authority of the United States. He shook hands with the president of the Philippines when he got off the boat. He is not a refugee by any definition of the term, under the laws of any nation, or international law. He is a decorated veteran of the German Army in the First World War, where he valiantly fought the American Army, and is a patriot of the highest caliber. He has lived in this country openly and freely for several years. He is a contributing member of society with sterling reports from his block manager, whose presence I can produce, but your honorable and otherwise worthy assistant would not allow me to do so. The documents are clearly in the file before you, sir. I believe it is the honorable prosecution who is being clever here." Hayashi smiled at his opponent with a slight nod. The prosecutor did not acknowledge him.

The commander tore through the papers before him with a frown. He looked at his female assistant. She shrugged. "Yes, yes. Partially true. He is a veteran, I see that. Do you deny he is Jewish, Hayashi?"

Hayashi paused and looked thoughtful. Like a prize-fighter, he saw an opening. He turned to Karl, leaned over, and whispered. "Do you deny being Jewish? It is permitted to do so, you know?"

"I...no. How could I? What should I say?" Karl stammered.

"You will ask permission to speak to the accused!" the commander shouted angrily at Hayashi. He did not like being ignored.

"A thousand pardons. He does not deny he is Jewish. I submit that being Jewish is not a charge herein, sir. Nor is it an established crime punishable by Imperial law. We would require notice of any extended charges of such nature. This is the procedure sanctioned by..." The commander raised his hand brusquely.

"Is that entirely correct? I assume you heard the speech of the German ambassador upon his recent visit? I assume you heard the follow-up radio program on this subject of Jewish refugees? You are aware of the atrocities these people have done on the European continent? What they have done to Germany?" the commander asked.

"My apologies, Commander. I may have been—wrongly—preoccupied with the war, and my duties on the night of the ambassador's program. Although his hosts received him politely, I would stress at this juncture, the views of the most honorable German ambassador are not necessarily those of the Empire. The European cultural viewpoints so expressed are not those of the Greater East Asia Co-Prosperity Sphere. The Empire has refuted all Western manipulation and colonization. In accord with the 'Eight Roofs' Policy, I submit that all races and cultures are to live in peace and harmony in our Sphere of influence."

"Are you lecturing me, Hayashi? This sounds like a lecture."

"No, Commander. I only serve as the accused's advocate, as my most humble duty demands. With all due apologies for the same and my devotion to said duty."

The prosecutor stood and bowed. The commander motioned for Hayashi to sit. "Speak!" The magistrate ordered the prosecutor.

"I believe I can settle the issue, Commander. We

are not pressing the matter as to the status of the accused being Jewish, or a veteran, or even a refugee. We have clear and convincing evidence that he was fleeing the country, which is illegal, not only under martial law, but the peacetime law of the land, and he tried to escape to a nation with whom we are at war. This is an act of hostile subversion and not the conduct of a loyal citizen invited to live here in productive peace."

"That is a supposition," Hayashi interrupted. "There is no evidence of any such hostile acts. Where is the documentation? He was arrested during an innocent holiday visit, appropriate to his...misguided...and unworthy...faith. Which is also alleged, but not documented, I must point out. And I must also note, people often change faiths."

"Do not interrupt your colleague!" said the commander. "You are stealing his time, and my time! *Thief!*" Turning back to the prosecutor, he shouted, "Proceed!"

The prosecutor smiled triumphantly at the defense before continuing. "The arrest report reflects the accused was caught in the act of fleeing to the residence of a conspirator, one Bernard Koch, now properly executed in accordance with due process, who was a known confidant of the most notorious American agent, Mademoiselle Rossier, who has also been rightfully disposed of. Accused Weitz and his brood were all bound for a ship covertly under the Australian flag. These facts are undisputed." A unanimous and audible gasp arose from the room. The hiss of "Rossier" lingered in the stuffy air.

The prosecutor sat down. "Very well. I believe we have heard *just* about enough in the matter of...what is it...*Weitz*? We shall now deliberate," the commander announced.

Hayashi stood. "I had not quite finished, honorable Commander. Some prejudices have been unfairly interjected into the consideration. Deliberately, I might add. There are certain critical nuances overlooked here that can be easily cleared..."

"You are finished. We have wasted more time with you than with any of the other matters today. You act like you own these proceedings. I have spoken. Sit. We shall deliberate." The three magistrates put their heads together, talking very low and fast. The commander did most of the talking, and one magistrate said nothing, only sleepily nodding his head.

Nakaya faced the room with his most arrogant expression, jaw raised and chin muscle tight. "We have considered the matter of Weitz and it is now concluded. After careful consideration, and with much deliberation disposed toward the most goodwill, it is decided this same Weitz is to be executed." The commander shoved the papers he held into a folder. "I am not going to set the date until the connection to these other agents of espionage are further explored. This notorious ring has yet to be fully exposed. Explain this to the accused, Hayashi." Nakaya looked around for any challenging faces, and finding none, proclaimed: "Long live his majesty, the emperor!"

Hayashi sat closely beside Karl. "You are to be executed," he said, confidentially. "That is to say, shot, honorable Weitz. The good news is, it will not be immediately, as is usually the case. And even better, you will be tortured here locally, and not in one of those terrible jungle camps. The soldiers there are very rough. And, I must add, being shot is not the worst alternative in this situation."

"I...but...why...what happened?" Karl shrank white with horror against the wooden bench and could barely speak. They had seemed to be doing so well, until the sudden final turn of events.

"I'm sure they will not kill you until the invasion begins. They will want to beat you to no end, to get more information out of you about the Mademoiselle Rossier, and the Jewish fellow, Koch, who led you into this illegal matter. He was bad for your legal defense. You should have told me about all of that. It is never good to withhold information from someone trying to help you. You left me astonished and speechless with embarrassment. Nevertheless, I forgive your shamelessness under the circumstances. No apologies are necessary. Next time...well...never mind."

"I know no Mademoiselle Rossier!" Karl exclaimed. "I know no such name. Why would they torture me? What can I tell them?"

"You can try that approach, certainly. It is not very convincing. Personally, I would prefer to make something up, to prolong the torture. Keep them interested. Tell them you have connections to this General MacArthur. They hate him."

"What about my family?"

"Oh, my, yes. I forgot." Hayashi jumped to his feet and addressed the court. The tribunal was packing up, anticipating a well-deserved break from the tedious proceedings. "The accused has one question, Commander. Due to my own foolish oversight, I am afraid. Ten thousand pardons. He wants to know, what will become of his unfortunate and...extremely innocent, and...very uninvolved family? This issue has not been disposed of in the deliberations."

One of the magistrates had already left the podium. "They will be shot as well, of course," said the commander, without looking up. "Was that a serious inquiry?"

"I must protest this," said Hayashi. "We had no notice. This is a separate issue. They were here only as observers. Notice is clearly required..."

"You need no notice when the same individuals are captured in the commission of the same crime with no distinguishing features. Martial law is well defined in that respect," Nakaya snapped. "You act as if you know nothing of justice. If, it is an act."

"I must protest. The children are minors. This one does not even know her colors yet. The woman had no such knowledge of anything. They were tricked by the dastardly criminal Weitz, snickering there at their discomfort. There are *most* distinguishing factors in each case. I insist on time to prepare a defense," Hayashi demanded.

"The order has been signed," Nakaya returned angrily. "And there is room for one more name at the bottom, if you care to protest again, and make yourself a part of their undistinguished conduct, and sentence?"

Hayashi bowed. "The defense humbly accepts the decree of the most honorable tribunal without protest. Justice has been served." The glum Hayashi sat, staring straight ahead. Karl faced the defender open mouthed, until a soldier took the prisoner under the arm and led him away. Hayashi drank from his water glass. What a bad day he was having! And, it was getting worse. His next case was an American.

* * *

"SERGEANT! The colonel is on the radio!" Blackwell called. "He told me to move the set somewhere the Madam couldn't overhear your conversation. I told him we had a headset, but he didn't care. So, I set it up in the galley. He's waiting on you now."

Hawk rushed into the kitchen and ordered the few idlers lingering there out of the room. Blackwell remained, easily able to hear the shouted conversation over the headset in the relatively quiet room.

"It looks like the Rossier woman is playing both sides of the fence, Sergeant. And that's with me giving her every benefit of the doubt," the colonel said. "She may just be on the wrong side of the fence. A lot of people are turning up, and they're talking about her. She's running a business there for her own profit. She gets along with whoever she has to get along with for her own good. Do not divulge to her, under any circumstances, the purpose or operation of our mission. Do you read me? Consider her a prisoner, not a rescue. Over."

Hawk looked at Blackwell. "Now, he says this shit? She knows every move we've made. Last time, he told me that he's sure she's dead."

Blackwell said nothing, as expected.

Hawk pressed the transmission bar. "Yessir, I got the message." Several thoughts ran through his head as he listened further to the colonel. *Had she in fact deceived him?*

"Good. We've run into some minor trouble. We have what looks like a problem with your escape route. At this stage, it doesn't look like we are going to be able to forestall the attack on the city, and you'll need to evacuate. Otherwise, you could end up on the wrong side of it. Have you ever heard of a Type 7, 30 centimeter Howitzer?" Over.

"Uh oh," said Blackwell under his breath.

"Not specifically, sir. I imagine it's an artillery piece. Over," Hawk replied, rubbing his hand roughly across his face as he waited for the other shoe to drop.

"Yes, and a big one. The shells weigh eight—nine hundred pounds. Got about a twenty-foot barrel. I would describe it as resembling a mortar. They only had four of them in the Philippines. Damned, if one of them hasn't turned up just south of you there on that route you took in, and it's blocking your way out. Something like that can easily sink a ship. In a way, this is a golden opportunity, and it's just good foresight that I kept you in reserve there. I knew I could put you to use somehow, in a forward position like that. We need you to get a handle on that gun. In fact, you or someone will have to get rid of the bastard before even considering getting you out of there. Read me? Over."

"Get rid of it...with what, sir? We don't have any explosives. We have a few hand grenades we could tape together. And some bazooka rockets. If we could get close to it. It must have a big crew. Over."

"No, no. A hand grenade isn't going to do anything to a chunk of iron that size. You'll have to utilize material you find at hand. My recommendation is to set off the ammunition they're using for it. Don't worry, we have a backup plan. If you cannot blow it, you have to get us an accurate location, so we can take it out by air. The main thing is *find* it. They fire it about once a day now. They're testing and waiting for some of the better targets of opportunity. We haven't been able to get a good reading on it. Spotter planes haven't seen anything in the general sector. Triangulation says it's in the grid

4ZVR, other than that it's like the damn thing is invisible. They can't hide a gun that big forever. Over."

Hawk did some fast thinking. "We haven't heard it. I recommend we locate it, report the location, and leave it alone, sir. We're not adequately equipped. We'll compromise our position here if we attack a big crew defending the gun. We can't get out of here after giving ourselves away. Over."

"That is *not* accurate. Overwhelming American forces are preparing to move into that sector right now. You will be able to intercept one of our units and link up. In any event, I am suggesting a hit-and-run operation, where you return to your current base there. You hit it, and you disengage. You do not stand and fight. My suggestions are subject to what you encounter on the ground. There are other ways to disable something besides explosives. I repeat, if you're afraid to attack it, get us the location. Simple as that. Over."

The ever-attentive Corporal Canlon entered the kitchen as the colonel spoke.

"Hey, is that Clark?" Joe asked, in his loudest, and stupidest voice. Blackwell and Hawk batted their hands at him angrily.

"We will lose our escape route, sir. Over," Hawk did a little repeating of his own, unsure if his message got through, due to the distracting entrance of Joe. Also due to Joe, his message was not as subtle as he would have preferred, upon further reflection. It came across as a bit desperate, rather than a plain statement of fact.

"You *have* no escape route. You *cannot* get yourself out of there, off that island, in the middle of a Nip held city. *We* have to get you out. Repeating. You are to locate the gun, disable the gun, if possible, record the location if it's not possible, and return to your base. Send six of your best men. If they disable it, they should be able to retreat in the confusion. We are not trying to engage the enemy any more than necessary. That's the Army's job. You were requisitioned a bazooka, as I recall? Over."

"We have it. It has a few bullet holes in it. Over," said Hawk, without enthusiasm.

"Sounds good. I have to shove off. You have all night to take care of it. You should have been able to hear the gun firing from there. You need to pay attention to your surroundings. Once they fire it again, you can get a fix on it. I'll check back with you in the morning. There is still no definite time set for a general attack on the city. Don't concentrate on those documents anymore, for now. The papers are probably not going to matter at this point. The priority is this gun, being set up on the coast along the bay, to sink some of our landing craft. Evacuating armies don't set up shore batteries. There is no actual beach in that sector, it's a swamp that blends gradually into the ocean. They've probably found a little solid ground in that maze to set the thing on. Find it, and good luck. Over and out."

"Man," said Joe, in the following silence. "That sounds like shit."

"We're gonna get trapped here," said Hawk, his fiery blue eyes burning through Joe as if he were not there. "Or, out there."

"But, it's like he said," Blackwell answered, "we're already trapped here. We can't get ourselves out."

"Man. We're trapped here, and we're gonna go way out there, even farther, stirring up shit, looking for some crazy thing," said Joe. "But don't worry, you got *all night*. And don't worry, you don't have to blow it up, you just have to disable it." Joe shook his head, looked down, and then quickly looked up at Hawk. "Who are you gonna send? I guess Baker could lead it," he hypothesized, managing to leave himself slightly above the pay grade of the suggested participant. "He's good at stupid shit like that."

"I'll lead it. What do you think?" Hawk answered. He sighed. "I gotta go out there and back before daylight. If they don't fire the bastard, I don't know how I'll ever find it."

"That didn't sound like what Clark said," Joe replied. "He said you're supposed to 'send' somebody. You're in charge here, you have to stay."

"Right," Blackwell agreed. "The colonel said six of your best men. If you yourself left, that would violate protocol."

"Like when I went out there and got Ulupong? I don't give a shit what he said," Hawk snapped, resigned to go on a deadly mission he considered ill advised. Welch flashed across his memory. Blackwell and Canlon discontinued the argument. The decision revealed no surprises, only typical James Hawk behavior. That did not make it right, or any less aggravating. Their only leader would be dueling with death in the unknown night, rather than staying here, securing their base of operations as it faced collapse. Joe put that part of the multifaceted problem aside for the moment.

"What about the bazooka? It sounded like he wanted you to hit the gun with the bazooka," said Joe.

"I don't know. It's full of holes. That tube is supposed to be a vacuum for a reason, and it ain't. The propellant might explode the barrel on us, or blow out all over us," said Hawk. "I don't know enough about it. I know I wouldn't shoot a rifle with holes in the barrel. I thought about using the rockets, though. If a bazooka rocket can crack it. He's giving us a lot to figure out here.

You need engineers for all this shit. Them guys can measure the power of an explosive, compared to what it has to explode. I'm just guessing, based on things I've seen. And my guess is that none of what we have will work."

"There's some gasoline cans out in the storeroom. They must have used it for a boat or something. You could try that. Those five-gallon things are kinda heavy to be luggin' around, though," said Joe.

Hawk rubbed his chin slowly. "Might try that. First, we have to find the son of a bitch. That might be as far as we get." He pulled out the map, shoved some cut vegetables aside with their cutting board, and spread it out on the wet counter. "Okay, here's the grid square, where he thinks it is. 4ZVR. That's one over from here, so it might take us an hour or two to reach it, dependin' on our Jap buddies out there. Then, it's two kilometers square, so God knows how long it'll take to bump into something like that in the dark." He blew out his breath. "I think we're gonna be out there a while. Awright. Let's rub some ashes on our face."

Joe and Blackwell sat stunned and speechless. The "let's" implied they had just been elected to be members of the latest of the colonel's risky ventures.

"What about the radio?" Blackwell asked, knowing Hawk would not carry it into this perilous situation, risking its loss; and also knowing, he himself went where the radio went.

"Leave it. Van Houten can handle it. I need you with us. In case, somebody has to tell Clark...the story." They did not miss the implication: in case somebody had *to live* to tell the story, and it would not be Hawk. Joe saw no reason for himself to be a part of the search, but he knew that he was going to be. Hawk must have grave misgivings about the venture, if he wanted the careful hand of Joe Canlon along.

* * *

HAYASHI MADE his way quickly toward the *Buntai*. He had a full day's work ahead of him. He had to be on time because his entire docket consisted of bad cases. He would be suspected of delaying the proceedings on purpose. All of his accused were Filipino partisans, and he had virtually no defense for them. It surprised him that they had not already been executed in the field. It never occurred to him that they were innocent, and had not come from any field. The streets were not as busy today, as most of the terrified civilians had already made their preparations for the invasion.

Hayashi hated losing. He knew his clients were enemies of the Empire, who had done awful things, but he still preferred winning his cases. He dreaded the day ahead of him. Commander Nakaya would be merciless. He feared one day the commander would carry through with his frequent, deadly threats against Hayashi, should a defense prove too zealous. Today, he had only zeal, and no law or facts at his disposal. He paused before the corporal at the door of the courthouse and straightened his uniform. The guard saluted the lieutenant.

"I am sure Commander Nakaya will be in fine form today," Hayashi joked with the corporal, before entering the lion's den.

"No, Lieutenant. Captain Nakaya is no longer stationed here," said the corporal. Hayashi showed his astonishment. This was like hearing Mount Fuji no longer resided in Japan. It could only mean the officer had been transferred to a unit assigned to defend the city, and very possibly Hayashi would be next.

"I hope he is well, and has received a promotion?" the lieutenant probed.

"No, sir. He has been shot, executed for treason last night."

Terror descended throughout Hayashi's chest and out to his extremities. He knew chaos had descended upon the city, but not to this stage. If a *Kempetai* commander could be shot for disloyalty, what would happen to him, a bold defender of the enemy? "But that is impossible," said Hayashi.

"No, sir. The rumor is he was discovered to have had a role in supporting the disappearance from custody of the most notorious Mademoiselle Rossier." The corporal leaned forward and whispered: "The new commander is not as nice."

* * *

As SOON AS twilight turned dark enough to safely cross the narrower side of the barge canal, Hawk led six men out of the Club. Their hulking shadows, lit from below by the water's surface, flickered larger than life across the walls, dwarfing the actual proportions of the real travelers, until they descended silently into the dirty canal. They waded along the course of the destroyed bridge, which once connected the shore to the island. The dappled shadows remained close to the broken supports of the span, still jutting from the water, to guide them along the shallowest route.

The patrol carried three bazooka rockets, five gallons of gasoline, a gasoline-filled whisky bottle with an oily rag in it, and several hand grenades. Not long after crossing the canal, as if fate smiled upon them, (or frowned upon them), they heard the thunderous report of the massive Howitzer in the distance. The ground shook.

"Shit. Can't be too far away," Joe said in a low voice. "I ain't heard *that* before. I don't know if I ever heard anything like that before."

"Too bad they didn't wait till we got closer," said Hawk. "We'll have a hard time finding it in the dark, if they don't fire it again. The damn thing sounds like it's everywhere."

The late January full moon had only slightly waned, leaving a good deal of illumination after the shifting eyes of the wary men became adjusted to the dark. While the light provided an advantage for traveling quickly, it also created a disadvantage as far as concealment. Each of them carried a silver outline of his figure with him, and they moved unsurely in the night, like wandering ghosts, drifting behind their more resolute leader. The powdery moonglow did not attach itself to Hawk, as he led them into a deeper, eternal darkness. He alone appeared to have no living soul to light him from within, or perhaps it was just that the brighter parts of the universe wanted nothing to do with him. In his natural element now, the deadly night, the other stalwarts followed his malevolent lead. Only on an outing such as this would anyone find any comfort in the presence of Sergeant Hawk.

Passing the outskirts of the shantytown, they followed the coast within the cover of the trees, some fifty yards from the ocean itself. The ease of tracing this route soon ended, however, when they encountered the swampland replacing the beach. The only advantage to the new and unwelcoming terrain lay in the assured absence of observers. The moon shrank smaller here, turning from silver to a jaundiced yellow in the fetid humidity. Competing tribes of reptiles and amphibians droned a grinding, rhythmic melody, covering the stealthy sound of humans passing through their thick, liquid domain. Wading in the waist-deep silt became a dubious task, there being no clear demarcation between swamp and the open ocean.

Hawk kept the men within the confines of the clawing trees, most of which appeared stunted, dead, or dying in the salty brine—knowing for certain at least some sort of earth lay beneath their boots, in order to support the withered trunks. A half mile away, back in the forest and running parallel to the jagged coast, lay the comparative comfort of the road they had first traveled by buffalo cart into the city. Hawk noted the proximity of the throughway, considering it a good means of retreat, or an alternative emergency exit, from this hair-triggered undertaking.

For now, however, he had to remain in the swamp and within the view of the ocean, if he wanted to ever locate the elusive Japanese gun. As long as they could see the bay in the darkness, they knew where they were. While the others may have thought of Hawk as one with the clandestine mission, Hawk himself actually disliked the whole operation. He considered it a remarkable stroke of bad luck to have been stationed in the vicinity of this hidden artillery piece. While Clark patted himself on the back for such a happenstance, Hawk kicked himself a little lower down the spine. The sergeant believed his men over matched by their lofty goal, though he understood the importance of the objective. More than anyone, James Hawk knew his limitations, as he usually found himself functioning along the edge of, or beyond them.

Dangers even greater than the obvious mounted against the odds for success. While a gun of such size could have a crew of well over a hundred troopers to be dealt with, the entire Japanese infantry roamed about as well, their lines moving with fluid urgency, preparing for the imminent American attack. All of the enemy activity necessarily attracted the interest of numerous groups of Filipino partisans, combining to make the murky coastline a boiling cauldron of murderous intentions, through which the Americans had to pass as unobtrusively as possible. Many of the partisans were little more than adolescents, dashing boldly about with quick and unrestrained bravado. Hawk could only hope the reported intentions of Yamashita to retreat toward the north contained some truth and that things would remain relatively calm here—at least for the next few hours. He had no aversion to shooting his way out of a tight spot, but this situation had the potential at every step to engulf his patrol with something more than they could handle.

Hawk called a halt after more than an hour of walking the tense tightrope between muddy swamp and lapping ocean—a stark portrayal of the real devil and the deep blue sea.

The precise dividing line was a matter of judgment as to where the sluggish marsh surface ended, and the gyrating surface of the bay began. The small ocean waves looked like thousands of little pointed tents, with their tent poles constantly pushed up and down by carousels of manic creatures under the water. Sometimes the first row of these watery tents extended right into the shade of the trees, sometimes they remained bashfully out in the open bay.

"This is the about the border of the grid square, and we ain't seen nothing," Hawk announced in a half-whisper. "I ain't seen a place you could put a big gun. It has to have a steel base to swivel on, and they usually stick them in concrete." He wrestled with his map and took out his flashlight. The others fidgeted uneasily, listening to the eternal breathing of the wide ocean and smelling salt and dead sea life. "Clark could've been wrong. It might be farther along, in the next sector."

"It's got to be back toward the road, on solid ground," said Joe. "We probably passed it."

"Might have," Hawk answered. "Or it could still be up ahead a little. Epley, you go on farther and see what's up there. We're halfway around the bay, the terrain's gotta change soon. Maybe things will be more solid. We'll wait here. Then we'll double back, halfway between here and the road, and give the dry ground another going over, just for old Uncle Joe here."

"It would be easier to follow the road," said Joe. "And anyway, the thing has to be close to the road to bring in the ammo. Hauling stuff through the brush around here is too hard. You can't be manhandling all that heavy shit in this mush. What good is us walking in this?"

"A little water ain't hurting you none. Might get rid of some of that funky rotted hay odor." Hawk turned off the flashlight. "We'll see. We'll check it all. Ain't got nothin' but time. Take off, Epley."

"How far do I go?" Epley asked.

Hawk looked out over the ocean, the gentle wave tops winking with glittering reflections of a lunar sheen across the protective bay. The peaceful scene helped him think. "Give it twenty minutes. It'll take you another twenty to get back. That's far enough. That'll take you just into the next sector. If it's not there, we passed it. It'd be nice if the son of a bitches would test it again."

"It probably takes over an hour to load it," said Joe. "And it's a lot of work. They don't want to waste those big rounds. Japs are real cheap, you know. They ain't got America sending them scrap iron anymore."

Epley moved off, waiting to hear no more of their theories or any newly assigned duties. Going alone through this abyss, even for only twenty minutes, made for as unwelcome an ordeal as he cared to shoulder.

Hawk chewed silently on tobacco, trying to formulate any plan providing some hope for success. The others talked in low voices. Joe expressed various ideas of his own, after each man muttered an opinion. Hawk wished he had brought Baker instead of Joe. Joe thought too much. He originally wanted him along for his sense of caution, but Hawk didn't want this much caution. It did not help any that the corporal posed fairly logical theories and misgivings. Joe was indisputably good at figuring out what could go wrong. Hawk didn't really need that right now. Baker was better at finding solutions. He could always come up with something, even if it involved an idea as suicidal as jumping on a rotating pump blade.

"Shut up," Hawk finally interjected.

Epley returned in twenty minutes, instead of forty minutes.

"There's something up there, all right," Epley said. "There's Japs talking and messing around with something. It looks like it might be a pier going out into the water. I didn't want to get into the middle of them. It sounded like a bunch of them. We can't get by them."

"No gun?" Hawk asked.

"Not that I saw," Epley answered. "Just Japs. All the Japs you'd ever want."

"It don't sound like what we're after," said Hawk. "The bastards are right in our way, too. I guess we better check it out, it might have some connection." He looked at the map. "This would be a good place for something, the way the coast dips in, if they just had some solid ground around here. It's probably hard to get a good view of this area from the air." Hawk held his breath for a moment. "This place reminds me of Louisiana." He looked at Joe.

"I say turn around and go down the damn dry road," Joe said quickly.

"What the hell for? Just ease your ass out of gear." Hawk raised a hand. "I have to know what's up there. Whatever it is, it's in a bad spot. If we have to evacuate our base at the Club, we'll have to come back this way, and deal with it then anyway. We gotta check it out a little better." Joe said nothing. It didn't sound like the location of the gun to him, from Epley's report. Hawk waded slowly into the darkness.

"What if you don't come back?" Joe called after him.

"Go back down the road." Hawk smiled to himself in the dark.

The sergeant soon heard enemy voices and smelled cigarettes before he saw anything. He slid farther into the trees for concealment and away from the edge of the open ocean. He spotted what Epley had called a pier, but it did not look like a pier to him. A low and narrow shadow extended a few feet out into the ocean. The surface of the coastal swamp water grew shallower, making him feel more exposed. Hawk crouched as he walked, holding the submachine gun in front of himself with one hand, and clutching the passing branches for support with the other, lest he stumble in one of the many holes in the swamp floor. Mud grabbed his boots, trying desperately to make him fall and create a disruption. Fish and frogs jumped up and plopped down on all sides.

He halted when he came to a cleared area. At first, he saw little evidence of the enemy. He heard them, however, and knew he had encountered a sizable camp. The sound of metal sliding upon metal drifted across the open space, along with the grunts of great exertion. Hawk settled his elbows in the fork of a wet tree, and stood waiting for the appearance of something to explain the noise. The shadows of half a dozen shirtless men appeared, bent over, and pushing a heavy object with great effort. It rested on a low tram, which rolled with a grudging squeal on strained rails.

Hawk noted the relevance. A man could not carry an eight-to-nine-hundred-pound artillery shell around, in order to load it into the big gun. Several men would have to roll the damned thing or operate a crane to lift it. He also noted all of the struggling by the Japanese took place on solid ground. The proximity of the enemy caused no fear in the American observer, only the old raging anger that possessed him every time he met them. He suppressed his overpowering, crocodilian instinct to empty a .45 magazine into the soulless targets. He knew he had to think clearly—humanly—in order to understand the operation here, and thwart it. He had not actually seen an artillery round yet; or more importantly, a gun to fire it.

The watcher pulled his arms from the fork of the

tree and crept closer to the road, still under the cover of the damp, dragging tree limbs. He sought the dry ground that the enemy soldiers made use of, and ultimately found it. On the ground, next to his soaked boots, he saw two narrow gauge parallel rails. He drew back and away from the rails, going to his knees first and then lying down. The steel path ran toward the ocean.

How could that be? Sufficient room did not exist for a gun emplacement between him and the ocean. Were they hiding their cargo under the water? Had the giant gun been set up back toward the road? It certainly wasn't here. None of it made sense. He could not imagine what they were up to. He had to get closer to the point where the rails intersected the ocean to understand the reason for such a watery destination.

Going closer to the bay required unimaginable nerve. Due to the foresight of the United States government, the backwaters of that great pioneering nation had been scoured, and the individual with the right evolutionary qualifications had been placed at the scene. What would seem an insane course of action to anyone else, struck Hawk as perfectly acceptable. It didn't mean he liked the looks of it any more than a normal person would, it only meant he would readily do it. He crawled along the rutted ground, and over the rails to the other side, as might any other nerveless reptile.

Trucks and heavy equipment had left evidence of their passage in the soft earth. His slithering over, along, and through the ruts resulted in a thorough mud bath. The caked patina of wet earth only served to greater conceal him. A shout from the darkness, off to the left, caused him to freeze in place. Other voices answered.

Sweat poured down Hawk's earth-covered face. The damp layering over his body only augmented the heat being generated within him, like a blanket. He paused in the middle of a shouted conversation. Recovering his sense of purpose, he continued crawling toward the ocean, moving steadily in the same direction as the rails.

He crawled over iron equipment that he knew from experience represented a pile driving frame, lying unassembled and horizontal on the ground. Anyone unfamiliar with construction would have thought it a discarded derrick of some sort, and given it little thought. He didn't give it a lot of thought, but he could identify it from personal experience, and it would later help him to solve the puzzle of the Japanese intentions.

He darted over the top of the iron frame, his eyes focused on the men moving around the halted tram in front of him. He looked back to see dripping mud scraped over the metal where he had passed. He heard newer voices arriving behind him. Footsteps approached. He was in the middle of these rotten bastards. The incomprehensible words were so close they dominated his eardrums, drowning out the sighing of the bay and the love calls of the swamp creatures. He slunk desperately against the horizontal iron derrick. The openings in the latticework were too finely spaced to squeeze into, but his tense body tried mightily to do so as he pressed against it. He was certain whoever was coming had to see him. But, as it happened, when they did, they saw nothing more than a darker shadow in the lighter shadows around them, and even that, only in their peripheral vision as they passed by the American. They had looked directly at him and seen nothing. He nonetheless flipped the safety off his weapon and prepared for flight toward the road, or at worst, a fight to the finish right here.

The two passing soldiers joined the others along the little railway, giving no sign of having discovered him. Fast talking and laughs followed, restoring Hawk's peace of mind. All of the enemy workers slowly drifted away from the presumed artillery round resting on the tram car and appeared to be retracing their route along the rails, which led to the road in the tree-shrouded distance.

After a minute, Hawk allowed himself to take a breath. He pushed the safety on again. He reached for his pocket and the block of chewing tobacco. Steadily, his hands lifted it to his mouth and he bit off a large portion. He considered abandoning his investigation. Things were getting a little tight around the seams here. It looked quiet down toward the water, and this served as an irresistible temptation for him. Like a compulsive gambler, who cannot admit his winning streak is over, he crawled onward, beside the rails and toward the bay itself.

He did not have the self-awareness to know this madness was his *raison d'etre*. The powerful rush of adrenaline saturating his body created an addictive euphoria that would make it impossible for him to ever give up this kind of life in the future—if he had a future. There was a good deal of heroism in it, of course, but some of it was merely the lowly burglar's fascination with his power over the belongings of someone else. In spite of all of that rush, however, Hawk was supremely aware of a desire to avoid getting shot full of holes. The rat seeks only the cheese, not the spring-loaded trap across his neck.

As he neared the water, he discovered a tarpaulin

had been draped across the rails. He could think of no purpose for doing this, consistent with construction practices in general. It did not serve as protection for the tram, only the rails themselves. Who worried about rails getting wet? What did the tarp conceal? He looked over his shoulder. All remained quiet behind him. He heard no other voices or footsteps. He lifted the tarp. As he suspected, beneath it lay only the rails. His hand felt oily and slick. He held his hand under the tarp, and taking his flashlight in his other hand, flashed the light on the oily hand. Blue paint, melted by salt water, covered his fingers.

The rails led directly into the bay, but a protective barrier had been built on either side of them, holding back the water in some sort of drydock. He lay the submachine gun on the tarp and slid into the jostling waves. Holding the top of the barrier dam, he followed it deeper into the water, until it rose chest high. A blue tarp still covered the top of it. He ran his hand under the water, feeling the protective wall before him, smooth and metallic, and implanted in the ocean floor. He ran his hand along the top of it, and noticed a different, rougher surface on the inside of the barrier. He pieced the puzzle together now.

The outer part of the barrier consisted of flat steel pilings, and the inner palisade was made of wood. The enemy had constructed a cofferdam here, with the pile driving equipment he had found on the shore. The rails ran on a dry bed right into the bay, in an area already well concealed by trees and the natural lay of the land. The blue tarps covered the top of the dam as it ran into the open water, camouflaging it to look more like the ocean's surface from the air.

"Crazy bastards," he whispered.

He looked out across the bay. A companion wall had to be on the other side of where he stood. He could not see how far this odd structure extended, but he knew what it meant. Somewhere, out there in the bay, lay the gun at the bottom of a wider cofferdam. No sooner had he made this discovery, than other thoughts flooded in. Being James Hawk, they were not thoughts of wonder at the engineering ingenuity employed by all of this. His thoughts were only of the structure's vulnerability to immediate destruction.

The frustrating part of the speculation was that he could not do the destroying. It should be a simple matter to breach the wall of joined beams at some point, breaking the seal, and putting an end to the relatively frail house of cards. But he wasn't going to be the one to do it, with hand grenades and a whisky bottle full of gasoline. If the demolition were to be accomplished tonight, a generous contribution of explosives would be required from the Empire of Japan, and it had already turned the lights out at the company store. He decided the matter required greater thought, and the thinking should be done elsewhere.

Easing out of the water and recovering the Thompson, he peered around the dam at the point where the rails descended into the partitioned off bay. There on the tram car, where the crew had pushed it by hand, lay parked a large cylindrical shadow. He felt along the top of it, to allow for certain identification. It resembled two oil drums lying lengthwise together. He knew one oil drum weighed about four hundred pounds and a thing this size could easily weigh eight hundred, commensurate with the dimensions given him by Colonel Clark. The presence of the shell only confirmed his assumption as to the whereabouts of the gun.

12

THE PAGES IN A BOOK

HAWK RETRACED HIS ROUTE OVER THE DERRICK AND THE rails, and back into the swamp. Once there, he heard the growl of trucks, drifting from the road, not so far away. The sound of an army on the move closed around him. He heard large numbers of men marching, with occasional shouts carrying back through the low brush and sparse stands of trees. Wherever the well-organized juggernaut came from, it now headed toward Manila, guaranteeing a great confrontation in the making, with Club Arashigaoka resting directly in its path.

"There goes our way out," Hawk said to himself. "Joe ain't gonna like that." He wound his way through the moonlight splattered mire, until challenged by the voice of Moreno, and he quickly answered. The men gathered around him.

"Took you a while," said Joe.

"Yeah. I found the damned thing," Hawk said. Several grunts of approval followed. "It's kind of a... buncha shit. They got it down in a hole, out in a cofferdam in the middle of the bay. We used to build them things in the Mississippi. It ain't no small-time operation." A stunned silence followed the revelation of the unexpected development. Astonishment had not been the intent of the Japanese, of course, their object being concealment. The intricate scheme had now been exposed, *if* the seven Americans in the swamp lived to tell the tale. "They drove piling all around it, and laid rails down into it."

"How can they do that?" Epley asked. "Won't water be inside it?"

"Once it's built and dammed up, you pump the water out and let it dry. They must have started on this a hell of a long time ago. I saw one of the shells for the gun, too. It's...big," Hawk continued. "And, a little bad news about the road. Their whole army is moving down it. They'll probably beat us back to town, because they have trucks."

Joe cursed. "We gotta go back through all this mud and shit again?"

"Yeah—if we're lucky—and if we have anything to go back to. Baker is gonna shit. Are the Japs going toward our army or running from it? I tried to come up with a way to shut down the gun, but I don't think we got what it takes. We need a pack charge, or a bunch of them, to crack this levee thing. It's double-walled. Looks like it ain't our night."

"How come they can't see all this from the air?" Hobby asked.

"It's in the curve of the bay, and trees hang out for a ways, but mainly, they got blue tarps strung over the top of it, to look like the color of the water. I imagine you can see it, but you would probably have to know it's there." Hawk lit a cigar. "Finding it was our job. We did it. I guess we're done here, boys."

"We could swim out to it, and throw a grenade inside," Moreno offered. Joe cringed. He did not like encouraging Hawk with stupid ideas.

"Could do that." The sergeant nodded. "It might kill the crew right there in the hole with it, but it ain't gonna do much to the gun. Then they'll know we're here, and that we found it. That ain't scientific enough, to suit me."

"How about if we could shoot one of those big rounds in the ass," Moreno continued, "bust it like a firing pin?"

"And blow a hole the size of Cincinnati in the shoreline, with us in it," said Hobby. Joe nodded approval at Hobby's rebuttal.

"I don't believe that would do it," said Hawk. "It ain't like a bullet. The explosive, and the fuse and timer, and *all* that shit, is in the nose of them things."

"Not always," Lawson said.

"Then shoot the nose," said Moreno. *What's with this guy?* Joe thought. *Is he in a hurry to see St. Peter? That's the problem with this Marine Corps thing, you get all these uncouth son of a bitches in one place.*

"I don't know," Hawk answered. "This round is big, and it's got a thick skin. It would take a lot to blow it. The weight of it falling out of the sky onto the nose is what trips it. I imagine a bullet might just bounce off. And tell the Japs we're here."

Lawson, who had five gallons of gasoline strapped to his back, spoke hesitantly. "We could set it on fire. Heat would do it. I heard of an ammo dump going off in a fire."

"Trucks go up all the time with a little fire," said Moreno. "And we got these bazooka rockets. They told those guys in training that one of them went off when somebody just dropped it out of the tube."

Hawk removed his helmet and let it float in the water. He rubbed his face vigorously, unintentionally removing most of his makeshift ash camouflage and some topsoil. "Maybe y'all are right. But the way I see it, we ain't got enough gasoline to get it hot enough. It'd burn itself out in a couple minutes. I've seen them bazooka rockets get shot without ever doing nothing. That's one of them things that only happens when you don't want it to happen. You can't be countin' on shit like that in the middle of a bunch of goddam Japs."

Joe liked the way the conversation tended. It was his turn to contribute. "Like you say, we need some satchel charges. Dynamite, plastic, fuses, and detonators. We can go back, and maybe they can airdrop us something." Joe stressed the key phrase: *go back*.

"Yeah," Hawk agreed, but still sounding reluctant. "Coming back for it would be up to the colonel. It won't be as easy next time, with all them son of a bitches moving around out there. I'm startin' to wonder about the Yamashita withdrawal business. Looks to me like he might be withdrawing in the wrong direction. Where are all of them coming from? Where the hell is our Army?" Hawk took out his map and turned on his flashlight. He rummaged in his pocket for a pencil and began writing on the map. Joe noticed he wrote on the blank, back side of. it The intense scribbling went on for a while.

"What are you doing? Writing your will?" Joe asked.

"Yeah. I'm leavin' you Colonel Clark." Hawk kept writing. "Be sure and kick him in the ass twice a day.

Helps his digestion." He began tearing the bottom of the map into pieces. He handed each man a piece. "Now, listen up, y'all. I gave you the coordinates to the gun location. Keep it outta the water. Try to memorize it. At least one of us has to get this back to the radio, and tell Clark. A lot is riding on it. One shot from the giant piece of shit could sink a ship and kill a thousand men, see? It's important. If battalion tells you, 'but them numbers is out in the bay,' tell 'em the whole story. Say, that's right, that's exactly where it is."

"What do you mean, *one* of us?" Joe asked. "We're splittin' up?"

Hawk sighed. "Not yet. But I ain't gonna tell you no boot camp fairy tales. One of us gets shot up, we carry him. Four of us, five of us, happen to be shot up, it gets a little different. All kind of shit can come to pass here, buddy. Somebody's gotta get these numbers back to the radio. No matter what."

A solemn pause followed. No one cared to express any ideas on this point—to Hawk, at least. As grim as it sounded, however, Joe decided the splitting up scenario was ten times better than Moreno's idea of trying to 'bust' one of the rounds with a bullet. That was a disaster of the more instantaneous variety—even if it worked.

"Like Joe said, they might be sendin' us back out here to blow the bastard," Hawk added. "This ain't over. I don't think the Japs are gonna leave their army parked around the gun like it is now, not after going to so much trouble to hide it. All them men and equipment only draws attention to it. They're just passin' through. But for right now, they're a *major* pain in the ass." He dropped the cigar and it hissed in the water. "Let's shove off."

Hawk quickly waded beyond their sight. Epley's wide eyes met those of Joe Canlon. Joe smiled and slapped him on the back. "Don't worry, kid. I ain't gonna leave you behind. He's just talkin' shit. That's how those crackers are. It's all that inbreeding. They can't tell the horses and cows from the people."

Epley wasn't sure if Joe was right. He knew he felt a stronger bond with Joe at the moment, one he did not feel with the obsessed Hawk. Joe represented the Marine Corps. Hawk stood for his own idea of the Marine Corps. Men like Hawk could not be a part of anything. All of the rumors about Hawk's viciousness came back to Epley; about how the sergeant had been a criminal, and rules meant nothing to him. While Epley had been playing adolescent team sports in high school, he recalled others, dirty vagabonds, like Hawk, hanging out at the trainyards stealing freight. It bothered Epley. He did not like being subject to the power of such a man. Not here, not now.

Epley knew that his mother, his pastor, the town council, his football coach, and even the Commandant of the Marine Corps, would not approve of his being subject to this man. Rayburn certainly would not have approved of the idea of splitting up. But then, Rayburn was a thief; and a *bastard*. Of course, Epley was only half right; as true as it was that Hawk had never been a team player, he had also never been in high school, or had the luxury of a freight yard to steal from. Epley had no frame of reference with which to even imagine the elemental background of a James Hawk.

The patrol stayed as close to the ocean, and as far from the road as it could, much as it had on the journey out. The return promised to be routine, until they spotted a bright light knifing through the trees ahead of them, illuminating the intricate patches of wet roots and bark; making them whiter than the noonday sun. Broken streams of the slashing brilliance lanced deep into the forest, made sharper by the shadows of the branches. Hawk dropped into the water until only his eyes and helmet were visible. The others followed suit, half of them saturating the written gun coordinates newly conferred upon them.

"Goddamn patrol boat, out in the ocean. Stay down, they cain't see us up in here," Hawk advised them. The searchlight jerked back and forth, high and low, every motion creating uncomfortable sensations in the bowels of the men hiding in the water. The disturbing brightness produced an occasional opened eye from the countless sleeping birds. Hundreds of little red orbs reflected the piercing shaft from the searchlight. The Americans heard the calm and idle chatter of the crew on the nearby boat as they swung the powerful lamp around.

The Japanese had cut the engine, leaving only the sound of the lapping of the tame bay waves against the bouncing hull. For that reason, the Americans had received no warning of the approach of the enemy craft. The prevailing silence and the dancing, blinding brilliance, combined for a chilling effect. Hawk rose to a crouch and motioned for the others to follow him. He veered away from the boat and toward the road, the dry ground, and the sheltering darkness in that direction.

After a few minutes, Hawk spoke. "We come close to running into that son a bitch. We might not be as lucky next time. They're watching the coast, and they might be watching the road. They could know something."

"I thought the Jap column was on the road," Joe said.

"Why are we going that way?" Hawk stopped and turned around impatiently. He reached for his canteen.

"Have you ever seen a compass? How many different directions do you figure we got left to go here?" Hawk asked, tilting his head back for a drink.

When they came to the highway, they did not hear the approaching column. Trucks on the open road should have already outdistanced them and reached this point by now. Hawk peered from the high stalks of grass at the edge of the empty road. The stalks closest to the highway were covered in powdery dust, and it wasn't long before the men were as well.

"They must have stopped," said Hawk, pulling back into the concealment of the grass. "Maybe they set up camp for the night. I thought they were making a night move. Maybe not."

"They could have turned off on another road," said Lawson.

"The only other road showin' on the map is this here Highway 17," said Hawk. "It's paved and farther to the east. I figure they'll stay off it. There's nothing else big enough for them."

"What do you expect from a Standard Oil map?" said Joe. "Let's take this road and get the hell out of here. It can't be much farther to the Club. If they went off and took the paved highway, we'll have clear sailing." Joe's idea made sense this time. The wide, dry, and quiet path stretched before them was too inviting to pass up.

"Stay along the side of it, so we can jump in the weeds if something comes along," said Hawk. "Drop that gas can back there in the brush. We may just be able to do a little double time along here."

After navigating the dark and unfamiliar roadway, the sight of the barge canal appeared like a haven of safety to the patrol members. Upon reaching the Club, and its radio, Hawk did not wait for the colonel to contact him. When they contacted battalion, however, Clark turned out to be unavailable.

"He's sawin' logs," Joe commented, a little bitter his own night had been exhausting, among other things. Hawk delivered the coordinates of the gun to the radioman on the other end, with the instruction to get the information to the colonel as soon as possible. Hawk thought it worthwhile to repeat the purpose and urgency of their mission, and what the coordinates meant. He stressed that his men were unable to disable the gun and detailed its unique location. It was much easier to deliver the information, without having to debate matters with the colonel, but it was also difficult to tell if the radioman on the other end was getting it all.

Blackwell turned off the radio, saving the battery. "I ain't real happy with that, but it's all we can do for now," said Hawk. "Let's get some shuteye. I think the shit's gonna hit the fan tomorrow. The Jap column must be coming into the city somewhere and going down to the harbor. They might do some sightseeing in our direction. Leave the radio on."

About the time Hawk fell asleep, Blackwell awakened him, with news that the colonel waited for him on the radio. Someone must have thought the incoming message important enough to wake the colonel.

"Good job, Sergeant." Clark sounded a little weak this morning. "What's this about the gun being out in the bay? Did you know those coordinates are out in the ocean? Why didn't you do something out there? Over."

"It is out in the ocean, sir. The coordinates are accurate. The gun is in a cofferdam. We didn't have anything that could crack all the steel and wood beams with us. It was too dark to find any enemy materiel to blow it. The Jap army is moving into the area and was all around it at the time. We think they were headed toward the city, but we lost track of them somewhere in the dark. There were ocean patrol boats. It's getting crowded in that sector. And around here. But where the gun is sitting will be wide open to an air strike. I didn't want to let the Japs know we knew about it, by pulling some botched job on it. Over." Clark waited a minute before answering.

"Yeah, okay. Good call. Maybe. They're telling me now that we can get it by air. Maybe. They're moving some ships in with aircraft. It might work out. Did you ever find those damn documents I sent you out there for in the first place? Over?"

Hawk looked darkly at Joe and Blackwell. Now, the documents were back on the table? "No, sir. We just got back. Over."

"Yeah. Okay. See what you can do. Try to stow the excuses next time. Some things have happened here tonight. We're getting information indicating the Jap army is moving up behind you. I believe this definitely rules out the evacuation of Manila as an open city. And *you* are...temporarily...cut off. We can't get to you right now. You have no escape route. The order for now is stand and hold until we can get to you. Maybe we'll know more after the gun is taken care of. We definitely can't be jeopardizing that operation yet. You'll just have to wait. Over."

Hawk clenched his teeth. "Aye, aye, sir. Over." Another one-minute pause followed.

"All right, Hawk. Try a little harder out there. I know you aren't as helpless as you act. Get on the ball. Good luck. Over and out."

"Stand and hold?" Joe repeated. "*Son of a bitch!*" He stood. "What is this? The Alamo?"

"Well, we don't have too many places to run anyway. But I think I'd rather take my chances hiding out in the swamp, and in the grass, down there, instead of sitting here," said Hawk.

"Me, too," said Blackwell. "Are we gonna run for it? It wasn't so bad out there. They'll never be searching that swamp for anything. They're busy doing other stuff. Boats can't get into the marsh, where we were. We proved we can get through there. We could just find a place to hide out and wait. This place sticks out like a sore thumb, in the middle of a big stupid river."

Hawk looked at him. "Stand and hold, kid." Blackwell and Joe both started talking loudly at once, each becoming more excited as the volume increased. Hawk raised a hand at the incomprehensible babble of noise. "Hang on, hang on. *Shit!* I'm in charge here. We can... reassess...the situation, if we have to. Right now, we can't take a chance on screwing up them planes bustin' up the gun, like the colonel done said. I wouldn't get my heart set on heading into the swamp back there, either. We might could get through it, awright, if we could get to it. But there's a Jap army on the other side of the bayou out there by now, between us and it. All we proved is that we're stuck on this island."

* * *

AN UNUSUALLY RELUCTANT dawn approached as Hawk slumped in the big chair opposite Eugenie. He watched her staring at him. *What is she thinking? I don't get her.* She did not look panicked by any of the developments he had just explained to her. He supposed being a prisoner of the *Kempetai* could make other things less alarming by comparison.

Finally, she spoke. "I can save you," she said. "And you can help me." She came around the desk and in one swift motion, suddenly sat on his lap. "You are frightened?"

"Uh, no more than usual, I reckon. But I gotta do right by the men down there. The colonel is putting us on the spot here, and me, especially. Everybody's gettin' a little high-strung. We're used to playing the waiting game, but not behind the Jap lines. There's a *lot* of Japs out there, baby, and the lines are changing places every minute. They got wheels."

She began to stroke his hair and hum a low song. "I can save the men for you as well. You have nothing to fear. Have you heard this song?" He listened to the soothing tune for perhaps longer than he should have. He didn't particularly like music, but he liked her voice.

"I don't think so. I don't follow songs much...and all," he said. His fingers tapped steadily on the arm of the chair and to a quicker beat than the time of the tune.

"You wouldn't know it, then. It is French, a song from the streets, from the people. Music has been my life. I am always singing to someone, but no one sings to me. It is very sad, don't you think? Life is so sad. We get so little of what we want from it." Her long, flare bell sleeve brushed his face.

"What's the purpose of that?" he asked, pushing the sleeve away. "Looks like it would be aggravating as hell, getting in the way of stuff."

"It is elegant. It is not part of the traditional Mandarin gown, it is my addition—my genius. You must sacrifice, to be a genius. Is that not true?"

"They wouldn't let you work in a war plant with them things."

"The sleeves? They worry you too much." She reached under a fold and unsnapped the sleeve, and then the other one. "You see, they can be taken off when necessary." She lay them aside. "Now, I can work in the war plant. And wash the dishes here, when my song is over. We have saved the world." She brushed his face with her bare arm. She began singing again, and he stopped tapping his fingers. Unmarked time passed. Time, that could be spent doing...something.

"You're putting me to sleep. I guess I better get out of here."

"Not yet. You haven't heard what I have to say to you."

"I didn't? Aw'ight, shoot."

"First, you must sing to me. You love me, don't you? You will sing for me because you love me. No one sings to me. But you will do it."

"I don't exactly sing for nobody," he replied. "I don't know no songs to sing. I ain't the musically inclined."

"As a child, no one sang to you? You never learned songs in school? You have never been to a concert?"

"I didn't go to school much. I always turned off the radio, when the singers came on. How about cadence, you know what that is?"

"You forgot what I asked—what about as a child? No one sang you to sleep? You heard no songs at Christmas?"

"No, if there was anyone around, they put me to sleep with a boot upside the head. I guess I do remember hearing *Silent Night* a time or two. Somewhere."

"Only *Silent Night*?" She looked toward the faint

glare of the rising sun through the open door and the bedroom window. "I am afraid that the sentiment is inappropriate for us. We are deprived of heavenly peace. You know no others?"

"I know some of *God Bless America*," he said.

"Because it fuels your martial spirit? There will be plenty of time for that. Anything else?"

"There was this spiritual, I kind of remember people singing. I don't know many of the words. Like I say, me and music really never jived."

"Ah. A spiritual? Like a folksong of the people from your homeland? This should interest me. I am of the people, too, you see? You don't know the words because you never listened. The melody is enough without the words. I understand the language of music, in here," she touched her breast. "You must try to have a heart. It is hard to live without a heart, but even harder to die. You must try, for me."

"Okay, but I really gotta shove off." He answered impatiently. "It was called, *I Wonder What They're Doing in Heaven Today*."

"Let me hear the melody. Your voice is so deep, from your chest. You are like a horse. In many ways."

"Yeah. I've heard that mentioned. Especially in the Marine Corps," he smiled. "The part of the horse that don't do the calculatin'. Now, that I think about it, I don't know the melody, either." He shifted nervously. "I gotta get going. Looks like a bad day ahead of us."

"Ah, I was just becoming serene. But of course, nothing lasts. Then, for business. Now, I shall save you. Your colonel is trying to kill you. You know this?"

Hawk laughed his raw, tobacco-soured laugh. "I've had some suspicions along that line."

"*Mais non—he is*," she insisted, raising her eyebrows.

"So, you will listen to me. The case, with my property in it, you will be sure to take it with you when you leave here?"

"I gotta real short answer for that one, sugar, because I don't have your satchel," said Hawk. "Sorry, if you don't believe me."

"That is not the issue for now. Do not argue that with me. You *will* have it when you go. It will leave here, because no one would leave it behind. Leaving it is not logical. There are valuables in it. The one who keeps it hidden now will take it out, and no one can get past you. Everyone is afraid of you."

Hawk laughed again. "Yeah, except maybe the emperor."

"You underestimate your power. Everyone respects a brute, even if they will not admit it. Listen to me. You remember the *Kempetai* station, the one I showed you? Where we heard the executions taking place? There is an unfortunate family there, and they are trying to escape Manila. They have fled hopelessly around the world. They have been condemned to die and will be executed behind the *Buntai* courthouse sometime within the next two days."

Hawk looked up, brought out of his pressing thoughts by the introduction of the totally irrelevant story. "Yeah? Why?" he asked, although not especially interested. "Filipino? Americans?"

"No, they are...German. There are many charges against them, but they all come down to one, really: they are Jewish. It is especially sad because there are young children. You may reach them through the tunnel I showed you. Two nights from now, a river barge will be waiting for them, also at the place where I showed you. Here, is the unsolved part of my problem.

It is the last part—so, you pay close attention, and don't act stupid with me. Only a complete madman would be able to remove the family from the hands of the *Kempetai*." She smiled broadly. This was not the somber face in the portrait. "Now. Tell me. Do you recognize *your* part in this passion play?"

"Uh..." She put a finger across his lips.

"There will not be many soldiers there. Your men can overpower them. You will tell the pilot of the barge my name, and he will direct you aboard. He will take you down the canal to the harbor, where by that time, your people will have already occupied a large portion of it. I know this. Once you cross your lines, you will be safe. You will give the family my case and its contents. All of your lives will be spared, and all of the lives of your men. If you stay here, you will all die. And the family will be executed. You may not think you will die here, now, on this quiet morning. It will not be this quiet for long. By then, you will understand better, and forget this colonel. So many of the Japanese will come, and they will be so bloodthirsty, you will have a clear understanding of my meaning."

"How did you set all this up? You ain't been nowhere."

"There are ways to do anything. You have been listening to colonels for too long, who tell you that you can do nothing, and nothing can be done."

"Right. Was it Ulupong?"

"Ulupong is despised. But he can do things no one else can do. You, more than anyone, should appreciate this as a virtue?"

"Yeah, that's for sure. But the thing is, I can't just go around doing whatever I want. I could run the story past the for you, I guess..."

"*No!* He will refuse. He does not care about the family. Or me. Or *you*," she said angrily. "He wants you to stay here and burn. You must forget this...this colonel...this saluting, this walking back and forth funny game...this trinkets on the shoulders. This is only a man, a bad and stupid man, lusting for more trinkets."

"Yeah, well, I mean, like if they were Americans, or resistance fighters, or something, I could probably do something. See, I'm in charge of these men down there. Me, the colonel, we're parts of this...thing. I can't risk their lives on something like that. Stuff like that has... you know...repercussions."

"All of a sudden, you know the big words! I told you, you are strong enough to overpower the Japanese there. If you stay here, you will die. That is your *repercussion*. You are not strong enough to withstand an army, the army coming here to Arashigaoka. Whatever you have seen, wherever you have been, you have never seen an army of such size."

"Well, maybe not, but there's a lot to this...why do you care about this one bunch, with everybody about to die in truckloads around here?"

"Has anyone ever done anything for you? Have you ever been grateful for help when you needed it most?" She shook his arm roughly, hoping to bring out some tender emotion she knew in her heart was not within him.

"What are you talking about? Ain't nobody never done shit for me. Them cards ain't in the deck, baby."

"Yes, I know. We are alike in that. But once in my life, when I was very small, the grandfather of this man I am sending you to, was kind to my father in Europe. I owe no living person anything—but there is this man and his family. I must do something for him because of his grandfather."

"I imagine grandpa's dead by now," said Hawk. "Put up your checkbook."

"No one who does good is ever dead," she said. "That is why we are here. This is our chance. Yours and mine. We have come thousands of miles through two lifetimes to this place to do this. For them. The young."

"That's another thing that don't ever come my way—chances. I can't do it."

"Because they are Jewish? You do not want to do it because they are Jewish?"

"What? Look. It don't take many reasons for me to go bump off a few goddam Japs, but like I say, it ain't just me involved here. I got these men. I got orders."

"And you have never disobeyed orders?"

Hawk did not like that question. He liked the answer even less. He thought of Welch and the young men who had died on the ridge because of his wrong-headed decision to rescue third squad. Some sort of shame left him silent. He didn't know exactly what he was ashamed of: was it that he had disobeyed orders, or that he would not do it this time? She did not wait for him to figure it out. She knew he was not accustomed to moral dilemmas of any sort.

"It does not matter what you say to me or your big words. You *will* do it. I came here for you. Pay attention to what I have told you. Remember my words." She continued to stare angrily at him. "You will do it, in the end, not because you are afraid to die. I know you, I know you are not afraid to die. You will do it because you love me." She looked intently at him, as if teaching a lesson, and continued.

"You and I are the short-lived young, who know

what the old ones know, who know time does not heal all wounds, and that there is not always a tomorrow. We know evil and death will find our dreams. We know you cannot change the regrets of the past with hopes from today. We have learned it is not our past that is dying, it is our future."

Hawk had no response to any of her insight. This supernatural creature had chosen the wrong person to impart her wisdom upon. Sometimes, he thought they had a language barrier. He was certain there was a barrier of some sort; and she was on the talking side, and he was on the doing side. He could only meet the mysterious, accusing eyes burning into his with his own blazing defiance, firing a borderless neon splash that fused the two of them together in the crowded little room. Did his inability to answer mean she had won the argument? A low rumble, that could have been thunder, came from above them. They knew immediately, it was not thunder.

"We better see what's going on," Hawk said, helping her to her feet, and glad to end the discussion. They made their way quickly up the narrow steps to the tower above. Hawk rushed to the railing to look out over the city. Beautiful old Manila still spread out there, as forged from its earliest days, and its Spanish days, and even its American days. He could see the Intramuros, the old walled city; the sturdy and ancient bastion of civilization being turned into a crude Japanese defensive stronghold.

Today, in this part of today, it was still the city where Asia met Europe. There stood the columned post office, the historical, domed cathedrals, the wide old plazas and grand hotels; some newer, ambitious office buildings, mansions, towers, contrasting with the low, teeming, leaning architecture of the impoverished. All of the structures, those with cheap tin roofs and those with dignified red tiled ones were all connected by the bright green tree canopies, looking like a movie set where someone was filming an epic about a lost city. The stadium, the hospital, and the intricately carved old cemeteries—each awaiting with geriatric fragility the harsh new order about to visit them, the apocalypse in fire and brimstone. In the distance, a preview of what was to come blighted the horizon.

He watched a line of black explosions extend across the northern edge of the city, sprouting with mechanical precision. Seconds later, the sound of each detonated bomb reached them, thundering in the air and eerily crackling along the ground, and through the foundations of Manila and its people alike. White smoke separated from the black ugly fountains, and rose heavenward in flowing balloons, like spirits, as did no doubt, the real spirits of the stricken humanity below. All of it—the vast, jumbled old city, the panoramic expanse of the fire and smoke—reminded him of how he lived and breathed, like some vagrant here, halfway around the world from where he belonged.

"I guess they done found Yamashita," Hawk commented in a brooding, low voice.

"I told them he was leaving. He is not here. Why are they doing this?" she said with tears in her voice. She dug her fingers into Hawk's shoulder, demanding an answer.

"I don't know. Maybe if we had found the papers," he said.

"The papers were *my* papers. They said what *I* said."

"I told Clark that. He's just a colonel. This came

from the top. They probably didn't pay much attention to him."

"The Americans wanted to do this all along. It would not have mattered if there were not a single Japanese soldier left in the city," she said. "They want to destroy."

"Well," Hawk said, "I can tell you, there's more than a single Japanese soldier left in the city. It's hard to fine tune things when you're dealing with Japs."

She clutched him to her. "I do not want to leave you. I am not ready for this. This cannot happen yet. We were going to stop this, you and I. We were going to be together."

"Don't worry. We're taking all of you with us," he said gently, bending his head over hers. "Nobody's leaving you." Another frightening series of explosions came from afar.

"No, don't you see? I am here only to save the others. And you. If I cannot, I have no reason..."

She buried her face in his chest, crying. "Remember everything I told you. And that I love you." She pulled away from him and turned her back to him. He stepped away from her, toward the railing to watch the rising chorus of evaporating, fiery orbs.

"It is sadder to live, than to be dead now," she said to him.

He studied the distance. Everything remained far away and had little impact on him. An entire culture was about to be destroyed, but in this moment, it still breathed out there. He wondered what had been happening at battalion. The colonel had given him no warning of any air raids. Between the explosions, he heard something like the turning of the pages in a book, or more like the wind whipping quickly through them.

It seemed like it was only in his head, compared to the distant thunder. "Oh, I wouldn't say that," he finally said, trying to ease the catastrophic mood. He turned around with a subdued smile, "stuff is always gonna happen..."

She was not there. His eyes met only the pale blue sky above the half wall on the other side of the tower. Far away, over the undisturbed side of Manila, a thin cloud coasted peacefully by.

He glanced around the deck of the tower, finding he was alone in the sighing wind. "Aw, hell," he growled. He bounced his way down the tiny, winding stairwell. The bedroom below presented itself to him just as vacant. He stepped into the adjacent office, and she was not there. "What in the goddam *hell*?"

He opened the door of the office and stepped out onto the third-floor balcony. Hobby leaned over the railing a few feet from him. He frowned at the look on Hawk's face.

"Did anybody come outta here?" Hawk asked.

"No. No, Sergeant."

"Son of a bitch. You been standing here long?" Hawk walked behind him, toward the stairs.

"Yes, I've been here ten or fifteen minutes," Hobby answered.

Hawk descended the stairs. People milled about as usual. About half of them were staring out the windows, all were listening—waiting, for something. Joe Canlon passed by and he stopped him.

"Have you seen Eugenie?" Hawk asked.

"Not in a while," said Joe. Sensing something was wrong, Joe added, "Is she missing?"

"I was up there talking to her, and I had my back to

her, and I turned around, and she was—just gone. I mean—gone."

"Probably pissed her off," said Joe. "Want me to find her?"

Hawk leaned heavily against the edge of the banister. He could not explain it. "Yeah. Yeah, hurry up." As he looked aimlessly around the room, his gaze finally came to rest on the giant portrait. He closed his eyes.

13

ENCOUNTER WITH THE UNSEEN

JOE SHOUTED ORDERS AND PEOPLE WENT FROM ROOM TO room, calling the name of Eugenie. No one had seen her go into the kitchen. Hawk inspected the tunnel. After entering for a few steps, he called into it, and only the echo of his voice came back. A twenty-minute search of the Club produced no results.

"Let's go up top there," Joe told Hawk, who remained slumped against the stairs, watching the proceedings. "Show me what happened."

"Yeah. Okay." They ascended the stairs and Hawk hastily recreated the scene. At first, Joe became more fascinated with the bombing north of the city. The far explosions rolled under the ground and ended with a snap beneath them, at the foot of Club Arashigaoka. Joe finally focused on the problem at hand.

"Well, shit," said Joe. "She fell off when you weren't looking. There's a high wind. It's pretty obvious to me. Look at this damn wind. Not much of a mystery."

"Without screaming or nothing?" Hawk answered. "Just fell off?"

"Yeah, see..." Joe walked over and sat on the short wall surrounding the deck. "She sat here and was talking, kind of involved in what she was saying...next thing you know, she's head over heels. People do that in New York all the time. I tell you, this rail here? It wouldn't meet the code in New York. With people drinking and all? Shi-i-t. Not to mention old people and stupid ones, stumbling around. This wall is too low. That's non-union labor for you. She just tipped over it. Pretty obvious."

"And when they fall in New York, they scream like bastards, too," said Hawk. "You don't just go falling off something clammed up like a rock."

"I don't know. Maybe not. You didn't hear nothing? No, *oops,* or anything?"

"I didn't hear *shit.*"

"I guess she was too surprised." Joe shrugged. "You had that noise going on out there, too. But, that's what happened," said Joe, getting off the wall and walking to the center of the deck. "She walked over, like this, sat down," he repeated his demonstration of sitting on the wall, "and she was talking and got real involved in..."

"Okay, don't say that shit again, or I'm shoving *you* over. I told you, she didn't fall," Hawk angrily stopped the repetition of Joe's performance. "You don't fall without screaming, or stumbling, or doing some damn thing."

Joe looked thoughtful. "Okay. Say...she didn't fall. She jumped. Happens all the time in New York. They call 'em jumpers. She wasn't surprised, because she knew what she was doing. She planned it out. Didn't want anybody stopping her. So, no screaming." He got off the wall and looked over the edge. "She done it on purpose. But...I don't see no guts down there."

Hawk walked over to him and looked down. Nothing extraordinary appeared to be on the grass or rocks below. "That's not where she was standing, anyhow. She was over there on the other side, where I just was," said Hawk. Joe crossed the deck and looked over the opposite side. "We were talking. She didn't jump. She was in the middle of a goddam sentence." He paused. Or had *he* been in the middle of a sentence?

"Yep. You were right. Yep. That wasn't the place. *This* is the place where she jumped," Joe said, looking down. Hawk rushed over. He again saw nothing below.

"Why? What are you talking about?"

"The water comes right up to the bottom of the building. There's just that little edge of the bulkhead sticking out there to stop her. She bounced off it and fell in the water. It knocked her out, and the channel carried her off. Or probably, she just sank." Hawk leaned out over the railing. It creaked, leaning with him. This time, Joe's theory made sense, a lot of sense. It was the only theory that had made *any* sense so far.

"She *jumped*? Why? She didn't say, 'I'm going to jump.' I...didn't hear...anything." Then, he heard the wind turning the pages of a book in his mind. Yes, he had heard something, and had mentally dismissed it. Was that what that sound was?

"Hawk, them people don't always say why. They do it all the time in New York. They call 'em jumpers. It's just the way some people are wired. I guess times get tough—all that shit, you know how it is. The pressure. They don't drink, and got nothing else to do." Joe sat down heavily on the groaning little wall again, ignoring its frailty. "Like, I'd get drunk, myself. I'd never jump into the goddam drink. They usually do it when they lose their money. I ain't got no money, so I ain't got nothing to worry about, as far as that goes. That's what happened, though. Don't you see? She always acted funny, if you ask me. I know you don't like hearing that."

"Come on, let's go down there," said Hawk.

"Outside? With all this shit going on?" Joe asked, pointing at the increasing explosions north of the city. But Hawk was already halfway down the stairs, Thompson in hand. Joe cursed and rose to follow.

Traffic did not navigate the canal in the early hour. Perhaps the sound of the bombing kept people indoors for the morning. Hawk and Joe rounded the front of the building and went toward the back, which faced the narrow and shallower part of the channel, the side never hosting marine traffic. The bank opposite them looked larger, closer, and ominous here in the outdoor daylight. Its innocuous, stunted grass and half-grown trees appeared threatening in the foul-smelling dawn ground fog. The fog creeped slyly across the water toward them in rotating swirls, and stopped in midstream, like malicious, taunting ballerinas.

The two reached the point along the bulkhead, below where they had been standing in the tower. The corner of the mansion came very close to the fog-covered water, with a sharp edge of the protective barrier of rocks jutting out beyond even that, and into the canal. The actual surface of the grim liquid was a good six to eight feet below them. Unbroken rainbows of oil floated on the motionless water.

Hawk looked into the murky, iridescent liquid. but it refused to give up any secrets or answer any of his questions. Joe, however, had more of an investigative mindset. He wanted to bolster his theory. He spotted something on the edge of the bulkhead, a couple of feet down. Leaning over with a grunt, he plucked it free, from where it lay jammed there.

"Here you go," said Joe. "It's one of them deals that were hanging on the arms of her shirt, or dress thing." Joe held the black cloth out to him.

"Those are called sleeves," said Hawk, staring at it blankly, his words sounding far away.

"Yeah. That's what it is, all right. Got...snaps...on it." Joe thrust it at him again, and Hawk took it. Joe cast a nervous glance at the bank opposite them. He felt exposed out here, after all of the time they had spent hiding indoors during the daylight hours, afraid to even pass by an uncovered window. "She bumped her head on this sharp rock here, see? On the way down," Joe offered quickly, waving his arm and trying to rush the investigation. "Don't see no blood, though. Well, she had all that goddam hair. Knocked her out, anyway, and she drowned. You want me to jump in and see if she's under there?" Joe was an excellent swimmer. "There ain't much current on this side. Hell, she could still be lying under there. Now, it ain't gonna be a pretty sight, you know?"

Hawk went to one knee. He cast a wary glance at the bank looming opposite them, just as Joe had done. "Nah, I guess this is how she wanted it," he said.

"Yeah," said Joe, not wanting to sound impatient by rushing things. "They call 'em jumpers."

"Yeah. I remember you sayin' that."

"Hard to figure," said Joe. "I'm thinking it's on account of she lost all her money, and the business. You know? That's probably bad for some people. When you ain't got nothing, like us, you don't understand all that kind of shit. Money? That's hot shit, for people that ain't got much else going on. Money kind of protects 'em from real life. But, then too, she was funny. Some people ain't right in the head. I know you don't want to hear it. But they just do stupid shit, to be doing stupid shit."

"Yeah." Hawk answered absently, his gaze dropping from the water to the bulkhead. He noticed something at the tip of his boot. A wire extended over the edge of the broken pieces of concrete, winding downward through the cracks of its stacked rocks, and down into the water. "Look at this thing," he told Joe, his voice still somber. He lifted it with a finger. He stood, leaning his weight on the Thompson as he rose.

"A telephone wire?" Joe asked. "Goes to the Club?"

"The Club's phone wire was on the front of the building. It had been cut," Hawk said. "It was a bigger, commercial wire, up on a pole."

"That's that kind of wire like they used when we were kids. I see it still around, sometimes. Probably real old. Maybe it's a field telephone," Joe said, fidgeting. "You think we oughta go back inside? Lotta people are waking up by now. All *kinds* of people."

Hawk nodded. American field telephones used black, insulated wire, with copper and steel strands twisted inside it. The wire resting across his finger consisted of two insulated brown strands, braided together.

"It's a field telephone, awright. A Jap telephone," said Hawk.

He pulled the wire forcefully from under the three inches of soil covering it. A line of wire lifted the sand, and uprooted weeds with a snapping rip, all the way to the building. They followed it. The strand extended up the corner of the hall, inconspicuously attached to it, within the edge where the corner boards met, by means of U-shaped staple nails. The heads of the two men fell back as their eyes followed the wire up toward the tower, which leaned over them in the clouds, creating the optical illusion of its swaying.

"It's a Jap city. What else would it be? You gotta expect Jap wires," Joe reminded him. "A Jap telephone in a Jap assed place."

"I don't expect nothin'. The Japs weren't supposed to have been *here* for more than a few minutes the night they took her. What the hell is this son of a bitch wire doing here?" Hawk asked. "Running under the channel?"

Joe rubbed his nose vigorously. "We better go inside and find the other end. Probably just leads to some old shit," he said. "A goddam toaster, or something."

"Probably," Hawk agreed. The wire disappeared from sight in an area under the third floor. "C'mon."

Climbing the stairs inside, they once again entered the office of Eugenie and looked at the floor, where it met the walls. Seeing nothing, Joe noticed a single sheet of paper on the desk, with writing on it. He slid it from beneath the Statue of Liberty figurine. But then, stepped back, and left it there.

"Look, a note. Jumpers usually leave a note. This proves it," said Joe.

Hawk picked it up, and silently read it.

"The family—Weitz. The barge man—Leo. Dawn, day after tomorrow."

He handed the note to Joe, who also read it. "Hunh," Joe commented. "I guess it ain't a note. Just some kind of crazy crap. But that was her—crazy."

"Hmph," Hawk answered. "The wire ain't in here, it must be in the room next door there."

"It has to be," said Joe. "What is that room, anyway?"

"Nothing. Somebody called it an attic. I don't know. I

looked in there once, and it was empty. Let's check it out."

They walked outside the office, onto the mezzanine hallway, and into a smaller hallway that had a single, low door as the only entrance or exit to the attic space. Hawk opened the unlocked door. An odd odor wafted out, but otherwise, he found a bare, unfinished room, having no paneling or wallpaper. The lack of a light source made it difficult to see inside the cramped area. The orientation of the hallway and balcony blocked the outside light.

"Not much to it," said Joe. "Of course, I think somebody might have shit in here. Too goddamn lazy to go outside." He kneeled on one knee, near the back wall of the attic. "Look, here the damn thing is." Hawk leaned over beside Joe. The corporal ran his fingers along the braided strands of wire to show him. The line entered from the outside of the building, ran across the wall for about six inches, and then back into the wall through a small hole drilled there. Joe pulled at it, but it was tightly nailed down.

"What in the...stomped up hell? Where does that go?" Hawk said, tugging at the wire as well. "It just comes in and goes out."

"This attic must be between her office and another room. See, there's some little space between us and the outside wall," said Joe. "This room is only half the attic. There's an even smaller space over there."

"I never noticed that. There's no door to the other half, how do you get into it? It must be wasted space."

"Could be some little closet or something," said Joe. "Let's look." They went back out to the hallway. If another room existed, it had no entrance. Hawk backed away from the blank wall.

"The wire goes into the walled-off room, or closet, or whatever it is," he said.

Joe laughed abruptly. "Well, if it does, it's the only damn thing goin' in there, because there ain't no door. I don't think that's big enough for a room. It's just a little space."

"I'm tellin' you, the wire goes in there. Why would you have a room with no door?"

"Construction error," said Joe. "They didn't have all this modern technology when they built this place. They just kind of played it by ear. Non-union labor." Then he suddenly cocked his head. "You know, I remember this old guy in Buffalo who had a big house like this, and he had a room right in the middle of it with no doors, just sealed up tight. Like this."

"For what?"

"They said his wife was in there. When she died, he put the casket in there and walled it up. Kinda spooked me, you know? We never talked to him about it. But that's what people said. You know how people talk." Joe shook his head. "This big place here is spooky, like the old man's place was, with all these secret rooms."

"Aw, horseshit. That's ignorant," said Hawk. He walked out of the hallway, back out onto the main third-floor mezzanine, and leaned over the railing. "Hobby!" he shouted.

Hobby came out of the kitchen. "Get the axe on the back wall of the galley and come on up here."

Hobby soon stood next to them, axe in hand, facing the blank wall, as did they.

"Somebody forgot to put a door here, kid," Hawk said. "Knock a hole in the wall, wouldja? Right here."

"You mean...start chopping into the wall?" Hobby

asked. He remembered Clark's order about not tearing things up.

"Yeah. Knock the hell out of it," Hawk answered.

Hobby reared back and buried the head of the axe into the wall with a hollow thud. He wiggled the blade free and swung again. But before the axe head struck the splintered wood a second time, a loud blast engulfed the hallway, sheetrock spat outward, and a fine hole appeared in the wall. Hobby flew backward against the opposite side of the corridor. He slid to the floor, groaning weakly. The axe continued forward, however, and stuck in the paneling. Joe and Hawk jumped backward, away from the wall and the unexpected gunshot. Hawk raised the Thompson and fired three or four rounds through the wall, a few inches below where the axe hung in the wood. Smoke filled the tight quarters. In the ringing silence that followed, they heard the animal-like sounds of thrashing behind the barrier and a small squeal.

Hawk and Joe retreated to the main balcony in a crouch, awaiting any other response from the hidden room. Smoke sifted through the railing. Hobby lay crumpled and still, dead on the floor in front of the mysterious lair.

"I think maybe you just killed your girlfriend," Joe whispered.

Hawk frowned, feeling some regret for his impetuousness, but after glancing at Hobby, nevertheless fired three more rounds into the wall, this time, closer to the floor. They heard boots pounding up the stairs behind them, as some of the others came to see what had happened.

Hawk slung the Thompson and entered the hallway again, first checking Hobby for a pulse. There was nothing to be done for him. His chin was on his chest, as if he were napping, which he had so often done. "Okay, stay back, goddammit. No sense anybody else gettin' shot here," Hawk said, pulling the axe free. He swung it angrily. With three furious strokes, half the wall fell away from him. A strong odor immediately filled the entire club, as the subdued light revealed the confines of the forbidden chamber.

On the floor inside the little space, which did not qualify as a room, lay a dead Japanese soldier clutching an 8 mm assault rifle. In a corner, stood a full bucket of feces, next to a blanket. Beside the bloody, dead man was a box containing a field telephone, splintered by several forty-five slugs. In the other corner was a large canvas bag, with carrying handles. Hawk knew immediately what the bag represented. It did not look as he had imagined it, being bigger and shapeless. Joe stepped inside to investigate the scene. He was surprised he did not find a riddled Eugenie Rossier on the bare, boarded floor. He looked up and poked the ceiling with his rifle.

"Here's your door," said Joe. "Trapdoor in the overhead. Guess we were wrong. Every room's gotta have a door. Except for the old man's place in Buffalo." He stepped up on the broken radio to look inside. "Goes over to the attic."

"Get the bag. Lawson, throw that bucket of shit out the window," said Hawk. He didn't mind risking his life for the others, but underlings did come in handy for certain tasks.

"*Man*—don't need that," said Joe, as Lawson carried the bucket past him. He put his hand over his mouth and nose.

Hawk walked inside, giving the tiny space closer scrutiny. Loose papers with handwritten notes in

Japanese lay on the floor, spattered with blood. Being neither a natural sleuth, nor a great military strategist, Hawk did not first reach for the bag, or the dead man. Being instead a natural killer, he first picked up the soldier's weapon, and looked it up and down. He held a Japanese manufactured version of the German StG 44.

"Look at this son of a bitch," Hawk told Joe. "Pretty damn nice for a Jap."

"It's an automatic," said Joe, glancing at it. "He could have killed all three of us."

"No," said Hawk, "he could have killed *all* of us, period. Bastard must have been in here all along. All he had to do was walk out to the railing and wipe us out any time."

"Why didn't he? Looks like he killed Rayburn for the bag, and then just went back to hiding," said Joe.

"I guess he wanted to see what we were up to. Those son of bitches put him in here before we even got here. They knew every move we made. And still do."

"That means," said Joe, "this Jap probably had a friend in high places at the old Club Arashigaoka. I hate to say it." Hawk looked over his shoulder at Joe.

"You didn't like her much, did you?"

"It's not a matter of liking. She was kind of loony," said Joe. "I don't like people actin' weird. Because when you're actin', you ain't bein' straight. You knew her better than I did. Are you sayin' there *wasn't* something wrong with her?"

"I don't think she was in with the Japs. She told me she wanted me to get this family down the river away from the Jap police. If she had any pull with the Japs, she could have saved the family herself." Hawk finally picked up the bag.

"Why? If, she had your dumb ass doing it?" said Joe.

Hawk glanced at Joe without expression. "Let's get Hobby downstairs. Moreno, throw the goddam Jap in the canal," said Hawk.

"Somebody'll see him," said Joe.

"That's their problem." As Moreno and another man lifted the dead and filthy soldier out of the dark space, Joe had another idea.

"Maybe...maybe we oughta watch them throw him in the water," said Joe. "See how he does in there, you know?"

"Why in the goddam..." Hawk paused. "Oh, yeah. I guess we should." Joe was suggesting an experiment to determine what had happened to the body of Eugenie. The sergeant dropped the bag on the roulette table on the way out, and he and Joe followed the two men carrying the dead enemy soldier through the door. They prepared to sling him into the channel.

"Wait up," said Hawk. "Take his nasty ass around to the back. The water's different back there."

The little funeral procession rounded the building, and without pause or ceremony, the pall bearers tossed the body with a cartwheeling motion into the oily back-waters of the barge canal. The virtually nonexistent current did not carry him off, nor did he sink. He floated there, face down, rotating only slightly.

"Hunh," said Joe, as Hawk silently watched. "In New York, they call them floaters. But, *her* lungs would have been full of water. It wouldn't have been that way for her. He wasn't killed in the water. The extra weight in her lungs, you see, would make her heavier and..."

"Aw, shut the hell up," said Hawk, turning around.

"Leave him floating like this?" Moreno called after them.

"Yeah. He's doin' just fine," Hawk replied.

Upon returning inside, Hawk overturned the satchel of Eugenie. On the table lay various items: jewelry, each piece carefully tagged with a tiny piece of paper containing illegible writing; a heavy stack of documents, many in the handwriting of Eugenie; a considerable amount of American currency, banded together; and the colorful Japanese occupation currency.

Ana stood beside Hawk and picked up the Japanese bills.

"Mickey Mouse money," she said. "It was never worth much. Now, it is worth even less. But it was ours, it was our pay. It is everything we had."

Hawk shuffled through the papers and threw them back in the bag. "Keep it," he said. "We don't need it." He scooped up the jewelry and the American money and dumped it all back into the satchel. Ana asked no questions, nor did she express any gratitude. She turned quickly and walked away with the money. After she left, Joe reached boldly in and pulled out the bundles of American money.

"This was mine. It ain't much, but it was my pay," Joe said. "It is everything I had." Hawk slapped it back into the bag. The sudden disappearance of Eugenie and death of Hobby had not left him in the mood for humor.

"We found what the colonel wanted. Which means, I guess, he doesn't want it anymore. Blackwell, better get him on the horn," Hawk said, hefting the bag. "I don't see how we're ever gonna get this thing to him now."

After assigning Ana, Marie, Van Houten and two others to peruse the documents, Hawk was later informed the pages contained not only Yamashita's plans to abandon the city, but those of Iwabuchi to set up a less well-manned and last-ditch defense.

It took a while, but after Blackwell had contacted Clark, Hawk quickly related the discovery of the hidden spy behind the wall, and the recovery of the satchel.

"That Jap must have been there when you got there. Those people there with you, all knew about him, Sergeant. Make no mistake about that. He had to get food and water. Watch your back. That woman knew about him, too. The police left him there to get those papers, and to keep us from getting them. The Jap wanted you to find the documents for him, and he killed your man for them. He listened into everything you did. That's why they attacked your patrol when you went after the Ulupong agent. Over."

"But they didn't stop us from finding the gun in the bay," Hawk replied. He didn't buy much of the colonel's explanation. He winked at Blackwell.

Clark had a ready answer. "Because I told you to move the goddam radio away from that woman. She didn't know about the mission for the gun. She relayed everything you did to the Japs. Better tie her up right now. Observation of her isn't good enough anymore. You need to restrain her before she flies the coop. Or kills somebody. Over."

"We think she might have killed herself. Jumped in the canal." Hawk answered. "I...don't know why. Over."

"I can tell you why. You found her body? Over."

"Not yet. It just now happened. There's been a lot of things happening—all at once."

"Yeah, yeah. Get the effects of the dead and put them in a safe place for graves registration. I mean our dead. Don't worry about her. We'll be there soon to pick you up. Manila is as good as ours. Those little bastards will be running for the hills. Over."

"The Japs must know we're here, sir. Maybe they

know we got their man. They'll be coming for us. You'll never get these documents if they capture us," said Hawk.

"Things are not as simple as they were Hawk. We destroyed the gun, but that area is still heavily occupied now. You can't just walk out of there, like you did when you came in. It may take us two or three days to get through to you. But we will, you can count on that. Enemy units are going to be collapsing all around you. They'll be too busy running to take prisoners. If it looks like they'll get the papers, throw them in the canal. It's not imperative that we have them now, but we don't want them to have them. I'll check with you soon—to see how you're doing. Over and out."

Hawk tightened his lips and looked at Joe and Blackwell.

"He ain't real worried about us," said Joe.

"He said he would get us out," said Hawk. They both looked at Blackwell. Blackwell shrugged. "That's what he said," the young man affirmed the conversation. "Soon," he added with some irony.

"It ain't gonna take 'em too long to figure out their boy's met up with his ancestors," said Hawk. "Then, they have no reason not to blow us to hell. We can hold this place for a while, as long as it's just those local police coming after us. If they send in regular army, with heavy weapons platoons, we're on borrowed time."

"Yeah, the colonel didn't mention any of the details about that kind of shit," said Joe.

"Maybe he'll come sooner, if that happens," said Blackwell.

"I think you missed something," said Hawk. "You had to listen close. He explained it all, when he said to throw the bag in the canal. And—that the Japs ain't taking no prisoners."

After a moment, Joe nodded. "Yeah. I guess he did. It sounded better when he said it."

Hawk slapped Blackwell on the back. "Well, kid. If you ever wanted to kill some Japs, this is your lucky day."

The words proved to be truer than expected. Within minutes, a cry arose from the front windows. A patrol boat approached. Hawk rushed to the window and gently pushed the curtain aside. A small boat sped across the middle of the canal, headed directly for the front door. Its prow parted the waters into two threatening white curtains, exhibiting absolutely no hesitation or caution.

"They didn't waste any time," said Joe.

"I don't know," said Hawk. "I only see a half dozen of them in the boat. It don't look to me like this bunch got the message. They must be doing a routine search on their own. They ain't being too careful, to my way of thinking."

"Whatever they're doing, they're coming *here* damn quick," said Joe.

The launch passed the halfway mark across the canal and roared purposefully toward them. Hawk thought quickly. "They'll be coming inside," he said. He raised his voice. "First section get along the back wall, second over by the booths. We let them inside and catch them in a crossfire. Use the tables for cover, if you can't find nothing else. Don't let 'em see you. We let 'em get all the way inside, and I'll open up. Then everybody fires. Move the civilians in the galley." A mad rush of activity followed. Hawk dropped the curtain and dodged over to Baker. "You stay at the window. They'll leave somebody outside. When we open up, you nail whoever they left in the boat." Baker licked his lips, and touched the muzzle of his MI to the window, with a metal on glass click. The plan had been quickly formulated, and now, it would have to be quickly executed. The men waiting had no wiggle room for mistakes. But then, they had known since they arrived here, this moment had to come.

Hawk joined the group hiding along the wall by the booths. His hand caressed the pistol grip of the submachine gun. It slid up and along the receiver, as if he had never touched it before. In the moment, here was his truest friend, his only family, and his guardian confidant: an empty-souled metal contraption. Crouching there, he could hear the speed and volume of the launch motor slow. His breath grew short, and then stopped altogether as the boat idled, and the vibrations of the motor ceased. He lifted the freshly oiled submachine gun beside his face and rested it there.

"They're getting out," Baker said in a low voice that carried up to the windblown rafters. "All but two of 'em. Coming up to the door."

"Stupid bastards," Joe whispered. "Why didn't somebody tell them we were here?"

"Too busy, I guess," said Blackwell. "They're just like us. When you tell somebody something, nobody pays any attention to you." He swallowed. "Unless—somebody did tell them. They could set a charge."

A voice shouted from the other side of the door in Japanese. Hawk realized he should have kept Ana, or Ferd, with him, to translate. Now, there was nothing to do but wait. He had no idea what the man outside demanded. He wondered if the group came to offer them a chance to surrender. Or, if the Japanese thought civilians hid inside. The insistent Japanese visitor shouted again. Every man within the darkened interior tensed with expectation, as they heard the sound of shuffling boots on the porch outside. Thumbs and fore-fingers pressed heavily against the familiar steel of their rifles, hoping for the best from their trusted armament.

"They *must* know we're in here," said Joe. "Why's he yellin'?"

"Yeah," said Blackwell, his voice high pitched with the fear of the unknown that was to follow.

Mercifully, the sounds of hands clawing at the front door could finally be heard. Clearly, the visitors intended to come in. By all indications, they had assumed the building vacant, as they did not surround it, or exercise a great deal of additional caution. It looked as if Hawk's plan would go forward. Had the intruders continued to stand outside shouting demands, Hawk had not prepared an alternative course of action. The door swung open, and a triangular pyramid of light lanced the interior. The Japanese outside consisted of mere leaning shadows on the floor, for the moment. They talked in low voices. Baker raised his elbow, taking aim at the men in the launch bobbing out front.

A pair of boots stamped boldly inside. A lone soldier stood within the doorway, letting his eyes become accustomed to the shadowy interior. He shouted again in Japanese and took a few steps toward the middle of the room. Four other soldiers followed, each looking around nervously. Hawk liked that. It looked certain the visitors did not know the Americans were there. They would not have entered in such a casual manner. No doubt the intrusion indicated a routine check of vacant structures.

Hawk rose deliberately, without any suddenness,

like the predator that he was, and held back the trigger of the submachine gun. The room erupted in deafening and blinding gun fire. Angry, coruscating sparks lit the gloom here and there. A pane of glass in the front window shattered as Baker fired an entire clip through it. The brilliant, flashing explosions illuminated the walls inside and could be seen through the windows outside. The vividly flickering convulsion lasted only a few seconds. The five Japanese lay in a stack of torn clothing on the floor, the room filled with circling dust and smoke. At the end, the investigators had seen Hawk loom up before them and little else. They did not return fire.

Hawk ran to the front door. The two men in the boat lay draped lifeless over the gunwales. Baker had done his part. "Baker! Sink that boat. Open the bilge drain, or whatever it takes," Hawk said.

Joe ran to Hawk's side, and detained Baker with a hand. "We could use the boat to get out of here," Joe suggested. "Somebody had to hear all of that noise."

"It ain't big enough. It's in the way. We gotta get rid of it, fast," said Hawk, motioning Baker outside. "Drag these bastards out of the doorway and shut it."

With one problem solved—an unexpected one at that—the rest of an anxious day dragged on. What would happen next? The sounds of massive explosions across the city grew in intensity. Were the enemy too preoccupied to deal with the Club Arashigaoka? Had no one heard the gunfire here? Were those who once monitored the Club's occupiers with a spy now engaged elsewhere? Perhaps the leisurely rescue proposed by Colonel Clark might be allowed to unfold after all. The almighty wisdom of the superiors would prove correct again. The Americans inside only waited, as ordered, attentively watching both sides of the ship channel for signs of activity. Commercial traffic had all but ceased.

Hawk knew this was precious time, and that it was wasted. Still, he waited for the colonel.

After finding some rusty ball bearings among the tools behind the kitchen, one of Hawk's men, Manfredi, came up with an idea for repairing the bazooka. He heated the tube of the rocket launcher, and hammered the ball bearings into the bullet holes, using a Japanese rifle thrust down its bore as an anvil. The amateur craftsman brought his handiwork to Hawk for approval.

"Yeah, that might work—once. Not a bad idea. Keep it ready," was the sergeant's offhanded opinion on the repair. "Things'll probably get bad enough to want to use anything." He paced behind the men watching the windows and did so on into the night. In the back of his mind was the fate of Eugenie, and her directive as to the rescue of the Weitz family. Every consideration, however, was overruled by the last order of Colonel Clark: stand and hold. And wait. He will contact you soon.

That night, the last night, Hawk went outside in the depths of the early morning darkness, dimly lit by stars. He let his legs catch his weight as he slowly dropped from step to step and went down to the front bulkhead. Behind him and above him towered windblown Arashigaoka. He sat down there, legs dangling over the canal, looking across the water at Manila. Most of the city lights that had shined on the previous nights had been extinguished now, for fear of what was to come. Long ignored blackout curtains came into use. But a few glimmers still twinkled here and there. Did they belong to soldiers, schemers, drunks, or lovers? Were people alive behind those windows or only ghosts? Did they look back at him? The ethereal glow reflected from the water flamed rhythmically up and across his face.

The night deepened, and he sat alone on the broken pieces of concrete, occasionally raising a knee, sometimes lifting his head to face the broad waters, and thinking—not pleasantly—of the many things that he had to think about. Among them was why and how a woman he had trusted, against all advice, had simply abandoned him. His lips tightened. As with life's other cruelties, he was no stranger to abandonment.

14

COVENANT WITH THE EARTHBOUND

THE DIMMEST LIGHT POSSIBLE PRECEDED THE SUNRISE, bringing increased anxiety. Haze or some weather event blinded the day. The patrol spotted enemy troops crawling on the banks of the narrower branch of the barge canal, with the intruders deliberately trying to conceal their presence. The rear side of the building had a limited number of windows, compared to the front. Only two small apertures faced the nearest bank from each floor. It was difficult to ascertain the intentions of the gathering Japanese—at first.

When troops also began to mass on the banks of the far, broader branch of the channel, their intentions became a little clearer. A full assault on the Club's island inevitably shaped up. A dozen boats had poised to cross the channel on the wider side. The congregating fleet consisted of landing craft, powered by aircraft motors from the rear, each of which could carry an entire platoon. Machine guns shined from each bow in the soggy light.

No signs of any watercraft could be seen at the

disposal of the troops on the rear side of the club. The enemy knew they would be able to wade across the canal at the point where the bridge supports thrust out of the water. It would have been more difficult for them to assemble any landing craft on the closer bank, having to transport them across both branches of the canal in order to do so or bring them very near to the building itself. With their wading restricted to the narrow, shallow area that supported the former bridge, they promised to make themselves excellent targets.

"We're trapped like rats in here," said Joe, watching the enemy come together in groups across the channel. "They're heading this way."

Hawk lit a cigar. "Nothing worse than a cornered rat."

"Look at the ammunition. We'd have to hit three Japs with each bullet to get out of this alive," Joe continued.

"Gotta hit four." Hawk walked toward the back of the hall to check the situation there.

"What did he say?" Blackwell asked Joe.

"Just stupid shit. I'm getting nothing but 'stand and hold' out of him," said Joe.

"We don't have much choice now," said Blackwell. "It's an island, and we're on it."

Things remained tense but quiet for a long while. The quiet could not last forever.

"They're shovin' off," Baker finally called out in a low and even voice from the front window. "They'll be here in a minute." Hawk ran down the stairs and opened the front door. He had not detected any aggressive movement toward the rear of the building but expected a coordinated attack would soon be launched. Having several men with automatic weapons already in the rear windows, he chose to place the patrol's lone machine gun facing the approaching landing craft in the open front doorway.

Ordinarily, a stubborn defense could dampen the enthusiasm of such a frontal attack. Everyone knew, however, that particular strategy did not apply here. Nothing dampened Japanese enthusiasm until the last man on one side or the other had been killed. This was the only strategy left—for both sides: it was the strategy that summed up the Pacific War—kill until no one was left to kill you.

"Set the thirty caliber up in this door," the sergeant told the machine gun crew. "We'll let 'em get a little over halfway across. That oughta be close enough," said Hawk. The machine gun team stacked a few thinly topped tables across the door for cover.

Hawk turned to Manfredi. "I can't risk that thing blowing up on us. Are you volunteering to operate it?" Manfredi had grown accustomed to the bazooka after working with it. He trusted his crude efforts to restore it and had confidence in its functionality.

"Yes, Sergeant. I don't mind," Manfredi answered. "I'm sure it will work."

"I like your spirit. Then, get up in the tower by yourself. You don't need no loaders getting' blown to hell with you. Those boats ought to be a solid enough target to set off the fuse in the rockets. Once we open up, pick out one and sink him. If that bastard works, and don't backfire on you, check out the barrel, and maybe try for another one. If it's meltin' down, or don't look right to you, just ditch it and come down here with your rifle and help us out."

"The only thing is, the rocket may not detonate,"

said Manfredi, "it might just burn right through the side of the boats."

"Yeah, I don't know. That's what comes from a lack of schoolin'. The bazooka team says it don't take much to set 'em off, and I gotta go with that. We ain't gonna have to wait long to find out," said Hawk. "The experiments just ended. Take off."

Manfredi scrambled up the stairs carrying the bazooka, which had been assigned to almost everyone in the patrol at one point or another, except for its original team.

"I wish he would give the word to open fire," Joe said to Blackwell. He sighted down the barrel of his M1, every muscle tightened down for action. Joe glanced back at Hawk, who was the only man on his feet, as the others tensely crouched in position to meet the attack. The sergeant paced about in the middle of the room, only occasionally eyeing the oncoming boats through the large, high windows. He did not have to look at them to know where they were. The motors grew louder, with the sound carrying along the water's surface, and drifting through the open door, and vibrating through Baker's broken window. And loud they were, like so many airplanes, jammed shoulder to shoulder, buzzing in a cracking rage toward the island.

"The farther away they are, the better. We might be able to turn them around," Joe added. "If he would just *do* something."

"Yeah," Blackwell answered. "Maybe so. Hurts my ears."

Seeing Joe and Blackwell together made Hawk think of moving the radio to the safety of the galley. But then, was the galley any safer? The kitchen had a lot of blind spots, and an explosive could take out a wall. Before he could arrive at a decision, other things began to happen, and he completely forgot about the radio. Under intense pressure now, he considered the objectives of the oncoming enemy. None of them boded well.

The Japanese immediately clarified their intentions for him. The foremost enemy boat opened up with a machine cannon. The glass of the front windows exploded down over the residents of the Club, with glinting, gleaming panes shattered into a colorful tempest, raining prisms of crisscrossed morning sunlight from one end of the large ballroom to the other. The clinking sound of the breakage was lost in the roar of the splintering impact of the big slugs on the shuddering back wall of the dance hall. The fountain of window debris splashed over the standing Hawk like large and clear droplets from a waterfall. A shard of glass slid under the brim of his helmet and stuck in his forehead, just above the eyebrow. He reflexively pulled the triangular missile free of his skin, and a stream of blood rolled down and into one eye. Batting at it with the heel of his hand and having little success as far as accomplishing anything, he charged half-blinded for the front window and opened fire on the closing flotilla. The distinctive sound of the Thompson was the signal for all of the others to open fire, including Manfredi's rocket launcher in the tower.

The American thirty-caliber machine gun concentrated on the lead boat, spitting a deadly volley up and down the center of it. The open landing barges provided little cover on the sides or front, and the occupants crowded helplessly together amid the leaden chain of lead whipping through them. Joe heard the bazooka discharge above him and saw the trail of the rocket's propellant streak toward a landing craft in the middle of the enemy formation. Immediately, a v-shaped, black discharge snapped skyward, causing the boat to pivot, throw out half its crew, and split in half. The wreckage struck two other landing craft, blocking them from any forward progress.

"Right on target!" Hawk shouted.

Rubbing his eye free of blood, Hawk noted the chaos caused by the sinking craft with approval. Two baffling engineering questions had just been answered for him. Would the damaged bazooka tube explode? And would its rocket detonate when striking an unarmored object? The favorable results increased his chances of inflicting greater losses on the enemy but by no means indicated he could forestall their victory.

Joe tore a bandage from its package and handed it to Hawk, who pressed it to his forehead. He crouched at the front window with the others as he batted at the irritating flow of blood leaking into his eye and blurring his sight.

Machine guns on the attacking boats opened fire, sawing back and forth across the ballroom, peppering the walls with bullet holes. Another bazooka round from Manfredi blazed down into the canal, striking a second target and jamming the progress of at least three more craft. The man in the tower had arrived at the conclusion the mended, thin metal tube proved itself worthy of further use.

The Marines fired into the confused attackers, who now slowed, unable to proceed through their own wreckage. They tried to turn their prows around for a retreat back to the far side of the channel.

Having temporarily staved off the frontal attack, Hawk turned to check on how the men in the rear of the building had held up. He heard intense automatic fire and knew instinctively the Japanese must be attempting to wade across the other branch of the barge canal behind them. He would have to climb the stairs or go into the extreme rear of the galley to confirm this with his own eyes. The enemy fire continuing to pour through the shattered front windows, ultimately discouraged him before he could crawl halfway across the room.

Although in retreat, the fire from the fleet of the Japanese did not completely let up. A heavy barrage chopped at the wooden wall shielding Joe and Blackwell, forcing them to duck and flatten, as part of the windowsill and the remaining glass flew asunder in front of them. Joe raised his head from the floor to see the smoking radio before his eyes, jagged and shredded by a half dozen machine gun rounds. Colorful wires and shiny metal flowered in every direction. He crawled away from the stricken instrument and toward a portion of the wall affording him greater cover.

Hawk turned around and squirmed on his belly toward the front wall, near the position of Joe and Blackwell. He dropped the bright red bandage from his hand, having sufficiently staunched the flow of blood enough to allow him to see again. He sat with his back against a part of the wall without a window. On both sides, he could see where 20mm machine cannon rounds had ripped through the outer and inner walls, assuring him his chosen spot for cover could not stop the jets of steel from lancing through the exterior of the Club. He had cover only from the eyes of the Japanese and not from any of random shower of penetrating lead.

"Hawk!" Joe shouted. He kicked at the blasted radio, shoving a severed part of it toward the sergeant. "The colonel caught one in the ass! You're in charge now!"

Hawk looked at the pieces of the burned radio, recalling his plan to move it. *A little late on that one.* He looked up.

Across the room from him, high on the wall, the placid face of Eugenie Rossier stared down at him. A scar of bullet holes stitched the bottom edge of the portrait and part of the wall, like the rising and falling line on a graph. With bullets setting ablaze the very air above his head, he recalled she had offered him a way out of just such an occurrence as this. But if he took her up on it now, he had to keep the other half of the bargain as well. Or he thought he would have to keep it. It no longer mattered what a faraway colonel thought of the matter. What would his men think of her offer of escape? Theirs were the lives on the line. Eugenie had known what Hawk would do and had told him as much. This had made him resist the idea even more—until now. He crawled over to Joe.

"We can get out through the tunnel," Hawk informed Joe. "And we might be able to get on a cargo boat down at the end of it, parked on the canal bank, if we keep a deal I made with the woman."

"What the hell are you talking about?" Joe asked.

One of the machine gun crew, having little cover of any substance in the open doorway, was hit by the retreating Japanese and lay dead on the floor. He had made no outcry. The enemy fire slackened as the logjammed boats managed to pull themselves free and return to the far shore. This made the rest of the confused flotsam an easy target for the men in the Club.

"We have to get a civilian family out of a police station down where the tunnel opens out before they'll let us on the boat. Are you in or out?"

"In or out of *what*?" Joe growled through clenched

teeth. "If there's *any* way out of this shit, you better take it—fast."

Hawk nodded. "That's what I figure."

A moment later, Manfredi sprinted across the floor and slid beside them, still holding the bazooka.

"What the hell are you doing down here? Did the thing break?" Hawk asked. "Why ain't you up there?"

"No, it's holding up fine. I think it's a permanent repair. The range isn't that great. I came to tell you more boats are coming down the canal. I saw *a lot* of boats. You can only see them from up in the tower. They're still a little way off, but they are coming this way."

"Shit." Hawk took off his helmet and combed his hair back with his fingers. It had been plastered to his bloody forehead. Not only could he not see this new advancing threat, he had no suitable way to fire at the reported second fleet, due to the way the building was situated: other than from the tower, and neither the floor's load capacity nor space could accommodate the entire American contingent up there. Even if it could, they would be trapped in the little area when the enemy inevitably closed with them. Otherwise, only a blind northeast corner of the club faced the portion of the canal from which the newest assemblage of boats came.

"How's the rear holding up?" Hawk asked Manfredi.

"They drove the Japs back across the river, but they'll be back," said Manfredi. "The water is full of the dead ones. They don't stop." A new sound, a jolting explosion, lit the bulkhead in front of the door. Another struck near the left rear corner of the tired old manor. Everyone reflexively ducked at the unexpected threat. Hawk recognized the blasts as being issued from a 50mm knee mortar. The Japanese had no shortage of such weapons. Enemy grenadiers sighted in on the

American machine gun and appeared to be only slightly out of range of it.

"Get everybody in the galley. Everybody, now!" Hawk ordered Joe. "Hurry up while the fire's slacked up." He turned to Manfredi. "Get upstairs. Get everybody down here." Manfredi leaped to his feet as if hit by a cattle prod.

Hawk stood, in spite of the occasional random shot still passing through the building with a deadly hiss. He raised his shoulders as another mortar round hit the island near the rear of the hall. The position of the Club had been bracketed. The old walls shuddered and shifted. He walked over to the machine gun crew and ordered them to withdraw and to bring the man killed with them. Hawk walked back to the portrait and looked up.

"You win, lady," he said and pulled the picture from the wall. He carried it with him into the galley and opened the passageway to the tunnel. Placing the portrait inside, he waved each man through the opening as they arrived from above. "Get those lamps," he told Lawson and Moreno. "Blackwell, go back and get that damn bag off the table." The last to enter the tunnel, Hawk shut the pantry door and the concealing shelf behind him. He had no way of knowing if the Japanese already knew about the tunnel, or in the alternative, how quickly they could find it. He only knew he had something of a head start on another upcoming, unwelcome, unauthorized, and thankless operation at the end of the tunnel.

* * *

KARL WATCHED SOLEMNLY as the guards stood before the terrified family in the cell next to him. Only one of the guards spoke any German, and very little at that. It was easy to tell what was happening, however. The drama transcended human language. The Japanese unlocked the cell door and swung it open.

"You go now," said the head of the guards, "You time now. Out!"

"We have done nothing. What are you doing with us," said the frightened prisoner. The man had been moved into the cell, briefly reunited with his wife and two children, under circumstances similar to those of the Weitz family.

"You time now. All you Jewish over," said the guard, motioning urgently. "Station closed. No more. All prisoners go, now." Karl's heart stopped when he heard this. "Out!" The guard screamed as the man shrank back.

"We are not Jewish," said the man. "We are Turkish, and we are German. We are Muslim. You have our papers, you know who we are. My name is…"

"No talk. No Jewish, no more. No lies," said the guard, motioning for his men to enter the cell and force the occupants out. They did not have to seize anyone, as the points of their bayonets were sufficient enough to pry the horrified people out of the corners of the damp and dirty little cage.

The Weitz family watched in stunned silence as the *Kempetai* pushed and shoved the inmates down the dark, narrow corridor and into the warmth of the dawn outside. The man pleaded for the guards to listen to reason, the woman shrieked, and the children cried. The seams of hell had burst.

"Dear God, we're next," whispered Marta. "Look at that!"

"No, no," said Karl, "they are keeping us for interrogation. Mr. Hayashi assured me, you heard him. We have nothing to worry about. They have not questioned us yet."

"Karl, you heard what that soldier just said," Marta insisted. "They all lie. Hayashi, too."

"That soldier doesn't know what he's talking about," Karl replied. "There is obviously a problem with the understanding of the language here. Hayashi was very honest with me."

"You had better fight them, Karl. There is no sense in being led outside willingly. Once they have us outside, you can hear what is happening. We must fight them while we can," she said.

Karl bit his lower lip and clutched the bars. "Yes. If they come back. They probably will not come back. I think they are frightened. The Americans must be coming soon. It sounds like they are evacuating the courthouse," he said. "I hear people leaving through the front. I have heard they are evacuating the Japanese women, the court personnel."

Gunshots rang out.

"No, I hear none of that. It sounds like something else is happening to me," she said.

* * *

HAVING WAITED for the night to pass, Hawk pushed the branches shielding the tunnel exit aside. His instructions from Eugenie had been to attack at dawn. Visibility improved with the slow sunrise dispelling the darkness. He could hear an occasional gunshot coming from the *Kempetai* station on the bank above him. The police must have been in a good mood and gotten an early start on their workday. He could also hear mortar rounds in a distance not far enough away, no doubt leveling Club Arashigaoka.

"Wait here," he told the others. "I'm gonna check on our ticket out of here, before we get into anything we can't get out of."

Leaving the tunnel, Hawk walked down toward the bank, where he immediately spotted the barge that he had been informed would be moored there. The air was cool, and thick with the port smells. He unslung his Thompson. He had to make sure the boat had not been commandeered by the Japanese. A man stood on the bank in civilian attire, smoking a cigarette. The orange tip glowed in the half-light. Hawk studied him silently.

Daylight had not fully lit the scene. The sky looked strange, as if a storm approached, or some smoky density obscured it. This desolate, abandoned locale was not the sort of place where anyone was likely to happen by. And yet, Hawk relied upon his breeding and instincts; instincts similar to those of a Mississippi wharf rat. When the whole world hates you and wants to kill you, you develop heightened degrees of sensitivity. But to survive, the successful rat must also take chances. No one caters his meals.

Hawk finally stepped into the open. He had to get the show on the road, one way or the other. The man waiting there expressed no signs of alarm at seeing him. The American left the muzzle of the Thompson pointing downward, for the moment.

"Leo?" Hawk called.

"Yes. Hawk?" the man answered.

"Yeah, we made it. Eugenie Rossier sent us. We're ready to go down to the harbor. Have the Americans taken it yet?"

"A part of it. It will be dangerous, but we will make it. I was surprised to see some barges are moving today. I don't think anyone will stop us," said Leo.

"You have taken the people from the police already?" the man asked.

Hawk wondered what the man would do, if Hawk just told him that there would be no rescued captives from the *Kempetai* going with them. But he didn't say that. He had thought of doing it, many times, long and hard. Instead, Hawk answered: "Not yet."

He lit a cigar. Rats have to take their pleasures where they can get them. "Sit tight. We'll bring 'em on down here, directly." Hawk blew out the smoke. "What is this thing, diesel?" He looked down the length of the massive craft, deep and partially covered with arching metal. He knew it was not going to be a fast mover.

"Steam," Leo answered. "The towboat is steam. This barge has no motor."

"Ah," Hawk said. "You the...pilot?"

"Yes."

"What are you haulin'?"

"Sand and gravel. And...you."

"Yeah, right. Okay. Just wait, and I'll be right back. If you hear some noise, don't get edgy. That's just how we do things."

"I understand," said Leo. "Hawk?"

"Yeah?"

"The *Kempetai* are very bad. It is not so easy. They take pleasure in the things that they do."

"I know. We're here to straighten all that out. They're fixin' to get some Sunday schoolin' with Jesus, in just a minute."

* * *

KARL DID NOT HAVE the opportunity to fight, as Marta had wanted. The captors swung the cell door open and kept their victims at rifle length with sharpened bayonets in their faces. Karl was led out first, looking for any opening, but finding none. The children followed, peacefully enough, as if being shepherded by their kindergarten teacher. Marta came out last. Before taking ten steps, Marta shrieked in horror and fell to wailing on the concrete floor.

Lieutenant Hayashi heard the commotion on the rear courtyard from his seat in the hearing room. He had not worn his uniform today. On the days when he conferred with his clients, the commander required him to wear an ordinary business suit, so as not to intimidate them. It was assumed they would more readily confide in him without his uniform. He was scheduled to discuss the final outcome of his negotiations over their fate with the Weitz family, and to give them the bad news.

Hayashi had not been informed by his superiors that under the pressing circumstances, his daily conferences had been deemed a waste of time. Maintaining the charade of justice was not as important now with American bombs falling in the vicinity. The local master of ceremonies, Commander Nakaya, had fallen victim to the show trials himself. The Weitz family was next. It made Hayashi sick. He had grown to like the children, especially. He wanted to leave the premises, but the newly appointed commander would not allow it. Since no accused remained to try, there was no need for Hayashi to stay. The only reason for the public defender to be here was as sport for the commander to irritate, or...worse.

Hayashi put his hand to his forehead as he sat at the

counsel table, listening to Marta's horror-stricken voice crying in the distance. He was pleased to be out of uniform today and experienced some of the terror the residents of Manila felt upon seeing the crisp *Kempetai* attire on the martinets around him. The female stenographer sitting next to the commander pointed out the sluggish conduct of Hayashi to her superior. Every move, every facial expression, had become suspect in these desperate days.

"Are you ill?" the commander shouted at him. "What is wrong with you, Hayashi?"

"Oh, no. It is nothing, Commander," Hayashi gasped. The merciless screaming continued outside the room. No one here had ever liked Hayashi much, because of his role as public defender. Would he be taken out back in Manila's final moments? Would he scream like Marta?

* * *

HAWK RETURNED TO THE TUNNEL. He quickly explained the situation to his men. Six would climb the bank with him and scout the police station. Baker and the rest would guard the rear and the access to the barge. Joe would go with Hawk, as would Moreno, and Lawson.

They climbed the steep embankment with slow and deliberate steps. "Why don't we just take the boat from the guy and hit the road?" Joe whispered. "Are we supposed to be doing shit like this?"

"Sometimes you gotta do the right thing, even when you don't want to," Hawk answered. "If a man can't solve a problem for somebody now and then, he might as well give up."

"Yeah, okay." Joe bit his lip. *More of that shit*, he

thought. *God, I swear, if only I was in New York right now, I would never listen to that kind of shit again.*

Upon reaching the top of the embankment, they saw the low, squat administration building, where justice had been swiftly dispensed by the Japanese for the last three years. A cinder block wall surrounded the rear courtyard of the structure. The wall may have been placed there for decorative reasons, long before the station's dedication to its current purpose, because the top of the blocks rose to only about three and a half feet in height. Each cinder block had two holes completely through it, so that the public could see through the wall, adding to its aesthetic appeal. But then, equally decorative and aesthetic low shrubs had been planted before the wall at a later time, obscuring the ability to see through it, for the most part, and defeating the original purpose. The Americans found themselves positioned on a side of the building running parallel with the canal, rather than at its rear. The outside of the premises remained unguarded here, for the moment.

Hawk bit off a plug of tobacco. "Stay here. I'm gonna have a look see."

His men remained lying on the bank, with only their heads peering over the top of it, and at their objective. Hawk crawled rapidly toward the wall. Voices spoke calmly from within. The damp canal morning muffled the sounds. He reached the cinder blocks and pushed back a woody plant in order to see through one of the decorative holes in the cement.

The first sight he encountered shocked even the callous Sergeant Hawk. Inside the courtyard, the bodies of men, women, and children lay piled to one side in a large sloping jumble, looking like bundles of used clothing with an enormous pool of blood under them.

Eyes and mouths of the dead stretched wide open, their arms and legs askew. It took him a moment to be able to look away, as he silently cursed.

A half-open door gave access to the station itself. Artificial light came from the doorway, providing subdued illumination. Five soldiers lounged about, smoking cigarettes and talking. Each carried an Arisaka rifle, which Hawk noted, they kept in their hands at all times. The rear wall of the courtyard had been stacked with another layer of cinder blocks to serve as a back-stop for a firing squad. Hawk crawled back down to the bank.

He outlined what he had seen, without elaborating on the magnitude of the dead. "We can take them bastards pretty easy, but I don't know what's inside the place. I think I gotta go around to the front and check it out real quick," said the sergeant. "I'd like to get the people we're after out of there before they get all mixed in with the soldiers. We need a clear field of fire, so they don't get hit."

"Let's grenade the ones that are outside now, while they're all together," said Joe.

"Might," Hawk answered. "I gotta find out where our people are. We can't go doing anything yet." He spat and poked Joe in the shoulder. "Here's what you do. Take the men up there where I was. You can fire through the holes in that wall. Spread out along the whole length of it, and pick a target. They won't know what hit them. I don't think you'll even need a grenade. But you don't fire until I do. I'm gonna try to come through the station house and up behind them. Don't go making *any* noise, because when you get up there, you're only gonna be about twenty feet from the son of a bitches."

Joe nodded. "Somebody's gonna spot us with all this moving around. You better hurry it up," he advised.

Hawk didn't answer. He crawled up the steep, dew-wet bank, and this time passed the wall and edged along the roughly textured side of the building, ducking beneath a set of windows. Reaching the corner of the brick *Kempetai* station, he ventured to look around it and toward the anterior part of the structure. The building fronted a street and faced several buildings on the opposite side of the road. Two guards stood on either side of the entrance. They were not the biggest problem.

On the other side of the street stood two more guards, with a full view of the front of the station house. It would be impossible to try to reach the men guarding the entrance, without the two across the street seeing his approach. Hawk pulled back quickly before any of these four could inadvertently spot him. He sat calmly against the wall, taking a moment to assess the situation.

His choices dwindled: he had to rule out a stealthy entrance into the well-guarded front of the building. The only means of entry through that door would be with guns blazing. It would be difficult to coordinate such a blitz with a rear attack. He returned to Joe and the others, now hiding in their position near the cinder block wall.

"They got the front staked out pretty good. I saw four of 'em, and there may be more. It'd be too big a run-in there. Real noisy. We might have to just go through the back and skip the front," Hawk announced in a low voice.

"And that ain't gonna be just as noisy?" Joe asked.

"I figure we can knife 'em. We go over the wall all at once and swarm their ass," said Hawk.

Joe had a pained expression. He did not like such maneuvers. In his estimation, a hand-to-hand free for all did not compare well to shooting your target from ambush. Fate intervened, to relieve Joe of his concerns.

"Sergeant! Something's happening!" said Lawson.

Hawk peered through the shrubs. Loud voices preceded jostling shadows across the half-open rear door. The door opened fully and a woman was tossed several feet across the courtyard, where she fell on her hands and knees. Several children ran behind her screaming, and two guards shoved a man out the door and shut it.

"Son of bitch!" said Hawk. "That must be them."

"They're gonna kill them," said Joe flatly, involuntarily focusing his eyes on the pile of corpses. A trail of blood extended across the paving stones, from the backstop wall to the stack of dead, explaining the procedure that was about to unfold. The prisoners would be shot and then dragged to the corner of the courtyard. "They'll put them against the wall."

"Awright. This is it, then. Let them line 'em up. When they separate from the prisoners, we'll cut 'em down." Hawk raised the Thompson. The demands of the predicament eliminated any further planning. Instinct and skill would have to take over. How they would hit their targets without hitting the prisoners, and what would happen inside the building after the attack, all had to be left to the devils of chance.

The position of the Americans helped to solve the biggest problem. They saw the entire murder scene from the side, with the executioners on one end of the courtyard and the victims lined against the wall on the other. They had a clear delineation between friend and foe. The officer in charge pushed Karl against the wall with the others, where he slumped, half standing with a hand pressed against the cinder blocks to keep himself from falling. The children stood at attention, looking proud. Marta never regained her feet and was shoved and slid into place near Karl. She ceased struggling and sat on the ground, reaching futilely for the youngest child, and calling to her.

Upon the order, the six soldiers raised their rifles in unison and aimed at their targets. Unlike an American firing squad, every rifle was loaded, and the executioners would be allowed to fire as many shots as necessary. There was nothing unsure or hesitant about the movements of the rifle team, they were obviously experienced.

Hawk knew that the enemy soldier closest to the position of his men would prove the prime target for them. Each executioner after that in the line, located progressively farther toward the center of the courtyard, would be more difficult to hit. The officer at the far side of the line had the greatest protection, afforded by the cover the bodies of his men provided him, and by his distance from the source of the American fire. The sergeant therefore chose the officer as his first target. Fortunately, the Thompson submachine gun had little respect for the human body as a shielding object, and the close quarters were ideal for its limited range.

The officer in charge raised his sword overhead. Hawk had to stop the proceedings immediately, with no time to think about it. He aimed down the line of men, between two heads, and at the officer with the raised sword. He held back the trigger. The shuddering flash from the muzzle nearly reached out and touched the firing squad. Two intervening heads partially exploded, and the officer behind them disappeared in the gyrating arms and legs that followed the American volley. After the explosive barrage stopped, the officer still stood there, holding his sword, with a look of astonishment on his face. A single shot rang out, catching him between the eyes, and he fell on top of his dead or writhing men.

"I got him," said Joe with some relief.

Hawk vaulted over the wall, checking both the wounded and the condition of the Weitz family. The family lay stunned and frozen in shock, probably expecting that the deafening outburst had been directed at them. They appeared to be unscathed.

"Finish off these bastards," Hawk shouted over his shoulder as he ran quickly to the open door and into the station house.

He passed through an empty line of cells and threw open the door to another room, an anteroom to the larger courtroom beyond. Without hesitating, Hawk plunged into the heart of the building. The huge rising sun flag was the first thing he saw in the hearing room. At his elbow, a uniformed officer sat at a high bench, peering down at him with a puzzled expression. Hawk raised the submachine gun toward the underside of the man's jaw, touched the trigger, and blew him out of his swiveling chair with a short burst. The new commander had expected a short tenure in his post, but not quite that short. Only a woman and an unarmed man, wearing a suit, remained in the room.

Hawk passed by them and walked quickly on, toward the front door. As he reached the door, it flew open in his face, revealing four red-faced guards. They carried rifles across their chests and would have become tangled with one another, had they tried to aim them.

They never found the opportunity. The American easily reacted first, firing the remainder of his magazine into them at a range of two feet. One of the victims tried unsuccessfully to grab the flaming barrel, but that was the group's only resistance. Hawk stepped out onto the sidewalk, his hands automatically replacing the clip as he looked both ways down the street. He saw no other guards or anyone else approaching. Two children stared at him from several yards away. He waved at them.

"Hey, kid, whatcha know?" he called.

The sergeant returned through the open door, stepping over the slain sentinels. The little man in the suit ran headlong into the Marine's bare chest and bounced back as if he had collided with a steel pylon.

Hayashi's jaw dropped as he looked up in horror. If ever one had seen a vision of the destroyer god, Hayashi could empathize with them. The piercing blue eyes in the brutal, cold and slashed face looked right through him. The little man's lips trembled as he slowly backed away from certain death, his arms outstretched at his sides and his fists clenched.

"Beat it, Tojo," Hawk growled and stepped past him. Hayashi was left standing there, rooted to the floor. Hawk returned through the empty building and entered the main room.

The woman still sat next to her slain commander, unable to move. "How are you, ma'am?" Hawk said, grabbing the telephone in front of her and violently ripping it from the wall.

She shielded her face from the outburst and pointed fearfully at something on the bench a little farther down. Looking where she pointed, Hawk saw a radio, futuristic in appearance and more compact than its American counterpart. He latched onto its carrying strap and prepared to smash it against the floor. He hesitated. His patrol no longer had a radio or any means of communicating with anyone. He had seen Marines operate Japanese radios on Guadalcanal and knew that it could be done.

"Thanks," he said, throwing the strap over his shoulder.

Hawk ran back through the empty holding cells, and into the courtyard beyond, where single shots rang out, as the wounded, former executioners were disposed of. In a matter of seconds, the judicial system of an entire district in Manila had been overturned.

The Weitz family had remained in place since the Japanese threw them before the wall. Speechless, they watched the American attackers attend to their work. Hawk finally swept up the littlest girl in one arm with a smile. Karl watched, still stunned.

"What do you say, sweetheart, wanna go on a boat ride?" Hawk set her up on the wall. "Sergeant James Hawk, United States Marine Corps," he said to the others. "I imagine y'all would be the Weitz family?"

"Yes, yes, we are," said Karl. "Has...the city been liberated by the Americans? How did you know our name?"

"Not exactly," Hawk answered. "You been liberated by us, and that's about all you're gonna get for now. We ain't out of the woods yet." Hawk took Marta by the hand and pulled her to her feet. She felt as if she had been seized by a dragline, so powerful was the grip. "Can you walk, ma'am? Are you hurt?"

"I-am-not-hurt," she managed to stutter each of the words out.

"Well, that's good. We got a little traveling to do.

What do you say we get over this wall and on down to the river?"

"How could you find us?" Karl had the presence of mind to ask.

"Eugenie Rossier," Hawk answered.

Karl's face only registered amazement. "Mademoiselle Rossier," he repeated.

"She's the one," said Hawk. "Come on, General. We can tell all kinds of funny stories later."

15

THE DARK GLOW OVER MANILA

Joe led the group down the bank to the barge, still waiting in the water below the *Kempetai* station. Baker joined them with the rest of the men, who had been guarding the tunnel and the path to the mooring. The Americans, the Club employees of Eugenie, and the recently rescued family, all climbed aboard the huge barge, and down below its thick, ten-feet high walls. Hawk swung up to the wheelhouse of the tugboat, where Leo prepared to push the barge from the rear. Leo had a crew of three, besides himself. With the word from Hawk that all was ready, Leo cast off, and the bumping, tandem crafts lumbered underway, their old tire fenders bouncing against one another.

Hawk ran along the gunwales of the moving tugboat and leaped down onto the elevated partial deck in the stern of the barge. He and Joe stood together, placing their elbows on the wall there, in position to watch the progress of the barge's departure from the *Buntai*. They could see the men moving about in the wheelhouse of the tugboat, swaying to and fro, high in the water behind them.

"Easy as fallin' off a log," Hawk commented.

"Yeah," said Joe. "Are we moving?" Generally, when a boat leaves shore, there is the illusion that the earth is moving, rather than the boat. In this case, it did not look like anything moved.

"I think so. Steam, you know? It's a little slow," said Hawk. "But steady."

"Yeah, right. We ain't gonna be winning any races. Hey, look at the Club back there," said Joe.

Tracers arched into the empty windows, and an explosion snapped here and there along the sides of the badly leaning structure. The Japanese airboats fired at will at the mansion from the very edge of the bulkhead. The scene resembled a combination of a fireworks display and a house fire, with the boats pouring more fire, rather than water, on the blaze.

"The stupid bastards think we're still in there," said Hawk.

"Why don't we just get on the tugboat and ditch this tub of shit?" Joe asked. "We're going nowhere fast here. This chunk of iron might sink. Them guys ain't far enough away for my money."

"I don't know, I didn't set any of this escape plan up. But I got a feeling we're about to find out why we're in a barge." Hawk gestured at a small, dark figure on the surface, approaching them at a high rate of speed from across the canal. "At least this damn thing is bulletproof."

"Shit! A patrol boat. They've already spotted us," said Joe. "That didn't take long. Somebody at that place back there must have tipped them off."

"Get down. They'll talk to the guy in the tugboat. We

should be okay. They think he's hauling sand and gravel."

Joe dropped below the gunwales in the main body of the barge, where the sides rose much higher than in the stern. The deep belly of the boat had been built to carry cargo, and the little, raised deck in the stern made up a navigation and operation platform. "I sure hope you're right. We're sitting ducks in this bastard. Large Slow Target."

"It don't matter. We can kill the son of a bitches if we have to," said Hawk. "It ain't but one little boat."

Joe hated Hawk's easy satisfaction with violent solutions to all of life's problems. "Yeah, how about the next fifty boats they call up to help them out?"

"Yeah, it'd be better if they would go away, man. If they don't, they don't. We'll take care of it."

The ponderous barge moved toward the middle of the channel. The patrol boat intercepted the tugboat and pulled alongside it. The free-floating barge, which had been deliberately left unsecured, continued coasting ever so slowly, with a gap widening between it and the tugboat. The people in the bowels of the barge could hear the pilot and the Japanese police shouting back and forth to one another.

"They are asking for his permit," Ana relayed. "They are telling him that the harbor has been destroyed. It is closed to traffic, and it is very dangerous for anyone to go any farther." She looked from Hawk to Joe, watching their reactions to the news. "The *Kempetai* are telling him that the Americans are down there, and that they will kill him," she added.

"I hope to hell the Japs are right. Every cloud has a silver lining," said Joe, tensely. Hawk removed his helmet and tried to peer toward the rear. He wanted to study the interaction between the tugboat captain and his interrogator, lest unexpected sparks fly. The back and forth shouting continued. He could see Leo emotionally waving his arms at the Japanese officer in the boat. He noticed that the other soldiers in the patrol boat did not act especially concerned, or alert. Some sat, only one held a rifle, and even he failed to point it at anything.

"Leo is telling them he has sand for the Japanese soldiers to use in their sandbag defenses, and that the Japanese port authorities have told him that he must go on," said Ana. "The Japanese officer is saying that there are no soldiers in that direction anymore, and he should turn around. They act angry with one another. You know how men cannot just speak to one another like human beings."

"Ain't that the truth," Hawk answered distractedly. "Son of a bitches."

Meanwhile, as the animated conversation deepened, the barge coasted on, drifting slightly toward midstream and leaving the tugboat behind.

"This is great," said Joe. "They're gonna get fed up with that bastard and shoot his ass."

"Probably so," said Hawk. "They ain't much on conversation." Then he shook his head in exasperation. "Nope, worse than that: they're coming this way, to have a look at the barge, and us." Hawk ducked and replaced his helmet.

"Now what?" Joe asked.

Hawk waved Baker over.

"Pay attention," the sergeant told Baker, draping an arm over the other's shoulder and pulling him closer. "The lady is gonna shoot the shit with this asshole. You gotta get up on the high part of the stern and th'ow a grenade in that boat while the chit-chat is going on. They might see you, but they might not. We ain't got much choice. Read me?"

"Got it," said Baker, squinting intensely, with a full understanding of the situation, and his importance relevant to a favorable outcome of the matter. Hawk turned to Ana.

"You're gonna have to climb up there and talk to this Jap boat nut. See what he wants. Tell him there's nobody else on board. If everything goes right, we'll blow 'em out of the water without them ever knowing we're here. If it doesn't go right," Hawk paused, "we'll have to shoot it out with 'em."

"I don't want to. They will just shoot me. I am frightened," she said.

"Yeah. Well, me, too. You got to. That's the way it is," he said. "Climb up there and just talk that stupid Jap shit to him. Say whatever you want." He lifted her like a child onto a stack of crates, so that her head protruded visible above the gunwale.

The patrol boat left Leo behind and coasted beside the barge. The officer shouted at Ana through a megaphone and they exchanged a few sentences in Japanese. The irate Japanese began to tell her that he had to come aboard and check the cargo. She countered that the boarding was not necessary, although she failed to manufacture a plausible reason as to why it was unnecessary. Hawk, following none of it, nodded at Baker, and Baker stood, with his arm whipping downward in a fast and violent motion. Hawk yanked the back of Ana's dress and she screamed, falling backward into his arms, just as the grenade detonated in the patrol boat. Setting her down, he bounced up onto her place on the crate to check the damage.

Two of the enemy appeared to be badly wounded, floundering in the water, and two more lay stunned or dead on the splintered deck of the launch. The last two sat up, holding their heads. Hawk swung the Thompson over the wall of the barge and fired into them. A grim smile touched his lips. *The no-good son of a bitches.*

The operation was not quite as successful as he first thought. When he looked around, the tugboat no longer bumped along behind them. Leo had completely passed them, and proceeded on toward the safety of the harbor alone. Joe jumped beside Hawk and aimed his M1 at the wheelhouse of the fleeing tow boat.

"He sold us out! Want me to kill him?" Joe asked, sighting in on the back of Leo's head as the pilot spun the helm. It looked as if Leo had decided he only wanted the US Marine Corps in his rearview mirror, without realizing that that was not always the best location.

Hawk stared at the retreating tugboat, without answering for a long minute, as he considered Leo's treachery, and the predicament within which they now found themselves.

"Nah, let him go. Lost his nerve, I guess," Hawk finally said.

"We ain't got no motor, we ain't got no rudder. What do we do here?" Joe asked. They looked at both of the tantalizing banks, floating peacefully past at the speed of the almost nonexistent current. Hawk called for Blackwell. A bend in the canal drew near, and Leo disappeared around it. The clumsy barge wobbled adrift in the middle of a deadly nowhere.

"Did you figure out that Jap squawk box?" Hawk asked the radio operator.

"Yes, Sergeant. It works swell, it's a good one," said Blackwell.

"Get the battalion or get anybody. Maybe they know where we are. See if they can get their ass here," Hawk ordered. Blackwell ducked into the darkness below the shade of the barge's wall and turned on the radio. After manipulating a few dials, he was soon shouting into it.

"Too late," Joe reported. "Baker says we got more company coming." Hawk climbed up to the raised part of the stern where Baker sat, with an excellent view of the canal behind them. In the distance, three more enemy watercraft followed them. They bore down quickly.

"It looks like some of those big ones that were attacking us at the Club," said Baker. "They can rip us a new asshole with those machine cannons."

"There ain't gonna be no surprising them this time," said Hawk, nodding toward the still smoldering patrol boat that they had tossed the grenade into. "Get the machine gun and the bazooka back here. Move it!"

"Shit!" Baker grunted as he leaped down to the deck.

The barge slid slowly past a wooden sign on the shore, hanging vertically down from a bomb-blasted pole that had once supported it. The whiteboard read: "Wharf 119," in painted black figures. For some reason, Hawk remembered the number. Perhaps he thought he would have to pass one hundred nineteen more signs to reach safety, which was daunting at best.

The advancing airboat began firing at the aimlessly adrift barge. There would be no opportunity to try any subterfuge with this new contingent of landing craft; the Japanese already knew the barge contained a hostile force. Of some consolation, however, was the discovery that the Japanese machine gun bullets could not penetrate the thick hide of the tough old freight hauler—a marked improvement over the crumbling walls of Club Arashigaoka. Hawk assembled the men in the stern, training fire on the attackers. The civilians huddled below, under the safety of the high iron walls and piles of sand and gravel in the main body of the vessel. Once the American machine gun had been set up in the stern and turned loose, the closing enemy slowed their waterborne charge. Slowing the speed did not, however, lower the decibels of the aircraft engines reverberating inside the metal well of the barge.

The protective walls jutted no more than two to three feet high in the stern of the barge, requiring the Marines to lie prone as they trained fire on the enemy. The three airboats split up, with two of them proceeding along the starboard side, and one moving to the port side. The strategy produced little success, as they could see nothing but the high walls of the barge above them once past the stern. The Japanese would have no targets unless they came directly at the stern, where withering fire awaited them. Their maneuvers could be tracked by virtue of the incredible noise generated by the airplane motors.

Hawk well knew that tactical problems would not long trouble the enemy. They had a history of welcoming frontal attacks, no matter how costly. Each of their boats held as many enemy soldiers as the total number of Marines the barge carried. He could hear what sounded like one of the enemy airboats ramming the port side of his lame transport, in an effort to push it toward the bank. First it rammed, and then it scraped savagely against the giant, dead, floating leviathan, trying to steer it aground. The other two attack boats had returned to the stern and stayed only a few yards behind the barge, trading fire with it.

"They're pushing us ashore, so their goddam army can board us," Hawk told Joe. "Where the hell is Manfredi? Get him up here with the rockets! We have to cut the odds."

Joe held his head low and rolled down onto the safety of the cargo area below. He soon returned with Manfredi and the bazooka.

"Try to knock out one of them!" Hawk told the man with the rocket launcher.

"You better get back," said the other, lifting the tube of the bazooka onto the stern's gunwale. "It's loaded, and it could explode. Things are rattling loose."

"Right." Hawk pushed Joe, and the two of them dove onto the deck below.

Manfredi rose only a couple of inches, in order to lower the sights of the rocket launcher on the nearest boat. A couple of inches was all the waiting enemy machine gunners required. A line of shells rained across the barge's stern like hail, shafting through Manfredi's helmet, and up the barrel of the bazooka, ripping it from his hands and spinning it into the canal. Manfredi's helmet flew back into the faces of Hawk and Joe, and the stricken man was lifted from his feet, clutching his head, only to be riddled with another burst of fire. His body spun in midair, toppling over the gunwale and into the water. Hawk tossed himself up, twisting back up to the elevated stern, slamming his forearm and submachine gun flat onto its deck. He saw the enemy boats advancing to only a few feet from him.

Joe, looking up at Hawk, only muttered, "We needed those rockets."

While the determined airboats nearly touched

them, the proximity meant that the Japanese could no longer elevate their machine guns high enough to fire at the defenders. The Americans had the ability to reach over the gunwale and fire down into the crowded landing craft with their rifles. The Americans' advantage soon evaporated, however, as the platoon of previously unengaged Japanese troops began firing their own rifles upward. The uncoordinated rifle fire proved to be less intense than the relentless automatic American weapons, and the Marines inflicted heavy casualties on their unprotected adversaries, while taking few of their own. All through the vicious exchange, the hollow, metallic ramming and scraping could still be heard coming from the port side, where the enemy tried to steer the barge to shore.

"Shit! They almost got us onto the bank!" Joe screamed. "We're gonna have every Jap in Manila on top of us!" Hawk sprang back down onto the deck and ran toward the sound of the enemy boat colliding with the barge. He saw the dented inner wall where the landing craft had been ramming the outside. Taking a grenade, he pulled the pin, and without counting, arced it over the iron wall, where he judged the enemy boat must lie. After the expected explosion, the ramming continued unabated. The grenade had accomplished nothing.

Blackwell grabbed Hawk's shoulder. He had to shake the sergeant vigorously to get his attention amid the deafening sounds.

"The colonel!" Blackwell shouted, handing him the headset to the captured Japanese radio. The gong of the airboat rammed the wall next to his ear.

"You're under attack! Why aren't you at the Club? How can I link up with you, if you aren't where I told you to be? Where are you? What the hell are you doing? Over." Hawk had caught the words in mid-transmission.

He shouted back an answer. "The Club is *gone*. We're on a barge in the canal. They're pushing us ashore with motorboats, right into the lap of the Jap army. Over."

"I repeat, where are you? I need a traceable location. What are your coordinates? I can hardly hear you with all that noise. Over."

"I don't know. We came down the canal toward the harbor!" Hawk paused when the broken signboard flashed in his memory. "I saw a sign that said Wharf 119. Over."

"Pier 119? Wait one. Over."

The enemy boat rammed the side of the barge with a renewed vengeance this time. It sounded as if it intended to come through the wall or destroy itself in the effort. The Japanese landing craft circled repeatedly, making suicidal, full speed runs into the side of the barge, gradually driving it ashore. It sounded as if the hull of the old tub was finally grinding into the rock-strewn banks of the channel. The bow lurched skyward, and Hawk grabbed the dented wall to maintain his balance. Gunfire from the stern intensified. He could not see what was happening down there, but he imagined that the changed elevation at that end of the deck had made it easier for the enemy to board them. It felt as if the entire starboard side of the barge had been grounded onto the bank, with the stern end driven higher still.

"Okay. Sergeant. Hear this," the colonel continued, "Pier 119 is behind American lines. You are in friendly territory. You have entered the harbor, and it is under the control of the US Army. Over."

"Yeah, well. These Japs ain't so friendly!" Hawk

shouted. "They're crawling all over our goddam boat. Over."

"Listen to me. There are no Japs in that harbor, or on that side of Manila. You are being attacked by patrol boats from down the ship channel. They are coming into that district from another sector. They are not a threat. Hold them off. Planes in the area are on the way. The enemy will be cut off without support. Over."

"Not a threat," Hawk repeated to himself.

He dropped the radio and ran to the stern where the obviously threatening shooting had increased. His men fired their last few rounds down over the gunwales, but he could see enemy bayonets already lancing up at them. A little over a dozen of the Americans could fit onto the stern to hold back the onslaught. Unless they had been reinforced with even more troops, the Japanese consisted of three platoons crammed onto their attacking landing craft. The Marine ammunition had been exhausted as the final clash descended upon them.

The two pursuing landing craft managed to race headlong into the stern, colliding with the barge once it had been beached, and creating an upraised ramp for the attacking Japanese to climb onto the back of the stranded freight hauler. Hawk squirmed into the forefront of the battle and fired his last magazine into the faces of the struggling enemy soldiers. A phalanx of jabbing bayonets charged at him where the bows of the crashed landing crafts met the barge, and he bashed them backward with his empty submachine gun. As they wilted before his fury, he climbed up, with one leg on the wall of the stern, and threw his empty weapon into the teeth of an attacker.

Epley stood next to Hawk, frantically shoving his

empty rifle barrel at the oncoming mass of furious and grimacing humanity. An enemy marine chambered his rifle and aimed it point blank at the young man, having saved his last round for just such a moment. Without hesitation, Hawk stepped in front of both Epley and the rifle muzzle. The weapon misfired, enabling the sergeant to seize the enemy soldier's rifle and bayonet. He slashed at the oncoming horde with this new weapon, ripping streams of blood from heads and necks, until the bayonet broke free of its rifle, and a half dozen of the frenzied attackers tackled him. The clawing mob, with Hawk at its center, fell over the side of the barge and onto the muddy shore below.

A stunning and awkward landing from the substantial height did not cool his ferocity. Fighting from his knees, he ripped at faces with his fingernails like a wild animal. The enemy kicked and tried to pile onto him, only to be beaten blind with iron fists. He held one man in a choke hold until he stopped moving while kneeling on the head of another, pushing him into the drowning mud until his resistance stopped. Hawk managed to push the others off him. They floundered in the muck, dazed, disoriented and trying to regain their feet. More of the Japanese discharged off the third landing craft, running along the bank in an effort to join in the melee, to finish off the outnumbered but still vicious lone American demon on the shore. The newcomers, however, had fully loaded rifles and would not have to rely on the limited powers of human strength to settle the matter.

American fighter planes swept low over the chaotic scene, their loud engines drawing the attention of the Japanese. The enemy shouted excitedly at one another as they pointed skyward. Those still able withdrew from the combat and ran back for their one, still functioning landing craft. One or two fired their rifles with futility at the aircraft roaring above them. Left alone, Hawk kneeled in the bloody slime, his utility jacket torn almost completely off, and blood streaming from the cuts on his head and face, including the first one from the flying glass at the Club. He watched in surprise as the remainder of the Japanese dropped from the lofty heights of the barge above him and ran for their departing landing craft. He had never seen the enemy so readily quit an engagement. He dimly deduced that these were not the battle-hardened troops of his past engagements.

Hawk lifted his knee off the head of his drowned antagonist, mud still gurgling from the dead, open mouth. He jolted himself wearily to his feet as the planes chased the remaining enemy boat out into the channel. The Americans in the barge shouted encouragement to the fliers. Hawk climbed back into the stern and stood beside Joe and Blackwell to watch the outcome. The three planes repeatedly passed over the fleeing vessel, strafing it mercilessly. The enemy troopers dove into the water in an effort to free themselves from the pounding inferno.

There would be no rescue attempts, however, nor any humanitarian efforts. The planes continuously flew back and forth, scouring the gray surface with lead until every flailing swimmer had disappeared or stopped moving. Shouts of approval rose from the barge as blood saturated the surface.

"Goddamn Japs got no respect for air power," said Hawk, his chest still heaving with exertion.

"We could have used them planes yesterday," said Joe with a relieved smile. A dozen of the enemy dead lay across the gunwales and on the raised deck of the stern. More lay on the earth below and in the wrecks of their landing craft. There were several wounded, and they were twice blessed, for the defenders had no ammunition left with which to cure their ills. For this reason alone, they would be transported to American Army hospitals, where they would likely survive the war.

Hawk turned his back to the channel and leaned against the bloody gunwale. His head hung down, and he batted his eyes to clear them. He told Blackwell to contact the colonel and told Joe to bring the civilians to him. Blackwell arrived first, with the radio.

Hawk waved him away. "You talk to him. Tell him it's over," Hawk said, his chest heaving with labored breath. "Tell him...tell him he was right about everything. Agree with all his stupid shit. And...and don't forget to thank the son of a bitch for the planes." Blackwell withdrew, leaving Hawk to face Ana, her fellow Club workers, and the Weitz family. They had huddled in terror throughout the engagement, and looked in relatively good shape, compared to the torn and bloody warrior panting before them.

"They say the harbor is liberated, folks. You're in American territory now," Hawk announced weakly. He was not at his best, in order to serve in his capacity as representative of the United States government to them. "It don't look like much right now. You know your way around this place better than I do. You're free to go, if you want. It sure as hell don't matter to me," Hawk said, guessing that perhaps some of them, for reasons of their own, had no desire to meet with the American authorities, and would just as soon disappear into the landscape.

Karl Weitz stepped forward, tears of relief in his

eyes. He grabbed Hawk's vein-corded arm. "They were certain to have killed us," he said. "We were dead until you came. I've...forgotten your name. But I promise I never will again."

"It don't matter. I got something for you. Joe, go get that damn bag," said Hawk. "Mademoiselle Rossier left you something in her will."

"Mademoiselle Rossier?" Karl asked, stifling his pent-up sobs. Overcome with relief, and with knowing what these strangers had done for him, unplanned praise burst forth. "I am afraid we owe her more than I could ever repay. I never even knew her. She helped so many people, who never even knew her."

Joe handed Hawk the satchel. "Yeah, she was a real looker, too," Joe told Karl. "She reminded me of Hedy Lamarr, didn't she?" Joe asked Hawk, who didn't answer. Joe, therefore, as was his way, repeated his opinion. "Didn't she look kinda like Hedy Lamarr? Maybe not exactly."

"I don't know," Hawk answered sharply, while he rummaged through the bag. Blood dripped from his face across the sides of the bag, and he paid no attention to that, either.

"Mademoiselle Rossier was perhaps...Jewish?" Karl asked.

"Hedy Lamarr used to be Jewish," said Joe. "A guy in New York told me that. A lot of people in New York are Jewish. Maybe Rossier *was* Jewish. Was she, Hawk? Hawk knew her better than us. Was she?"

"I don't know. *Goddamn.* Go away. Go check on the wounded," said Hawk. Joe left with a defeated expression. He did not like the rebuff. "Some of these bastards are kind of ignorant," Hawk explained to Karl, pulling the jewelry out of the bag and rubbing his face. "This is your property, I think. It has name tags on it and all. I'll turn it over to you, and leave it up to you to clear it with the colonel. I'm giving it to you now, so we don't have to jack with the goddamn Army. She was...you know... worried about that."

"Oh, my god," said Karl. "She gives us our lives and this, too?"

"Yeah." Hawk looked at him from beneath his brows, his face swollen from the battering it had taken by rifle butts. "To tell you the truth..." Hawk said, but he didn't seem able to finish the sentence as the two of them stood facing each other.

"Yes?" Karl finally encouraged him, coaxing the words out. He sincerely wanted to hear the words of his savior. "Yes?"

"To tell you the truth, I don't know what Hedy Lamarr looks like."

Karl laughed. "Nor do I." Hawk reached into the bag and pulled out the American dollars.

"It looks like the people in the city got the short end of the stick," said Hawk. "Maybe you could divide this up somehow. She would want that, to help them get started again. I mean, otherwise, some son of a bitch'll just steal it, and buy his ass a Rolls Royce, or whatever cheap chiselers do. This kinda shit wouldn't last long."

Karl took the bills. "She must have been an angel from heaven."

Hawk drug a forearm across his eyes to clear them of debris, yet another time. "Yeah, that crossed my mind. But I don't think so. She was from...somewhere." He coughed. The air filled with smoke from the burning port. For the first time, able to reflect on his surroundings, he noticed that the world seemed to be on fire. "Looks like it's everybody's lucky day, huh? Maybe...

maybe not everybody," he added, as smoke swirled between them. "Good luck to you, Mr. Weitz." Hawk clapped Karl on the shoulder with a raw knuckled, bloody hand. He dropped the bag on the deck and turned back to the gunwale, to look across the channel, where the bodies of the unfortunate vanquished floated. Their youth wasted for—essentially—nothing.

Behind him, the harbor visibly collapsed into fiery shambles and the black fumes from petroleum-smelling flames drifted overhead. The Japanese had chosen to destroy the port before leaving. Off to the left, he noticed that they had set fire to much more than the harbor area. The glow of massive spires of flame could be seen pulsating in the sky. The entire city burned. Joe caught Hawk's eye. Joe also looked in amazement at the destruction over the channel, purposely ignoring his indisputably rude sergeant. Joe could be sensitive at times. Hawk supposed he had been a little harsh with his friend and comrade at arms, in the midst of all the excitement.

He walked over to the frowning corporal, who no doubt indulged his own feelings of thanksgiving and relief at the brutal outcome of the final encounter with the Japanese.

"That was a close one, huh?" Hawk asked him, throwing a friendly elbow at him, but missing. "Japs got no respect for air power. It'll get 'em someday. This ain't the first time it saved us, huh?" Hawk looked smaller, drained, pathetic, and far from the avenging coiled spring of violence he had been an hour earlier.

"Yeah," Joe agreed, but did not encourage any further conversation. Hawk stared ahead and then looked down; in spite of the outcome of the battle, he was a defeated spectacle. He was not good at making amends. He needed tobacco, but it had disappeared with the majority of his shirt.

"Hey, podnuh, I wanted to ask you something," Hawk said at last. "I was...thinking."

"What's that?" Joe replied, still reluctant to welcome any small talk.

"Where did you first see Eugenie?"

Joe considered the question briefly. "With you, sitting in that booth, in the dark. Where did you first see her?"

"On the stairs, somewhere in the dark," Hawk answered. "It never really made sense. She told me two different things. She said she came in the door, and then later on, she said she came in through the galley. Nobody ever saw her do either one. All them people there? That's kind of impossible, don't you think?"

"Ah, she was crazy. She lied about everything," said Joe. "I bet, if you think back, she never said she came in either way. There ain't no way to know. I stay away from women like that. They'll tell you any goddam thing."

"Yeah. I don't know. She was pretty straight with me. The whole thing...just never made any sense. She never exactly lied to me..."

"Well," said Joe, softening a little. "She never exactly told you the truth, either, or we wouldn't be standing here talking about her, wondering how the hell this all happened. We know one thing is for damn sure. We know what happened to her, because we found her sleeve on the rocks."

"Yeah...I guess. Except...she wasn't wearing those sleeves at the time," Hawk answered. Joe studied him with a puzzled expression. "You were sure right, though, she looked kinda like..." His voice died in his throat. He had forgotten the name—which he had only known for a few seconds. Hawk turned away, striking the gunwale lightly with a torn fist, as might a judge ending a case with his gavel.

Hawk did not look back toward fiery Manila. Smoke blocked the sky, turning its day into a roiling night. The rhythm of distant explosions was punctuated by the closer ones. He slumped to sit against the wall of the barge and stare instead at the blood-stained deck: large, endless red swaths smeared over the dirty rust. Whose blood? No one cared anymore. Its importance was lost to the world around him. He studied it as droplets of his own fell into it.

Sergeant Hawk no longer had any reason to watch Manila. He and Eugenie had failed in everything they tried to do for the old city and for one another. What had happened to her? It didn't matter, because one thing really was for certain: she had left him. Whatever means she chose, she was gone. It seemed that the loss of the Pearl of the Orient had meant more to her than a mere man, such as he. Too late, he realized that she was right about her power over him. Now he felt the power, and little else. If he could have saved the city, would she have stayed? She had believed in him for a while. She believed a lone man could save a country. What did he believe?

His head fell back against the metal and he closed his burning eyes. His heartbeat slowed. If he were thrown in with the dead, it didn't much matter.

Was there a dark-haired beauty, alone in a black cape, walking the earth on a hillside somewhere, sadly watching the holocaust below? Was she even now in the camp of one army—or another? Because he had seen so many die, he knew that it was only chance leaving him on this earthly side of life's great divide. As to death, he had more answers than most men his age, but he also had more questions. Where was she, and what *was* that divide that had always been between them? Could a man cross it? Were there secret passageways through it that allowed you to go back and forth? Did beings glide through it on a frail scent or a remembered sound, bank, and return from whence they came? Was it nothing more substantial than a soft footstep on the stairs, or the wind whipping through the pages of a book?